BETTER TO BEG
FORGIVENESS...

Baen Books by
MICHAEL Z. WILLIAMSON

Freehold
The Weapon
Better to Beg Forgiveness...

The Hero (with John Ringo)

BETTER TO BEG FORGIVENESS...

MICHAEL Z. WILLIAMSON

BETTER TO BEG FORGIVENESS . . .

This is a work of fiction. All the characters and events portrayed in this book are fictional, and any resemblance to real people or incidents is purely coincidental.

A Baen Books Original

Baen Publishing Enterprises
P.O. Box 1403
Riverdale, NY 10471
www.baen.com

ISBN 10: 1-4165-5508-0
ISBN 13: 978-1-4165-5508-7

Cover art by Kurt Miller

First printing, November 2007

Distributed by Simon & Schuster
1230 Avenue of the Americas
New York, NY 10020

Library of Congress Cataloging-in-Publication Data

Williamson, Michael Z.
  Better to beg forgiveness— / Michael Z. Williamson.
      p. cm.
  "A Baen Books original"—T.p. verso.
  ISBN-13: 978-1-4165-5508-7
  ISBN-10: 1-4165-5508-0
  1. Civil war—Fiction. 2. Political fiction. I. Title.

  PS3623.I573B48 2007
  813'.6—dc22
                                                  2007027930

10 9 8 7 6 5 4 3 2 1

Pages by Joy Freeman (www.pagesbyjoy.com)
Printed in the United States of America

For Ron and Vicki
Who weren't sure I knew what I was doing,
but gave me the benefit of the doubt . . .
and a long time to prove it.

CHAPTER ONE

Basically, I'm in it for the money," Aramis Anderson said. "Who can turn down entire weeks' worth of pay per day?" He sat back in his couch and sipped his drink. He'd already finished his lunch, and the sandwich must have screamed in terror, seeing and then disappearing down that voracious maw.

"Yeah, but I figure they pay that for a reason. This won't be easy." Former Captain Alex Marlow, USMC, remembered being young and stupid. That's why he was *former* captain. Granted, he'd gotten the job done, but Anderson's ego was larger than his had been and potentially a problem, despite all his training and experience.

"No, not easy," Anderson agreed. "But it's better pay than the infantry, better rules of engagement than the infantry, and better gear than the infantry."

Anderson kept bringing up the infantry, by which he meant the U.S. Army infantry. "All Marines Are Riflemen First," but the Army's riflemen were often condescending to the rest of their servicemates.

I'm probably being too harsh, Alex thought. *I was much the same and grew out of it. He's well trained, and he follows orders.* He didn't need to let immaturity and abrasiveness cause tension. You had to get along with your team even if you didn't care for them socially. The kid did well at the Academy, did have limited real world experience, and was quite bright. He'd keep an eye out, and say something if he needed to. After all, he'd agreed to bring the kid along as muscle with brains.

"I've never guarded a head of state before," said Eleonora Sykora, leaning back in her couch and clearly enjoying the smooth flight of the luxury aircraft. The plane was soundproofed, and even her soft tones were audible. She was a Czech from Earth, but spoke good spaceside English, if a little rough on pronunciation. She was female, slim, and elegant looking, not exactly the image of an executive security professional.

Of course, Alex reflected, that understatedness probably was to her advantage. She was not a small woman, but didn't come across as imposing, either. She had good credentials and Jason, his deputy and friend, spoke highly of her. They'd been on contract together.

"So we do what we always do. Bound to have some advantages and disadvantages," he said.

Ripple Creek Security sounded very sophisticated and classy. They charged accordingly, and paid their operators likewise. But if need be, that sophistication devolved to six or eight nasty operators with guns, who carried their principal to safety while shooting anything in their way. Their primary clients were governments and multinational and multisystem corporations. It was said they rarely lost a principal, but of principles, they had none.

"So what would be each?" Sykora asked.

"Oh," Alex replied, and engaged his brain from peripherally alert to responsive. "Likely to have decent quarters for us, and lots of indoor time. Likely facilities to check incoming individuals. Likely to have good control of vehicles and facilities . . ."

"Likely someone has a ChiNaTech Mark Fifteen missile with a microburst remote control aimed at the palace, a few planted informants in the existing indigenous security, bugs and a horde of savages outside?" Sykora asked.

"Elke, you've been doing this enough months that's a rhetorical question, right?" Alex asked back.

She nodded with a wry smile. She ate steadily and neatly from the tray, not in the ravenous fashion Anderson had. She was always methodical and thoughtful. You had to be to work with explosives.

Bart Weil had sat next to her when Anderson hadn't. Weil was poring over maps of Celadon, their destination. Weil was a big, grizzled German, a wet-navy vet turned bodyguard. This was a different mission from guarding idiot musicians and their retinues, but

Weil did both well. He could be as polite or intimidating as necessary. He had the most actual security experience, and Alex aimed to exploit that. The man was quiet but not slow. He recalled their duty together during the meteorite strike on Novaja Rossia, keeping a starving mob in a blasted wasteland from looting supplies that had to be issued in a proper program. It wasn't easy telling families with hungry children to wait, or threatening fathers who were trying to see that those children did get fed when they cut the fence. At least, it wasn't easy for Alex. Bart was coldly professional.

Across from Bart, occasionally pulling the screen flat to see better, Shaman read the same maps upside down. He was slim and looked the part of an executive. He was also a damned fine doctor with lots of combat experience during Liberia's Third Civil War (or Eighth, depending on who did the counting), more than once using rigger tape, rags, and a pocketknife to perform lifesaving surgery. Horace "Shaman" Mbuto might leave you a scarred mess when done, but you'd probably be a *living* scarred mess, and reconstructive biosculp was covered under Ripple Creek's generous benefit package. Alex wasn't sure if the native rituals Mbuto used alone and on patients were a religious matter for him or simply an act meant to disturb and creep out observers, and wasn't going to ask. The man was one hell of a cutter and one hell of a shooter with years of experience.

Last on the couch was Jason Vaughn, with his attention focused on his computer.

"What are you writing, Jason?" Alex asked.

"Letter home," Vaughn said tersely. Vaughn had a wife and kids on Grainne Colony. He'd probably memorized the maps already, and his eyes kept flicking up and forward toward the flight deck, in nervous habit. Vaughn was a pilot if need be, an armored vehicle driver if need be, a mechanical master, and very professionally paranoid. He swung from reticent to lecturing, and if he said something was so, it almost always was. Alex was glad to have him along. Great operator.

They were all great operators. That's why they got paid better than doctors, lawyers, and most corporate mid execs. If you wanted someone with that skill set and talent, who'd put themselves between their employer and an incoming bullet, you had to pay. *Contractor* had been the polite term for a long time now, but the proper term was *mercenary*.

They were on contract to guard Balaji Bishwanath, the incoming temporary president of Celadon on Salin. Celadon was a backwater haven for terrorists and pirates, and enough events had finally happened to draw notice to those facts. The UN Forces were pacifying it, at least on paper, and the Bureau of State moved in the interim president selected by the Colonial Alliance while a new, functioning government was created. Many of the gangs, syndicates, clans, and tribes didn't want the peace Bishwanath promised. Contingents from every faction on the planet wanted him dead.

That wouldn't really matter in the long run. More troops would come until the UN/Alliance's goal was accomplished. But as with common criminals, there was a mind-set with certain people that such fights were "winnable." It was only fair, and professional, to give Bishwanath proper security presence while things settled down. The fact that he was seen as such a figurehead was, in fact, a boost to his credibility.

"Do you think we can get other contracts here, boss?" Aramis asked. "We've got diplomats, Assemblypersons, CEOs, and executives. I figure this could last a decade."

Money was one of the big appeals, Alex admitted to himself.

He replied, "The execs want to invest in—by which they mean exploit—a developing economy, and need protection from the exploited. There's an occasional correspondent who can afford our rates for a few days who might sign on, too. That's Corporate's job. We're Operations. We beat on enraged peasants and dedicated assassins, and cash our checks. Do it well, I'll give you a good review, Corp will find you jobs."

"I'll do my best."

Bishwanath rated more than six guards. They were just his immediate circle of "civilian" guards. Around and outside were plans for eighty-four more, four platoons of what were called Long Range Reconnaissance troops. At one time, such were called "Special Operations," but the euphemisms were all designed to make the military sound not quite so violent to an increasingly sensitive culture. A decadent, wimpy one in Alex's opinion.

Alex, Bart, Elke, and Jason all knew a cross section of those Recon soldiers. They'd served with them or across from them. Shaman Mbuto and Aramis Anderson hadn't moved in that circle, but Shaman had an existing history and was respected. Anderson was the new guy and took it personally. At the same time, youthful troops were valuable in part because of their need to prove themselves. They could be prevailed upon to perform suicidally dangerous tasks, and sometimes survive. Older, more cynical personnel were not so image driven. Not that Alex intended to waste the kid cavalierly, but if heroics were called for, it was Anderson he was going to call upon to jump on the grenade.

For now they were en route to Celadon and casually dressed. Much of this contract would be in suits, in limos and offices but it would also be outside at times, though, and Mahore, the capital of Celadon, was in a tropical latitude near sea level. It ran warm and muggy. Vaughn and Anderson fit suits right off the rack and looked great, wonderfully photogenic. Elke needed hers tailored, but with her short, fluffy hair and fine features she looked like an executive or a personal assistant, not a bloodthirsty bitch with kilos of high explosive. Weil needed suits specially made and bulged out of them, looking like some legbreaker with his broad features and chest. Mbuto just looked silly in them. He looked comfortable and respectable in shorts or casual clothes, and even in robes or ritual garb that would fit Carnivale, but a suit on him was out of place. Alex in a suit was just a guy in a suit.

That rogue's gallery effect was another useful feature of his team. Hide the discipline and weapons, look like showpieces, and be prepared to deal out wholesale death if there was a problem.

He turned his attention back to the shifting landscape below. The Broadwing aircraft had a stately, fuel-efficient speed and flew at a low enough altitude to allow a good view. That wasn't intentional, but Alex and Jason were both taking advantage of it now.

The landscape was patchy jungle of mixed Earth and native growth, with farms, ranches, and mines hacked out geometrically here and there.

"Fewer roads even than the Hinterlands on Grainne," Jason said without looking in.

"Mostly hardpan dirt, some fused. I don't see the highway."

"It is not visible from here," Bart said, indicating the map screen.

Things looked slightly odd in the orange-tinged light of Bonner Durchmusterung +56°2966, which was far too complex a name for a very unremarkable K3 star. Many settled people just called their local star "the sun." Some had shortened versions of the star's Earth name, like the Grainne Colony, which called Iota Persei "Io." But "Bon" or "Durch" wouldn't work well. That was a catalog name. The declination number or whatever it was wouldn't work. Here, for some reason, the star was locally known as "Bob." There was no figuring that, so Alex watched the terrain.

Scattered villages dotted the farm areas, or sprouted around crossroads. There were few towns. Little of the local life was compatible with Earth life. That was good and bad. Bad, because it meant nothing local was edible. It also meant, in this case, that the pheromone- and smell-driven local predators took no interest in Earth life. The only threats were those man brought along, mostly himself. Not that his team should ever be stopping in the remoter areas, but it never hurt to scout things out.

The buildings in the settlements were prefabs and huts of native materials. Prefabs marked the "official" buildings and those sponsored by investment. Peasants had huts. Sunlight, or Boblight, was polarized by and reflected from water bodies, but not from glass or metal structures, or polished plastic. There weren't any. This place had started drab and run-down and then slid.

Stretching, he took a sip of water. The seat was very comfortable, covered with a finer fabric than most commercial liners, and powered to support his neck and back automatically, shifting as he did. Military flights didn't rate such expensive but spine-saving hardware.

Alex wouldn't admit it was his first trip off planet. The star flight had been smooth enough, and there wasn't much to say, so he ignored it. Both Elke and Jason had been off Earth, and Jason now lived off Earth, retired to a wealthy colony. He'd retired from the military, not from working in the field.

Anyway, it made sense to soak up the view, get firsthand intel. There was nothing wrong with being a paid tourist, either.

Salin was just a planet. It had analogs to much of Earth plant life, and a few lower animals. Not much local was above very simple amphibians, though the seas were fairly active. There were a few reptiles including some flying types. That meant a lot to the scientists who studied such. To him, it meant few nonhuman threats, which was fine, as there were enough of those. Salin was smaller than Earth, but had similar gravity and lots of metals in its core. Bob was a flare star, with periodic outbursts that weren't dangerous to a human with good UV block or a hat, and barely noticeable for their small violence. As with everything else around here, it was unspectacular. There was also a certain amount of metal in the asteroids here. Those were potentially profitable, being easy to transport through jump points, but the two large and one small nations on Salin had never been able to come to an agreement about them, so they remained unexploited. Planetary exports tended to be technology, foodstuffs, tourism, or rare minerals or gems. On the planet itself there were few people with education to create new tech, there was nothing rare here, barely enough food for subsistence and certainly nothing exotic, and the ongoing tribal wars and desolate or uninteresting terrain prevented any kind of tourism.

What a hole, he mused.

He tensed slightly as they landed. This mission was still being put together and the Ripple Creek oporder did not have much information on infrastructure. It lacked details such as whether the port was automated, or if pilots had to manually land and if there were even navaids. All these intelligence holes were information he needed to get the job done, but he'd have to make do. The landing was uneventful as it turned out, and they taxied up to a very basic, sheet-roofed building that served as the terminal. That summed up what this place was like.

As soon as they rolled to a stop, he said, "Okay, debark, Elke and Bart, grab our weapons, and let's meet our principal at his new home."

Their craft was a civilian Broadwing, but was on contract to the military. Again and again that was happening, and Bart Weil didn't like it. He remembered when everything had been done at great expense with armor and combat craft. This was allegedly cheaper, but it was not safer and contractors weren't always reliable. He hated using them. Then he caught himself and laughed inside. He was a contractor and wouldn't be here otherwise. He'd done executive protection for years, but only been on military-type contracts a few months, like most of the team, and was still adapting to the mind-set.

He walked aft, out through a wave of heat and down the ladder rolled against the fuselage. They were debarking on the apron, which said what was needed about this backwater. He started sweating, but it was only from the weather, not from any threat. Yet.

There was a crew already unloading the hold, but not in the briskest fashion. That might be partly diet and climate—they had starvation-and-manual-labor physiques, even in this lower-than-Earth gravity—but he suspected a good part of it was laziness. Why work harder if it would not pay off?

Their pallet came out on the forks, and he waved to the operator for attention. There was a moment's mixup as he used a hand signal he thought meant "down" that the operator understood as "tilt forward." Bart was almost responsible for the pallet dropping and shattering, because it was the ground guide's job to direct; the driver couldn't see anything at that angle. Bart hated being in charge, or having to rely on someone, so neither side of this was good for him. He also knew there'd be a lot of that this tour. He was already tense from it. The operator, at least, had been competent if not industrious.

But he managed to guide the load down, and he and Elke snapped the wheels out from where they served as dunnage, to proper road position. The pallet could be driven by attached or remote control for as long as its ampacitors lasted, towed as a trailer, or pushed if it had to be. By itself it was an expensive piece of equipment, and what it contained . . .

The others were around shortly, having brought all the personal gear, which was piled on the crates for easy transport. They took the spare time to examine the surroundings in person.

There were moister, cooler areas near the poles. These temperate and tropical zones were dusty and dry, largely, even close to the coasts. Rivers were few, small streams meandering into swamps being more common. Here was simply bright yellowish Boblight, flat terrain with local gingko analogs, and Earth palms with some coastal pines. The dust was dun.

No one commented. It was a place. That was all that could be said.

"So who's our escort? Paras?" Bart asked.

"Just an infantry convoy," Alex said.

"Great. A moving wall of raw meat to soak up fire. I hope they're large as well as stupid." He said it mostly to twit Anderson, and it worked. Bart could see his teeth grind. That made them even for the navy jokes the boy had been telling. "Sheep would be obvious" indeed. Humor was only funny when you intended it to be.

They sat on their crates. They had their personal gear and

water, with a few rations in case of long delay. Ideally, they would have armed up at once. Unfortunately, a combination of factors prevented that.

First, the crates were heavily sealed and would require equipment to open. That was to prevent theft of their very high-value items by assorted elements. BuState was also worried about "weapons in civilian hands," which was very annoying. The team would not be the agents of that distribution. Still, until they were on-site, they were "civilians" and couldn't touch their own gear. Always politics, always in the way of getting the job done.

"It would be nice to fly in," Bart said. "In a vertol or even a helicopter."

"It would," Vaughn replied with a nod, "but there aren't proper facilities. They never had a pad at the palace, and the only aircraft here so far are the Army's. They're trying to avoid this whole 'BuState mess,' as they call it."

"Well, their priority is fighting the war," Anderson said. "You can't blame them for that." He was picking at loose pieces of plastic on the crates.

"I am not blaming them," Bart said. "I would do the same. But it would be nice."

"Give it a month," Vaughn said confidently. "It'll change."

"Must be our convoy," Sykora said, pointing across the high, dusty apron to an approaching line of vehicles, most of them military.

"Probably," Jason agreed. He hadn't done this for long, but he had been in the military for years, and his assessment of the convoy wasn't a pleasant one. Mostly wheeled vehicles, almost no tracks, thin-skinned and fine against small arms but no good against any kind of support weapon. Inadequate crew-served weapons aboard. Likely great air support nearby, but that took seconds in which troops could die. The UN didn't want to appear like an occupying force, so they were using the minimum amount of armed and armored military gear. Yet another way to sacrifice troops for appearance. He was again thankful he'd accepted retirement.

He couldn't wait to get to somewhere where he'd have Ripple Creek's own drivers and support. What a sad statement that he trusted them better than the troops.

The irony was that the Army felt exactly the same way about

contractors. How could you trust someone who fought for a paycheck? How could you be sure they wouldn't bug out? Why trust people who were outside the chain of command, and exempt from the Military Code of Justice?

The reality was, all those same rules applied on contract, and they'd forfeit their pay and face criminal charges if they bailed. They had some wiggle room, being an independent command, so they could dispense with a certain amount of stupidity and paperwork. After all was said and done, however, they were still soldiers.

The convoy was accompanied by a wave of dust. Everyone squinted as it rolled up. There were twelve vehicles; quite an entourage for six bodyguards. Jason surmised that the rationale was probably enough vehicles to dissuade attack—on the troops, not on their "civilian" passengers. Alternately, they'd had errands to run.

"Ripple Creek?" someone shouted from the second vehicle.

"Yes," Alex agreed, and showed ID. He was motioned up close and touched in a code on a proffered pad screen. After checking that and his picture, the officer nodded. Jason took in the exchange, and looked at the officer closely. He was perhaps twenty-five, though his face was lined from exhaustion and sun.

"Have your people climb in the grumbly," he said, indicating the next-to-last vehicle.

"Check," Alex said. He waved and pointed, and the team rose and moved. Bart had the controller for the pallet, and rolled it closer to the line of vehicles to make attaching it for tow easier. In only a few minutes they loaded up and were ready.

The grumbly, so nicknamed for the low exhaust note of its cycloidal engine, seated eight. This one was configured with an open top, and had two pintles epoxied to it for mounting guns. That meant plenty of visibility, and no armor.

Eight was the nominal capacity. There were six on the team, the driver and codriver, and then four more troops squeezed in to the seats and adjoining bed. They were armed, so no one complained, even though it meant being crunched against dusty, sweaty soldiers with bulky gear.

It was a military convoy. That meant the seats were coarse, not well-padded, badly worn and flattened, and only better than nothing for reducing bumps from spine-shattering to mere bruise-causing. The drivers were going balls-out, and the reason became obvious.

It was a local sport to take potshots at convoys. The access road was straight, flat, and had ample clear space around it. Behind rises and distant buildings, however, a number of locals were shooting.

"Which faction are they?" Jason asked the sergeant in charge of their detail.

"Does it matter?" the sergeant grinned. "They shoot at everybody. It's just what they do."

The distance was far too great for any incapacitating weapon. The gunner above and behind had a real machine gun, and rapped off a burst here and there. Responding to every instance would waste ammo, so he was judiciously choosing targets he had a chance of at least disturbing, and ignoring the rest.

"Kinda fun. Can't wait until we play," Aramis said.

"Yeah. Fun," one woman rasped. "I ain't paid enough to call this fun." She flicked her eyes at Aramis, blazing jealousy, then turned back to the panorama, watching for threats. At least she took it seriously.

Jason took in technical details. It was a talent, a skill. He might not notice the contents of an adscreen unless it changed, but he'd damned sure notice additional wires or a ladder. The grumbly was worn, one pintle had been replaced and there were two extra ammo cases jammed in storage against a seat back. He also noticed definite tampering with the safety cover on the machine gun. That was supposed to be personalized to the operator and no more than two backups because of civilian paranoia about "weapons getting into the wrong hands." Soldiers were far more paranoid of not being able to return fire, with good reason.

"The safeties are pulled," he said softly to Alex and Elke. "Which I'm glad to see."

"Yeah, some regs are meant to be disobeyed," Alex replied. Elke just nodded and glanced over to confirm the fact.

Alex had been briefed on friction between contingents. Most of the military were not happy with the Executive Protection Details. EPDs could use nonstandard weapons, lethal force, and were almost immune from prosecution for all but deliberate murder. If the local government didn't complain, BuState wouldn't follow up. Then there was the EPD pay, which started at that of a field grade officer and went up.

Of course, in exchange for that money, the EPs were expected to throw themselves on grenades or take bullets for people they might rather see dead. The job wasn't about supporting their buddies or getting the benefits, it was about killing or dying for a buck. Aramis wasn't the only one who saw it as a way to make money and nothing else. Though most who'd done it for a while also had professional pride and the love of the challenge. They were still soldiers, just hired for specific operations.

He'd seen similar friction between active and reserve units, combat and support and various branches and nations. That was settling down a bit now that all militaries belonged to the UN's central alliance. Standards were leveling out and your backup could be almost anyone, which led to greater trust after a few missions. Contractors were always on the outside, though. That distrust worked both ways, but these soldiers appeared to be decent so far.

Shortly they were in town. That was a lesson itself.

Rough shacks lined the streets, interspersed with small stores. Some had electricity, generally wired straight down from a pole and looking improvised and unsafe. Several blackened rubble heaps might have sworn testimony to that, though they might also have been from arson, fighting, or other domestic causes.

Some of the buildings had windows of unbroken glass. The broken ones showed it to in fact be glass, not a modern poly. The construction was anything from native cut stone to hewn lumber to scavenged lumber and fiberglass or fiber panels. The roads were in poor repair, some fused, some paved with asphalt or concrete, and all broken and crumbling from age, wear, and the occasional explosion.

Then there were the people. They sat on porches or in yards staring aimlessly or wasting time with simple games. Many had the glazed expressions of alcohol or drug consumption.

"Nice place," Aramis murmured. He alone of the six had not actually seen combat or fire, though he'd deployed in some pretty nasty places.

"How . . . familiar," Shaman said.

They were all alert. They'd had photo briefs and text, but actually seeing it with the Mark 1 Eyeball made a difference. The streets were largely straight but with some shifts that made clear fire awkward and offered defensive positions. They were also fairly narrow—two or three lanes generally.

"This is a bad place to convoy," Bart said. "Too many ways to get blocked in."

"I think some of the central streets are wider," Jason said. "Though the layout sucks."

"Odd to have broad streets further in but not out," Bart said. "I wonder why that is?"

"Not a lot of traffic. Nothing resembling suburbs. Most people on foot," Elke said.

"Ah, yes," Bart nodded. "That would make sense. Streets are only needed in town."

The troops ignored them, apart from an occasional glance. There was a glacier of ice there to be broken before any real cooperation took place. Alex frowned. They'd have to get on good terms with their backup.

Elke was antsy. She had no weapons, none of her explosives, and was dependent upon people with far less training to protect her. She was gritting her teeth and would deal with it, but that didn't make it fun.

It wasn't just the training. She was thirty and experienced. She had the maturity and psychology to work with large amounts of explosive. These *blbé* kids imagined a firefight or two made them professionals and veterans. Some of them talked like it on boards and fora, and when at parties.

Getting shot at made you experienced in one thing and one thing only: getting shot at. It didn't mean you were trained well with your weapons, or that your opinion on anything was any more relevant. It just meant you knew what it felt like to have your life in the sling.

There were construction people who knew that, not to mention explorers and mountain climbers. Demolition experts knew it, too. Every time she set a charge, she held her life in the balance.

While she mused she watched. The locals had been shooting singly, but were starting to bunch into small groups and offer greater volumes of fire. Most were inaccurate, but sufficient volume increased the odds of a hit from astronomical to . . . what would it be called in English? Atmospheric?

She leaned out to get a better view as the vehicle bounced over the rough road, the trash, occasional sticks and roofing materials. The breeze cooled her slightly, but it was still humid and smelly.

There were clumps of natives behind barricades of cars or rubble, but they didn't seem to care how good or bad the cover was, or whether or not they were seen. She squinted and considered.

The fire picked up. Closer.

It wasn't well aimed. Some of the locals, "skinnies" in military slang, were holding their weapons sideways to spray. Some were holding them overhead. Others were firing single shots for better effect, but ruining that effect by snapping the weapons down, as if using them to throw bullets. None of them were in cover now. They'd swarmed out of squat, blocky apartments built of extruded concrete, now chipped and broken. They darted around in the streets shooting at each other mostly, with an occasional burst toward the convoy.

Still, there was a lot of metal flying.

The vehicles accelerated, and Elke wondered why there weren't more closed and armored vehicles. Oh, yes. The goal was to appear "nonthreatening" because they were peacekeepers, not combat troops. Apparently no one had told the locals about that.

Then she heard screeching fiber tires on road and crashing brush guards and bumpers, and the convoy bound up in a cluster. They were among two- to three-story buildings with empty windows, interspersed with sprawling town houses from the early years of colonization.

Okay, that was bad.

Whoever was in charge, that lieutenant, was a *zkurvený* idiot. You *never* let this happen. You sent out point vehicles, outriders, had satellite or air images real time, and had enough power up front to drive over or blow through obstacles. Whatever it took to prevent being boxed in.

Elke took in the surroundings as dust blew by, stirred by the tires scraping the surface. Her hair felt as if it was standing on end, despite the dust and sweat starting to cake it. She'd kept an alert eye for critical issues. Now she looked in depth. The skinnies were pouring out of somewhere, and had decided the convoy was a target. She doubted it had been planned, because the initial attack had been incompetent and undergunned, and the arrivals were not in any order, just groups.

She felt a jerk as they started moving again, but slowly. The convoy was still bunched up.

Large population, low employment or usage, lots of weapons.

That was a bad scene for trouble, because it became entertainment. And yes, there were people cheering on factions in matching colors, waving banners. One group was behind a cluster of armed men and boys, who were shirtless and wearing sandals with their rifles. Another was on a rooftop some distance away. They seemed to abide by the formality of separating combatants and noncombatants at least.

The fire was increasing. Most of it wasn't aimed, but it was certainly concentrating more toward the convoy, and the law of averages said a hit would occur sooner or later.

Elke swapped glances with Jason next to her and Alex a seat forward. Their movements were imperceptible, but their expressions were clear. She knew Jason from a previous contract and trusted his input. His look agreed with hers, and that wasn't good for her confidence.

They were all wishing for armor, weapons, and contact with their people. While the soldiers had more familiarity with the area, they didn't seem to take it seriously. Familiarity was leading to contempt, but casualties were inevitable even from idiots if one didn't take precautions.

She leaned out again to assess threats. Two things happened.

A round snapped by, cracking the air and making people duck. Then, the soldier nearest her reached out an arm and said, "Miss, I think you better sit down. It's getting a little hot—"

"Just get out of my way!" Elke snapped. She got very tired being the object of protection. Especially by some twenty-year-old infantry kid she could best use as a sandbag to tamp a shaped charge with. He did move, though, even if he seemed offended. He was marshalling his thoughts for a retort but she turned away and ignored it.

Her brain caught movement, she identified a threat, and pointed, "Grenade, there, now! The rocket!"

"Huh? What?" the kid replied, looking vaguely in that direction. He clearly didn't see it.

Which was fine. Forearm between body armor and face shield, right under the chin, a twist to the grip of his weapon and a pull, and Elke raised it left-handed to her eye, clicked the safety, and squeezed. She felt it thump her shoulder as it banged.

Oh, good. His safety was cut, too. Otherwise, she would have looked very silly, right up until they all looked very dead.

"God damn you, bitch!" the kid shouted, and tried to wrestle it back. She could have kept it, but she'd accomplished what she needed to and let him take it.

"Thanks," Alex leaned back and acknowledged. He'd seen the same threat.

"No problem," she nodded.

"What the fuck do you think you're doing?" the kid asked, snarling. The patronizing politeness was gone now.

"Your job," she replied as she turned back. They were just roaring past the building corner she'd pointed to. Her grenade had blown the motor compartment off a ground car, and shredded some indigene with an antitank launcher. She pointed again for emphasis. She controlled the shaking she felt.

The grunt looked offended. Likely that wasn't due to her gender, just due to his attitude. Somebody needed to remind him that all Ripple Creek Executive Protection Division contractors were military veterans, and either special operations vets or civilian security vets as well.

Hopefully, they'd quickly be at their destination, where her better, high-quality weapons were waiting, along with her crate of toys.

She grinned and felt a tinge of lust.

CHAPTER TWO

They traveled in silence the remaining few kilometers to the palace, the troops fuming and distant, even if close enough to touch.

As they neared the edifice, Alex assessed it with a practiced eye. He recognized it from photos, but it was a bit worse for wear. Random fire had hit it, and not much maintenance had been done. It was apparent why the press always showed it from a distance, even apart from security concerns. The palace had never been impressive architecturally, merely large. With a scruffy façade, it just wasn't eye-catching, especially through heat-crazed air.

As they got closer it grew larger, and didn't get much worse, but certainly not better. There were desiccated lawns around it, with some weeds creeping in, and low walls and spike fences that had been more than decorative at one point, with sensors and stunners and other defenses. The bright sunlight just seemed to point out the current lack.

Then their grumbly peeled out of the convoy and drove into the palace grounds. There were security present; locals with rifles, in actual clothes. They all wore identical near-new boots. Those and jackets with a logo on the back were their "uniform." At first, that wasn't reassuring. Then it was, because it meant *someone* was trying to create a semblance of order and professionalism.

Of course, the smoking, drinking, and lolling about with elbows on the wall, or lying unconscious on the grass, spread-eagled and snoring, didn't help that image. The entire team groaned.

The female sergeant who'd looked jealous earlier now snickered and said, "Better you than us, contractors."

"Thanks, troops," he said with a nod. He wanted to be on as good terms as possible, because they'd have to work together. He gathered his team by eye. Bart had the controller for the pallet and brought it forward on capacitor.

"Thanks, Lieutenant," he added to the convoy commander as he walked forward. The rest apparently didn't feel like talking, at least not to their hosts.

The troops were behind, as were the palace guards, and ahead was the palace itself with more troops waiting. Still, they moved cautiously from habit. Nothing around here registered as safe.

As they approached, one of the real soldiers—not local—took a half step out.

"ID, please," he said.

Alex stepped up, showed his, flashed his orders on a chit to match those on the screen. In turn, the rest of them cleared themselves in.

"We need to unload our gear," Alex said.

"Yes, sir. Right through the arch and you can go through the double doors." The attitude here was a bit more professional. The guards were Marines, he noted with a tinge of pride. No, he was not a Marine anymore, dammit.

"Thanks." He kept his thoughts to himself. This wasn't the place.

The entrance was up a few steps. Bart negotiated the pallet over them with skill, and then through a massively armored entryway. The outside doors were for show. Inside that were vaultlike doors, a portcullis, a vehicle trap, fighting shields that could deploy from the walls . . .

After a glance, Elke said, "The walls are armored against explosives, and have periodic breaks to let the pressure vent before it reaches inside."

"So it would smear any attackers?" Jason asked.

"And then spew them like stew, yes," she said, while pointing at a joint. "See here?"

"I'll take your word," Jason said. He was technically trained, but that was pretty esoteric. Alex had no idea on the subject, other than the basic manuals for placing charges.

Well inside now, surrounded by enough assets for a small town, some semblance of order was achieved. They each shouldered a ruck, a duffel, and weapons, leaving one of the NCOs to watch the rest, which he assured them would be delivered. The pallet would go through a cargo route upstairs that was less awkward than this route, but longer. Besides the Marines, there were a few support personnel passing by. They were probably honest, but it was a lot of gear the team were each and collectively signed and accountable for.

Once they were a way down the hall, Jason asked, "What the fuck happened to my Army? It used to be professionals and they were competent." He glanced around in case he'd offended any lurkers. He didn't seem to really care, but there was this image to maintain.

"Politics," Alex said. "The last SecGen drove out the good ones. Now we have a war with what's on hand, which isn't much."

"It's scary. Depressing. Fuck." Jason apparently didn't feel like discussing it further.

The first point of business was to coordinate the operation. A female Aerospace Force Tech 1 in spotless, almost unused battledress led them through cool, lit hallways. Her name tag said "White." With her was an AF security NCO named Buckley. White had a pistol, he had an abbreviated combat load: all weapons, no ruck.

The team had memorized the floor plan, but this area had not been on those plans. They swapped guarded looks. Not in concern over the screwup. That was expected, inevitable. Their concern was about the potential threats that had not been uncovered yet. Glancing around, they determined these corridors were little used and rather old, with a hint of dust and must. Hopefully, that disuse meant they were not a well-known route.

But they would be soon. There were other personnel walking around the maze, all potential leaks, and one such group fell in with them.

A dusty officer with a ragged voice asked, "Agent Marlow?" His uniform was not spotless and unused. He wore a well-broken-in harness and carried a scratched submachine gun, commo helmet, and strapped gear. So did his men. They were all male, all serious business, and clearly professional.

"Here," Alex agreed.

"I'm Major Weilhung." He paused a moment with a hint of challenge in his expression, that seemed to say, *Yes, that is my name, can we dispense with stupid jokes and move on?* "I'm commanding the palace and movement security."

"Good, glad to meet you already," Alex said, offering his hand. They swapped firm grips. It was true, and diplomatic. The six of them were the immediate escort for Bishwanath. They alone couldn't stop a serious force. They could only get him out of line of fire, secure a room, and call for extraction. Weilhung was the officer in charge of said extraction. Good relations with him were necessary. Thank God he seemed competent.

"Yeah, likewise. It's a bit disorganized out there," Weilhung said.

Seeing the expression on his face, Alex said what Weilhung couldn't. "You mean it's a massive wringer and sledgehammer party and all of our balls are hanging out?"

The AF escort choked and tried to stifle a grin. Unsuccessfully. She made no comment.

"I would never put it that way," Weilhung said, then whispered, "where I could be heard and nailed for it." Their boots clattered on tiled floor and hid the comment from casual hearing. Raising his voice again, he said, "But that's an interesting comment. Yeah, it's a mess and going to get worse. You know the background here?" He waved a portable damper to show they were secure against surveillance. That was interesting, because on-site with the principal nearby was a very unusual place to hold a no-shit briefing. Apparently, Weilhung was short of time.

They were approaching a pair of wood-façaded security doors that looked elegant when closed but like vault doors when opened and visible from the edges. They led into the palace proper; Alex recognized the room beyond from maps: it was the conference room in the third basement.

"Weak government," Alex replied. "Largely symbolic, allowed massive tribal chaos and all kinds of off-planet piracy and terror. Got out of hand, Army came in and put in the boot, Bishwanath is a temp at least, maybe longer, because he's a known quantity with a background. Tribes are still fighting, crime syndicate is still operating, with the equivalent of national armies to protect them, several other factions all wanting their ideals to be the new order, and nuking the whole planet from orbit is not an option."

Elke muttered, "I hate that last part. The mushroom clouds would be so pretty in a glowing honeycomb hex," as Alex bit down and said evenly, "Have I missed anything?"

Weilhung nodded as he pointed to chairs. "That's a good synopsis. Things are coming apart fast, though. BuState keeps talking about a peaceful solution. General Ellis wants to use force, I want to use a lot more, and the locals are already doing so, even if not in a very effective manner."

"That's why they pay us the big money," Alex quipped. He looked around. No damage down here. So the palace was decent cover, and the lower areas had not been breached in the fighting. The tunnels were an obvious bolt-hole, and might still be secure for now. He'd still want those mapped and any exits sealed.

"Yeah, but you have to see the locals to believe it. They're more dangerous to themselves than each other, but there's a lot of stray fire, and twenty million of the twits. And the flipping media makes them out to be some kind of romantic heroes."

"We saw some of that on the way in," Alex agreed. "Common morons with guns. Bad concept."

He took a long drink from the straw on his ruck strap. The water was cool but not cold. They were inside, facilities were nearby, and he was thirsty. There were good tactical reasons not to drink too much when convoying. There were good tactical reasons to stay well-hydrated the rest of the time.

The gear was heavy, cut into shoulders, and caused his people to make occasional grunts from bumping each other or walls. No one said anything. That was part of the job. It was going to be like this for months, which is why they got paid as they did.

Tech 1 White held doors for them, then hurried ahead. She was decorative, but she was also very practical, which Alex appreciated. He didn't like comments about support people. You lived or died depending on how support staff did their jobs or didn't. White was familiar with the surroundings, glad to help, didn't get in the way, and seemed discreet. He made note to make use of her if she was around. You thanked such people by giving them enough work to stay busy and letting them know they were useful and needed.

"Right in here," she said, speaking for the first time. "This is the Private Parlor, where President Bishwanath will be working. Through there are his apartments. Through here"—she opened another door—"is the Front Parlor. These rooms to the side are yours. I'm at six-three-nine-one if you have any questions."

"Thanks, Tech White," Alex said. This time, the others chimed in. That they felt more gratitude to a functionary than the grunts was telling, Alex thought. He frowned. That would have to be fixed somehow. They couldn't resent the people they worked with.

White and Buckley left, they started unpacking gear, starting with weapons, and looked around. Paneled wood, rugs on polished floors, minimal artwork, comfortable furnishings. They each had a private room with a shower. That was all they had time for, but it was certainly much choicer facilities than the holding barracks Corporate had kept them in on arrival the night before in Kaporta. The Front Parlor did connect directly to the President's quarters, so they could guard both entrances. Both entrances were on the same end of the hallway. There was no real alternate way out. That would have to be fixed.

"Cover those damned windows and get some shutters," Bart muttered. Past him, Alex could see a lizardlike bird analog, tiny and cute and with feathers that were almost scales.

"Indeed," Jason agreed. "Cover and concealment. I don't care if it's a courtyard, I don't want to be a target."

"I already was apprised of that and put in a work order with the engineers," Alex said, trying to soothe nerves. "It may be a week."

"So everyone watch your profile," Aramis said. "Shaman doesn't need the work."

"I can always operate on the coffee table," Shaman joked. "It is broad, flat, and a good height if I am sitting." Or was he serious?

"Everyone got local time?" Alex asked.

"Yes," Jason said. "Twenty-one hours, twenty minutes, and some odd seconds, Earth time, divided into twenty sixty-four minute hours, with a second very slightly shorter than Earth's to account for the difference. I've got Zulu Time on one screen and Local Meridian time here on the other."

"Good," Alex nodded. "Everyone else?" There was agreement.

"Going to take a bit to get used to a short day," Aramis commented.

"Eh, I just sleep when not working, read when I happen to be awake, and work out before breakfast," Bart said. "That is left over from idiot synthmod stars who perform until oh two hundred and party until oh nine hundred, then sleep before traveling."

"You're not coming from the ten div or twenty-eight-hour day I'm coming from," Jason groused. "Try that."

The second bundle of gear came up on the cargo elevator and was delivered, which was far better than having to go back down for it. While unsorting that, Alex's phone beeped. He used no music, colorful auras, or other expressiveness because it was strictly a tool, and encrypted in several layers to keep it secure. He had his set to beep and tingle, so he'd be aware of it.

"Marlow," he answered.

"Alex, Massa here. How goes it?" a deep voice asked. Agent Massa was the District Agent for all RC contractors in the capital and surrounding areas, which pretty much meant this continent.

"Good, sir. We just rolled in, got our basic gear. I'm going to ask again about more weapons."

"Yeah, and then you'll ask again until I buy some out of pocket to shut you up. Feel free to acquire some. My hands are tied by the BuState assholes."

"Understood, sir. Local purchase."

"Yup. For cash. We'll cover you but don't know about it." At least with the Company, when they said, "we'll cover you," they actually meant it. That still meant the hassle of acquiring weapons they should have been able to bring. BuState was bent on this being a "low-key" operation.

Bishwanath was a president. There would be nothing low key about guarding him, Alex feared.

"Got it. I'm on-site and you can log me in. I'll send my updates when you ask."

"Weekly will be fine unless I call. Good luck, Alex. Massa out."

"Thank you, sir. Out."

He had no sooner disconnected than it buzzed again. He answered.

"Agent Marlow, this is Tech White," she said with a clear, perfectly modulated voice. "President Bishwanath is on his way up, and would like to meet all of you."

"Of course," Alex said. "We're a bit grubby, though." Sooner or later, they had to find out if the President was a straight shooter, or a stick in the ass. Now was as good as any.

"I'll forward that information. White out."

"Marlow out."

He turned to the others. "Head's up. The VIP is on his wa—" he was saying as there was a knock at the door frame, followed by it opening.

Bishwanath came in.

It was obvious who he was. No one else would be traipsing

around the palace in a suit, surrounded by Recon soldiers with carbines and other lethal hardware.

Without hesitation, they stood to attention.

"Sir!" Alex said crisply. "A pleasure to meet you at last."

"I rather think we are meeting at first," Bishwanath said, eyes twinkling behind his glasses. Glasses, not contacts, not surgically corrected. That's how far back this place was. "You would be Agent Marlow, and this would by Sykora, Weil, Vaughn, Anderson, and Mbuto?"

Alex didn't raise his eyebrow, but was impressed. He'd taken the time to learn about his contract underlings. That spoke well of him and was definitely a hint as to why he'd been chosen for this. His English was English. Where had he gone to school? One of the Oxford colleges?

"Correct, sir," he said, and shook the offered hand, then moved aside to allow the rest access.

Over his shoulder, Bishwanath said, "Thank you, Captain Nugent, I appreciate your escort."

"No problem, sir. We'll be around for backup whenever you travel, and on patrol in the palace at all times." The captain was in armor and field gear but with short sleeves. Still, full gear in the palace showed that the President wasn't a wimp, understood practicality, and was a gentleman who could handle any function.

It also meant that large numbers of professionals felt that such garb was needed, despite large numbers of professionals. So the local security had to be just the shit.

"Excellent."

Ugly, Alex thought to a completely different conversation than the audible one.

Nugent saluted Bishwanath, nodded to Alex, and left with his troops.

"Agent Marlow," Bishwanath said as he turned back.

"Mister President. How may I help you?"

"Please sit, and get on with whatever tasks you have. Can I have some drinks brought? Ades? Fizzes?" He produced a small pod and flipped it open.

"Could we get some tart lemonade and a sport ade, sir? That's very thoughtful, thank you." Alex wasn't going to serve his troops sweetened goo. That was on their own dime.

"Absolutely." Bishwanath tapped an order into the handheld

while Alex studied him. The man came from the local warring tribes, but knew several languages and was quite at home with modern technology. He seemed to understand the accepted courtesies of space-based society, as it was called, though it was hardly an accurate term. They were here in space on a rock that was a desolate hellhole.

But Bishwanath was well above that. Dapper, even elegant in appearance, dark olive skin with graying hair, on a slim but healthy build, though shorter than Alex by several centimeters. The man was cultured, urbane, and sophisticated.

"All I want to do," Bishwanath said, "is learn a little about you, find out what I can do to make your job easier, and if there's any support you need." He met Alex's eyes and seemed casually relaxed for any input. Diplomatic.

"Well, sir, we have issues of travel, palace security, communication, support, and then our personal issues," Alex itemized as he thought on the fly. "Travel we'll be examining as soon as we can, both the vehicles and routes to be used, and our tactics will be predicated on whether the trip is for appearance, or if a discreet approach can be used. That's the realm of myself and Mister Vaughn."

Vaughn stood from his gear and nodded at the introduction. He'd been stowing rifles and ammunition in a rack, after function-checking them and loading them.

He said, "Yes, sir. I'll look over the vehicles and routes, and I'll assign our personnel where needed. I'll coordinate with the military convoys, and with your personal guards as needed."

"Yes, my personal guards," Bishwanath said with a frown. "How do I say this diplomatically? You are far better trained than my palace guards, and I place more faith in your contractual detachment than their loyalty, if you take my meaning." At that moment, a servant brought in a broad tray with pitchers of lemonade, and electrolytic drinks, glasses, ice, and a plate of cookies.

"Thank you, Rahul." He turned back and said, "And you may confide as you need to in Rahul. He's been my right hand for decades, even if he looks domestic. In fact, that is his greatest cover."

"Ah, yes, sir," Alex said. "Make note of anything you need that the guards can't handle and I'll see it's taken care of without mention. A pleasure to meet you, Rahul."

"And you, sir," the man said. He was fairly robust and broad but looked meek, until you saw his eyes. The man had been in some action. His voice was deep and a little gravelly.

Bishwanath continued as if there'd been no interruption, as Rahul left. "Excellent, Mister Marlow. And Mister Vaughn."

"Palace security," Alex continued as if he hadn't just been told the locals were full of leaks and potentially corruptible as neutrals or enemies, "breaks down into external and internal. The military has external, though we'll watch this immediate perimeter. Inside, it's the domain of Miss Sykora and Mister Mbuto."

They stood. Elke was sweaty from shifting boxes of gear, mostly explosive. Shaman was carefully cleaning his hands from handling nonmedical gear. He did that almost constantly and without conscious thought.

"I will be setting up monitors and reactive devices on several internal perimeters, sir," Elke said. She took a healthy gulp from a glass of lemonade. She gasped when done and said, "Even if we are not around, there will be defensive mechanisms. I would like to install some in your private apartments, if you will trust me."

Bishwanath looked slightly tense, then fought it down. "How much eavesdropping is required?" he asked.

"Sir, I will be happy to shut it off at any time on your order. If you need privacy for political or personal considerations, it's none of my business to monitor. At the same time, automatic systems should be armed, and you can override on a word if you need to. The more I can monitor from here, the better. I'm sure you're worried about publicity of secrets—"

More likely publicity of girlfriends, Alex thought.

"—but my system is programmed not to keep logs of that. You are welcome to come look for yourself anytime. But only you or one technician you escort, to keep my material secure."

"And I would like to monitor your vital signs, and also air ducts, windows, and food," Shaman said. "Let me know of exercise and I can instruct it to ignore high metabolic readings. I would like to make periodic inspections of the quarters, and I will escort you on each trip. After any attack, I will examine you for external injuries. It is possible not to be aware of them."

"Yes, I have had that happen," Bishwanath nodded. "I agree. Please pardon me. I'm not used to this level of attention and it feels not only odd but intrusive, even though I know it is necessary." He looked disturbed and sad, then resumed a professional mask.

Alex recalled Bishwanath was married, but his wife would not be along until things stabilized. She was still on Earth as a moderately wealthy exile. Of course, that "moderately wealthy" had translated to "hugely wealthy" here. That had to be a lifestyle change.

And that wasn't his concern. His concern was keeping this principal safe. How was Bishwanath dealing with the separation? That was something to follow up on.

Few people realized there was a necessary rapport between guards and their principals. You had to learn their mannerisms, quirks, how they'd respond to requests, demands, being slammed to the ground for cover, how to motivate them to keep their morale up in a crisis. A polite, intelligent, and friendly charge made it easier, but it was possible and just as important with a jerk you hated, as long as he understood you'd do your job.

Bishwanath was easy, so far, but any VIP at this level had to be hiding secrets. Alex didn't need to know those secrets, but he did need to have a feel for the man.

"And what of Mister Weil and Mister Anderson?" Bishwanath asked.

"They're our youngest and toughest, sir," Alex said, without adding, *and most expendable.* "They'll be close in, and prepared to carry you if needed, block you from harm, aggressively protect you from threats. At the same time, we are specialists in our fields but each cross-trained to some extent. At any moment, the operator on scene or seeing a threat may take charge, and we will follow those orders until circumstances resolve. So if Mister Anderson locates a threat outside while I'm still in the car, you can expect that I will do as he tells me as far as reacting and responding to it."

"And you'd like me to do the same, you are saying," Bishwanath said with a nod. He didn't seem bothered by the idea. In fact, he seemed glad of the discussion. Good.

"Exactly, sir, and I appreciate your understanding. It helps us do our job."

"We should talk again, then, when I have time. In the meantime, I think we should look over our upcoming itinerary as soon as we can."

"Excellent, sir." Alex waved and everyone moved in close. He noted with approval all now had body armor, carbines, and pistols, and were assembling commo rigs. They'd do everything in that basic gear except shower, for the duration of the mission.

Bishwanath opened up his doccase and started fingering commands. He had the latest style that worked on finger movement without any actual contact with keys, and wasn't popular because it took a lot of sensitivity and training to operate. That was another sign that he was comfortable with modern, even futuristic tools. The device clashed with his glasses and archaic suit.

"These are times, locations, and purposes," he said. "You'll notice several are to smaller venues to meet with tribal leaders. I cannot insult them by demanding they be disarmed. Your Bureau of State would like me to not make those appearances, but I must."

Alex cringed. Yeah, he had issues with that. Huge ones. He glanced around. Elke was grinning, probably at the thought of gadgets and explosives. Aramis seemed to like the idea of being Billy Badass to the peasants. No doubt he could clobber several of them at once, but the idea was to avoid engagements when possible.

Alex said all he could. "We'll manage. Do you have body armor yet, sir?"

"I do, but could use advice on it."

"Mister Weil will work with you. That's his field." In part because he'd done more actual close-in bodyguarding as opposed to combat missions. That would not be a good way to phrase it, however.

"Thank you," Bishwanath said, and Bart nodded.

"My pleasure, sir. I think I shall enjoy your attitude in contrast to some of the celebrities and corporate managers I've protected."

CHAPTER THREE

Bishwanath left an hour later. They knew his approximate itinerary for a week, and it was a packed one, and had learned some details about him.

"So, how's everyone feel on this?" Alex asked.

There wasn't any hesitation. Bart had the most experience as an actual bodyguard and said, "Good man. He won't cause a lot of problems or pull an attitude that I can see."

"I also will work well with him," Elke said.

"No problem," from Aramis. "He's honest and open."

"He is a bit reserved in my area," Shaman said. "I will need to watch him, but I don't expect him to hinder me treating him."

Jason said, "Things look so good as far as he's concerned, I expect everything else will be screwed up beyond belief."

Alex nodded. "Good principal. We have most of our gear. The military has made contact. All we have to do for now is our job. Let's finish."

There were nods and the work of setting up resumed.

"These are severely nice digs," Elke said, the odd word choice garnishing her accent.

"Yes, they are," Alex acknowledged. They each had a small but comfortable room, two shared bathrooms, and the common room decked out as conference or reception room with a living area near a vid console. He sighed and said, "Aramis, take your feet off the table, please. If you need a foot stool, there's one over there."

"Hell, boss, they'll charge it off as wear and tear, no big deal."

But he did comply, removing them from a very expensive octagonal table turned and carved from wood, and putting them down on a hand-stitched rug that had to have taken years. The issue was more a matter of the item's location than value. Still, feet didn't go on furniture. As long as he complied, the talking back was a quirk. Irritating, but a quirk.

Getting settled in was a major operation. Weapons were now scattered about, though that "scatter" was intentional and precise, putting them within easy reach of anyone, anywhere in the room. Those weapons either had safety circuits disabled, or were programmed to recognize any of the team's grip or DNA to activate. Civilians and politicians insisted on the "safety" interrupts to prevent "criminal use." Criminals destroyed those circuits on stolen weapons, and professionals did so whenever they could get away with it, laws be damned. The circuit might work the first time 499 times out of five hundred. But Murphy said it was that five hundredth time your life would depend on instant operation.

"Nothing like legal and diplomatic bullshit to fuck things up," Aramis said. "I want my fucking knife."

"Yeah." Alex agreed with him totally on that. Celadon wasn't stable, so they'd entered through a starport in Salin's other nation, Kaporta, which was where they were officially operating from. The local laws there prohibited large knives, as well as axes and shock batons. There'd even been an argument over "guards" having lethal weapons rather than crowd-control types. However, the lethal hardware was corporate issue, so it had reluctantly been cleared. The knives, tomahawks, and batons they'd wanted for close quarters had all been put in bond until their departure, as a "courtesy." It was a courtesy none of them appreciated. They'd been able to bring some of their folding knives, the smaller ones.

That and the tension with the Army weren't a good sign of how this operation would go. There'd be more territorial infighting than shooting of targets, if Alex's guess was correct.

One of their items was an upright "wardrobe" that was a rotating arms locker. Much of their support gear was within. Pistols were loaded and placed butt out on racks where they could be easily grasped. They were stowed near ground level. Doctrine held that one used a pistol to fight one's way to the rifle one should have had all along. Ground level made them accessible while diving for cover.

Above those hung rifles and a machine gun. There were spaces for more machine guns, but they had only been authorized the one. Alex would be making connections to acquire more hardware. Each of them was proficient with American, European, Chinese, Russian, and Brazilian Federation weapons.

Once everything was checked and unloaded, Alex called Tech White again.

"How may I help you, Agent Marlow?" she asked.

"Yes, ma'am," he said. She wasn't a ma'am, but more smoothing. You were never wrong to call an AF member "sir" or "ma'am." They liked their politeness. "I'd like to look around, and if Major Weilhung is available, I'd like to go with him so we can discuss our protective strategy."

"I'll give you a contact list and put you through," she said.

Twenty minutes later, the two commanders were patrolling the palace, and the entire EP team was out separately, except for Bart who was guarding the entrance to the President's quarters proper. Alex had debated bringing him along too, but they didn't want to suggest to the military that any of their EPD duties could be taken over by soldiers. That type of bureaucratic authority grabbing had happened before.

Alex and Weilhung both carried two floor plans, one on computer, one on paper. At each door they made notes and marked distance, then entered to mark windows. Lots of those windows had been blown out in fighting. They were now being repaired. Because the locals were largely unskilled and unreliable, the work was being done by military engineers and contractors at Earth taxpayer expense. Not that there was any guarantee there weren't infiltrators among the contractors, who might plant sensors, beacons for missiles, or just an outright bomb, but the odds were against it, and odds were part of the game.

"Obviously not made to make our job easier," Weilhung commented.

"Yeah. Pretty, but not well-defensible," Alex said. "What do we do?"

"All we can do with the politics," Weilhung said with a twist of an eyebrow. "I have good people on regular patrol, I've got cameras and sensorwebs coming. I have regular but handpicked sentries at all entrances, and you saw the vehicle barricades."

"Yeah. What about those indigenous guards? Our principal doesn't like them much himself."

"Oh, you saw them," Weilhung said, with a smirk that turned into a grimace. "They're trip wires. Best they can be."

"And an invite to test the rest of the defenses. I expect some action," Alex said.

"Right. They also look like shit in the press. Wonderful setup. It's going to be a long job."

"I'm going to work on our setup," Alex said. "This floor and the apartments. That's as far as we should get from our principal."

"That makes sense," Weilhung said. "I'll finish securing the rest."

"Right. I'll be in touch."

Overlapping with that discussion, the EP team was out in rotating pairs, assessing and taking photos, then planning defensive movement and positions around what they had. Every exit, window, cubby that could be identified was checked, marked, and regarded. While Alex kept Weilhung busy, Jason figured it was his job to get things done quietly. "I can lay a gun here and cover the loading dock," Jason said of a small service restroom that was largely non-functional and very remote. Likely, it had been abandoned for years.

"Is it better than that shielded balcony, you think?" Aramis asked.

"Not as good of cover, but much less obvious, and allows an enfilade."

"Yup. Mark it."

"Got it."

The palace wasn't excessive, but was as large as a typical hotel. In fact, it appeared to be built on the same frame, with a fancier shell stuck over it. The dressed stone and carved points were all attached to the aluminum trusses that supported it. With conference rooms, guest suites, and the President's personal area, all down long hallways, it was easy to see the shape. That private area was being stripped of the previous occupant's décor and belongings, which were variously being sold, taken to museums, or recycled, meaning "looted," and being refitted for the new administration. The team went through everything they could find to look for traps or threats, and to set up potential escape routes and defenses.

"I don't like those stairs," Elke said. "Far too open. I'd like to mine them."

"Mine them how?" Horace Mbuto asked. The two of them were together. He had worked with Jason and Alex before, but Elke was new to him.

"To collapse from the top. We have better ways out. Stairs need to be wide enough for us, not much wider or narrower. I want to equip all the narrow ways with fragmentation, and the wide ones to be taken out of the picture. That leaves us the elevators if we have escort, the six staircases that work best for us, and the roof or window slides."

"Ask Alex. Makes sense to me."

"Alex, take a look at this image." She captured a shot of the stairs through her shades. "They're too wide and I'd like to be able to remove them."

"How long to set up, how dangerous?" he asked.

"No danger. I'll have a keyed device. Not long. I can do it now."

"Do it."

"Roger." She looked at Horace and said, "Cover me?"

"Surely."

It was good practice and safe procedure. He scanned both directions in the upper mezzanine, then over her and down the marble stairs with their neo-Southwestern carpet runners. They looked to be real nylon, not Dacron or any of the modern substitutes.

"How is this done?" he asked.

"Charges under the carpet," she said. "Word might get out, but that helps, too. It means no one will risk coming this way. I can drop the entire second flight straight to the floor. That's ten meters."

"With concrete. You'll make work for me, girl," he said. Some of the paintings on the wall were real pieces from Earth. A pity they were faded or damaged. He examined them for known names. Yes, Lubov. Garner. Likely some others. Two hundred or more years old. People didn't expect a man like Horace Mbuto to know his classics and finer points of medicine. He enjoyed breaking the stereotype.

"No, because these aren't people we're going to worry about," she grinned while she worked. "I'll also run wires into the power system that I can trigger by frequency modulation. Even if the power is out, I can detonate."

"Nice. How much explosive do you have?" He peered down quickly, then went back to scanning for threats. She had sliced and peeled the carpet with surgical precision.

"I ordered a mixed tonne. They let me get five hundred kilos through. I'll have to arrange another shipment."

"Hidden how?" Five hundred kilos of HE. The woman didn't do dainty.

"Oh, not hidden. That was just a safety limit on that aircraft. The rest will arrive in a few days." She seemed comfortable having a conversation behind her back without turning.

The bureaucrats might be a bigger enemy than any faction, he thought. And they couldn't be shot. Though the temptation to arrange accidents had occurred to all of them and was a regular subject of discussion. It was always like that.

Danger aside, the team was hired for having outrageous amounts of competency in the core tasks involved. Their strong, silent demeanor on duty was practiced to make them both discreet and seem unthreatening. Professionals knew what they were. Bystanders had no idea other than vague notions of guards against attackers, or more likely, annoying people who wanted to meet the celebrity/public figure. That left an undefined group who thought them easy marks.

That was the group they liked meeting and disillusioning. Horace was hoping they'd be alive so he could show them his medical skills. He'd be frugal with the anesthetic.

Back in their den of professionalism, Alex called another conference. Once everyone sprawled on couches and chairs, or in Aramis's case, flopped down on the thick rug and fondling a carbine, he pointed to the vidwall.

"Okay, let's look at maps and routes. We're here, and the parliament is there. The convention center where most of the meetings will be for now is there," he indicated with a laser pointer. "He'll have to make public appearances several places. Those will not be outside, but will be accessible to the public." The map was large scale and had holograms of the key buildings. It was quite recent, having been constructed by Aerospace Force intel, from aerial and space images, but stuff changed daily around here.

"Is Recon dealing with the interdiction problem?" Aramis asked.

"Yes, crowds and security will be handled by Recon and Bashinghutch contractors." Alex said.

"Oh, them." Aramis sounded disgusted.

"Yeah, them," Jason said. "But even though they're not well

paid and don't have high standards, we can hope the reality of this place makes them alert."

"I doubt it," Alex said. "They're local hires." Aramis was right to sound annoyed.

"Ohhh, shit." Jason sagged back on the couch. He kept switching from confident to cynical. His worldview was being challenged.

"Yup. Both Weilhung and Corporate have complaints in about that. Maybe it will get somewhere. Hopefully we, meaning him, will get to vet them. Dunno. Just assume everything is a threat. Also remember, we're civil guards."

"Meaning what in this case?" Aramis asked.

Shaman grinned hugely, clapped him on the shoulder, and boomed, "Meaning we have to wear suits and look 'professional,' not helmets and hard clamshells."

Aramis didn't say anything. He just shared a look with everyone else.

"Yup," Alex said. "We look like suits. Soft impact armor underneath."

"Issue with that," Elke said.

"We all have issues with that, but go ahead," Alex said, looking at her.

"Do we have armor tailored for females, so I don't look like I'm stuffed in a sack and obviously wearing? Or should I wear it oversized, chop my hair, put on my shades, and look like a young male?"

"Good question. I'll find out. I'm not sure about tailoring it once it arrives."

"That's my concern, yes," she said. One didn't just sew ballistic armor. Then, the cooling vest she wore underneath would have to be adjusted. Both modifications took special tools. Aerospace Force likely had some along. The Army was supposed to, but that was a long bet.

"The other concern is that any female family members or guests of Bishwanath will have to have you as an escort everywhere, including the bathroom. You're also the only female. That means you'll be alone in threat zones."

"I'll go in. Stick Anderson outside the door. He's young enough to pass as a girl."

"Hey! I—"

"Can it, both of you," Alex said. While the kid brought it on himself, they were all determined to throw it back at him, hard. He needed to perform well in his first few engagements and they'd leave him alone. Until then, the hazing would continue.

There were nods, and they gathered around the maps. The holosheets showed buildings and terrain, as well as the flat features of roads. Controls allowed traffic flow to appear, approximating what had been last recorded. There were a lot of buildings and vehicles. Few of them were intact or operational.

"This place is regressing fast," Jason said.

"About like Liberia or Cameroon twenty years ago," Shaman said. "And it's an older story than that. War interrupts development, scavenging starts, it turns into a cycle. Only outside help can do anything at that point."

"And then there's who wants Bishwanath dead," Bart said.

"Everybody," Elke offered.

"Pretty much. Everyone except the Bishwanath clan."

"There's one other problem," Alex said. "Having to deal with the military. Regs aside, it's the bureaucracy. It can take weeks to get anything resolved. We'll have hours at best to deal with threats, possibly seconds.

"We'll have him secure here and we're backup to them, we move him where he needs to go, military keeps the perimeter secure, we bring him back. Those exchanges from military control to us are going to be where he's got the most protection and the most exposure, and some idiot arguing about precedence or jurisdiction to screw the works. Then there's the cops . . ."

"And BuState," Jason said.

"Yes. They want everything done diplomatically. You can't use diplomacy on an illiterate peasant with a rifle, unless you define 'diplomacy' as 'shoot him.'"

"I have my explosives," Elke offered. "If there's too much talk and not enough action, I can 'create a diversion' as they say, so we can snatch control again."

Alex just stared at her.

"Elke, that's outrageous, insane, and even the suggestion could get you charged with terrorism."

"Sorry, sir," she said. She looked depressed. He still wasn't sure if that was an act or if she really liked explosives that much.

"Don't be. It's brilliant. We're debating with the dips, there's a bang, we toss a 'fuck you' over the shoulder as we head for the car. I like it. But you *have* to be totally discreet or we'll get burned. Use it as a backup measure only."

"I can have a charge ready to go and leave it somewhere on-site. We only need to detonate it if there's a problem."

"Is that workable?"

"It means wasting explosive I don't get to blow." She pouted, looking put upon. "And if . . . when . . . anyone else finds them, they'll report it as a potential threat and terrorism."

"That keeps us employed. Even better," Bart commented. "More threats."

"As long as they don't trace it back to Elke . . . ?" He looked at her.

"I will use locally obtained materials," she said.

"Oh? What do you have?"

"I will tell you that when I obtain some," she said with a confident smile.

"Okay," he took a moment to digest that. Her wit was very dry. "What other diversions and arguments can we have ready for this crap?" Alex asked.

Elsewhere, a parallel discussion about interacting was taking place. Lee Weilhung was forced to be an observer. He tried not to speak.

Colonel Weygandt would have been a smoker in an earlier time. Instead, he fidgeted with a pen. Since this wasn't his desk, he couldn't shuffle ripsheets or fiddle with the computer.

"The Army does fine, why do we need them?" he asked. Which "them" he meant was clear from inflection.

In reply, Colonel Kieso tiredly said, "The Army relies on large numbers of people in organized but inefficient groups to accomplish big goals in a messy fashion. These people are precise and discreet and experts at close-in security. Unless you want to borrow some experts from General Kell's security detail?"

" 'Discreet'?" Weygandt asked, voice raised. "We have four complaints already, including one weapons theft." He was pacing, too.

"Which was returned." Kieso didn't leave his desk. He'd been at this too long to be surprised or bothered. "And should have been coded to avoid outside use." Weilhung heard the hint that too tight an adherence to regs would bite them in the ass. Weygandt didn't seem to get it.

"I'd be inclined to forget that, sir," Weilhung advised, sticking his neck out. "If word gets out that our soldiers can't hang onto their grenade launchers, and that the coding has been disabled, and that a contractor took control of the weapon for combat operations, well . . . you'll have a lot more work, Colonel."

"Yes, you make sense, but I've still got an incident report to write up even without that," Weygandt groused. It was his sorry lot to explain all the discrepancies in this operation, and hand them, as appropriate, to public affairs, the MPs, or the legal office.

"Look," Kieso snapped, "we have contractors all over the place. Admin. Services. Construction. Rebuilding. Perimeter security. Executive protection. Deal with it."

"Oh, I will."

Yes, he'd deal with it, Weilhung could tell. The proper reports and evidence through the proper Assemblyperson's office would deal with it. Never *piss off a lawyer*, he thought.

"And what do you think, Major Weilhung?"

Weilhung had managed to get discreetly back in the corner again, and at mention of him, Weygandt twitched slightly. Weilhung smiled to himself. Lots of intel was gained just from watching and listening when nothing blatant was being discussed.

"I think they seem professional, I know some of them by reputation, and I'll work with them as called for. There's always friction between military and BuState, contractors and soldiers."

"Well, Major, I respect your professionalism. Do please keep an eye peeled. If any of them do anything we can call them on, I intend to pull the contract and have them off planet at once. Your people can take over. People in the chain of command."

People you think you can shove around, Weilhung thought. *Not on my watch, asshole.*

"I advise against that, sir," he said. "They're on the same side. Tactics like that could make them not. Then we'd have trouble. Our goal here is to keep the President healthy to settle things down, not have jurisdictional disputes. It takes a thick skin at times." *And you, you fucking bureaucrat in uniform, don't have what it takes.*

"I'm not talking about a jurisdictional dispute. Army and Marines have jurisdictional disputes. UN and national forces have jurisdictional disputes. I'm talking about fucking civilians taking orders from those BuState whining socialists stepping into a military venue." Weygandt was bent out of shape over an incident that in retrospect was quite minor. That said to Weilhung that he was unsuited for any command. Likely why he was handling legal issues.

At the same time, the audacity of taking a loaded weapon from a troop, then handing it back was impressive and troublesome. Certainly, you did what you had to in a fight. Still, to even consider that method showed an extreme arrogance and lack of respect for the soldiers in question.

"I'll keep an eye out, sir," he said. *For my reasons, not yours.*

But, while he respected the professional capabilities of the EP team, he did not trust them completely. Regardless of contracts, they were not bound to the military system the way he was. They could always play BuState off against MilBu, and use Bishwanath for pull. Weilhung could do that, too, but he'd still be accountable to the military after he left here, and to the same officers. And he had less access to Bishwanath. So he could bend the rules a little and be okay. The contractors could just say "fuck you" and do as they wished, if enough money or power was at stake. Weilhung had no doubt they'd do so to save Bishwanath or themselves, and leave him out to hang.

Weygandt and Keiso were hashing something out. He headed back to the palace as soon as he made eye contact with the colonel and received a nod of dismissal. He wanted those sensors in place now, so he could track those jerks, as well as potential threats.

The military had problems. The civilians had problems. Put both together, and the advantages disappeared to leave just the problems.

Doug deWitt didn't like his putative boss. He knew that was mutual. DeWitt had been here for two years, from when it was just a nowhere place, a colony that was failing into subsidized poverty. His suggestions had been ignored then. Now it was the center of a small war and a gross inconvenience to this sector of space, and he was still being ignored. LeMieure had rolled in here fresh from a SecGen appointment, with neither experience nor professional credentials in any related field. There were a number like that who were all either in BuState supervisory positions or diplomatic positions. Certainly there was always some of that, but it was getting out of hand.

He also wasn't sure why the cretin was up this early. His reputation was for sleeping in late. He did know he didn't like sitting here blinking himself awake with coffee, wearing the same scratchy shirt as late last night, and having to explain information he'd already forwarded as text, video, and slide.

Calm.

"So, what do you think of the 'contractors'?" leMieure asked.

DeWitt shrugged, trying to be noncommittal and relaxed. *That's my favorite chair you're sweating into, you troll.* LeMieure smelled even from here. He was sour, stale, and not generally pleasant. In lieu of a suit or sweater, he wore cheap slacks and a turtleneck. Comfortable, certainly, but not how a professional presented himself to other professionals.

He finally replied, "They have excellent credentials on paper, and the company guarantees their work. They have teams here already under DA Massa. He gave me dossiers on them."

"Dossiers? Why didn't I get dossiers?"

As soon as leMieure said that, and started sounding petulant, deWitt knew it had been a mistake to mention it.

"I'll see about getting them sent back so you can look at them, sir," he lied. They'd been destroyed, and were on a need-to-know basis. So far, BuState, the military, RC, and deWitt had not seen a need for leMieure to know. He wasn't career service, he hadn't been checked, and was a known loudmouth and liar. Even if deWitt didn't care about revealing data on the team, they wouldn't appreciate it, and he had to work with their liaison and various other contractors.

"Good," leMieure said while rubbing his shaggy chin. "I need to know about these people. I don't understand how they think or why they do what they do." He looked agitated, almost scared.

Likely, deWitt thought, because that was one of the few things this man had ever said that was true.

Of course, not giving the man the information he wanted was going to continue that problem. DeWitt wouldn't trust him to properly blow the lid off a story he wanted publicized. Keeping secrets was out of the question, especially as he was already working on an "inside" docufantasy.

DeWitt sighed. Nothing was making his job easier, and there were going to be more problems.

CHAPTER FOUR

That next morning, ready to start their nonroutine schedule, Alex entered the common room after his briefing by secure vid with the higher-ups. He was tired already.

"Okay, we have another issue. . . ." He paused automatically, knowing there'd be groans. He waited while they tapered off. "BuState demands we make an attempt of nonlethal force."

He paused again. They noticed the box under his arm, of course.

"It's not that bad, guys. I spoke at length with a Mister Doug deWitt, and this is largely a public image issue. They want the appearance that we're ready to use nonlethal force, and if it turns out it's not possible, we can shoot the skinnies the way we should anyway."

"Yeah, but that image can get us killed," Jason said. "What happens when we're busy putting on a show while someone uses real firepower?"

"Gotcha covered," Alex nodded and grinned. They were going to *love* this.

He popped open the box and pulled out the baton.

"This comes from a company that specializes in police 'tactical' products. Corporate told them what our requirements were, and they came up with this, and I, personally, like it."

He raised the device, pointed it at Aramis, and gave him a moment to prepare, then pressed the button. The resulting flash was bright enough to overbear the daylight for a moment, and Aramis recoiled.

"Goddam!" he shouted.

"Yup," Alex agreed. "Two thousand lumens. In less than full daylight it'll stun someone to the ground. It's also a solid chunk of high-density polymer that can crush pipe," he said as he leaned into the kitchenette and cracked it hard against the worktable. Pieces flew. Not from the baton. "In case you need to hit someone. You'll notice the bulb end is serrated, so if someone tries to grab it they'll slice their hand up. You can also jab with that and then press again." He did so and an arc crackled between the crenellations. "If you have to, you can aim it—" He chose Elke this time, who stiffened slightly but nodded as he continued. "—and press." The stun function zapped and made her twitch in her chair, eyes rolling back for a moment before she shook her head woozily and recovered.

Into the appreciative silence he said, "And that's as nonlethal as I plan to get, thank you." He took another swing at the bench and left a depression in the slick polymer.

"So after we light them up and zap them, can we juice 'em a second time and then crush their skull?" Aramis asked. He seemed eager to try the concept.

"I believe that would constitute excessive force," Alex said. "We just want to be able to say we tried. Just be glad we have Mister deWitt at BuState. He's slightly to the right of Genghis Khan. How he got a job with those fluffy bunnies I don't know, but we'll take it."

"We have a schedule yet?" Aramis asked.

"Yes, we're escorting the President to make his introductory speech in four hours. Both the military and I suggested he do so from his office by camera. No go. He has to be in public." He didn't mention the argument he'd had over their weapons.

"Is the military coming along?" Elke asked.

"Yes, Elke. They have outer perimeter, we have up close. So our lives depend on them doing their job right." There were groans.

"At least they're Recon and not just maggots," Jason said.

Aramis was clearly getting ticked at the comments thrown back at him. "Jason, just what the fuck did *you* do in the military?" he asked with a stare.

"Knuckle dragging engineer, son. I dug the holes for us to die in." His own stare was confident and arrogant without being cocky. He was too experienced to be twitted, and seemed to like the sparring. "I knew my job and yours."

Aramis didn't respond. Any response would escalate things and get nowhere.

Alex did nothing, but waited to see if it would die there. It did.

"Recon is good, has a mission, and is keen on doing it. That's the best we can hope for. We're taking two vehicles for us, and will be together. I plan on fifth and sixth position on the way there; we'll randomize on the way back. First two cars will look like the official ones and have goons. Next two are Recon. Then us. Then more Recon.

"Any armor or real military vehicles in there?" Bart asked.

"Nope, this is a civilian mission. We'll all be in civvies. Body armor underneath, no helmets once we arrive."

"What is with helmets anyway?" Bart asked. "If we are being discreet, we can't wear them. If we are in public, we can't wear them. Needless weight."

"Well, just in case we do find a need, we have them," Alex said. "I won't require anyone to wear them, but do have them here. Elke, does that modified armor fit?"

"I'm wearing it now," she said. "And I still look like a girl. Though I would like a higher neckline, even under a suit."

"Is it a problem?"

"No, just personal choice in coverage. This will work. I have three small distractions in my pockets," she said, and slipped one out. It was a flat packet in the palm of her hand.

"A candy bar?" Jason asked.

"It was at one time, and it was delicious. Now it will give you heartburn," she smiled.

"That tiny thing?" Aramis asked, incredulous.

"This tiny thing," she confirmed, "will remove a limb within a meter. Bright flash. Loud bang. Much smoke. I have another that will bounce across the floor and make four small detonations mimicking mortar fire, and one other that is just a tremendous flash. We will take suntan from it."

"Excellent. I'd say stick with the first one for now."

"I will do so. Should I deploy it on arrival, or wait for orders?"

"Wait. We'll see what happens. Can you sleight-of-hand it if needed?"

"I could also plant it and recover it later, if it is outside."

Alex pondered that. Any lurking around without orders or some justification would draw attention. They could justify going in early. Not hanging around afterward. The security profile would change before the next trip, so it would be shaky to claim it.

"Hold it for now."

"Yes, sir."

Tech White came up, with Sergeant Buckley guarding her and some flunky named Wilson. Wilson was an older AF master sergeant, and motherly in a bitter fashion. She fussed over their appearance, criticized their shirt fronts and gloves. The process was three minutes in when Elke said, "Sergeant Wilson, can you advise me on this?"

"Hmmm? What is it?"

"My collar. It's not standing right."

"Oh, I see . . ." While Wilson fumbled, Elke shot a sly grin to Alex and the others and mouthed, *You owe me,* silently. The men grinned. While Elke still looked female in her tailored suit, even with the body armor, the gear underneath made her look about ten kilos heavier, all muscle, and the glasses and earbuds made her look not at all dainty.

But Wilson worked at some faint wrinkles, lint, and creases, and by the time the fussing was done, it was time to leave.

"First gig, let's make it a milk run. Tech White, please lead the way."

"Yes, sir. President Bishwanath is waiting." She held doors and Buckley acted as extra security. He handled his gear well, Alex noted. He hadn't said anything to anyone so far, any time they'd met him.

The team waited outside the door while Alex entered to see Rahul prepping Bishwanath, in detail. The President was impeccably dressed in charcoal gray, a genuine Saville Row suit that must have cost a month's wages for a contractor. He looked nervous, but only normal stage nervousness. He didn't seem afraid of violence.

Weilhung was in the suite with him with one soldier he didn't introduce. Both were dressed to fight and had minimal gear strapped on and accessible. They had carbines slung muzzle down. They clashed with the President and the fine appointments of the room, done in earth tones and cool tans of wood and leather.

Meeting Alex's eyes and nodding, Bishwanath said, "I am ready. Can you please review for me?"

"Yes, sir. We'll be taking two vehicles in the middle of the motorcade. I'll be in with you, along with Weil and Anderson. The others will be in the vehicle ahead. They will dismount and clear a path to the entrance. I will confirm, and we will move out behind you as they come to take the front. Once inside, we will wait in your vicinity, rotating as needed and patrolling likely threat areas. Departure will be similar. Major Weilhung's soldiers"—he indicated with an inclusive wave—"will also be in the convoy and on-site. They will provide what we call proactive force against potential threats. We are more reactive if there is a problem. I don't anticipate any, but am prepared.

"I see you have your briefcase and umbrella. Later on, we'll need to review and practice using those, sir, if you don't mind. For now, please do bring them and do your best if there's an incident." The umbrella was made of ballistic cloth and the briefcase unfolded to hang in front as additional torso armor.

"Excellent." Bishwanath nodded. "Then I am ready. Please lead on." He nodded to Rahul and Weilhung and started to move.

The team formed up on him as he moved through the outer parlor, and guided on his steps by the time that door was reached. By the end of the hallway they were pacing him. They took the stairs tactically, for practice, one pair moving down to each landing with pistols still holstered and batons in hand, then falling in behind as the entourage passed.

The motorcade waited in the archway outside the long corridor. The drivers were Recon soldiers in suits. Theirs were not as confining and pricey—they only had to look good at a distance. The soldiers inside the compartments would not be in suits, but in urban battle gear.

Situated just inside the door was the clearing barrel. Elke drew her pistol, slipped the muzzle into the gasketed opening, and fired one round. Between barrel and weapon muzzle chamber, it made only a heavy slamming sound, not a sharp report. She reholstered it and grabbed the door as Shaman function checked his. In turn, each of them fired one test round. The weapons were top of the line and Jason had flogged them over. A live fire test before each maneuver still made sense.

Elke and Shaman held the doors open. There was a light breeze as cool air rushed out and down under the summer heat rolling in above, the thin dryness a palpable thing. Bishwanath exited with Aramis ahead and Bart and Alex flanking, with Jason bringing up the rear. Jason moved around the body of the formation to get the limo door, and Elke and Shaman filled in behind it. Aramis stepped inside the vehicle, followed by Bishwanath. His other two personals climbed in with him and moved to front and back seats, Jason closed the door and checked it, then stepped in behind the others as they circled the limo for the car ahead of it. Elke had the door and climbed in behind him.

It was a finely choreographed dance routine. Except that this one was designed to take, and took, the President from the palace to his car with no immediate notice, in the space of too few seconds for most shooters, and with most of him covered by bodies.

Jason called on radio and said, "We're buttoned up."

"Rolling," Alex agreed. "Driver, we're ready. Major Weilhung, at your call."

Weilhung said, "Roger. Rolling."

Once moving, Bishwanath said, "Agent Marlow, I am very impressed by how your people work. It's like being inside a machine designed to protect me. I appreciate it."

"Thank you, sir. I'll be sure they know. Are you ready for your presentation?"

"Yes, I am. Oddly, stage fright doesn't bother me anymore." He chuckled.

The trip wasn't long, and Alex plotted the route on his handheld, tracking civilian and military vehicles, air cover, and nearby assets. He knew Jason and Elke were, too. It was habit and training more than precaution. There was no reason for a military convoy to get lost, and the area was saturated with troops. When his eyes ached from the small screen, he took another look at the limo. Roomy, tall, lots of luxury features, armored enough for any small arms and some support weapons. While not a tank or APC, it was far better than anything smaller. They had "minimal" weapons aboard—enough for an infantry fireteam.

"Incoming fire!" someone said, snapping him alert. Then he heard some pops. Bart had his pistol out, cradled in his lap, hands covering it for control and discretion. Aramis was a moment behind. Alex reached for his, but paused with a hand in his coat and decided to use his radio instead.

Clicking his transmitter to Weilhung, Alex said, "Sounds like light arms and normal harassment. Concur?"

Weilhung replied, "I agree. Hostiles do not appear to be targeting us directly, nor accurately. I'm watching it and continuing on mission profile."

Nevertheless, Alex checked his pistol under his coat again, and noticed Aramis and Bart kept theirs out for now.

Despite the sporadic fire, there were no actual direct hits. The trip proceeded well enough. Just more skinnies shooting it out for macho factor.

"Stand by," Alex said.

"Check," said Jason. Transmitted information was kept minimal. They all knew the drill; commo was just to coordinate.

Shortly, they pulled up in front of the Civic Center, which was the only public building in the district large enough, still intact and with the proper dignified presence to be used for this meeting. The Senate Building, the Federal Courthouse, and the National Building were all rubbled ruins.

There was a crowd here, Alex noted without surprise. Mostly media, some supporters, a few opponents. He briefly considered a comment to Jason, but Jason had done this before and knew what to do.

"We'll wait for them to clear the route, then proceed," he said while looking at Bishwanath. He also meant it as a discreet reminder for Aramis, on his first high-profile mission.

The vehicles stopped. Local police had the plaza clear, which made Alex frown. Not the most reliable support. Shaman and Elke got out and each took one side of the line, walking up toward the entrance. Jason stood by the car as cover. Assorted dignitaries and suited Recon got out of the other vehicles and began walking in. At this point, no one should know where Bishwanath was.

Then Elke and Shaman were walking back, and Alex's radio said, "Clear" and "Clear." He nodded and Bishwanath and the others tensed slightly.

Jason stood by their limo and opened the door, letting a wave of hot, dry air rush in. Bart got out first, then Aramis. Alex nodded to the President's attentive gaze, and Bishwanath stepped out behind them and started walking. Alex hopped lightly out behind him, Jason closed the door and fell in, then Elke and Shaman came back and alongside. They were halfway up the long, tessellated walk before anyone recognized him, and inside before there was any response more than a few shouts.

Perfect. It was a nice omen and a good first impression to be absolutely flawless.

Almost flawless.

The Civic Center was under control of the military, specifically, the Army. There was a checkpoint manned by bureaucrats in uniform, not five meters inside.

Officially, they were Recon, too, but it took only a glance to determine they lacked the skill set or intellect of Weilhung's people.

"Mister Marlow, hi," one of them said, without looking up from the screen. She offered a hand perfunctorily, which he shook to avoid friction. "You can check your batons and sidearms here, and there's a waiting area set aside for you. I'll have you escorted."

"There is going to be a problem," he announced. His voice was on the loud side of conversational, and he recognized that. *Deep breath. Don't kill the flunky. Yet.* He was also sweating in the cool, dark foyer.

"Sir?" At last, the sniveler looked up.

"Unless the President releases us, we are staying with him. And we do not disarm." There. Calm and straightforward.

The response was one of those smug, condescending grins he just wanted to smash with the baton.

"Mister Marlow, this facility is under military control, and safety is guaranteed—" Alex flicked his eyes at Elke and made a bare shake of his head. She smiled and crinkled her eyes, but nodded the same way, no more than a half centimeter. She would not give lie to that statement. Yet. "—and it's best for everyone's safety if we keep control of all weapons. You understand of course."

Bishwanath wasn't happy, and was in fact, getting angry. This was his nation, but both UN BuState and the Army seemed to think he was a puppet to push around. They denied that status vociferously in the media, but went right back to setting his schedule and "advising" him and shuffling him around like a flunky.

He wasn't going to say anything yet. He wanted to see how Marlow handled it. Was Marlow another puppet, and would he accept the role? Was his loyalty to BuState, Bishwanath, or himself?

Marlow seemed moderately agitated. There was a pause that lengthened, while the officious little twit stared in growing confusion.

"It's 'Agent' Marlow," Marlow said. "Not 'Mister.' And my contract isn't with the Army or BuState, it's with the Office of the President of Celadon, which is the Honorable Balaji Bishwanath. I take orders from him, or from my chain of command. So if you can reach my District Agent, or if Mister Bishwanath concurs, we'll check our gear."

"Very well, if you wish to be formal," the woman said—she came across as a "woman," not as a "soldier." She still hadn't stood up from her desk. Meanwhile, people were milling about. Bishwanath saw three District Representatives from the capital, two others from outskirt regions, and Mister deWitt from BuState, who was looking rather amused at the exchange.

But then the . . . soldier was addressing Bishwanath. "So will you please relay our request to your contractor, sir?" She made the word *contractor* sound like a cross between "pet dog" and "maid." And since Bishwanath's mother had been a maid for most of her life, he really got annoyed.

"I will not," he said. He waited for the confused look to return, then grinned. For a moment, he saw Marlow's face, which was also grinning.

"But, sir, Army policy—"

"This is not an Army function," he replied. "This is a formal meeting of the District Councils and myself. The Army's function is to keep outside threats outside and away."

"But we've taken control of this building," the woman said stupidly. She'd already lost the debate and didn't have any grasp of it.

"It is a civic building, and falls under the Office of the Mayor," Bishwanath said. "As Executive, he answers to the Executive Branch. That is me. If he gave you such authority, I am revoking it. Did he?"

"Er, well, lieutenantcanyouhelpme?" the woman said, turning.

The lieutenant was already standing behind his poor, outgunned sergeant. However, the question was one he hadn't been prepared for. "Er . . . I don't know if he did or not, sir. To be honest."

"Well, it's quite simple," Bishwanath said. "If he didn't, your presence here is not authorized. If he did, I can countermand it. Now, for the sake of good relations, getting started on time, not making a scene, and not interfering with the Army's ability to perform its mission, I will allow you to stay. I see no need to change a plan that's working in the middle. We shall discuss who has what jurisdiction afterwards." *Yes, indeed, we shall. You bastards.*

"And in the meantime, it pleases me to have Agent in Charge Marlow and his team escort me to my booth, and to sit nearby. I also believe their apparent civilian presence will improve the perception that I am actually in charge here, and not a mouthpiece for the UN SecGen and Assembly . . ." He paused a moment, watching the expressions of embarrassment, discomfort, and anger, before concluding, ". . . as some have implied in the news."

The lieutenant actually looked relieved. Possibly not having to put his name on the decision?

"Very good, sir," he said with a slight sigh as he exhaled a held breath. "I'll relay that at once to—"

Bishwanath didn't wait to find out who he planned to ask to be the next obstacle. He turned and said, "Agent Marlow, gentlemen, lady, please escort me."

Then he turned his back on the Army and walked past the booth. He was quite confident that . . . and yes, there they were. The team was around him again, in a perfect square, guiding off his steps. Miss Sykora was slipping what had to be some kind of small explosive back into her pocket.

He grinned. No, he had not been intended to be a sovereign, only a figurehead. But that was changing. Oh, yes. The mobs, gangs, and clans had been warring over this land for a hundred years. He didn't like the waste and suffering from that, and he was damned if the UN was going to add its different, more evolved, but still corrupt influence to the mix.

Behind them, the Army was having a shouting match over who had authority, and who might be prevailed upon to destroy their career by stopping Bishwanath. He smiled. Now if only the negotiations ahead would go as well . . .

CHAPTER FIVE

President Balaji Bishwanath. The title sounded like much more than it was. At best, he wielded the power of a mid-sized town's mayor on Earth. Despite its population, Celadon's economy was small.

He entered his apartment and turned to his escort. "Miss Sykora, thank you. I appreciate your efforts."

"Thank you, sir. Let us know when you need help," she said. "Delivery complete." She nodded once more and turned as he closed the door. He'd never get used to them speaking into the air. Their transmitters were dental plates that sat on the teeth and were all but invisible. The receivers were those tiny buds in their ears that also worked as amplifiers and filters. The equipment wasn't even particularly high-tech, but it was higher than anything here.

He exhaled heavily at once, and pulled his tie the rest of the way off, then started on the shirt and jacket. He needed a drink.

Bishwanath was tired. At every step, he'd had to debate not only his opponents, but his allies. It was infuriating. BuState, with good intentions and a committee of political scientists, was prepared to create his government. They were smug and not very discreetly condescending about his thoughts on the subject.

They wanted to "modernize," and in that he agreed. However, they had different definitions of "modernize." Their definition would make Celadon a molded copy of Zimbabwe, and Bolivia, and Borneo. A second-rate nation stuck with the expensive trappings of first-world pretension in the capital, with an ongoing struggle for relevance. Too, they expected that the same infrastructure would be used, which would destroy any national identity. No culture, trade, or tourism, just one more cog in the machine, providing raw materials at a horrible exchange rate, with the cost of interstellar travel.

He sat in one of the broad, stylish chairs. "Stylish" in a fashion of two decades ago. They came from no real culture, were just castoffs from the modern world. New, but not original. All of Celadon was like that. All of the planet, in fact.

It wasn't just that they were poor, uneducated, and undeveloped. They had no cultural identity. No reason to care. Each tribe had leftover scraps and machismo, and xenophobia of other tribes, from back on Earth, mixed with their development here. They all regarded it as important to keep the others down, and thus never made progress.

Earth made him think of Abirami. He'd promised to send for her soon, but he wasn't sure that would be possible. Until the threat level came down, it wouldn't be advisable. No doubt Miss Sykora would be happy to escort Rami around, but a single principal, as he was called, was easier to guard. Best she stay on Earth in the town house in Connecticut, conveniently located close to New York. Her photos showed it to be very pretty in fall, and she had things to keep her occupied, if she was lonely. Once he had things in better mettle here, then she could come home.

He needed a drink. He also needed to avoid falling into it as a trap. One double of a fine bourbon would help his tension and anger, which was tightly controlled and eating at him. He must keep his poise, invite others to see him as a voice of reason in the scrum.

Bishwanath knew the solution. He was willing to make the sacrifice that must be made to accomplish it. That would win him no friends and lose many he had. He was already seen with distaste by his would-be handlers. He would be reviled by many here, including his own people. He had no idea how history would view him, but that wasn't important. What was important was a nation, a people.

The sipping that had brought him through the first half of the fine amber liquid was not enough. The rest disappeared in a gulp. Elijah Craig probably wouldn't have approved of his whiskey being guzzled. The man had come from a culture with an identity that lived on, though its geography was now merely part of the North American urban sprawl. Celadon did not have that.

But in Balaji Bishwanath, Celadon, BuState, warring tribes, and now the Army, it seemed, had the one thing they all needed to get past the obstacles and solve problems.

They had a person to bear the blame.

"Okay, so what went right with that operation?" Alex asked.

Jason sat back in his chair and didn't put his feet up on the table. He knew where this would go, and was curious to see if the kids got it. He met Alex's eyes and both of them nodded a bare fraction of an inch.

Bart spoke first, after considering for only a moment. "It was smooth in transport. Movement on the ground was excellent." His voice was clear even from across the room, where he was guarding the other entrance to the President's quarters. As soon as possible, there would be a barricade in the hallway and any supplicants would have to come through the team first.

Alex said, "Good. Next?"

Aramis said, "I think commo was clear and concise. There was nothing confusing." He was obviously thinking about it at length, which was the point of this.

"Right. Elke?"

She stretched upright and erect and said, "I had the resources I need, a good amount of intel to start with, and our position was understood by our immediate allies."

"Exactly. Shaman?"

"We had control of the situation door to door." His voice boomed even when conversational.

"Jason, what about you?"

Leaning on his arms, deliberately looking casual, he said, "We had room to maneuver and the crowd was at a distance, plus we had backup."

"Right," Alex nodded. "We weren't alone in this. So then: what went wrong?"

No one spoke for a moment. He pointed and said, "Aramis?"

"Er . . . we could have had a better look at the cars ahead of time," he said. "All we had for info was 'limo' and 'enclosed estate type.'" He looked nervous, afraid of making a mistake.

"That's one. Elke?"

"We needed better planning with the facility security ahead of time. They had a very different oplan than we did." She didn't hesitate.

Nodding, Alex moved along the couch. "Shaman?"

"I would like to see a full medical kit onboard in case I need it. What was there was marginal."

"Good point. I'll make note of that." He scrawled. "Bart?"

Bart considered again. His English was excellent, but he definitely seemed to translate as he went. His grasp wasn't instinctive. He said, "I believe we could have used more gear aboard as well. Backup weapons."

"Almost got it," Jason said. "What the hell was our backup plan, and what were we going to fight with if the convoy got attacked and split up? We let someone corral us into traveling in a civil convoy, under military control, with dispute between departments over who was doing what, and all we had for ourselves and our principal was pistols." He hadn't liked it from the moment they started downstairs. He should have made a stink then, when Alex didn't.

"Right," Alex said.

After that sank in, he said, "I should have been more on top of that, and I'm sorry. Recon has a hate truck, but we don't. Six of us is almost a squad, we should be armed like it—grenades, support weapons, sensors. I'm getting with Corporate and BuState, and I've also been authorized to spend some money locally. We can 'get weapons off the street,' as the press likes to say, and use them to our advantage. I'm also going to be leaning on the military to get more independence. They seem to think contracted to their operation means we take their orders. They've got grunts for that. We're specialists."

"What are you thinking of picking up?" Jason asked.

"Machine gun or two. Repeating cannon. Couple of antiarmor rockets. Extra ammo. Shaman's field surgical kit. Barricades. Antivehicle mines. All the stuff they wouldn't let us bring in. Problem is, I have to get it without the military knowing, and through shall we say 'discreet' sources, and I'm not yet plugged in enough to know where. My possible sources of information are indirect questioning of the military, especially that nice Tech White and her office, though I don't know them and can't really trust them. I can ask the President, but his office is monitored by his people, probably BuState and the military. I can try to ask Rahul. I gather he'd have some idea."

Jason spun it over in his mind. "I can get the info and the other stuff. What do I have to work with?"

"You can?" Alex looked alert.

"Sure. You want to scrounge common weapons in a war zone. Not a problem. All I need is a clear entrance into the building when I get the stuff. I can take any vehicle. I'll buy sundries while I'm at it."

"Do it. When can you go?"

"If I have ten hours free now, I can do it now. I think I can find a dealer, with enough money. What do I have to work with?" he repeated. "Cash?"

"Some cash, some silver, some gold, and a little palladium."

He choked. "Holy shit. Palladium? Don't even bother. No one here will have change for that, if they even know what it is. It's got little industrial use in this shithole. Gold, silver, cash."

"Ten thousand."

"More than enough." Sheesh. At least Alex was bright enough to ask for help, but the man was way too honest. "I'll need good backup that's not obvious. Elke?"

She nodded. "Sure, I can come along. Should I bring my shotgun and explosive?"

"And pistols and a couple of carbines," Jason said. "ID and a vehicle and commo. Please keep the radio hot? In case of problems or questions?"

"Will do," Alex agreed. "The rest of us will make space, check the palace over again, and work on ROE and MO for tomorrow. Another conference."

"We'll leave at once," Jason said. Sweet. He liked being a tourist, and it was so much better when you had enough firepower no one wanted to fuck with you. You could really see a town then. "I'll need some stuff from Rahul."

"Go ahead."

He nodded and rose.

Rahul was in the President's apartment, and answered the door promptly. "May I help you?" he asked in mock obsequiousness.

"Rahul, let's be honest. We need more hardware. I need some supplemental trade goods. Here's a list." He handed over a scrawled sheet, then reached over to jot one more item down. "The first section I need right now. The rest later."

The bulky man scanned the list, clearly literate in English, and said, "I will need a couple of minutes." His face bore a grin that was knowing and deadly.

A few minutes later, Jason and Elke were in an open bay of the "carriage barn" looking at a large Volvo estate wagon. He liked Volvos. Reliable, classy, and tough as hell. This one had moderate armor upgrades and a couple of largely useless gun ports. It was far too clean and nice to be unobtrusive, but some dust and mud would fix that. He put down the box he was carrying and drew two bottles from it. Rahul had found everything on the "now" list, including a case of wine, easily.

"Elke, can I ask you to get dirty for me?"

"As long as I don't have to get on my knees," she replied with a smile. "Yes, I can muck up the truck. Is that what you want?" Damn, she was perceptive. That was why he'd recommended her, and was glad to have her along.

"You are no fun to tease. Yes, please do. I'm going to ask some questions."

She nodded and sought dirt in an abandoned flower bed just outside the huge garage. This time of year it was all dry and crumbly.

Meanwhile, he sauntered over to the gaggle of local troops ostensibly guarding this area. They looked uniform from a distance, but up close, it was obvious their maroon jackets came from several sources, and varied in fit and repair. Their pants were black but not standard, and they didn't look and obviously didn't feel professional. As he approached, they nudged each other alert, rose to their feet, and turned to face him.

"Hot out here?" he asked.

"Sher be. You need we help wut?" one asked. He appeared a bit more alert and observant than the others.

"I think you need a drink," he said, raising two bottles of wine. It was a mass-produced Earth brand, but he suspected they cared more about proof than robust complexity with a well-worn boot-like finish, or whatever terms the wine snobs used.

"Yar, we cud. Tank and cheer." The man took the bottle, glanced at the label long enough to show he could read, and said, "Help you we?"

The local dialect was English, but God, it was a barely comprehensible mess.

"I could use an extra gun," he said. "No, not one of yours," he said to their shying movements. "I want to buy one for my collection. Where would I find one locally?"

"Ah, you want Jim. Cuzzin mine. Look for le harweer sto at Fitty Nye an Gee."

Jason translated that and noted it. "Should I tell him you sent me? Send a message?"

"Shi, not. I boom his wive las mont."

The delivery was deadpan, but the whole squad started giggling. Jason settled for a smile and said, "I'll look for him. Need anything brought back?"

"Yea, we gots no rifle bults. Pistole, do sho, but no rifle."

"I'll see what I can do," he lied. If they only had pistol, and none of them had rifle ammo, it was probably on purpose and he agreed with the probable reason. He'd weasel around that. "Thanks for the help."

"Ya, no probum."

Alex took a quick tour of the floor. It gave him time to think, and it let him keep apprised of any changes. There'd been some cleaning, and a couple of the rugs had been removed, presumably to be cleaned or replaced. The bare areas of inset wood were dusty from a history of improper cleaning, and paler and less worn. That said something about the past. Everything here was façade, but no substance, a pattern of laziness.

There was almost no one about. One staffer had wandered past, a woman he recognized vaguely and who was older and not a credible threat herself. Of course, she could still carry a bomb or pass information, but she was approved and checked. Harinder? Was that her name? Likely. He'd have to memorize all that data.

He snapped a quick photo and let the computer scan. It confirmed. Harinder, no last name, cleaner on this floor. He nodded and she smiled faintly without a word.

One soldier, with badge, walked down a crossing corridor. At the far end, he saw Weilhung, in the combat casual wear that was apparently standard in the palace. Alex ignored him and headed for the rear corridor.

"Agent Marlow, I need to speak to you *now*," Weilhung said loudly, as soon as eye contact was made.

Alex sighed. It had to be administrative. Had to.

"Yes, how can I help you, Major?" he replied as he turned back.

Weilhung thumbed back over his shoulder, gesturing down the hallway to the rich atrium.

"It's generally considered a hostile act to plant explosives inside your own perimeter," he said while glowering, almost snarling.

Oh, the stairwell.

Alex realized it had been several seconds and Weilhung was waiting for a response. There wasn't really an answer he could give. They weren't contracted to care about anyone except the President, they couldn't trust anyone anywhere under the circumstances, as either a threat or a leak, and, the embarrassing part, it hadn't occurred to him it might be a problem. The explosives had been an answer to a problem, so he'd let it happen and agreed.

Weilhung took the silence as a cue to keep talking, hand resting on his weapon but not threatening. "I believe I can figure out your intentions with that. I sure as hell would like to be in the loop so my people don't wind up dead. I don't have to tell them if you're paranoid about it, but *I am also tasked with the President's safety, and I need to know.*"

Weilhung was pissed, and had every right to be. Alex had insulted his professionalism and placed him at risk because he'd been thoughtless.

"Major, it was a slip caused by being busy, and it won't happen again. Besides the stairs, you'll find charges inside the elevator panels on each floor, and inside the window of the President's office." That should do it.

Weilhung was obviously still pissed, but nodded.

"Thanks. I'll note that privately and I won't tell anyone unless the mission dictates, said mission being protecting that same President. Are we agreed?"

"We are. I'll keep you informed."

Weilhung let his displeasure be known by nodding once again, curtly, and turning without a further word.

Alex turned and headed back for their dorm. He hadn't mentioned the charges under the floor in front of the President's apartment and office doors, or the ones in the basement elevator alcove. He didn't want to explain another discrepancy, and he'd play BuState against MilBu if need be. He couldn't trust anyone. Anyone.

There was a stranger in the room when he returned. He was standing, the team was sitting and no one seemed worried.

"Ah, Agent Marlow. Doug deWitt, BuState," the man said, offering his hand. Alex looked him over. He was tall, balding, and had a no-nonsense presence and was possibly former military.

"Good to meet you, sir. How can I help you?"

DeWitt smiled. "I'd give you a list of people to shoot, but if you actually did it, my ass would be in a bind. However, I thought you could use a sitrep."

"That, sir, will be very much appreciated. Please have a seat."

"Thanks, but if you don't mind, I prefer to pace."

"Suit yourself. Mind if I get others in on radio?"

"Please do."

DeWitt was a serious pacer. Back and forth between one of the couches and the coffee table, sideways to face his audience, he never stopped moving. He strode around looking at artwork, examining frames and tables, until Alex had Elke and Jason on a speaker. Their radios were quite decent even at this range, though much of that was the base station Jason had set up, wired into the mast antenna assembly on the roof. That was a military grade system, but Ripple Creek had its own encryption algorithms in addition to the factory codes.

"We're here," Elke said.

"Okay, we have an interaction problem with the Army and with the local palace guards. Each wants to be in charge. With the Army, they want total control of anything to do with the President."

"They likely figure they'll take the blame if something happens," Shaman said.

"Right." DeWitt nodded as he moved. "And we're the ones who have to cover the problem, which is why we hired you. At the same time, there are various elements in BuState playing this off against each other for advantage. I don't know who ultimately will be running the show here."

"As long as you'll back us up as you have, we'll manage," Alex said. "Let us know if we can smooth anything out and we'll see what we can do."

"Well, try not to borrow weapons from soldiers on patrol any-more," he chuckled. "Hey, I agree completely, but dammit, that made some sores."

"Perhaps we could offer some classes on weapon retention?" Elke snickered through the speaker.

DeWitt sighed. Obviously he wasn't getting the results he wanted.

"Okay," he said. "Look, I know you guys are way better than the average bullet catcher. I know you're the best there is at this. I expect you to do what it takes to keep yourself and the President alive. I know that means friction, but keep it to a minimum. I don't want any pissing contests, any dick measuring, or whose fart stinks more."

"Sorry, sir," she said, sounding remorseful. "I wasn't being entirely humorous."

"Yeah, I know," he said. "It's a sucky situation."

Alex said, "Can you tell us more about the parties we'll be meeting as we escort the President?"

"You don't have that long," deWitt said. "There are twenty-three registered political parties, most of which have some variation of *people's, progressive, democratic, workers,* or some other euphemism for 'property-stealing communist' in their name. Sorry, did I say that out loud?"

"Inside voice," Alex said with a grin. "Use your inside voice."

"Right. Then, there are at *least* two hundred clans in varying alliances. They shift daily. No one has any idea how, if they didn't grow up here. Hence Bishwanath as an attempt to create what has never existed here—a society as opposed to a mob. Then there is relatively peaceful but massively corrupt opposition from vari-ous sources. Like the mayor and representative of Vishnuabad, a district, technically a suburb, north of here." DeWitt squinted as if pained.

"Oh?" Aramis prompted.

"Known rapist, philanderer, indulges in sobriety once a month or so, drugged out of his mind and incoherent, gutless, fat, known to off people who get in the way—or have them offed. He'd never dirty his hands even if he wouldn't wet his pants in fear of an altercation, though no one has ever been able to prove a thing. Witnesses are either paid off, blackmailed, or threatened into silence. The locals slobber over him like some messiah. It's revolting."

"So he became mayor by being more brutal than anyone?" Bart asked.

"He's mayor because his father was president and got shot in a tribal dispute. The father was a mensch. The son played the sympathy card in his first election, and bought them after that. His main good points are that he stays bought, and buys people with lots of public services. Of course, he does that with other people's money."

"What's his name?"

"Kenneh Dhe."

"And why is Mister Dhe a problem for us?"

"He's powerful. That makes him a problem. He's complaining about the cost of security, the 'off-planet intrusion,' the 'second-class status for our people.' If he can get you out of the way, he's got a better chance of killing Bishwanath. Not directly, of course; he'll create an accident. Festering scum, but powerful, and will never openly be a problem, but watch for his lackeys, both paid killers and the frothing nutjobs of the People's Progressive Party."

"And what can we do?" asked Alex, pondering that if that was "relatively peaceful," either deWitt or the locals had a different definition than he did.

"His people want gear. If you're a source to him, he'll keep you off the target list for now."

"And our principal?"

"That's harder to say. Dhe can be bought, but Bishwanath is ethical."

"Not what I meant, but good," Alex said. "How do they interact? I don't want to try to involve myself in politics. It'll take me away from my real job."

"And I don't want you to," deWitt said, with a point of his finger. "But you need to be aware. If you need to trade gear for safety, I'll back you up. I'll be holding my nose against the stench, but if it gets us through this, I'll do it."

"Okay. What type of gear?"

"Intelligent question. Nonmilitary stuff is fine—fuel, vehicles, whatever you can acquire. If you can get his personal guard matching uniforms and shoes he'll owe you hugely. If you have to trade ammo or weapons, just keep it as low-end as possible. Sidearms, armor would be okay. Rifles are iffy. Do not give him anything larger. You're welcome to promise it if you must, but weasel out of it and call me if you need help. I'll try to protect you if you have to do it, but I can't ignore it."

"Well, we've got someone buying loot. I suppose selling it is ethical."

"Can't we order extra from Corporate?" Aramis asked. "Oh, right," he said, flushing as everyone gave him "What, are you stupid?" looks. Nothing with proper import papers or RC stamps could wind up missing without extensive documentation. Even in those cases, not much could go, and nothing accountable.

"Sounds like a goat fuck," Alex said.

"Ah, that explains the lanolin on our pants," Jason quipped through the speaker. "Well, I've been worse places. I think. Though I prefer not to."

"You know, there are two types of people on this world," Elke was heard to say.

"Yeah. Those we're going to shoot now, and those we'll have to shoot later," Jason replied.

"You don't have that much ammo," deWitt said. "And just keep the sentiment quiet. The less the Skinnies know about how low we regard most of them, the better."

"Of course," Jason said. "I was thinking more of politicians and mob organizers."

"Them, too," deWitt agreed.

"Any trouble with unions?" Alex asked.

"Heh. No," deWitt said on a turn, his head shake matching up so it looked as if his body pivoted under it. "This place is so far down in the shit that unions would help. They'd create some income, some incentive, and some kind of training program. As it is, the local operations hire ten times as many as they need, figuring to get one who wants more than drinking money, short-term rent, or who lied about skills and can't do it. And that's in regard to mostly unskilled farm and loading labor."

"Damn."

"How are threats?" Bart asked.

"Another good question." DeWitt seemed glad of it. "You can expect mobs anywhere for any reason. No pay, no water, blocked road, not enough jobs. They'll sit and sing and chant and yell until someone gives them money or shows enough force. They don't usually riot like chimps, but that can happen. Arson. Rape. Theft."

"Good, clean family fun." Shaman didn't sound surprised either.

"Yes. Mobs with clubs, machetes, and brush hooks, even hoes and spades. Rifles as far back as the twentieth century are out there, and even revolving pistols. Modern stuff you know about. Comes in by the shipload. Mostly projectiles. Explosives aren't common. Not reliable ones."

"No vehicular IEDs?" Elke asked, stumbling slightly over the long word.

"Not much anymore. They dropped below that level of technology about six months back. Trying to find anyone with a working phone is problematical. Finding anyone who knows the fundamentals of marksmanship is almost as hard."

"Good news."

"Mostly. There are still some bombs here and there, and mortars. If they can buy it they'll use it."

"No domestic production though?" Jason asked.

"Nope. Not even close. They did have a factory producing rifles under contract from Sulawan Industries. Closed. Ammo was coming, and still is in lower volume, from Olin's plant in Kaporta. They never produced any heavier weapons. They didn't need many support weapons and had a whopping six tanks and four howitzers. What fighting they did do was infantry backed with mortars and machine guns on light vehicles."

"And what about our window shields and an emergency exit for the President?" Alex asked. "Any word?"

"Only that it's pending." Alex started to fuss, but deWitt continued with a raised hand, "I even asked about an emergency elastic chute. Nothing yet."

Alex nodded. The man was trying. They had one ally, at least. "Thanks," he said.

"No problem. I'll keep on it."

CHAPTER SIX

Jason, at the wheel, was tired when the briefing ended, and not just from the information load. Even dirtied up, the vehicle was obviously in better repair than others—it had all its windows. The dome marked it as something luxury. He didn't mind getting screwed on the price of weapons based on that perception, because he would, even without being seen as rich. The attention and possible rumors he could do without.

The fatigue came from being hair-trigger alert for hours. He had to be prepared for any attack that might happen. Someone could figure him for wealthy, important enough to kidnap, want to steal the vehicle . . . the temperature was set at a cool eighteen degrees Celsius, but he was sweating, sour, flushed sweat. His eyes were gritty.

Elke was sweating, too, hair plastered on her head and stuck at odd angles. She had the entire arc from 90 to 270 to watch, and her fingers twitched on her carbine. Not dangerously; she wasn't near the trigger. More a case of caressing it and checking function. In the footwell was her riot gun, which was damned near a cannon for close range, with a selectable twenty-round cassette. She'd loaded it with buckshot for antipersonnel, compressed slugs for breaching doors, impact frags, and even finned reconnaissance rounds in case they needed aerial images. She loved it and even slept with it. He wondered if she slept with it in that way, too, the way she hugged it so much.

"Let me know if you see anything interesting," he said.

"Yes," she replied. Neither of them needed to say what they did. They were just confirming they were both together on the job.

"Hell of a situation, eh?" he mumbled, trying to keep alert with conversation. This all seemed so unreal.

"Very. Mobs with clubs and hoes. Sounds like a bad zombie sensie."

"About right, I think. They believe in zombies here."

"I believe in zombies," she said. "Drugs can do it. They don't have much else here."

Something heavy banged on the roof. Jason goosed the throttle and gripped the wheel during the downshift. Civilians learned to stop when unsure. Soldiers learned to nail it. He changed into the far lane, into oncoming traffic, and honked loudly as he accelerated around a slower sedan. Luckily, there wasn't that much traffic.

"Rock," he heard Elke say. "Thrown from a third floor. I see the man."

"Threat now?"

"No."

"Check." He braked carefully and slid back into traffic. "Asshole."

"Yes. Grinning. He wanted attention. It's a shame I can't give him some." She was twisted around backward in the passenger seat, one foot up, ready to pop through the roof if needed.

"So note the address. We'll be back this way." He shot a glance in the mirror but didn't see anything.

"Thank you. You are a gentleman."

"I try to always please my partner," he said. The banter wasn't sexual, wasn't even humorous. It was just contact. "Wish we had a drone overhead," he complained.

"It would be obvious we were important," she said. "This is an all-or-nothing environment."

"Yeah," he replied. "Don't stick it out unless you're ready to back it up big. And that's just against the peasants."

The streets varied. There was a grid, but it was overlaid with multiple local mazes of alleys and twisting side streets. Some even redrew existing streets, where there were vacant lots. Some of those larger lots had been broken up by squatters into several smaller parcels with odd geometry, and paths wended through the chaos, over what had been curbs and sometimes foundation blocks. As they bumped and careened, Jason was glad of the armored, resealing, and reinflating tires.

Some surfaces were glazed, some hardpan, some paved, some cobbled, and some mixed. Others were rutted, dried mud. Many of them were broad, like most colonial roads. Obstacles included running and broken vehicles and stripped hulks, pedestrians, bodies in the roadway that might be dead, drunk, or just fucking stupid, and God help you if you ran over them anyway. There were random cats and dogs, some ungainly ostrich-looking thing, chickens, draft animals—mostly mules—random men, boys, and gangs with guns . . .

"Not like Grainne," he commented, to himself but aloud. "We've got cities, the Hinterlands, the Habitats, and some slums, but I don't see anything here that is above slum, including the palace."

"No, nothing like this in Europe," Elke replied. "The worst areas of Bosnia or France aren't even close. Well, maybe the nastier parts of Paris."

They found the hardware store, or at least what should be the hardware store. The painted sign said so, and there were some tools and supplies stacked outside, but nothing to suggest it was doing real business. No one had money, and there was enough rubble to scavenge for building materials. Tools not already in circulation were likely stolen as opportunities presented. People loitered outside the store, either employees or day hires, to make sure nothing went missing. There was a donkey-drawn cart tied up to a rail.

"Dare we get out?" he asked.

"I think we have to," she sighed. "Park so we can run if we must?"

"Yeah, I'll back in," he said. They were taking delivery, offering good terms, and wanted invisibility. There were alleys on each side of the building, likely for that purpose.

"Arriving to shop," he said into his phone. It cost a lot to keep the circuit open, and he didn't care; it wouldn't be his bill.

"Location noted." Aramis had the duty.

"Roger," he said.

"Look at that place," he said in awe. It looked a lot like an American Old West store, complete to the deck and rail that the cart was hitched to.

"I'll get a snapshot," she said. Her camera was built into her belt pouch, and aimed by "eyeglasses" that offered no correction but acted as polarizing shields and ballistic armor. She'd been in this field a while and that was a ten to twelve thousand UN mark setup. Of the money contractors got paid, quite a bit came out of pocket for extra gear.

She was by far the most mature of the three younger operators. She had a lot of experience, even if she'd only been on contract for six months, with this as her second assignment. Not being military, Ripple Creek had no double standards. Elke wasn't small for a woman, but not imposing either. She was titanium under the slim outside, though. Jason was comfortable with her demeanor. She'd done well coming in, with the borrowed grenade launcher, even though on paper she'd seen little combat.

"Got it," she said. "Shall we go in?"

"Yup. Taking the keys, leaving it unlocked, got the wand if we need it." He'd lock it, remote start it, or trigger tear gas if needed; being a palace vehicle, it had several built-in features not found on standard models. But this looked to be a fairly safe location. Just smugglers and illicit arms dealers. No real threat.

There were four men lolling outside the hardware store. Lolling seemed to be the national position. None of them rose, even though at least two were armed. Were the rifles mere status symbols? Or enough of a threat to dispel plans of attack? The lazy attitude didn't mix well with the concept of ongoing tribal war. Though there were probably multiple nuances to the disputes. All four were skinny and pale, wrinkled and aged. They might have been anywhere north of forty, but were probably in their twenties.

"Good morning," he said. "I'm told Jim can help me shop."

No one moved. They watched him, and didn't appear threatening or threatened, but there was no response.

"I need to buy some stuff," he said. After a moment he fished a silver round out of his pocket and caught sunlight on it.

That caused stirs and eyes to widen. Plastic fiat money didn't shine like that. Two men stood up and went inside. He watched them expectantly, and with some caution. Elke was behind and to the left, and he could feel her facing out for potential threats.

Then one of the two remaining stood, stretched, and said, "I be Jim. Yo." He extended a hand then pulled it back. No actual contact, just a gesture, and likely proof he wasn't holding a weapon. He was tall, skinny, had a dopey look that was obviously an act to Jason's trained eyes, and was wearing a snug T-shirt. No major weapons.

"You be wanting de manly hardweer, yas?"

"Yes. What can you show me?" he asked.

"Depands on wut you show me."

The man was smiling, no threat. Elke was behind and they

both had carbines. Jason decided to show him a little. He slid out several silver rounds and a small gold bar. Replacing them, he flashed the edge of a roll from his other pocket.

"Not bad," Jim grinned. "Okay, let's shop. The woman she wi you?"

"Yes. She's with me."

"Come back," Jim said. Jason couldn't tell at first if he meant come back later, or now. But he gestured as he turned and they followed.

They went through the main store, which did indeed have a modest selection of tools and hardware in bins, in a style not seen on Earth in nearly a century. Further back were garden implements, largely untouched. Most people here didn't garden anymore, and those who did either had staff or used home-built implements.

Behind that was lumber and synthetic building supplies, in huge piles inside a fenced yard. Jim's two friends from earlier were here, now armed and standing over a neat pile of four- by eight-centimeter polymer studs stacked on three pallets spread on the dusty ground underneath as dunnage. The yard was compacted earth, not fused.

It wasn't hard to figure out what was next, and no doubt Jim thought himself clever. The top layer came off, and the lower studs were cut to hide a large crate. Inside the crate were samples.

Jim didn't know how to handle weapons, either. He dragged out a nice carbine, didn't check the chamber, and waved it around. Jason politely reached out, accepted it, and inspected it.

Well . . . it was okay. Bore was a bit worn, trigger was a bit loose.

"Okay," he agreed with a nod, to Jim's eager grin. "But I need something stiffer, longer, more powerful." He made an appropriately rude gesture with both hands and the rifle, and Jim giggled.

"I be have it, man," he said with a nod, while licking his lips. "Hold on." He reached in and hauled out . . .

"Oh, yeah, that's it," Jason said. He tried not to grin, but this was more like it—one of H&K's newer box-belt-fed machine guns. This one was crusty and beat up outside, but it didn't take long to determine the inside was clean enough. "What about a test fire?" he asked.

"Sho," Jim agreed, and slapped on a box. He knew how to load and fire well enough. The finer, snobbish points of safety and maintenance he eschewed. He got past loading without killing anyone, pointed out over the fence and pulled the trigger. The

H&K responded with a nice, steady roar and a scattering of case bases in a neat pile.

"Good mechanism," Jason agreed. "How much?"

"Two tousan," Jim said, and sounded very sure of that price.

"Fuck me what?" Jason said at once. You haggled by being offended no matter what the opening bid was. Then the amount registered. Holy shit, that *was* offensive. "Do I look like a masochist you can bend over and fuck?"

The look on Jim's face suggested he just might swing exactly that way. He raised his hands placatingly and said, "Nono! Two tousan list. For you, eightee hunnerd."

"Five hundred. It's stolen, used, and I know you didn't pay that much."

"Fiteen." He looked annoyed at being talked down. Not annoyed enough to suit Jason, though.

"How about I go somewhere I won't be insulted?"

Elke played along brilliantly. She tugged at his sleeve and said, "There was that guy by the port. I'll bet he'd start at a thousand. He had a new one, too. I don't really care if the UN is missing it."

"Twelf."

"Actual list is nine fifty. I'll pay that. I want three. You'll throw in ammo and tools."

"Hunnerd exta for that," Jim said. *Now* he looked disgusted.

"Done. I want hand and rifle grenades. I'll pay twenty per grenade. Two hundred for mountable launchers."

"Two fitty," Jim said, squinting.

"How about I leave this shit and go elsewhere?" He made as if to throw the H&K.

"Go!" Jim replied with an open hand. "You won' get cheaper."

"Six launchers, fourteen hundred."

Jim nodded. "Okay. Haf ta see if I have six."

Jason had expected as much. Jim was likely used to selling to local gangs, and would take whatever was on hand in trade. A "legitimate" arms smuggler would have set prices at a reasonable markup over list, with discounts in quantity, and parts on hand. Of course, all the "legitimate" ones were traced by somebody who could be made to talk.

"I want four cheapie Bushies, too. Something I can throw away."

"Fiteen hunnerd for fohr."

"Done." That was reasonable. Jim wasn't stupid, just small time and hopeful. Now they could bargain decently. Someone went running off to get the ordered goods.

Nosing over, Jason took a look in the crate. "Shit, what's that?"

"Old," Jim said. "No good."

"Let me see."

"Okay."

He took the weapon handed to him and drooled. It was well over a century old, and worn. It was an original AK-120, vintage twenty-first-century. A museum piece.

And Jason lived in one of the few nations where he could own a weapon. He'd have to find a way to get it home, but . . .

"Holy crap. I'll take it. Three hundred?" he offered.

"Yeah, sho." Jim seemed happy.

"Jim, I misjudged you. You're all right."

"Thanks. We friends?"

"Indeed we are. Where can I call if I want more?"

Jim scrawled on a card, and his writing was passably literate.

"Thanks. We'll wait in our car."

"Gotcha." The slang word was identical, even though so many proper words weren't. Jason smiled.

They walked toward the vehicle, feeling occasional wafts of breeze in the oddly humid air. All this dust and there was no real moisture, just humidity. Sucky climate. Humid one day, dry the next, but little actual rain.

Elke asked, "Are you sure that's safe? What if they decide to take the cash?"

"Small risk," he explained. "This guy makes his egg by selling. If he starts stealing, word will get out not to deal with him. Someone would take a hit. Someone else might see us in this luxury monster and try something. Can't be helped. But Jim we can trust to sell us stolen weapons and bad parts at an unfair price and keep his side of the deal."

"Right. There isn't much arms smuggling in Europe. Mostly explosive, drugs, and banned animal products. It is a more sophisticated, classy crowd." She said it with deadpan delivery. Her accent was a little noticeable, and her phrasing a bit too formal at times, but she knew English well enough to crack jokes.

Shortly, a rattly old truck with no windows drove up. It had once had windows, of silica glass, fragments still clinging on.

"Man. I didn't know you could find things like that anymore.

Must have been easier to set up a foundry than a capacitor plant."
Jason was impressed rather than amused. A certain amount of
smarts was necessary to use low tech.

"Is that the engine I smell? Petrochemicals?" Elke asked.

"Yeah, diesel fuel, I think. I've encountered it . . . here and there."
No need to mention that trip. Officially, it hadn't happened.

"Clever, resourceful. Also toxic and inefficient," she said.

Jim's friends unloaded a crate and two canvas bags that contained
the weapons. The containers were open, and the friends were armed.
Jason looked the packed weapons over and decided they were good.
Elke stood back, covering everybody. He figured the hand in her
pocket was near explosives of some kind. Jim stood anxiously, but
relaxed when Jason smiled and eased out money. Then it was time
to haggle over the appropriate amount of local cash, UN marks, and
gold. Jim didn't want silver. Silver was of more use industrially than
gold, and slightly cheaper, so easier to split. But gold was what Jim
wanted, along with UN marks. Local cash didn't interest him. Since
the local currency had been remonetized twice, at a hundred and a
thousand to one, and was still lousy in exchange, Jason didn't blame
him. The prices had been in UN marks and Jason had assumed that.

The deal acceptable to all, the friends heaved the hardware into the
back of the Volvo, thoughtfully not scratching the car, though that
would have made it blend in better. Then they were in and driving
as the locals evaporated, pretending nothing had happened. Dust,
trash, and ruined road kicked up under the vehicle and Jason was off.

He clicked his mic and reported to Alex. "Yeah, got some
groceries. Not much in the deli, but some basics that are better
than packaged."

"Sounds good. Are we cooking out tonight?"

"We can cook out anytime you like."

"Roger. When are you due?"

"Three zero minutes. Tell the gate."

"Understood. Out."

"Out."

Turning, he said to Elke, "So far, so good. You'll need to move
to the left in three turns."

"Oh, why?" she asked.

"So you can take a shot at that cocksucker who threw the rock
at us, if he shows his head."

She grinned widely. "I like you," she said. "That's very illegal."

"Yup. Going to do it?"

"Of course," she purred as she shifted over into the back and rolled the window down. That was potentially dangerous, and revenge wasn't smart, but the little bastard had pissed Jason off and he wanted some himself. She reached over and snagged her shotgun.

Three minutes later, he said, "Here we go." Nice house. American Old South style. Antewhatever it was called, in poor repair now.

"I see someone," she said. "Stand by . . . bastard, you mine." Her accent came through under stress.

There was the pitch, a high lob, breaking slightly inside, and there was the shot, and the kid spun around on the balcony clutching at himself as he died. The rock missed the truck this time, and Elke was a bloodthirsty bitch, because she switched to shotgun and took out three windows on the house as they barreled by, then climbed back into the passenger seat without a word.

"Dammit, I forgot ammo for the palace guards," he said.

"Didn't you plan to?" she asked.

"Yes, but I have to get them something. Liquor? Shoes?"

"I'll keep an eye out," she offered.

They settled on cheap Scotch and some cigarettes and chocolate. The chocolate was locally produced, and there was no telling how good it was. The smokes were Players from Earth. The liquor was a house brand. Again, the transaction had been UN marks.

"Should tell the boss local currency's effectively worthless," Jason said. "It's going to affect our deals."

"Yes. Want me to help hand over the stuff?" she asked. They were pulling into the palace grounds.

"Sure, after we clear security. Hope the bastards got the word."

"Yes, this could suck."

"Wait. Marines." The uniform resolved as they approached.

Jason slowed when the NCO raised his hand. Five U.S. Marines under UN flag were watching the post, weapons loaded and held ready. The perimeter was built of concrete blocks with cameras and remoted weapons. He had the window down and both IDs out as he stopped. "Vaughn. Sykora. Ripple Creek Security, contracted to Mister Bishwanath's personal guard."

The sergeant in charge nodded as he took the ID. "Your name is on the list. You know your last four backwards?"

Jason gave it a moment's thought and said, "one-eight-seven-one."

"Good. You have the countersigns and duress signs?"

"They haven't told us anything, Sergeant," he said with a head shake. "You can call up and Marlow will vouch for us." He indicated his radio mic.

"I believe you. It's been pretty screwed up so far." The NCO was young, but knew what he was about. "Countersign is any exchange equaling fifteen today. Plus, minus, multiply. I'd watch the dividing or roots or whatever. You'll confuse some people."

"Like the Army? Sorry, that was mean," he replied. "Fifteen. Got it." And Elke echoed "Fifteen" next to him.

"Yeah, but I wasn't going to say that." The grin vanished and the Marine said, "Duress words are *sombrero* or *flugelhorn.* 'Try to work the duress words into a conversation rather than using them without preface, in order to make them sound innocuous. Security personnel will be alert for their use.'" He quoted from some manual with obvious bemusement.

"Repeating. *Sombrero, flugelhorn.* And I'm supposed to work them into a normal conversation. Who the fuck came up with those? Army again?"

"Aerospace Force actually. How, I have no idea."

"Ah, well. At least we get to share the stupid. Is the rotating list of those with our people?" Jason asked.

"No, but it will be encryptmailed before midnight. If not, call down and ask."

"Thanks. I'll let our people know."

The radio said, "I heard. I'm tied in through Tech White's board at present. We'll get the words."

"Roger that and have a good day," the sergeant said to the air and waved them through. The other Marines moved back.

The local guards sighed and accepted the gifts with some enthusiasm. They really had wanted ammo, and may or may not have known why no one else wanted them to. Jason had guessed correctly that booze and tobacco would always welcome. They waved thanks as Jason climbed back in the vehicle and rolled the few meters to park it.

Caution was called for even inside. The weapons needed to stay hidden from anyone who might claim them.

"Alex, can you come down here?" Jason said. "Got some stuff."

"Already waiting in the back." More locals guarded the entrance to the large garage and maintenance bay, with an occasional Army patrol.

"You know what's scary?" Jason asked as he pulled into cool shadow and saw Alex and Aramis in back, looking casual.

"What?" Elke asked.

"These are U.S. soldiers. Anyone else would be worse."

"Europeans are still good," she said. "Also Japanese and Koreans and Turks. I agree on most of the rest. Those countries that are good are too few in number to deploy here."

"Right. That's part of it. The U.S. pretty much has to be along to make it stick. It's still frightening how bad things are. You always hear the old guys complaining about how much better they used to be, but it's true. Discipline, morale, and skills suck."

Elke shrugged. "That's why they pay us." She opened her door and stepped out.

"Yup. Though I'd rather consult and have better regular forces," he called as he did also.

"I agree."

Aramis was jittery excited, so as soon as Jason opened the back, he handed the crate over.

"Upstairs," he said. The kid grabbed the crate and moved. The young bastard was strong, that was for sure. Wiry, clean-cut handsome, highly intelligent, and a great shot. His only really bad trait was his ego. Of course, that sort of came with being good-looking, strong, and a damned good soldier.

Elke moved ahead, checking for foot traffic, while Jason followed, handling the doors. Aramis grunted with the crate but never put it down, even though it was close to forty kilos, a load even in point nine-two G. Alex slung the two duffel bags over his shoulders and shuffled a bit from the encumbrance. The only question was whether or not they'd be seen on video and if anyone would want to stop them.

Tech White called down briefly, and Alex clutched awkwardly at his mic. No problems, no worries, no, we don't need help, and a few painful minutes later they were back in their suite.

Everyone was eager.

"That's more like it!" Aramis said as he pried open the crate. "Three belt feds, a grenade launcher each, and some bammy bombs." That was a newer slang for hand grenades than Alex had heard. "Elke, can you even throw one of these fifteen meters to clear bursting radius?" It was a legitimate question. Most females couldn't. But his delivery was rude.

"If I have to. I generally hide behind hard cover up close, or soft cover at a distance. Like a dead Army puke. Or a living one, if I can't find a dead one." The grin on her face was not friendly, though it wasn't threatening death. She was just warning him that he'd crossed a line.

He looked about to say something, but Jason shook his head and said, "Don't," and he didn't. Smart move.

Jason turned to Alex. "How are we going to issue these?" he asked.

"I'm checking with Bishwanath. If he okays it, we'll be carrying the launchers mounted and have a machine gun here, one in the trunk and one in the passenger compartment. No luck on rockets, though?"

"No, I'll have to find another source. But hey, we're much better off now."

"Oh, yes. We can put out some fire instead of just stinging. Not a bad price, either." He frowned slightly. "So, palladium and local cash are nonstarters. UN marks and gold are preferred, it seems, and not sure on silver. Tobacco and booze trade well. Got it."

"I expect medicine and ammo would do real well, too," Jason offered.

"Yeah. They do so well they're banned and would get us jailed. Some logistics NCO got busted for that last month. He was getting food, capacitors, and luxuries his unit needed, like night vision and body armor. Then he got nailed anyway. Something about nonmedicinal drugs sneaking into the mix."

"Right." Yup. The Chain would overlook legitimate barter, until some asshole screwed it up with contraband. Then it all had to stop for at least a while. The moron in question had screwed things up for a lot of people.

"There is good news," Alex said. "Our gym is being set up. Came in on a Space Force logistics flight."

"Excellent. What do we have?" Shaman asked.

"Environment treadmills, so we have scenery to run with. Weights and tension machines and boards for push-ups and sit-ups. An interactive strike machine. Just the basics."

"At least we can do some exercise," Jason said. He didn't really care for exercise, but he cared for not exercising less.

"Yup. Down the hall on the right. The small function room."

CHAPTER SEVEN

A lex actually didn't mind the morning conferences down the hall. They were practical, which might be a first. Of course, most of the attendees were military, and not high enough rank to wax poetic. He was close to start time, and nodded to Tech White, Major Weilhung, and Mister deWitt as he entered. He grabbed a cup of real coffee, as opposed to the stuff that wasn't coffee but pretended to be that was served most places, and sat down. A moment later, Bishwanath arrived.

They all stood to attention, and of course he asked them not to, and they'd both keep playing their manners. Rituals were comforting. They sat back down around the long table. Alex wondered why there was wood grain to the artificial material. There were much nicer patterns possible by not pretending injection molded plastic was walnut.

Bishwanath wore an odd expression, part elated, part disturbed.

"Mister Marlow, I have changed my official bodyguard," he said, directly and without preamble.

"Sir?"

"The drunken rabble you've seen outside are gone. I have replaced them with more professional hires."

"Oh, good." He looked at deWitt. There was obviously more going on here.

"I'm going to be honest with you, Alex, Major, and so is the President," deWitt said. "The improvement comes with some strings."

"Hit me," he said.

"What are we facing?" Weilhung asked.

Bishwanath's voice was so melodious and pleasant, even when he relayed bad news. The man was a natural politician. "The new hires are from three different clans. This was to promote the idea of cooperation. None of them are from my clan. This was to show that I trust other groups. However, I cannot say that I am thrilled and comfortable with this, my press releases to the contrary."

"Understood." Right. Reality took another bite as maneuvering took center stage.

"Awkward, but good to know," Weilhung offered.

"Also," deWitt said, "besides the obvious potential for inter-factional violence, they still aren't up to the standards we'd like. They can be bought, and they lack the training of you or the Recon unit." He nodded to both leaders. "Hell, they aren't even up to the standards of regular infantry. You can't bet your life on them."

"It is entirely possible," Bishwanath said, "that they will rout, accept a bribe, or prove unable to offer the protection they claim. That latter is most likely. They may also brawl amongst themselves. I don't expect them to do more than brawl, having given their words, but fighting is considered both manly and recreational. I don't trust them, but I must pretend that I do for diplomatic reasons."

He paused for a moment, hesitating. Then he said, "To be fair, my own clan would not prove to be as well trained." He seemed embarrassed.

"Sir, I will not be under- or overestimating anyone if I can help it," Alex replied. "I do appreciate the info, and will keep it under advisement."

"There's another thing," deWitt said.

"Yes?"

"Officially, they are trusted. Therefore, they will be trusted to handle patrols and security. Including incoming vehicles."

Weilhung started. "Oh, no! Hell no! Not a fu— dammit." He looked *pissed* again. "I'll deal with that as I have to," he said, sounding sheepish and offended.

White said, "I have security issues with our intel equipment, sir. It can't be left unattended and can't be left accessible to people not cleared and clearanced by Aerospace Force." She looked as uncomfortable as the others. Despite her low rank, she spoke easily enough at high level. This was obviously a problem for her.

"Right," Alex agreed. "I propose an authorized personnel list for access to different areas, and badges. We can discipline and boot them if they get into needed-for-duty areas."

"Excellent idea, and I will endorse it," Bishwanath said.

"Yeah," Weilhung said. "I'll have to limit some of my people, but they've been exploring. Can't blame them, and ordinarily a good thing, but this helps."

"Good," Alex acknowledged. Yes, that was better. Not having even Recon skulking around meant he could better deal with security and Elke could wire more mines. He didn't have a problem with that at all.

And what was White's function? He wasn't sure if he could trust her or not. Did she work for Bishwanath, the UN, the Army on a share program, or some private AF operation? Or a combination?

She was the most inscrutable of the bunch, and it unnerved him. She was not a combatant, she was more than an admin type, clearly some kind of intel. She was of low rank but high position. She wasn't sharing information with him generally, so what was her function?

White felt his gaze and stared back, emotionless. No, not quite. She made a quick appraisal of whether or not he was a threat and what type, then seemed to rule him safe and ignored him. She was the junior military person here, but she obviously held some strings in addition to her position. What strings, though?

The three Army officers were another matter. Alex knew politicians when he saw them. These were them. He'd been read the riot act over Elke "stealing" a weapon, and a protest had been filed with BuState, quashed, and was now being appealed. They didn't want to let that go. There were ongoing disputes over guarding Bishwanath, and insistence that the military could handle all of it.

And he was required to be polite to these gentlemen, if they could be called that, out of both courtesy and a need to get the job done.

"I must prepare for some video conferences. If you gentlemen will excuse me?" Bishwanath said. Everyone stood to attention and waited while he departed.

As soon as the door closed, the temperature seemed to rise.

Colonel Weygandt said, "Mister Marlow, we need a chart of all your explosives and other booby traps in the palace, and keys so we can disable them until the appropriate time. It's not safe to have them armed constantly, even if they could be a useful tool in certain circumstances." His tone made it clear he didn't think they were useful at all, but in fact scared him.

"'Agent' Marlow, please."

"I didn't realize we were being formal," the man sniffed.

"*Agent in Charge* is formal," he corrected. "*Agent* is just a courtesy, like *sir* or *sergeant*. It is my rank. Then, approval for information release on presidential security can only come from the President." He kept his face neutral, but was guiltily enjoying torquing this clown.

"Oh, no. We're not playing that crap!" Weygandt smacked his fists on the desk as he stood. "You will by god give us that information or I'll see you're pulled and charged with obstructing a military operation!"

"Sir, that information is on a need-to-know basis. Approval for variations is myself and the President, depending on who's asking. You do not need to know that information, as you will not be in that wing of the palace. Major Weilhung"—he nodded to his military counterpart, who gave him an ugly look—"has that information pursuant to his duties, conditional on not releasing it. If I suspect the information is compromised, I will have to have the devices relocated."

"Marlow, I'll send a munitions disposal team up there to clear them out if you don't try cooperating."

"I'll arrest them and hold them for trial, assuming Major Weil-hung allows them through. You can argue with Mister deWitt over the authority."

DeWitt saw the eyes on him and said, "BuState, MilBu. Palace is a civil facility. I've got to back Agent Marlow up on this." The man really looked as if he needed a drink. The day had barely started but he was already having to piss on fires.

"I'll keep piling brass on you until you toe the line," Weygandt said.

"I don't take orders from the military. Military discipline applies per our contract. That does not put you in chain of command. Our District Agent for this nation can give me orders, or the President, for whom I work. Not you." He'd been a bit shaky, but dammit, this was getting fun. Weygandt looked ready to pop a vein.

"Do you really think that tribal drum-thumper is in charge here? You need to seriously consider who . . ." Weygandt seemed to realize he'd crossed the line.

"Who is in charge then, sir?" Alex asked and stared at him. Everyone else did, too.

Alex realized he also had gone where he shouldn't. It wasn't a secret that several groups were trying to control Bishwanath for the UN's benefit. That sort of thing had happened before elsewhere, but such things were never discussed, even among the parties involved. And half of those present were not involved.

Weilhung looked disgusted at Weygandt's lack of control. DeWitt fidgeted for a moment, then controlled it. Tech White was still inscrutable.

Alex said, "I'll relay all the information that is needed, and I'll make sure the President knows of your interest. If he says so, I'll keep you in the loop." It was a tense moment, with everyone trying to pretend it hadn't happened.

Alex at least knew why the requests for support weren't coming through. Someone didn't care. They didn't care enough that they deliberately weren't going to help.

Weilhung didn't like briefings. He'd rather be doing stuff. That his current rank and position required lots of meetings was a dark spot in his career. He envied the contractors in some ways, but wasn't about to switch. He couldn't say why other than being stubborn, and out of a certain amount of national pride, though the unifying of the major Earth militaries was a real bite in that. Still, he fought for someone or something, not for a buck. Already he'd seen that the contractors had no respect for any rules they didn't like. Like the worst of the new troops out there, only unable to be called to account, and paid highly despite it.

That meeting done, he was needed at once with the damned legal staff. They were called an "Operation Policy and Procedure Council," but they were lawyers. Their only concern was keeping the UN or the Army from being sued or seen badly in the press. How many troops died for that image, they didn't care.

But the really aggravating part was that he had to follow their orders. That he sometimes agreed with those orders was even more annoying when you thought the men giving them were assholes.

Weygandt was definitely one of those. Too high a rank and too stupid to argue with, and with an elevated sense of his own relevance and importance. He'd push for authority to make himself look bigger, and the worst that would happen would be he'd get pulled from that particular activity. The lawyers never got busted. They knew the law too well.

He wanted to keep a closer eye on the contractors. White's recon gear had shown him an incident while they were out acquiring weapons they thought he didn't know about. Personally, he approved of them bagging the twit throwing rocks. Officially, however, it was an unauthorized killing of a nonthreat. That indicated yet more disdain for the proper procedures.

Today's schedule was fairly quiet, and Aramis hated being bored. On the other hand, he loved handling weapons, and Jason had all the new hardware spread out on the rear floor near the kitchen when he came through.

"Mind if I help?"

Jason looked up from slipping the trigger group out of a machine gun. "By all means," he said. "Familiar with them?"

"Yes . . . but I could use some practice." Actually, he'd never handled this particular H&K, but it was similar to others and he thought he could figure it out, which was why he wanted to look at them now. That the other EPs were exercising or following up on paperwork made him more comfortable about asking.

"No problem. Take that one," Jason indicated with his head. "Tools are in the box."

Holy crap. It only took a glance to realize that Jason really knew his stuff. There were tools and spare parts in the toolbox's trays that could likely assemble the guts of four or five different weapons. He had nice tools, an electronic analyzer for trigger mechanisms, ballistic tests, and bore-sighting, as well as adjusting and programming optical sights, and some custom-made stuff. One of them was a highly illegal box for reprogramming or scrambling operator codes. That was how all their weapons had been made "any user."

It was hard not to feel out of depth, and Aramis knew he needed to back off. Dammit, he'd passed the same tests and training as the rest. He was younger, sure, but he was good for the job and was proving it. He had four years in the military, running good exercises and some real peacekeeping ops.

Jason, though . . . he'd been career and retired, and was still in good enough shape for this. The man knew weapons, medicine, could acquire stuff . . . and he never made an issue of it. Aramis found it aggravating, because he wanted to be that good himself. But that would take years and he was not patient.

This H&K wasn't too different from the one he'd trained with on duty, and they'd had familiarization at Ripple Creek's Academy. Actually tearing down the weapon you'd be using was a good move, though.

Jason didn't even seem to be conscious. His fingers took assemblies apart while his attention was on a screen off to side, which he paused to scroll periodically. Cleaning brushes, cords, cloths, and adjustment tools flitted back and forth, and in minutes, the thing was back together, sitting on the polished floor, its bipod feet padded against the fine wood.

"So why Aramis?" Jason asked.

"Huh?" Why what? It took a moment to catch the question. "Oh, my father was a Three Musketeers fan, when the sensie came out. Even named my sister d'Artagnan. We call her 'Dart.'"

"Have trouble growing up?"

"Because of the name? No. I'm Aramis Adam Anderson. I went by Adam or A or Triple A. I use it now because it's a neat-sounding radio call sign." At least he thought it was neat. Jason didn't seem to be the kind to harass someone over their name. He held the barrel to the light and checked the bore, clean, then picked up the receiver to work on the gas mechanism.

"Yeah, it does have a ring. Though you might have been better as d'Artagnan. And that buffer balancer retention pin comes out the other side, which is why you're trying to fight it."

"Right, thanks," he said.

"No problem. Look, I'm twice your age, and I remember being yours. I think you'll work out fine. Stop trying to prove it and just be yourself, eh? You could easily fit into a position like Bart's or Elke's in a couple of years."

"Ah. Elke." It slipped out. Now it was going to become an issue.

"Yeah, what about her?"

Aramis sat still for a moment, and pulled the pin from the correct side and found it *was* easier that way.

"I got nothing against her," he said with a shrug.

"Sure you do. I may even agree with you."

"Really?"

"I can't say if you don't talk. I can't advise you if you don't, either." Jason buttoned up the remaining gun and started stripping down a couple of the spare pistols.

"Well . . . EQ crap aside, women aren't as strong as men, don't have the endurance, and react differently . . . not necessarily badly, but differently."

"Yeah, I know that last part. And?"

"And her presence is bound to cause friction for the rest of us. Every time they've let women into combat units, it's screwed things up."

Jason just nodded. Finally, he said, "Well, all those statements are true. At the same time, people with her skill set are rare, and you adapt to the reality. She's also passed the Company minimum and then some, so even if we're both stronger, which I'm pretty sure we are, she's better than a lot of those infantrymen out there you keep talking about . . . infantrymen you are way above, despite any friction or attitude."

Aramis felt sheepish and flushed red. Yes, he was better than average, and proud of it . . . and it was uncomfortable to boast, even though he felt he should a lot of the time.

"Yeah, I know," he said. "And she seems to know her demolition."

"Seems to," Jason chuckled. "Look, I'm fine working with her. I know the kind of jazzy chick you mean. But there are jazzy guys, too . . . you just meet more and can empathize with them more, so you don't notice them."

"And they don't create a problem in shorts or half naked," he muttered.

"Heh. Get used to it, kid. I don't know what the Army's been doing, but it was pretty standard when I was in that you showered or dumped when you could, and your buddy or teammate was likely wired the other way. You deal with it." Jason didn't nearly look his age, but when he said things like that he came across as old and crusty.

"What unit? You said Engineer."

Jason nodded. "Aerospace Force Landing Field Engineer. I did electrical power and controls, and crash barriers and recovery, plus got shot at a few times by locals who didn't like dropships landing in their cornfields." He finished replacing the barrel on his pistol, cleared it, loaded it, and holstered it. "Let's get breakfast.

I'll check the grenade launchers afterwards." He stood and stepped into the kitchen.

Aerospace Force . . . and Bart was former navy. Elke had been with some regional paramilitary European unit that barely qualified as military for Corporate's standards. Alex at least had been a Marine . . . but Aramis was more of a "real" soldier than any of the others.

It was frustrating as hell that they all outclassed him.

Bishwanath felt an eager, nervous tension. One of his new duties, not discussed, was to protect himself. To that end, Agent Weil was teaching him how to use assorted tools that were designed to prolong his life. The necessity was not pleasant. The facts around some of the devices were even less so.

First came armor under his clothes, hot and restrictive, but able to stop most fragments and small arms. For larger weapons, Weil assured him it would "make sure you leave a good looking corpse." Hardly reassuring. Additional armor was laminated in his briefcase, which could unfold in four layers to yield an extensive front trauma plate. The umbrella was heavier than it needed to be. It acted as more armor, and the shaft was made of titanium, so it could be propped on the ground and used as a fighting position.

There was also a small plate that Bishwanath wore plastered to his torso, which he'd been warned to be careful of showing through his clothes. The device was a combination of a long-range transponder, by which he could be tracked in the first minutes of a kidnapping, before it was detected, and an emergency medical system that could both monitor and inject lifesaving drugs—shock reducers, stimulants and heart medication, anything that might prolong his life a short time if attacked. He didn't find it reassuring that such was needed. Nor were the drills pleasant. They were, however, invigorating.

"Go!" Weil said, and Bishwanath snapped his briefcase open, stuck his arms through the loops as the practice papers fluttered around him, popped open the umbrella, and ducked behind it. He shimmied back against a wall to provide maximum coverage of the large canopy of the umbrella.

"Not bad," Weil said. "Practice twice every morning and once at night. I will teach you pistol for defense in a few days."

"Please," Bishwanath said, smiling through sweat. "The Army is very much opposed to the idea. So I embrace it."

"This is going to be a very awkward tour," Weil said. "And it's not because of you, sir. You are a great principal to work with."

"I imagine the conflict between your factions is similar to that between mine."

"Yes, sir. That would sum it up well." Weil looked bothered by the conclusion.

CHAPTER EIGHT

After a week on-site, at last, the team went out in two rotations to get a tour of the area. Alex had gained grudging permission for them to be their own drivers. Before starting that duty, he wanted a thorough familiarization. Jason concurred. He had seen a little on his shopping trip, but there was more here than that, obviously. It was a complex nation. Primitive ones always were, and this was far more primitive than most. Social, economic, and job status could be told by clothing and mannerisms, if one knew what to look for. Tourists always found such displays "charming" and nonthreatening, and mentioned how safe they felt. That was because of different cues that didn't trigger any threat warnings. That made it even more dangerous, and this wasn't a low-threat area to start with.

Jason was still unhappy in the fancy Volvo. He would rather be in a dented and dinged Lexus or some other second-rate flash box. The problem was the President couldn't just buy such, Ripple Creek didn't have the money on hand, BuState wouldn't hear of it for image purposes, and the Army wanted something modern and "reliable," meaning "new."

He, Aramis, and Bart were out with one of the Recon troops, a Sergeant Raviti, who had been here for some weeks and done a lot of driving.

The man kept a running lecture going as he steered through traffic. "You'll notice no enforcement of road laws," he said. "All optional, and four-lane roads are used as five or six on a common basis. Pedestrians have right-of-way if they get in the way and might damage your vehicle or make you late, but can be safely run down and killed as long as the press isn't looking. Officially, of course, we have a policy against that. You'll see people merge from side roads without signaling, and across lanes. Very chaotic. Here we have a bottleneck because lights are ignored. Lights will also not work sometimes."

"Lights," Bart repeated.

"Yes, lights for traffic control, no automatic vehicle controls at all."

Jason made notes, as did the others. He'd known that intellectually. Now he had to actually consider it. That was why they were doing this recon.

"That's the plaza to our left now, yes?" Bart asked.

"Correct. And this is the end of the broad area of the Esplanade of the Nations. Largely used for parades and such during the early years. It is now a convoy road and kept well clear by patrols."

The plaza was paved with tessellated concrete flagstones. There were some elevated areas and other architectural features that had probably been striking when clean and painted. Now, it was cracked, filthy, covered with people treating it as a park and swap meet, with weeds growing through the gaps and cracks. Some stones were missing, stolen for construction or repair, or they may even have been borrowed by city engineers for official use that was more important than the public spectacles held here. When your choice was plaza or road . . .

"What about the plaza?" Jason asked.

"It would be impossible to keep clear so we don't try. That will be a problem for you at the palace."

"Yes, it's closer than we like," Bart said.

"This is a market on this side?" Aramis asked, pointing to a mishmash of tents, carts, trucks, and awnings.

"It is the official traditional market. Farmers bring produce here. Notice the rioting."

It wasn't quite rioting, but there was much pushing and shoving, money and goods being swapped and in some cases forced back and forth. Kids darted under the mob, likely pickpockets, and some shouting matches led to pushing and shoving. The likelihood of more than small-group violence didn't seem great, but was possible.

Someone looked back at their staring faces, then spit and made a rude gesture. The mercs were all dressed in cheap garb with billed hats, like the locals, and looked like contractors of some kind, for shipping, the port, any technical job. For a moment, everyone in the car discreetly reached for pistols and checked the locations of hidden carbines with their feet. All was in order, and no violence was offered beyond the thick saliva on the glass.

"There are other markets," their guide said, "outside abandoned shops or inside them sometimes. On corners that will overflow and block traffic. In the plaza. On the Esplanade. We'll turn down the Esplanade now."

"Only decent thoroughfare and it's largely foot traffic and animals," Aramis muttered.

It was broad and newly paved with once attractive trees lining it, but they were all dead or dry or withered now, with handbills taped to them and limbs broken from vandalism. People meandered across at oblique angles, or strolled.

"You can't run them down here," Raviti said. "It is considered a pedestrian route. You drive slow and polite and don't cause trouble or they'll roll your car." He drove very gingerly.

An ugly, ungainly looking bird strutted across the street. All traffic gave it wider berth than they did the checkpoints.

"What the heck is that thing?" Jason asked.

"The local name for that is a *ginmar*," Raviti said. "It's a mostly failed derivative of the ostrich. The intent was to provide a better, larger meat animal that could survive on the scrub growth. But while they were amending the metabolism, they came up with something even stupider than an ostrich, viciously aggressive, and very territorial."

"Dangerous?" Bart asked.

"Not as such. Apart from an annoying squawk. The claws aren't much. A kick could injure you, but it's not very coordinated. When it gets upset it sprays feces everywhere."

"So stay in front?" Aramis smirked.

"Yes, but it tends to spin around. The ranchers turned the damned things out. They can't tell friends from threats and attack anything. So they're all feral and largely useless . . . and would you believe the ecosimps have a fund for it?"

"Easily. Likely about how we created the problem, made it a victim, and are at fault, so we should correct our moral deficiencies and become more like this noble beast?"

"You scare me," Raviti said. "We had a group like that here last month."

"It stinks. Bad," Bart said.

"That's not the ginmar. They smell rotten, putrid. That's the chemical plants west of here, still working. We started calling this Ammonia Avenue."

"Good. Ammonia equals nitrates equals explosives," Jason said in understanding.

"Not so much," Raviti replied, shaking his head. "You'd think so, but they're largely nontechnical. I could do that from the factory. No doubt you could. Most of them have no clue. Occasional fertilizer bombs are about it. The real explosives, PETN and such, come in from off planet. The really sexy stuff, Orbitol and Smitherene, are furnished by some political group. We suspect Moveon."

"I thought Moveon was a peaceful front for progressive socialists," Aramis said.

"Right," Jason said. "And you believe that?"

Crump.

"Mortar fire," Jason said as everyone tensed. "Ah, the old days."

"There should not be mortar fire here," Raviti said, looking concerned. His hand went to the weapon under the console for reassurance.

Jason keyed his radio and spoke into the air. The transducer in his mouth picked up the speech. "Boss, we have mortar fire at this grid." He spoke the numbers. While that likely wouldn't matter, any intel was of use.

"Odd." He could hear Alex's frown. "Let me check with White."

"Please do."

Crump. Crump.

Those were slightly closer, and Jason was tingling. He wanted hard cover and there wasn't any that was viable. They were safer in the moving vehicle.

Alex came back on. "It's not directly related to you. Some urban faction and some rural one mixing it up. Jace Cady is on net. She says they're getting fire up north, too. Come on back for safety."

"Understood. Out." He closed the circuit and said, "Sergeant Raviti, we should go back, please."

"Yes, I was reaching that conclusion myself," the man said,

turning onto a side street and gunning the turbine to blow through some debris. There were a few derelicts in the way, who scattered. Someone threw a rock and someone else fired with an archaic cartridge weapon. Jason decided it wasn't worth the time to shoot back.

Then they were on another thoroughfare, though this one was dirtier, with shattered and missing sections of road surface. The buildings were further back from the road and most were abandoned: large houses, small apartment blocks—actual blocks—and small businesses, now closed.

"Roadblock ahead," Raviti said. "Suggestions?"

Jason looked forward and saw a handful of armed men with archaic rifles. They were affecting some kind of uniform. Where their loyalty lay was indeterminate. Their barricade was semiprofessional, steel tetrahedrons and wired lumber to bind and slow a vehicle.

"Change routes? Back up?"

"Other routes are unknown. We're only a block off the main route, but getting back could be an issue. We're also sighted. I'd rather not risk backing into another block and giving them more time."

"Makes sense. Get close, slow down, blast around the side," he suggested. "Everyone else be ready to initiate hostilities."

"Sounds good."

One of the men waved them down, with an avaricious grin, apparently looking forward to a bit of looting. Rape and torture might be in there, too. Jason had experienced a lot of things in his life, and preferred to remain ignorant of those. They had to be worse than being hijacked, and it was bad enough.

Raviti was slowing, blinked the lights once in acknowledgment, and made as if to cooperate. Meanwhile, all the passenger side windows were opened enough for weapon muzzles.

Raviti nailed the throttle, steered left around the barricade. The fit was tight and he left paint on a board. One punk tried to grab hold of the roof for some stupid reason, just as Aramis and Jason stuck muzzles out the windows and hosed. His face exploded into a mist with chunks of teeth and bone sticking to the window as he tumbled off, and the rest ran for cover while pitifully returning fire.

"Got some blood on you," Aramis said, as he fumbled for a bleach wipe.

"Thanks." Aside from the disgust factor, there was no telling what pathogens lurked here. But the smell of blood, propellant, bleach, and the local air was awful enough.

Three tense hours later, they were back, comparing notes with the others who'd been on the earlier tour.

"So what do you think of my nation?" Bishwanath asked when he visited a few minutes later. He'd been announced, but walked in and started talking without preamble.

"Very colorful and rich," Aramis said as he sat back down on the couch. He even said it with a straight face, Jason noticed with amusement.

"Potentially a very strong economy," Elke put in as she ran through protocols or scans on her computer.

"They are nothing but stinking, unwashed, illiterate hicks with no drive, self-determination, or self-respect," Bishwanath replied, facing the fireplace in the corner. He turned when the silence drew out.

To their uncomfortable glances he said, "I appreciate your manners, but please be honest with me. I get all the lies and sweet talk I can handle from tribal leaders and BuState. The most important thing any leader can have is honest input from unbiased sources. That is not your job, but it won't cost you anything and it will help me."

"I'd deal with the self-respect first, sir," Jason offered. "That'll give them a reason to improve the rest. I don't know how you'd go about it, though."

Bishwanath nodded. "That, Mister Vaughn, is the problem I face. I am president of nothing, unless I can turn it into something."

Jason had met a few local politicians on Earth. Without exception, they'd been self-serving assholes, greasing him up for votes and ready to renege on any promise, or weasel-wording their promises to mean nothing. The news, biased as it was, made it obvious the politicians higher up the food chain were sharks and wolves. Jackals even. This man was a mere local mayor, who had been thrust into a national position and was determined to see the job through.

It was admirable. The only question was, would integrity matter?

"I must impose on you further," Bishwanath continued.

"Yes, sir?" Alex asked.

"I am meeting with other leaders tomorrow. The meeting is in a park, with spectators allowed."

"I saw that," Alex said. "I'm told few will actually spectate? It's just for show?"

"Largely," Bishwanath nodded. "But they may heckle and there may be threats. There will also be the competition between factions, including Mister Dhe's powerful set, and I want to look as discreet and nonthreatening as possible."

"You want us with sidearms and looking casual," Alex said.

"If you can do so."

"Of course we can," Alex said. Then he said what Jason was thinking. "Of course we don't like it, either. I must continue to recommend a strong presence and safe zones to meet. The threat level doesn't appear to be reducing as far as I'm concerned."

"I understand, and I would like to please both you and my colleagues," Bishwanath said. "You can imagine that's awkward."

"Yes, I can. We'll handle it, sir. I do appreciate your willingness to discuss it."

"This is tomorrow's meeting with Mister Dhe?" Jason asked.

"Yes, yes it is. A dangerous man. Have you heard?"

"Yes. We've heard. We'll be discreet but ready." Jason expected Dhe was several kinds of cowardly asshole. If trouble was to start, it would be now.

"I appreciate that." Bishwanath seemed scared but determined, and braced himself as he left.

They all sat for a moment, to be sure he was gone and show some respect. That was ingrained into them.

After a measured five seconds Jason said, "We need some relaxation. Aramis, find us a stupid sensie to play in the background. Where's the inside phone?" He fumbled around on the couch. The damned thing was always buried. "Here. Kitchen," he said.

"Kitchen, sah," some young woman answered.

"Yes, this is us." There really wasn't any other name for them. They weren't staff and weren't the President. "I need some fresh vegetables and six large steaks."

"Would you like them with dip?" the cook asked. She was likely deputy cook, not the chef.

"No, I want raw vegetables, raw meat, and a rack of spices. We've got a kitchen up here and I'm going to use it. Bring us some Coke and a few other drinks, too, please."

Aramis punched up something on the vidwall. "That's more like it," he agreed, grinning.

It was obvious everyone liked the atavistic idea of just scorching some meat and eating, without any fine china or nicely laid out platters of anything.

Jason had landed his wife in part because he could cook. It also made him popular at unit parties. Anyone could apply heat, but to season properly and maintain juiciness and tenderness took skill. The food arrived already peeled and cleaned, which he appreciated, wheeled in by the elfin cook he'd spoken to. Tipping was considered gauche, but they thanked her graciously as she left.

In the kitchen behind the parlor he filled a pan with onion and mushroom as fast as he could chop them. They'd given him a good kitchen knife, too, almost as good as his set at home. With butter and beef fat to cook in, and garlic and a splash of honey to season those, he got to work on the steaks.

It felt great. It also reminded him of how much he missed Raquel, Quentin, and Rowan. The kids always loved helping serve, running around like little waiters with towels over their arms, taking drink orders. He and Raquel always included the kids in their life, and he couldn't even dwell on them now or he'd have trouble sleeping later. He let the memory linger for a moment and then squashed it.

"Aramis, how would you like your steak cooked?" he asked as fragrant fumes filled the area.

"Sure, why not?" the kid shouted back. Good answer.

"Elke, how do you like your meat?"

"Hot and naked, just like my men!" she called. Damn, she didn't need to go there. Sadistic bitch.

"Bart?"

"Trot it through the kitchen. I'll chop off some bits for Alex and ride the rest home."

"Shaman?"

"Whole. I need to practice my surgery."

"So now we know your secret. Alex?"

"Damn, I was hoping to shoot my own, then sacrifice it to Odin."

It was spur-of-the-moment joking, and great stress relief. It was one of those moments you could never tell as a story to anyone who hadn't been there themselves, and that was what made it great. They'd get through this and go home rich, and not just financially.

✧　　✧　　✧

Nighttime, and quiet, apart from distant fire that never stopped, and the buzz of aircraft. That was fine, and soothing, even. Elke kept her curtains open, the optical grid angled skyward, and lights off. There was nothing within weapons range that could see into the window from above, and staying away from it prevented targeting from below, in addition to the polarized grid. She liked the open feel of sky and stars.

Elke was not sexless, nor did she really get aroused by explosives. Well, not most of the time. However, she was not going to be a woman around some of the elements she had to deal with here. Aramis Anderson was a potential problem, though mostly tame. Some of the military and civvies, though . . .

She was not a woman when on contract. She was a shooter and an explosives expert, nothing more. But because she was as well trained as her comrades, but obviously not male, she was hard for the civvies to comprehend. That was an additional tactic in her arsenal.

Off duty, she did have a personal life. Currently, no one was in it, but it existed, and it needed to be fed for her emotional health. There were high-tech gadgets for that, too.

Her door was locked. She double-checked that. Both Jason and Aramis had been caught stroking off, and it was understood though still a little uncomfortable for the others. She was going to keep her aloofness as another defensive mechanism.

Unconsciously, she went through a checklist and prepared gear. Weapons and armor just in case. Computer. Goggles. Software. Files. Earbuds. Neural stimulators. Contacts and dildo. Bed cover. Pillow. Lie down there, with a translucent view of the window through the images that would follow.

The program was her own. Music and natural sounds and images flowed through a sunset and starscape, with a roiling gas giant and moons. The broad, paned window behind them made it that much more surrealistic.

The stimulators started on her muscles, relaxing tension away, then lightening to caresses on her nerves, whispery thin and ghostly. She clutched at the cluster of hardware between her thighs and held her breath tightly as her reactions climbed sharply. Tendrils on her breasts and sides and thighs resolved to fingers, if cybernetic, and the pressure throbbed and buzzed inside her as she spiked several times, surrounded by starlight and jazz and wafting scents of jasmine, shesham and cedar and a pulsing, throbbing urgency in her loins that rose to a level that made all her muscles taut and tense again, shoulders and heels driving into the bed as her hands grabbed at air and her abs and inner muscles locked tight, as tight as her lips and teeth clenched to avoid crying out.

The earthquake tremor aftershocks coursed through her for minutes, her entire body sensitized so even the cool air from the vents was a palpable touch.

It took five minutes to clean up and pack the gear in her private case while she pondered that all of them were performing some variation on the ritual, and would never discuss it.

Then she checked her weapons again and lay down for sleep.

CHAPTER NINE

Horace woke first. He was always like that. The tension of the pending operation would trigger some internal alarm several minutes before he planned to rise. He showered and dressed, and proceeded to the common room.

The servants were a great touch. Breakfast came up shortly, in variety. Horace limited himself to a piece of melon and a poached egg on toast sandwich. He never liked being full while operating. There were too many reasons not to have a full stomach when under stress.

Aramis came through next, grunted sleepily, and dropped for some push-ups. He wore trunks and a tight shirt. As soon as he was done, he plowed into a meal that showed he'd never heard the information Horace had. Ham, the sweet beans from around here, breads, jams, eggs, and potatoes. Well, he was twenty-two and could afford to be voracious. He'd be hungry again in an hour.

Slowly, the rest trickled in. Most ate then showered. Elke was clean, dressed in slacks and support tee, and simply threw her top on once done eating at the bar, though she hadn't spilled a crumb. Well, not "simply." She had her body armor, weapon and harness, light, radio, tool kit, armor, several flat pouches for explosives, her camera kit with the polarized glasses, and the capacitor chargers built into her shoes to power all that gear. She was fifteen kilos heavier once done, though she still was shapely enough and lean. All the compartments and pouches were shaped to her armor. He understood why the tailoring job she'd needed was such an issue.

All the while, Horace checked over his small kit. This time it was in a briefcase, to look unobtrusive. Other packing options included a backpack, a belt pack or pockets if needed. He counted trauma dressings, wound sealer, two pouches of emergency plasma, two more of hydrating fluid. Suture and splinting supplies, a medicomp that could read all vitals, defibrillate, seal a pneumothorax and time drug delivery, the appropriate needles and shunts for it and for delivering medications by hand, antivenin for insects, sedatives, stimulants, cold and fever medications, painkillers, hideously expensive nanobots that could help with trauma repair, scalpels . . . all modular and state of the art for this kind of work.

Jason sat on the couch, gear in front of him on the table. He had weapons, armor, radio, light, and lots of ammo, though his radio had an additional channel so he could split from Alex independently, and he had one kit with extraneous stuff and dressings. He also had a coder for locks and alarms and some old-fashioned breacher gear for breaking mechanical locks. He knew how to pick them, though he likely wouldn't. In this line of work, cutters or a wrecking bar were faster.

Alex had a briefcase, too. His was armored and contained additional computer gear and some extra goodies. He also had extra capacitors on top of the extras everyone else carried, and more maps, plus codes to let him call for backup from the military without wading through channels. They all had one emergency bypass for that. He had layered codes so he could call less than a total response.

Bart and Aramis were the muscle, so they had lots of ammo and heavier armor and just basic radios. Elke handed each a flat pack with another charge in it they could stick in their coats.

"Weather is going to be warm and humid," Horace advised them. "Hydrate now and bring a bottle."

"I figure to have water in the vehicles so we can refresh as we go," Jason said. "We can only carry small bladders under our suits."

"Good idea."

Alex was on the radio and turned. "Updates," he said. Everyone paid attention.

"We leave in two hours. We're driving, two vehicles, and there will be military escort to the three-kilometer line, so when we arrive we're 'civilian' for the news. The President is tied up with prep, so won't be joining us until we leave. He says he trusts us implicitly and will be ready. I am assigning him the code name *Dishwasher* for commo, and he's amused by that."

Everyone acknowledged and went back to eating and preparing. Horace was checking his sidearm when Elke came over and touched his shoulder. He looked up. Alex was with her.

"Yes?" he asked.

"Consultation."

"Of course. Do I need my bag?" He wondered if she were ill.

"No."

They moved to the corner of the room, to a table sliced of a local agate and set on sturdy, black wood. Like many Celadon products, it was good, but not quite good enough to justify export. Better marketing would make it exotic and rare, but that hadn't been done. So much like Cameroon and Liberia.

Elke placed her computer on the table, angled so it was hidden from the rest and from the camera that the military used to spy on their common room and didn't know they were aware of. So far, the AF had not mentioned any of their irregularities, nor had the Army, who presumably didn't know what the AF saw, or they would have complained.

"These are the President's vitals from last night," she said. There was an IR spectrum image of the room, taken at intervals, and one frame had Bishwanath in it, dressed in pajamas. His readings were . . . odd.

"Yes, he's medicated," Horace said. "I suspect for a stroke condition and possible liver disease. It looks to be controlled, but we'll have to make sure we have the appropriate medication on hand in case of emergency evacuation."

"I can reconnoiter his quarters and check my emplaced gear as I go," Elke offered.

"We can just ask Rahul. I expect he'll be willing."

"Both," she said. "He may be hiding information from his friend."

"I concur," Horace said. "It can be done tonight, or whenever is convenient."

Weapons cleaning, function checks, loading, observing each other so as not to "print" a weapon through clothing, even though everyone present would have to know they were armed, reviewing maps, routes, potential blockages and escapes, emergency procedures. The two hours before departure were filled with technical matters that most people wouldn't expect of "mercenaries" or "legbreakers" or even "bodyguards." Alex contacted Weilhung and White and got intel and satellite updates.

"I'm changing the planned route," he said.

"Why?" White asked on-screen.

"Because it means any planned trap won't work." Horace grinned from the couch next to him.

"And this is a more scenic route. That can be played in the press," Alex said.

"Good," White agreed. "He's visiting his people."

Weilhung sighed. "You realize I have many troops set up to guard the planned route?"

"I do, Major. Sorry. Is it that much of a problem?"

"Not for me or them, no," Weilhung said. "However, certain officers are going to scream."

"Aw, too bad." Alex was grinning now. "No need to say anything. You can move the troops as we go, they won't know why, which means no one else will know why."

"Yeah. Are you planning on telling me the actual route?" Weilhung asked.

Horace sensed tension. Did these two commanders trust each other? If not, how was it going to play out?

"Yes, I'll give you the route. Can you come up for a hard copy? And you also, White."

"I'll get both copies," she said. "It will take me a few minutes to clear my board."

"Understood. I'll have them here."

As he muted the audio and locked the camera, Alex looked at Horace and said, "And that'll delay things about until we leave," and winked.

"Don't we trust them, sir?" Horace asked seriously.

"I trust both of them implicitly," Alex said, also seriously, his face quite sober. "I have no reason to believe that everyone they deal with is trustworthy. White I imagine keeps everything locked tight and only shares it with her shift relief. Weilhung has to perforce share it with his subordinates. It trickles down from there to . . . who knows?"

"There are other snoops," Horace said, indicating the camera above with a flick of eyes only. "If Elke can read the President with her gear, so can others."

Alex looked disturbed.

"I keep forgetting how much surveillance goes on, even here. It's almost as bad as London, Chicago, or San Fran back on Earth."

"Assume everything is public," Horace advised.

The movement went well, as usual. They performed their dance through the palace and into the vehicles. Military vehicles led, limos in the middle, more military tailing. The new route was circuitous and led past the market, where some garbage was thrown.

A rotten cabbage thudded against the glass of the principal limo, and three EPs raised weapons, then holstered them again. Alex looked at Bishwanath, who shrugged.

Elke was jumpy. She wanted her shotgun, but it was stowed under her feet. This vehicle was well-armored, she reminded herself. No immediate danger.

The President said, "If they wish to express themselves thusly, I won't try to stop them. A few stains on my limousine just punctuate what our situation is like."

"It must be irritating, though," Shaman said.

"Enormously," Bishwanath agreed. But it anything, he sounded bored.

The route seemed to work. Nothing further happened. The chosen course into town paralleled and crossed the old one twice, and then looped around. Anyone trying to respond would not have much notice or time in which to do so.

The park in which the meeting was held could only charitably be called so. The grass was long, tufty, and choked by weeds. Several decorative paths were now broken and overgrown. The trees needed pruning, and several had snapped off in storms or been broken; it was hard to tell which. Elke saw trash, bare spots, areas that had obviously been campsites with fires until Dhe's goons had chased them out for this meeting.

"Oh, my," Elke said as the entourage pulled to the curb. Dhe's contingent was already set up and . . .

There were no words. His supporters were behind a rope that was patrolled by police and local soldiers. A few real soldiers, Turks and Bulgarians from the insignia, reinforced them to give some semblance of professionalism. Dhe had his own guards, too. Well fed. Overly well fed. They could certainly wave guns around, and they wore bright red pantaloons, white socks, flowerpot-shaped hats, and blue shirts with piping and braid. They almost looked like some ancient army from early rifle days.

The crowd . . . people in rags, flowery princess outfits, working clothes, fine suits, and the tuxedo tights of the wealthy, all here to show support for a politician who "spoke for the poor."

In Elke's estimate, the jewelry and limos of three or four of the guests on the bleachers could double the standard of living of ninety percent of the crowd. So much for the "graduated tax" Dhe was fond of.

The rich few were not only ostentatious, they were strutting gay peacocks. The poor were gutter poor, and the other groups were every flake and freak one could imagine. This was the so-called "People's Progressive Party." They cared about the poor.

Mister Dhe was sitting, but did rise to meet Bishwanath. Elke quivered alert. The crowd was largely uncontrolled; Dhe's men were armed. She knew the Army and the Recon troops were in a perimeter behind that crowd and on the buildings nearby, but it was still an area full of threats. Her professional instinct was to move in closer to shield the principal from attack, but that had been ruled out for appearance. She could be reactive only.

"Checking crowd, no immediate threats, nothing but freaks," she said. They all slipped out of the vehicles as one. Elke and Shaman took the front as Bart and Aramis moved in from the sides, and Jason slipped in behind next to Alex.

"Confirm freaks," Aramis said. She could hear sotto voce and the radio both.

"Bad terrain, multiple potentials," Bart said. He was referring to threat positions that could be occupied.

"Solid readings," Shaman said, referring to Bishwanath's vitals. "Nothing additional."

"Freaks and scum," Jason said.

"Consulting with Mama. Potentials cleared, and will be recleared." Alex had to be going nuts at the rear, watching Bishwanath walk into a potential trap.

Nor was it a paranoid fear. Someone might take advantage of the open terrain, or try to frame Dhe, or Dhe might make it look like someone was trying to frame Dhe. You never knew.

The press were out, of course. They were privileged, and considered threat free, which was ludicrous, even if you considered their lies and carrion eating to be nonthreatening. Media was a very easy way to insert a spy or worse, which was why most governments were so leery of them, while being required to cater to them.

Bishwanath smiled broadly. Considering his comments about Dhe, that had to be a fine acting job. Elke watched him and watched her sector of the guests and the crowd. She felt her fingers twitching and restrained them. No weapons, no explosives. Not yet.

The cameras and "official" guests made it a jungle for an EP. The only good part was that Elke looked less like a fixture as she wandered around, past fractured trees and the human buzzards perched below them.

Dhe's guards had earbuds, too. There were also three Recon troops she recognized, checking the threat zones that had been reported. Elke snapped photos with her eyeglass setup, and nodded to her compatriots. Recon, at least. She didn't regard Dhe's thugs as anything other than targets she couldn't shoot yet. They were all style, if that revolting combo could be called "style," and no substance to speak of.

She couldn't avoid looking at Dhe because Bishwanath was next to him. What a disgusting creature. Pallid, a corpulent slug, obviously drunk out of his mind—she could smell the ketones fermenting out of his body from here—stuffed into a suit, and unable to speak a full sentence without drifting into incoherence that was quickly masked by the applause of his bootlickers.

But Bishwanath smiled and was relaxed, and acted as if they were long lost friends. He'd even hugged the man and kissed his cheeks. Elke shuddered.

The event was canned, nothing but speeches and platitudes, which was reassuring. Both parties were showing their presence, agreeing that they could work together, and the pats on the back were just to locate where to stick the figurative knife.

Her attention was split between Bishwanath and the event. Nothing untoward seemed to be going on, and there were plenty of personnel around. Assuming Dhe's people cared about him, and he had competent friends somewhere, there didn't seem to be much to worry about.

Shaman walked past and just nodded, nothing to comment on. Aramis had, too. Everything seemed clean without any excessive neatness to suggest a setup. Nor was there anything to indicate

Dhe's people were anywhere good enough to set up something so clever that it would look innocent.

When the face-to-face finished, there was a brief question-and-answer. The whole thing was so predictable.

"President Bishwanath, what do you intend to offer to the unemployed, since Department benefits have run out?"

"Obviously, we will be creating a system of payments to ensure these people are taken care of. However, there are delays in the implementation, since we have to identify everyone and arrange for funds to be delivered. With the existing lack of infrastructure, this could take time, but you have my assurance it's high on my list of priorities."

Bishwanath was good. All the questions fell into the same pattern. How much, what benefits, what money are you going to give to group X to buy their vote and ensure they don't riot like chimps? Isn't it your fault we trashed and burned our society and now have nothing to show? What about Lady G, who's living on the street? Why do we have to wait? Can't money be handed out now? Make people happy and security won't be a problem. Look at the money being spent on your guards...

Then a reporter approached Elke. She tried to turn and be busy elsewhere, but a microphone was in her face, and she was on the spot. Their SOP was to give polite but uninformative replies and finish quickly. Elke could also pretend to speak no English, but she disliked doing that.

"Miss, you're one of the President's hired guards. How do you respond to allegations of waste on your contract?" The speaker had a practiced, pleasant smile and a huge set of tits that stunned Elke. They had to be natural, couldn't be comfortable, and the outfit was designed to make them very visible to the interviewee. That meant distraction. The woman operating them had to be bright and planning on being underestimated mentally.

"That's really not my place to say," she replied, programmed response. "The contract was arranged through BuState to my company. I don't handle such matters."

"Very well. What is it like guarding the President? How much time do you actually work?"

Inquiry of information not to be shared. "I really can't discuss that," she said, hoping to pass this off to Alex, but he was busy and she was in the crosshairs. "We have an ongoing task of planning and executing security in the palace and for events, rehearsing, training, making advance trips to locations. We're busy pretty much all day, every day."

"And what is he like, then?"

Personal. Be discreet. "He's a busy man, and we keep out of his way. He's been very gracious and hospitable with our facilities and support."

"Hypothetically, if there was an attack at one of these functions, would you work to protect other victims? Or is only the President your concern?"

Trap question! "Obviously, the President's safety is our primary concern. Once we have ensured that, we are available to help others, depending on the situation. If you'll excuse me, I have to escort the President."

"Absolutely, ma'am, and thank you for your time."

She fell back into position as Bishwanath headed slowly for the car, shaking hands and smiling. "Grip and grin" it was called. Necessary, if time consuming.

They moved in, passed off and surrounded the President, escorted him to the car, and slipped inside as planned.

Alex said, "Okay, wrap up and head for the barn." Bart drove the escort this time, Jason had the President. They switched off at random for further safety, and rotated on who was close to Bishwanath as well. The catch was that either Shaman or Jason had to be nearby for medical support, and Bart and Jason were the best drivers. Jason was also deputy, so either he or Alex had to be in the primary vehicle. Jason was really the person to watch.

The local police did manage to hold the press back as they boarded, Elke on duty with Alex, Jason driving, and the others in the chase car. Bishwanath gave a last wave as they pulled away slowly. That slowness was predicated by the crush of crowd the police hadn't managed to restrain.

Once through the crowd, Jason accelerated. Elke grabbed a water bottle and downed a liter.

"Thirsty," she said, suddenly feeling sweat in the air-conditioned compartment.

"Very," Alex agreed. Bishwanath didn't say anything. He also was drinking, also water.

Gulping, Alex said, "Three kilometers and we'll group back up. Shouldn't be any real—"

Which was of course when the attack hit.

Elke's bottle went flying as something crashed into the car. She let it fly and dropped down, grabbing one of the dump guns and reaching for her shotgun. Alex sprawled across Bishwanath, and she snagged helmets from the center mount, one for each of them, then grabbed for her own. She had the wrong helmet, she realized as she slapped it on. It was too loose, but there wasn't time to deal with that.

Jason yelled, "Incoming rockets, get the fuck *out*! Right!" and she took that as gospel. Alex had one of Bishwanath's arms, she had the other. She kicked at the release on the right door as she slid over, and raised the carbine over her feet.

Half the seventy-round stick evaporated into a roar and a sharp smell, with plastic vapor in the air. By the time the burst finished, three point two seconds at full rate of fire, heat waves were pouring off the barrel and distorting the image in her glasses, and she'd fanned the shots across ninety degrees of space in front of them. A second burst indicated Jason unloading. Right now, it sucked to be anyone in the area, because their only concern was saving Bishwanath, no matter how many locals took fire. *Innocent bystander* was an oxymoron when someone was bringing rockets to bear.

She dropped the dump gun and tumbled out, Bishwanath rolled over her, pushed by Alex and crushing her left breast between their weight and the sharp angles of the carbine. Luckily, the serrated cap of the suppressor wasn't where it could poke her. The armor was good against impact but was quite soft otherwise, which was a mixed blessing. Alex stepped on her shoulder, but lightly as he sprang, then he was lifting the President off her.

"Mister President, we have to move! Please come with me!"

First thing was to clear a perimeter, but Jason had mentioned . . .

SLABOOM!

Direct fire grenade. He'd said rockets, she thought through the ringing, and was glad of her earbuds. A glance back showed Jason patting Bishwanath down and slipping plugs in his ears, and Alex scanning. There were the other three. She'd missed their car being hit, but it was in pieces and flames now, everything forward of the passenger compartment shredded. Or maybe it going up had been the warning Jason had shouted. Bart limped a bit and curled around his left side, but was moving well.

They had a perimeter and their principal, and they were within a couple of kilometers of backup, including possible air cover. It was even possible Dhe's men would show up and be of help.

She shook her head, realizing she was a bit stunned to think something so silly. Those posers were useless even if they had courage, professionalism, or the desire to help, which they didn't.

"Report," Alex demanded.

"Argonaut, one, full, go, Dishwasher," Jason said. He had the President.

"Shaman, one, full, go, Dishwasher," Shaman said. Both medics had the President. No report of injuries.

"Babs, one, full, go," she said. Condition one. Her injuries were some scrapes, stings, and bruises, minor enough she wasn't going to report them.

"Brat, four, half, go," Bart said, indicating some injury and half ammo load.

"Aramis, two, three-quarter, go," Aramis said. Minor dings, a couple of bursts shot.

"Playwright, one, half, go, Dishwasher," Alex confirmed. "Cover and retreat. Say so?"

Both vehicles had been crashed with small trucks and then rocketed. That showed definite planning. They needed cover fast, and this was a largely residential area north of downtown with broad avenues and center islands. There wasn't much to cover behind except houses.

Elke heard a sound, identified it as nearby fire and a threat, then caught the movement.

"*Fire to our left!*" she shouted, and turned. Bodies stumbled through a doorway from an apartment building and headed toward them.

"Ground arriving, air en route, over," Weilhung's voice said.

Behind her, Jason had Bishwanath and turned for cover with Shaman. Aramis and Bart moved ahead to clear a building. Alex was moving to her right to cover her. In a few seconds, Recon should be there with the Hate Truck, but she had a fight on her hands now.

She raised her shotgun and shot at once, pointing center mass of the attacker closest to her. The others were spreading out slightly. She took a quick glance for threats while continuing to snap-shoot at the point. Fifteen meters wasn't enough distance to require aiming, and the pattern would be about fifty centimeters at that range.

The first two tumbled off the steps. The second one contented himself with twitching and clutching. The first one got to his knees and began to rise. Elke was already on one knee and shimmying behind a tree above the curb that would hopefully provide at least some cover from high-vel rounds. The skinny palm barely qualified as a tree and only her slenderness made it worthwhile as cover. At that, it wouldn't stop rifle fire, and maybe not carbine. Still, any cover was better than no cover.

One of the enemy was wearing body armor, and while she didn't believe it, a dress underneath. So that rumor really was true. A wiry, buff young male in a turquoise evening gown. His sartorial elegance didn't stop Death or her pellets from finding him. The first load shattered his hip, flashing crimson through the fabric, while the second, raised and right, went through his face. She was proud of that shot, but didn't stop to admire it. She scooted back, slip-stepping, to make sure she didn't trip on obstacles. Alex was in close with a carbine, chattering out bursts.

She tossed a retch-gas canister just downwind enough to be clear of it, a frequency tailored smoke upwind to conceal their retreat, and toggled her glasses to see through it. Then she swiped at a pocket to get a handful of what she called Nasty Pebbles. They were little balls of hyperexplosive wrapped around a kernel cap, with a fuse and microcontroller chip protruding enough so she could program them with the controller she had hanging under her right arm to counterbalance her pistol. She didn't waste time programming them under the circumstances. She just clutched and threw.

"Here they come," Alex said, and, "Dishwasher ready to be installed."

She was still slip-stepping backward as the pebbles started bursting with loud snaps. The smoke swirled and billowed, but she moved fast enough to keep it mostly between her and the threats. One more freak in a dress—a violet summer print with a fetching brimmed hat with a fringe—came running through, dripping blood where something had nicked him. She shot him. Slip-step might look like a silly pop-music dance step, but it also gave you a very smooth, level retreat that made shooting easy.

✧   ✧   ✧

Jason had point and led the way toward the nearest building, a small house that would become their redoubt of the moment. He bounded up two steps. There were no obvious threats, but it paid to be discreet anyway. He doubted there were any here, but he was not paid to make that assumption. He stood to at the door as the rest closed in, keeping his attention split between street and their potential retreat. He couldn't let anything flank them, but also had to be aware for a tactical shift that would require exfiltrating through another route.

Aramis came up next. Jason watched him. The kid was doing his job well despite being the new guy. He laid down good fire and moved in an orderly fashion. Then he was against Jason. A few moments later, Shaman and Bart joined the huddle and it was time to move. Aramis goosed him to signal readiness. That wasn't a prank; the buttocks were the easiest exposed contact. He felt the touch and moved to the left, shooting a solid load into the door's mechanism, wishing for Elke's shotgun with breacher loads.

Bart kicked the door off its latch and stepped back again. Jason crescent-kicked it back against the wall and charged inside, to their right . . .

Aramis was a few centimeters behind and moved left, as Shaman went straight, and Bart backed up behind Bishwanath. Alex and Elke tumbled up the steps and took position right inside the door. Elke reloaded at once and instinctively clutched a grenade. Bloodthirsty bitch. He was glad to have her along. He noted one civilian inside, not a threat.

Just outside, the Hate Truck rolled in. A crackle of electricity stunned all those nearby, then the troops inside opened up with the nonlethal hardware. Between stunners, weepy gas, and retch gas, psychoactive agents and foams sticky and slick, it was a matter of seconds before the entire streetful of locals started thrashing and puking, sliding around on the ground and sticking together, with the reek of shit coming from involuntarily voided bowels. Recon was required to use nonlethal force, but they used as much of it as they could get away with.

Aramis had wet himself. That of itself wasn't amusing; it happened even to experienced pros at times, and there were also times you had to go. It had really struck his macho ego, though, and he was trying hard to hide the dark stains down his legs. Elke snickered blatantly. She'd never had that problem that he knew of, but didn't think less of people who did. However, Aramis was now in a position of ruining his own image. That made it hysterical. Jason suppressed his own chuckle. *There's some humility for you, son.*

Bishwanath stood cautiously, as Jason and Shaman patted him down, looking for wounds or other damage. Jason took the rear, Shaman took the front with his kit.

"Thank you, gentlemen, but I'm fine," Bishwanath insisted.

"We'll check anyway, sir, just to make sure," Shaman insisted right back. "Pupils even and responsive, pulse, respiration, and blood pressure elevated but normal. No visible injuries."

"Right," Alex said. "Shaman, check Bart. Let's get the convoy."

"Let us say hello to our hostess," Bishwanath said, pointing.

Jason looked where Alex was looking. Ah. The old lady. Sitting in a chair and looking both disturbed and confused. This was her house.

"Er, ma'am," Alex said. "We, that is . . ."

"Just passing through," Jason offered.

"Have we a moment?" Bishwanath asked.

"Yes, sir," Alex agreed. "The street has to be cleared and transport must arrive."

"Good afternoon, ma'am. I must apologize for our sudden entry," Bishwanath said.

The lady finally recovered from the shock of having her burglarproof steel door kicked off its hinges and a squad of armed, dirty suits swarming into her living room.

"Mister President!" she said, squinting slightly. "What an odd way of meeting."

"Indeed, ma'am. I do apologize, and I will ensure your door is fixed at once."

There came the thumping of lifters overhead. It was a pity, and a crime, Jason thought, that they couldn't have those during the convoys, only for reaction. They'd been led to expect better support.

"I've told them where we are and that we're secure," Alex said. "Let's cover front and back and give the President a few moments. Elke, can you record?"

"I can," she nodded. Her record wouldn't be as high quality as production video gear, but it would make good copy. That would help. Jason stepped out front with Bart and Shaman as the rest covered the back and Elke recorded.

"Nicely done," he said to Bart.

"Thanks," the man offered, smiling for once. "It worked well. Though the limos are a mess."

" 'Well used' is the term. But when we make a mess . . . hehehe." He indicated the street in front.

It was an intersection with a divided residential street crossing a thoroughfare. Two limos and two trucks were smoking piles of wreckage, both limos with holes blown in them. The Hate Truck's ministrations had left dozens of gawkers and troublemakers twitching. A good dozen were dead from fire. Bart was the team's only casualty. . . .

"I think the ribs are just bruised, and your liver may be, too," Shaman said. "I'll check with the full scanners when we get back. You should be fine in a few days with therapy."

"Good. As long as you are not to cut or saw."

"I save that for my very best patients." Shaman grinned hugely.

A few moments later, they all proceeded down in a huddle around Bishwanath, into the back of a military armored troop carrier. The President seemed delighted to be in such a vehicle, though all the others had long familiarity and didn't like the heat, fumes, close quarters, or sharp corners.

"I'd rather do this every time," Jason said, loudly enough to be heard.

"It's exciting, but I don't think I like it quite that much," Bishwanath admitted.

"It's not the 'like' so much, sir, as the 'can't be taken out by small arms' bit."

"We are all prisoners of our societies and expectations, Mister Vaughn." Bishwanath was smiling, but looking tired.

"That we are, sir."

Shortly, they pulled into the palace, debarked under Recon guard, and made a point of thanking their backup. Aramis was especially enthusiastic.

"Nice with the gas," he said, grinning. "Nothing like watching the little bastards squirm and squirt."

"You're welcome," said one of the operators. He grinned back. "All I know is, we finally got to pop smoke."

"Yeah, thanks," Jason said. "Aramis, I could use a hand back here."

"Sure," the kid agreed. "Thanks, guys. Later."

Jason checked they hadn't left any gear behind that was either controlled or personal, then ran the vehicle's hatch up until it clanked closed.

"Jason," his earbuds squawked.

"Go ahead, Alex," he replied.

"Clean up, grab food here, we'll debrief in a bit."

"Sounds good. We'll be up in a few. Checking the transport, got some docs and a spare magazine someone left."

"We'll put it out for claim."

CHAPTER TEN

Jason felt a lot better after a shower. Damn, it was always a good day when you took fire, saved your principal, and got back unhurt. He didn't regard his bruised elbow or scraped shin as injuries. Those were part of the job.

As usual, the "news" was on for intel. Sometimes it gave advance notice of things they should have been informed of but had been forgotten in the frenzy. Of course, they had to immediately get the real story, which would rarely bare resemblance to the incompetent and ignorant ramblings of the press.

Elke was sitting back munching an apple, clean and calm and with a spreadsheet on her computer. Occasionally, she'd grip the apple with her teeth and type with both hands, then revert to one hand for each, or speak into the mic hanging around her neck; she wasn't bothering with headphones for interaction. This was all input.

She noticed his stare and said, "Running inventory of explosives, detonators, caps, remotes, circuitry, and triggers."

"Ah, right," he said. "I do mine old style. Sheet of paper and here." He tapped his head. A folded-up piece of paper with numbers was harder for someone else to interpret, but Elke kept tight control of her computer. Very tight.

Shaman scanned Bart with a handheld ultrasound unit, running it carefully over the dark welt on his ribs and nodding at the images on screen. He and finally sat back, waving his arms as if in some ritual. At least he wasn't wearing a mask.

"It is just bruising, but may have hit the liver, as I said. Watch how you feel and tell me if there are symptoms. Any symptoms from indigestion to fatigue or nausea to trouble moving."

Bart nodded and pulled his shirt down. "I did something similar when I was small, crashing into a tree."

Aramis was cleaning everybody's weapons. No, it wasn't punishment, Jason decided, looking at him. The kid had figured it needed done and looked very enthusiastic. He was also methodical and precise for the most part, with just a few pieces sliding across the mat. There was nothing wrong with him, really, except for maturity. He just didn't yet have internalized that there were some areas and times you didn't play around. Once he straightened that out, he'd be fine.

Alex had his computer attached to a large screen, and a map of the routes highlighted.

"Okay," Alex said, "now that we're all here, let's look at it.

"First, I should have given more thought to the closest few hundred meters, where we had limited support."

"I want to know where the hell the air power was," Aramis asked.

"They were there," Alex assured all of them. "They were definitely there. But once we were out of the vehicles, and the attackers were among civilians, what could they safely shoot at?"

Good point, Jason thought.

He said, "So someone competent set up a bunch of goons to try to pin us down. Luckily, we were faster and better than they anticipated."

"Right, Jason," Alex agreed. "This was a payoff for training and planning. We did our jobs and got out of a nasty situation. Great job, all of you. Elke, I loved the explosives. Bart, the camera is fuzzy but you bailed out under fire and didn't get hurt badly. Jason, Aramis, good fire on target, fast response getting to our ersatz safe house. Shaman, and Jason again, great response on the President. Fine operation all around, under the circumstances."

"There appears to be disagreement over that," Elke said, pointing at the vidwall.

They all turned to see what she indicated.

"—after a miserable failure at protecting President Bishwanath, these contract security personnel were rescued and escorted back to the palace by UN-commanded U.S. Army soldiers." Jason recognized the speaker as the redhead with the huge knockers.

"Just who are these 'contractors'? According to the company's official release, they are 'highly trained, motivated military veterans with exceptional ability in executive protection.' But what did we find when looking them over?"

The screen cut to a telephoto of Elke. "Checking crowd, no immediate threats, nothing but freaks."

"Confirm freaks."

The redhead said, "*Freaks* was their term for the loyal followers of Representative Dhe. This term was repeated several times—" Cut to Jason saying, "Freaks and scum."

Jason was pissed. He'd always regarded the press as traitors and barely restrained his desire to physically clobber them when encountering them. He glanced at Elke. Elke was glowing infrared. Utterly motionless. *Hell hath no fury*, he thought, and this woman scorned liked playing with explosives.

"We interviewed these alleged experts after the meeting, and here's what we were told . . ."

Cut to Elke on camera. "We have an ongoing task of planning and executing security in the palace and for events, rehearsing, training, making advance trips to locations. We're busy pretty much all day, every day."

Cut to a long range, fuzzy image of Elke dumping the H&K, then Elke, Alex, and Bishwanath tumbling out of the limo in an undignified heap.

"Hypothetically, if there was an attack at one of these functions, would you work to protect other victims? Or is only the President your concern?"

Elke: "Obviously, the President's safety is our primary concern. Once we have ensured that, we are available to help others, depending on the situation."

Cut back to her dumping out the carbine in the general direction of a crowd. Cut to close-ups of victims getting shot, though the light didn't quite match and it could have been taken anywhere.

Repeat: "Once we have ensured that, we are available to help others, depending on the situation."

Cut to them running for the house, explosions in the background. Then of the crowd writhing on the ground, though that had been caused by the military.

Cut to Aramis answering some question, "It would be a hard call to make, but passersby are not really our problem," then a close-up of dead bodies near where the attack had taken place.

Bart erupted at the screen, "That is one of the bastards who crashed into us!"

Back to the reporter. "So we have a team of what amount to mercenaries guarding the President, who regard innocent bystanders as merely obstacles to be shot and disregarded. They have at least once injured the President in the very act of 'protecting' him, and consider running from a fight and into cover as the right solution to the problem. This is putting strain on our already overworked soldiers, who must then clean up the mess left behind."

Weilhung appeared on camera. "There is some stickiness, seeing as we have . . . different procedures for operating."

"It's aggravating?"

"It can be, especially since they're not accountable"—there was a cut from his face as more of the attack was shown—"and some of our people resent the difference in pay scale."

Back to the reporter. "The contract for Ripple Creek is a round-the-clock deal. Each individual is on contract, not hired, and there are six for the President, plus two supplemental personnel. There are several others groups operating for various dignitaries. The cost on these contracts is ten thousand marks a day, for the six primary contracts. So what does BuState, who is ultimately responsible, get for all that money?"

Montage: "Not really our problem." Attacker moaning and bloody. "We are available to help others." Elke and then Jason dumping out full sticks. Screaming people running and hit in some engagement somewhere.

"There was a sad, ironic aftermath to this monumental failure," the reporter said, filling the screen again. "The house they chose as cover belonged to a senior citizen. Here's how her door looked afterwards. You'll notice that military engineers are repairing it, once again having to clean up a mess left by contractors. Here we can see the dozens of people who were filling the street at the time, some of them children, being treated by Aerospace Force medics after the response to this attack was to indiscriminately fill a block with incapacitance gas."

"That was the Army, goddamit," Shaman muttered.

Flash to Dhe. "Obviously, I am shocked and saddened that someone has attacked President Bishwanath. He and I had a productive talk on the needs of the poor, and I am glad to hear he is well. At the same time, the incompetent support he has is likely a big reason so many necessary programs are awaiting funding. It's not just his guards who are hindering operations.

"I, of course, would be happy to offer a contingent of my own executive protection people, at my expense. Being local, they have a far better understanding of the issues and threats, and certainly will not shy from the situation." Repeat the video of the dog pile out of the limo.

Miss Tits resumed her monologue. "The ultimate question, of course, is why a president who can't seem to actually get aid to anyone, other than some personal matters taken care of by the Army, and is protected by outrageously paid mercenaries with no regard for anyone but him, and little even there, is being considered for a permanent position. How will Mister Bishwanath rule without the military to bail him out? Will his budget actually be used for the public good, or just for his personal empire?

"And why has our administration, why has Secretary General Rove, set up such a situation? Is it incompetence or corruption? We'll look at that when we return."

Utter silence prevailed for several seconds. Finally, Jason said, "Turn. That. *Shit*. Off." He was too angry, his voice too wavering, to attempt it himself.

"Power off," Shaman said.

"Dammit, I hate this shit!" Aramis said. "We retreat under fire and then we get some shit about pulling out."

Bart tried to lighten it with, "Didn't you learn? Pulling out is not a sure way to prevent pregnancy."

"Yeah, and I'm tired of listening to you pull off," Jason said. "That's the job, you knew it when you took it, and that's why you're getting paid."

He couldn't blame Aramis. He was so fucking pissed himself. Aramis was young, aggressive, wanted to go after trouble, which was the one thing EPs could never do.

He still had his earbuds in, and White's voice announced, "Conference. We're coming up."

Alex reached into his pocket, grabbed his mouthpiece from its case, slipped it in, and said, "Understood." He pulled the transmitter back out. "Okay, everyone breathe deep and get the stress out. We're all on the same side."

"Right, officially," Aramis said.

"Have to be," Alex warned him.

The knock at the door was followed by White entering, who was followed a couple of seconds later by Weilhung and deWitt. There was obvious tension on all sides, but everyone had it firmly under control. They gathered in the area in front of the doors, an atrium delineated by furniture.

"I see the misquotes are all around," Weilhung said. He looked both angry and nervous.

"Yeah. What exactly did you say?" Alex asked. He was offering the benefit of the doubt, and was in better mettle than Jason, who wondered about that himself. The quote as presented had been damning, but was it what had actually been said?

"I said, 'especially since they're not accountable to the same chain of command. It means we have different ways of doing things which can lead to unexpected problems.'"

Everyone looked at him.

"I figured that was a story in itself," he said.

"It is indeed," Shaman offered. "But not the story these ghouls want."

"Yeah. I'm sorry." He looked sheepish.

"You saw what they did to Elke and Aramis' comments."

"I get the general idea of what they said. For the record, you did a first-class job of getting the President to cover. I am impressed, so are my guys, and congratulations are in order." He made a point of offering his hand to each of them in turn.

Jason was fine with that, and shook it. If nothing else came of this, it helped reinforce they were on the same side. A related side was their bureaucrats. The primary enemy was threats to Bishwanath. The press, as always, were a secondary enemy. Losers and dropouts who couldn't get real jobs, but Wanted to Make a Difference.

That settled, everyone looked at deWitt.

"Are you bearing the usual bad news in a moral support package?" Jason asked.

"Not this time," the man shook his head. "I have one concern here, and it's a sucky one, but I've got to relay it."

"Shoot," said Alex.

"Because of other situations with reporters and assorted groups, they're now whining that they're receiving threats."

"Gee, who woulda thunk it?" Jason muttered loudly.

"We don't get to help, right?" Aramis asked.

"You don't get to help," deWitt said. "And worse."

There were sighs and groans.

"Yes?" prompted Bart.

"There *cannot* be any killings of reporters. They'll claim it was a deliberate attempt to silence them, go after you in court, and go after the administration, claiming it was government sanctioned. You understand what that means?"

"It means the government will fuck us over a barrel to cover its arse," Elke said. Everyone looked at her. That was a graphic statement for her.

"That is exactly what it means," deWitt agreed. "Do whatever you have to, kill a fucking nursing *baby* if it's in the way, but *do not* hit a reporter. At all."

"When this is all over, I'll do a special on them," Aramis said.

"I'll help," deWitt promised. "We all will. But they are inviolate for now. *Capisce?*"

"Got it." "Yes." "If we must." "Sure." "Understood." "I'll make sure of it."

"New policy here," Alex said, catching everyone's eye, "is that we do not talk to reporters. Ever. Not even to say, 'That will have to go through Corporate, fuck you very much.' Not a word. I'll clear it with Massa."

"Suits me," Elke said.

Weilhung looked annoyed. "Damn, I wish I had that power. Regs require I deal with them. Require it. I am required to talk to them truthfully."

"What I want to know is, who hacked our commo?" Alex asked, tapping his ear and jaw. "These are supposed to be secure."

White said, "I'll see what I can find with my gear. That will mostly matter if they transmit. Detecting a receiver is much harder. I will put together a package for you to take on your next run." When she said, "I" in that context, it meant an entire staff. She was merely the one who did the public speaking for the others, and one of the four people who covered a shift at that station in the palace. AF kept very much to themselves, and didn't socialize. Jason wasn't sure if that was local to this operation, or a new policy. They'd been more congenial in years past, or at least his elements had. Of course, the Army wasn't talking to them, either, and he had no idea whether or not the military spent much time talking without contractors. Certainly they often appeared together.

"So why is everyone secretive?" he went ahead and asked.

"Jason?" Alex queried, but in a normal tone, no warning in it.

"We don't talk to them, they don't talk to us. Everyone talks to Bishwanath, putting him on the spot. Mister deWitt gets to relay policy that applies to us a lot and the military less, even when it goes through their chain of command, and Aerospace doesn't seem to talk to anyone, but has all the gear. Are we on the same team or not?"

After several seconds, Weilhung spoke first.

"We are on the same team, but there are some matters I cannot share. Threats, certainly. Intel on the locals, once the source is sanitized. Certain material has to be kept secret to protect capabilities."

There was a pause, and Tech White said, "The information isn't the problem. Sorting and categorizing it takes time, and then we prioritize by mission and unit."

"Is there something more important than protecting the President?" Jason asked.

She replied, looking suitably embarrassed, "Well, please remember that the priority lists are not drawn up by me. I have a list of functions that must be fulfilled before I can perform supplemental functions. The list comes down from Theater HQ, and I have to submit requests for variation up through them."

DeWitt said, "I can help with that." Everyone looked over at him leaning against the wall. "I'll lean on General Ellis and reiterate the importance of the Presidential Escort mission. You must understand, the military's mission is pacification. BuState's is diplomatic, and BuCommerce's is development. It's a massive pie-eating contest, and only one pie."

"I feel we've been eating something totally different from 'pie,'" Aramis offered.

"Yeah, that's about it," Weilhung offered. "Look, I don't bear you guys any malice. But we can't be friends. No matter what BuState wants"—he nodded to deWitt—"we're in different chains for different reasons. That said, I'll keep you more informed if you agree to the same."

"I'll share what we can," Alex said.

Jason tried not to sigh. All lies. There was no way anyone could share what they had freely, because there were too many leaks. BuState was full of fuzzy studies types who'd share the intelligence as bargaining chips and for their attempts at world building. The Army tended to get drunk and talk, or just boast, or could and had had bona fide spies selling intel. White had openly admitted that Aerospace had totally different goals.

And we are tasked only with keeping the President safe. Not with being team players.

There was nothing to indicate the situation would get better. Only that everyone agreed on the press as a mutual enemy.

And that fact just made secrecy all the more desirable.

CHAPTER ELEVEN

Colonel Weygandt braced himself for the pending visit. Dealing with BuState was always annoying. DeWitt was a pain in the ass because he was smart and at odds with UN HQ. On the other hand, that being at odds often meant he was supporting the military, which made him an asset rather than an adversary or hindrance.

The man on his way in now though, was none of that. If there was anyone in the BuState mission who could be dispensed with . . .

The door opened and in he came. His own "personal assistant" held the doorknob. Either Weygandt's aide had been pushed aside or hadn't wanted to get too close. Either was possible.

"The good news is, we can use this incident against those Ripple Creek bastards," Michel leMieure said without preamble. He was talking as he walked in. He seemed like the kind of man who should shamble. His assistant just slipped to the corner and started making notes.

A visit from the fat bastard was always unpleasant, Weygandt reflected. The man was everything a soldier was not. He was unkempt with greasy hair, unshaven but not actually bearded. He had the physique of a slug and he stank. He also affected "common" clothes.

"We do need to be careful," Weygandt cautioned. "There are people in BuState who endorse them greatly." Thank God the man didn't believe in shaking hands. Weygandt just sat up in his chair and nodded, hands evenly on the desk.

"Oh, like deWitt? Fuck him. Man thinks because he's posted here a year or two he's an expert. I've got my information from top sources. Not government ones." LeMieure's expression was a sneer. Weygandt was struck by how revolting this man was. Yet he'd been a darling of the intelligentsia as a troublemaker who started "dialogs." That semifame had been rolled into an appointment by the new administration.

He reflected that taking a shit in the middle of a conference hall would start a "dialog." That did not make it a desirable or worthy act. He'd have to have the cleaners come in and disinfect everything this man touched. He got queasy just looking at his sweaty figure. The assistant's presence didn't help. He was a progressive "cartoonist" whose scrawls offended a great many people, especially the military.

Weygandt kept his mask on and replied, "I believe Bishwanath might support them, too, in a crunch. He was a bad choice." But no matter how annoying Bishwanath was, he was at least a civilized man. A petty player and an upstart, certainly, but not the scum this man was.

"I was against him from the beginning," leMieure said, "but they liked his 'neutrality.' A man without strings is harder to work. Especially if he's a fucking idealist."

"Yes, he wants to build a nation." And was an idiot for it.

"And we want him to shut up and let us stabilize this hole. The minuscule improvements he could make are not worth the trouble of trying to put down every riot and insurrection that crops up. And they are going to crop up if we let them bring in development in technical areas. You start getting an educated and technical class, and a middle class of merchants that get wealthy, and all of a sudden it's a stratified society with class warfare."

LeMieure liked to talk a lot, Weygandt had noticed. He was never going to trust the man with anything relevant. He was never going to even mention anything relevant in case the rumors of how he extorted further info were true.

"Poor isn't desirable, but it's stable," he commented. He wished the man would just make his point and leave. Then Weygandt could make sure it didn't smear the Army. He'd so far managed to keep his secret that not only did he despise the fat cretin, he thought he was a blithering idiot.

What you needed was a strong leader. Class or classless society be damned. You set up someone with charisma and drive, told them what to do, and let them organize things. A central authority could slap down trouble and keep things stable, which ultimately led to a better society. Rights and development would come along once you proved it was stable.

"Who cares if they're poor? They don't know what it's like to be rich, except for tribal fathers like Bish, and that goddammed Dhe. Give them a few apartment blocks and running water for their village shitters, and they'll behave."

It was amazing how allegiances formed and crossed, Weygandt noted. The military, BuState, and contractors all hated the press. The press, military, and BuState weren't keen on the contractors, and the contractors and military hated BuState. You needed a dance card.

"Good point about him supporting them, though," leMieure muttered.

"Sir?" Weygandt prompted. Something interesting, no doubt.

"I'll need to warn the media not to accept any statements from Bish about his contractors. Not unless I write it for him."

"Good idea, sir," Weygandt said.

Well, at least he had an idea who'd fucked Weilhung over with that misquote.

On the other hand, Weilhung was an asshole. Let him take the heat.

"I want everything you can find on those contract fuckers. Those six specifically. I want to know every fuckup they've had. I want to know when they pull trains on that slut with them, I want to know what porn sites they cruise. Anything I can use to get them out of the way, so I can get rid of them. Preferably in shame and disgrace."

"I'll see what I can find," Weygandt lied. Though he wasn't going to protect them, but he wouldn't go that far. Just enough to suggest they be removed. "Aerospace commands the intel assets, and I'll tell them what I need."

"You do that. The moment Marlow started that 'we work for the President' crap he should have been gone the next day. They work for me. This is my project."

"I'm eager to see the end result, sir." It was true. Weygandt half expected this rotting toad to reduce the entire planet, both nations, back to the Stone Age.

"Get me that information. I'll have these fuckers gone."

He turned and left and Weygandt breathed a huge sigh. The odor lingered, but was fading. He would find that intel. It would take work, because he only wanted dirt on the contractors. As annoying as Weilhung was, anything that touched him would hurt the military. So he had to maintain appearances and find a more subtle way to get rid of him. But then, he was just a soldier. You didn't have to like everyone you served with. You just had to make sure they did as they were told.

The Ripple Creek contractors, as well as leMieure, were slime that weren't needed. Though at least the RC people were human.

Horace was just finishing his morning exercise when the call came. The buzz in his earbuds was Alex. He stepped out of the treadmill reflexively, as soon as he heard it.

"Fastball. We're moving."

Must be a schedule change, he thought as he checked his watch. They were starting earlier than intended.

Sighing, he grabbed a towel and a bottle of antibacterial goop, squirted a healthy dollop onto it, and started wiping down with the cool gel, which would have to do in lieu of a shower.

"I'll be up in two minutes. Please secure my weapon and a coat." He meant his carbine, of course. The pistol was in the gym with him, and his medical kit also. He grabbed for the slacks and shirt that he'd brought along.

He was dressed and heading up in seconds, and caught the team as they reached the stairs. Elke tossed him his body armor, which he slipped on, followed by his jacket from Jason and his carbine from Aramis. She carried her shotgun and looked much calmer. For her type, that was normal. For most people, it would indicate sociopathy.

"We're going early to avoid traps. I just felt paranoid this morning," Alex said.

"Very good." It made sense to do that now and then. One could be late, too, though that was riskier without an advance party to look for threats.

This was a factory opening. Purely show, no need for the President, but it was press. Let them see that he cared and it might carry over into the population. Horace doubted it would work, but it had to be tried.

The convoy contained both UN armored carriers and Regional Consolidated Militia vehicles from the local alliance that was now his official bodyguard. Those vehicles were . . . interesting. Ugly, but with a certain functionality. They were commercial light trucks with welded steel armor and epoxied ceramic and fiber panels. The work looked very professional and not at all slapdash. There were also gouges, dings, and craters in them. They'd taken small arms fire and some heavier HE. He didn't estimate any of them would take any kind of armor penetrator above a 7mm rifle.

Still, it was good to see a unit that had at least some of the courage and discipline of professionals. The question was, whose side were they on? The professional units in Cameroon had changed sides whenever anyone from the military had taken over a large faction, out of mutual respect, so to speak, and had generally allied themselves with whoever was stronger. Would Bishwanath be seen as strong even though most of his support was off world? Would this local unit help with that perception?

And would they suddenly turn out to be a threat in the middle of the day's proceedings?

Horace was with the President on this trip and Jason was not. That kept potential threats guessing as to which medic was on the bubble and where Bishwanath was. Bart was also along as driver, and Elke, but Aramis was in the other vehicle. All part of the dance.

"Oh, this is interesting," Bart said. His tone indicated it was the type of interesting that resulted in work for Horace Mbuto.

Bishwanath was on the news, while an overlay said, "Live."

"'Live,'" Elke said, with some dry amusement. "Well, he is alive, as opposed to dead. I suppose that is what they mean."

There were other, less obvious cues that it was not really the President. The light shifted slightly as the cameras cut back and forth. But that wasn't the most interesting part.

Alex's voice came through the net. "Are you watching Channel One?"

"We are," Horace agreed. "Most fascinating." Angering, even, because nothing good could come of this.

The "President" was saying, "Of course, while I appreciate the necessity of my security contractors, I am less than thrilled with certain recent events, and will be doing my best to address it."

"No more talking," Alex warned. Since they already knew their commo could be hacked, this was not something to debate on air. Even with the supplemental encryption White had provided them, they were leery of trusting their own commo.

Bishwanath looked sad more than anything.

"This is my country," he said. "Things would have been better all along if there'd been more attention to leadership and less to exploiting the resources and situation."

"Sir, this could set you and us up for a fall," Elke warned, pressing the mute button on her lapel. The annoying thing about the jaw transmitters was that they were always transmitting. It took a button or setting to switch them off.

"Yes, I am very much aware of that," he sighed. "Of course, the fabricators seem to have missed one point."

"Sir?" Bart asked. He was trembling and looked ready to destroy something. From the driver's seat, he couldn't see the image, but had heard it clearly.

"As a politician, I am free to contradict myself." He chuckled in an odd way that was both hearty and depressed. "It's not as if anyone on Earth gets the complete story anyway."

Bart said, "Roger," and accelerated. He pressed the button to kill his live mic and said, "Per Alex, we are speeding up in an attempt to arrive before this 'live' broadcast ends."

"Nice," Elke said, smiling with faint crinkles.

"I don't expect that will matter," Bishwanath said. "I've seen too many obvious deceits and lies covered up."

"No, but we have to try." Horace kept an appraising eye on medical readouts. Stress and situational depression could easily trigger any existing problems, including the prestroke condition that Rahul had reluctantly admitted to, then discussed in detail.

"Our speed is limited by your official bodyguard, sir. Alex wants to know how you feel about that."

"We must stay with them. That appearance can help counteract many other problems."

"No go," Bart said. "Cohesive movement." He nodded and said, "He's annoyed but he agrees. Not much else we can do."

The mock Bishwanath took a few questions on nothing significant. He promised money to various groups and then excused himself in a bit of a hurry. It was obvious that this electronic fake had been put together on short notice, and was being tweaked as they went.

"None of the reporters asking questions are the regulars we know," Elke said.

"Right," Bishwanath said. "They're all going to be out here. I would imagine some of the younger ones who appear are being bribed or cajoled into going along with promises of an 'exclusive.' The entire media knows how dishonest they are. They just don't care. Jackenas, all of them." He referenced a local scavenger known for eating the young of competing packs.

It was five minutes later when they pulled into the factory area, which was unremarkable; nothing but tower-supported polymer and blown domes with a magnesium-façaded office area up front and a small loading dock. For a change, everyone present seemed in favor of the President, probably because they all were expecting jobs and support out of this. No one wanted to tell them that the low-end tech gadgets they were producing were throwaways in any modern nation, and were being heavily subsidized to make them of interest to Earth consumers. These people needed the work, even if it was charity.

Of course, Horace reflected, bootstrapping had failed to work in most of Africa. A nation either developed itself or failed. Political scientists seemed incapable of figuring that out.

Professionally, he scanned the signs the crowd carried. "Welcome President Bishwanath" was neutral enough. "Work at Last!" was positive. "A Promise Kept" was clearly from a supporter, though it was possible it was a fake, too. Any excuse to get close to a target for assassination. There was little dissent. He saw a few grumblers a block away. He took a quick scan through the polarized canopies with binox, and was satisfied.

"Out we go," he said when he got the radio and hand-signal cues from Alex, and Elke nodded and opened the door as Aramis and Jason arrived to help.

Out into the cleared area, and cheering, with arms waving and possible threats making Horace go cross-eyed. A glance at the medical info. Bishwanath was elated and calmer. He genuinely wanted to help and this was a small step in that direction, even if he knew it was misguided. His official Bodyguard had the perimeter, and Horace admitted to himself that they did seem to be at least low-end professionals, if a little thuggish. That made them near elite by local standards.

Horace walked past one of the soldiers from the Bodyguard and indicated for him to follow. The man nodded and came along. He seemed fit if wiry, knew how to at least carry a weapon properly, and was a random choice so as to prevent anyone planning to take down Ripple Creek that way. They each had one local as backup.

Horace and his shadow walked their route in the warm air while watching Bishwanath.

The President shook hands with the factory general manager, shift supervisors, and some VIPs. He posed for photos. Horace and the others moved around in a rehearsed randomness that kept two of them near him at all times, two far enough back to provide crossfire and two more out patrolling for threats, each with their support. There was a hard perimeter of Recon backed up by more of the Bodyguard.

All in all, it went smoothly enough. One or two people were drunk, some were slightly belligerent but not disposed to fight professional troops, and in twenty minutes the ribbon was ready to be cut and Bishwanath was making his speech.

Which was when the trouble Horace had been anticipating happened.

His earbuds suddenly blared, "*Incoming fire!*" on a military override. UN military, not local, of course. Then he heard the whistle of artillery.

The six of them bulled through the crowd shouldering people aside and ignoring their local aides, in a frenzied rush to get to the President. Bart and Jason were already closely around him as Elke swarmed into the huddle, then Horace, Alex, and Aramis. They allowed just enough room for him to don his extra armor and open the umbrella, then pushed him down behind the reinforced podium and squatted against the impending blasts.

Alex pointed to the arriving members of the Bodyguard, then to the crowd and said, "Move them back and get us a hole to the ca—"

CRUMP!

Big mortar, probably 120mm, Horace thought. Indirect fire without terminal guidance.

WHAM!

Howitzer, large.

CRUMP! WHAM! CRUMP!

And now they're on target, he realized as the explosions tugged at his breath, sharp overpressure waves blowing by.

The factory took hits. Big ones. It was built to take the modest storms of this area, a light earthquake or a few minutes of heavy weather. Indirect high explosive fire was so far beyond that . . . and there went one corner, some of the framing. Chunks arced into the air amid gouts of smoke and dust.

Watching for assassins, Horace skittered backward in a crouch. He ached and it was tiring, because he wasn't young anymore. But he could still do it, and the whole group was like duckwalking crabs, to mix a metaphor, as they moved toward the vehicles.

Bishwanath swore and sobbed. "God damn them! Our people need that work. Damn them to hell! Please, stop it!"

There was nothing anyone here could do but get him to safety.

Three more explosions tore much of the structure apart, sending jagged splinters whistling through the air. The screams of the departing crowd took on an edge of panic as someone was hit. Debris and dust rained down, with a sharp smell of explosive.

The Bodyguard had cleared a good path, and had the crowd restrained without more than a few shoves. They actually did meet basic professional standards, which on this godforsaken world was impressive. They hadn't squawked and run, the way the previous hires would have. They'd made this job a hell of a lot easier, and Horace threw a finger to eyebrow salute when one of them met eyes with him. The kid looked scared, but determined as he waved back.

Then they climbed in, buttoned up, latched down, and rolled. Aramis was at the wheel and left marks on the pavement, using most of the emergency override. Turbine, starting fluid squirt, and capacitor load caused the vehicle to *move*.

Bishwanath was sobbing, but his vitals were healthy. A quick fumble under his suit and the briefcase body armor revealed no injuries. So Horace tipped out a double dose of an oral tranquilizer and passed them over with a drink. Bishwanath recognized the bottle, nodded, and took them without comment.

Back at the palace, the news wasn't reassuring, in no small part to bearing no resemblance to reality whatsoever.

Bart had become stoic about the treatment they were getting in the press, but this morning's complete fabrication of Bishwanath was infuriating. The current "news" on-screen was beyond belief.

First, the press made them out as cowards for not "stopping to help the unfortunate victims." After that, it was another round of inquiry as to whether they were worth the money. Then there were the incriminations, and attacks on the Bodyguard, who'd been brave and professional if inadequately trained through no fault of their own.

Representative Dhe came on-screen, and he wasn't any better looking even with video enhancement. There was only so much one could do, Bart reflected, to improve the looks of a pile of *scheisse*.

Dhe was as drunk as a derelict behind an Oktoberfest rubbish pile, but that didn't affect his ability to spew diatribe.

"Well, I hate to say bad things about our President and his staff," he said, then proceeded to do exactly that. "But you can't blame the attackers wanting payback because of the elitism of placing a factory there, where it only benefits the capital, of course. It's also not surprising that security didn't work. Keep in mind that the President's Bodyguard is just for show, around the contractors who take the credit and the military who does the work, because this whole presentation is one of waste and mismanagement, smoke and mirrors. This would not have happened in my district, where people want to work and the police are on the job."

"But what about the segment of the security force that were hired from your district?"

"Well, well"—it was amazing how the backpedaling started—"you don't expect the best to sign up for a position in a corrupt organization. If the President had asked me for help, I would have offered support, but of course, that would mean acknowledging that our society is broken . . ."

"I need hip waders even here," Vaughn growled in disgust.

"I wish we could drink," Bart agreed. Oh, how a few liters of beer would make this less painful. Or a few shots of good whisky.

"Who the hell is that fat toad? I recognize him," Aramis said, pointing.

Alex said, "Yeah, he was big on TV when you were about twelve. LeMieure. He rolled it into a job with BuState. He's deWitt's boss."

"No wonder Mister deWitt looks so unhappy," Elke said. "And no wonder he's not allowed to have weapons."

LeMieure's comments made his blood run cold.

"The President of course regrets the events, and has assured me that he will work tirelessly to provide a new solution, which is more equitable. He is unavailable at present, due to being stressed by the attack . . ."

It was right then the President stormed in from his apartment, past Shaman at the door. He certainly appeared to be stressed. He was not resting.

"How dare he? I made a statement, and that was not it! I aaeerggh!" His fists were balled, he was sweating, and his eyes bulged. He looked as if he were about to smash holes in the walls. Shaman hurried over for reassurance, but had a trank behind his back, just in case.

Incoherent rage didn't seem to indicate agreement with the program.

There was a knock at the door. Everyone tensed until Alex said, "It's White. I cleared her a few minutes ago."

White came in, along with deWitt and another AF technician. She raised a finger to her lips until her assistant, who actually outranked her, being a sergeant, fumbled with some gear and nodded.

"I've damped all the sensors in this room," she said as she sat on the corner of a table. Her uniform, as always, was spotless and she looked professional. That wasn't just a look for her, Bart realized. It was her normal manner.

"All of them?" Vaughn asked, sounding cynical.

"Trust me. Look at your own gear if you wish." She was curt and snappish, but it wasn't directed to anyone in the room that Bart could tell.

"All right, what's up?" Marlow said.

"You've seen the alleged news," she said.

"Of course," "Yes," "Yeah," and a growl from Bishwanath.

"All I can tell you is that there are serious attempts to hack your commo and network. We're here to strengthen it for you."

No one moved.

Finally, Elke said, "And will you have a back door?"

"I have a back door to everything," she admitted, "but I don't talk out of school. Not even about that conversation Elke, Alex, and Shaman had yesterday," she said. "Nor about Elke's game program of a few nights ago." Elke twitched at that but retained her poise. Bart had no idea which either of the references were to, but they seemed to reassure Alex and Elke.

It was true that White was inscrutable, and that their radios had already been cracked, while nothing he'd done or said had leaked out other than through the press's spying. Though it could have gotten to them several ways.

When Marlow looked his way, Bart nodded. It made sense. Better her than whichever scum were trying to run things.

"Do it," Marlow said, and the tech nodded and went to work. His name tape was off his uniform. That seemed to be a hint.

DeWitt finally spoke. "It should be obvious there's a power struggle going on here. I can't do anything about it. All I can do is offer hints and possible warnings of disasters. I'm not worried about my job, I'm worried about the lives of people I work with and care about. It's escalating to that level fast."

"What can be done about it?" Anderson asked. "Anything? Are we just puppets?" The kid was cool and attentive, all pretense gone.

"The President could do what people want him to do," deWitt said. "I'm sure that's not going to happen, and I don't suggest it. But that's what they plan to get."

White said, "I'm here for Major Weilhung, too. He's not happy with being in the line of fire of what he calls a 'pissing contest' between BuState and BuCommerce factions. So while he can't officially do anything, he's not a hostile at this time."

"Nice disclaimer," Vaughn murmured from his perch on the back of the couch, very close to the weapons locker.

She looked at him and ran a hand through her bobbed hair. "The way things are changing, I don't think anyone can promise anything, Agent Vaughn."

"Yeah, it's that kind of meat grinder," he agreed.

"What is Commerce's stake in this?" Shaman asked, looking from the President to deWitt.

"Same as always. Get a bunch of contracts for companies with connections to them or people they owe favors to," deWitt said. "They can't be too unhappy with factories getting bombed. More work for them."

"No one wants to stop the fighting here," Bishwanath said. "This isn't an Iraq or a China or an Indonesia. This is more like the American Civil War, where the British were happy to trade for cotton from the Confederacy and sell weapons to the North.

The only question here is who is going to control the market to the factions. I'm in the way."

"You've got a lot of courage, sir," Anderson said, and meant it. He appeared to be grasping that not all bravery was physical.

"And BuState is the referee?" Elke asked.

DeWitt sighed. "BuState is charged with developing the civil affairs of this nation. So the military has to clear through us on how much damage they can do, which they don't like, and I don't blame them. Commerce has to clear through us on how much money they can throw and where, which they don't like, and I don't blame them. Mister Bishwanath has to deal with us to *get* off world support, which he doesn't like, and I don't blame him. Same for all the smaller factions, the larger corporations, everyone except the media, who are trying to gain leverage over everyone so they can blackmail us into doing the things their sponsors want—more trade, better weapons. The reason Ripple Creek is taking a beating is because you don't have trillion-dollar weapons contracts, multinational ad campaigns, or a factory to sell. You're the little guy in the corner of the bar."

"It's my experience that that little guy is the killer to avoid messing with," Bart said in warning. He handed his fliptop over to the tech without protest.

"Which makes you smarter than my boss." DeWitt grinned sickly. "Look, I'm a career civil servant," he said. "I've been working here for years, and other unsavory places before that. I have a masters degree in the field, hundreds of connections, and have written operational guidelines that have worked more often than not. People like leMieure come in instead by sucking up to whoever is SecGen, President, Premier, or Prime Minister at the time, and show up for a year or so grandstanding. They know they won't have the job long, because only competent people do ultimately last, 'competent' in this context meaning getting the job done so the next leader doesn't have a mess to clean up. LeMieure knows he's back to making fifth-rate crap no one will want to watch within an election or two. So he's grabbing all the credit and blackmail he can now. If I do something that works, he'll claim credit. If he does something that fails, he'll try to pin it on me. So that means I am *also* looking for someone to take the fall, and because I'm ethical, I only want to take down assholes.

"You guys are assholes," he finished, "but not that kind of ass-hole. So I have my work cut out trying to piss on fires and find someone who needs a good humiliation session."

"Obviously, leMieure has help from the media if he can fabricate presidential appearances," Anderson said.

Bart took his computer back. Nothing seemed changed but a program had been added, labeled only "Games." He suspected it actually did contain games, as well as other software.

"He has help from my branch, too," White said, and they stared at her.

"I looked at the images as they came out," she explained. "Those were background shots that we arranged for as a courtesy, since there isn't a good studio or hall that size in the palace," she said.

"Correct," Bishwanath said, looking surprised. "I talk against a chroma key in the conference room. Everything else is assembled electronically, including the audience, who are in the studios set up at the Civic Center."

"So someone is selling your tech?" Anderson asked, sounding on edge.

"I think rather that they've cracked one outer layer of encryption to stuff like that of no military significance," she said as she ran a hand through her hair again. "But it's of political significance. I've told my bosses, who are not going to file a suit for infringe-ment yet, but can and will when it's appropriate. Meantime, I don't want to button up and let them know I know, and I have to secure what they don't yet have. When this asshole falls, it's going to take God to put him back together again, trust me." She sounded pissed.

"Does anyone have any evidence that Dhe was behind that shelling?" Marlow asked.

"Hard to say," White replied. "He might have been. His faction has the capability for it. I know the Army tried to interdict, but was hampered. No Air Defense close enough, because no one expected that and it's not really their lookout, and they couldn't counter fire. Not allowed."

"Can they at least tell us where?" Elke asked. "Knowing the weapons and range, if I can get a good location on origin we can look at images for camouflaged launch sites. Jason and I are trained for that."

"When I said 'not allowed to,' I mean the word came down from Army HQ not to turn the radar on. Officially so no one could track their location. Which, I admit, is a valid concern," she said with a nod.

"A convenient one, too," Bart observed.

"When I get a program of the players, parts, and staff, I'll let you know," White sighed. "I've never had this much hassle before. I had better see it reflected in my counseling and at promotion time."

"One way or another, I will see to it," Bishwanath promised. "All of you. Without you and Rahul, I would have nothing. My own staff are largely useless or ceremonial or both. Courtesy of Mister leMieure," he said bitterly.

Marlow said, "Tech White, when it's time to jump, will you give us a warning?"

"If I can," she replied. "And I may need a lift." Her eyes were wide and serious.

"Agreed," he said.

It felt like a wary retreat after a battlefield truce, as everyone split and departed.

CHAPTER TWELVE

Jason sat in the parlor, actually out in public, but all alone, everyone else long since gone to bed. He was often awake and alone, but liked the solitude, though not the loneliness. It was an interesting dichotomy he pondered often without resolution.

In the background he heard muted mortar fire. There was also small arms fire, but that couldn't be heard through the mass of the palace and the soundproofing. There was a bona fide civil war going on now, and the Army was stuck trying to drive wedges between factions to stop it, while being "sensitive" to the risk of civilian casualties. Always the way.

Jason wrote home often. He doted on his kids, and loved his wife more than anything in the universe. Long-term relationships and single households might be old-fashioned, but they worked for him. He had stability. That stability did help ground him here in this shit hole. Not the spiritual "grounding" the priests spoke of, though maybe it was. He hadn't been to Circle or to any church of any kind in years. Decades. It gave him some stability to know something waited for him.

And he missed them. This wasn't that long of a tour, but it was long enough. Especially when adapting from the twenty-eight hours and twelve minutes of Grainne's day to the barely twenty-one hours here. He wasn't a very social animal anyway, so stayed in his room asleep, exercised in the gym down the hall on treadmill, rack, and heavy bag, and crawled out to eat and go on duty. A semihermit, but it suited his temperament, so he often had night shift guard post.

The letter would go out electronically to whichever ship was outbound, be packeted, transmitted once that ship reached Earth's side of the jump point, then caught and transmitted again by a ship reaching Grainne Colony's side of that jump point. It might take two days if all went well, though three to five was more common and two weeks possible. That delay was part of what caused the loneliness. Granted, everyone from outsystem had the same problem. But there was regular traffic with Earth. Personally encrypted love letters zipped back and forth for hours at a time, several times a day as traffic came through. Grainne was another jump from there with more lag.

Dear Uberwensch,

Yes, I know I called you that last time. I'm busy here and having trouble being original. Forgive me?

I can't decide if you're being romantic or sadistic with the smut you send. I can't do much more than think about it. We don't have privacy to speak of in the palace, and while you said I can play, I don't have the time to work on seducing anyone. No locals I'd dare associate with, few military, and the one woman on our team is off-limits for that reason.

A shame. She's slim, healthy, has a darkly twisted sense of humor that helps keep me sane on operations, and she seems to think explosives are erotic. Heck of a woman. All EP women have to meet the same physical standards as men, so she can do 75 push-ups in 90 Earth seconds, at least 100 crunches, 15 pull-ups, and can run 3 kilometers in fifteen minutes with some light gear.

As to life, I can't complain. The pay is phenomenal, the colony doesn't tax external income because it's effectively an export (me exporting my skills), and the living conditions—the six of us have a suite, a private room each, and the run of a fucking PALACE that looks like the Bon Place hotel inside, only bigger. We have good gear.

We did get shot at today. Nothing serious. These savages have no concept of fire and maneuver, cover, advancing by team, taking objectives, and holding for reinforcements . . . it's more scream, shoot, thump chest bravely, get shot. They aren't even taking many casualties because it's not worth it to shoot them. Just let me say that everything you saw in the news about it, if you did, is complete and utter bullshit. Those cowardly, cocksucking pieces of shit will fabricate anything. When they got done, Julius Caesar would lose to Vercingetorix and Napoleon would just be a corporal.

But I won't lie to you. There are dangers here. The local guards of the Palace and elsewhere are drugged out, worthless, malnourished, and undeveloped scum. Crappy diet, poor social lives, no education. They can stop bullets, that's about it.

Then there's the Army . . . I am so glad I got out when I did, and I absolutely agree that the Colony needs to pull its troops out of the UN Joint Forces as soon as fucking possible. I know old-timers always bitch about how things are going downhill, but it's worse here.

The UN troops have good gear, and know technically how to use it, though they don't get much practice before arriving, apparently. No one wants to waste that valuable equipment for training, so they accept losses in combat. Equipment losses. That's the kind of leadership they have.

Worse . . . some commanders are following every order to the letter, including conflicting orders. BuState can give orders to MilBu. Yup, it's insane. So there are troops struggling with 70 kilos of gear, even in this gravity that's a bitch. Others are shrugging their shoulders and leaving it to the NCOs to deal with . . . but those NCOs come out of this same system. Some of them literally don't know how to request nonorganic transport. If it's not attached to them, they're helpless. They don't know how to use their assets.

And the troops . . . yeah, they have great technical training, but most of them are rebellious teenage punks from game clubs, or gangs. They weren't given any real discipline in basic. I watched a formation yesterday—they have formations constantly, in case anyone deserts in this dump? Maybe worried about AWOL and sex, which is forbidden. I don't know. All I know is, they don't trust the troops because they can't. As a senior sergeant, I wielded more authority than most CAPTAINS do in the UNJF. So they had a formation, and while calling roll, these kids were playing with game sets, computers, jawing, milling about. They can't stand still in formation and no one bothers to discipline them.

If the locals weren't the worst shit in space, these kids would be dying in job lots.

Sorry, I didn't mean to delve into politics. I know you never liked international relations in service, and don't as a civilian either. But that's what I'm dealing with. The "elite" forces are about as good as I and my buddies. Yeah, we're good. I don't feel we're abnormal. Certainly I wasn't in service. But now . . .

Hey, I'm fine and should be. Got good people around me, low threats, and lots of support. And the Army can always act as bullet traps.

Tell the kids I love them. I got the pictures and they're just still so cute. I sleep with that picture in my pocket to keep me warm.

Love you,

Jason finished, and looked up from his fliptop as Bishwanath entered the room.

"May I help you, sir?" he asked at once. Bishwanath's presence was probably unofficial but he kept a hand on his pistol and checked the location of his carbine. That was automatic, even though it was clear at once there was no threat. He wasn't keen on being a part-time servant. On the other hand, it was far safer than EP and he was getting paid the same either way. There was no harm in being nice, he figured. The man was decent.

"No trouble, Agent Vaughn," Bishwanath said as he closed the door quietly. "Forgive me. I can't sleep and I hate being by myself. Do you mind if I watch viddy in here?" He was dressed in a robe and silk pajamas with elaborate embroidery, and wore leather slippers that could serve as shoes.

"Not at all," Jason said. He couldn't expect any privacy in here anyway, and it was easier to guard the President up close. He jotted down the time in the incident log on the now scarred coffee table. "Principal entered common room. Unofficial." He saved and minimized.

"Is there actually anything worth watching on?" he asked. The President hadn't spoken any commands to the unit.

Bishwanath replied, "It's not so much watching anything I have in mind. It's watching . . . *anything*. Is that clear in English?" He was pacing slowly.

"I think so, sir," Jason said. Yeah, the man was lonely. He'd cut himself off from his own clan to maintain the perception of distance and neutrality. He couldn't trust any other clan. There were no other parties in politics awake at this hour . . . what could the man do after work? And he hadn't ever intended to have this much power.

"Sir, if you want to talk or run a net sim, just say so."

"Thank you, Agent Vaughn. I appreciate the offer. Though right now, I was thinking of a more cerebral pursuit which is hard to find."

"Reading a paper book? Logic problems?" Sometimes the man was too polite. That was better than the rude bastards they got at times, but still aggravating in its way.

"No, not quite like that. I wonder, Agent Vaughn," Bishwanath said, squinting slightly, "if you know how to play chess?"

Jason squinted in return and leaned back in his seat. "I doubt I'm in your ranking, sir, but I'll give it a try."

Bishwanath smiled, nodded, and walked over to a cabinet. That one had been filled on their arrival. Only a few items, but one of them . . .

The chess set he brought over was very elegant. Inlaid dark wood, possibly ebony, and light, burnished material, probably bone, were surrounded by a laminate of light and dark woods and set on a plain wooden base. He set it down, lifted it off a latched insert, and placed it in the exact middle of the table.

The pieces underneath were hand carved and had gold and silver wire pressed in. There were extra pieces, and it looked as if one could play several different variations with the same set. Jason lifted a king. It was near ten centimeters tall, a handful.

"Nice set," he commented.

"My grandfather's," Bishwanath replied. "He also like Persian chess and chaturanga."

"I can see."

"I try not to think about my family," the President said shyly.

"I'm writing a letter to mine," Jason said, tapping his computer. "Words on a page as well as the audio messages I send seem to add a level."

"Yes," Bishwanath agreed. "I write as I can. I did just now, in fact. I generally have little time, and my wife is not enjoying Earth. My children are grown and north of here."

Conversation tapered off to chess. Bishwanath was good, but clearly had his mind elsewhere. He built elaborate strategies but lost pieces from oversight, a forest for the trees issue, if Jason had to guess. Not being able to plan so far ahead, Jason used a strategy of clustering all his capital pieces and tromping across the board like a Roman legion, letting them support each other in a tight knot.

Meantime, Bishwanath muttered, occasionally talking.

"It's aggravating dealing with masses of people, all of whom expect that I will cut them some kind of favor. We had a deal once before. Their side supported some petty squabble. They have spongewood, which may be the only useful material export. They have an agreement with a chief of my clan." He sighed.

"I suppose the last one comes close to legit," Jason observed. He needed to open up his formation a little. They were crowding each other's lines of attack.

In a moment, Bishwanath was chuckling warmly.

"Mister Vaughn," he said, "*every* clan on this planet has some agreement with some chief of every clan. That's how business is done. Think of the corporate and union ties on Earth. This is like that."

"Sort of like winning the lottery and finding all the relatives you never knew you had?" he offered.

"Exactly like that. Exactly. All of them angry that I won't make favors."

"What problems are you having, if I can ask?"

"I can speak of some," Bishwanath nodded. "My own people expect position among the government. I am expected to guarantee this as a matter of course. Whether or not they are qualified for any position is irrelevant. They are entitled and I owe them, because we are kinsmen. What of their inability to do the job? I should hire a subordinate to do that, doing all the work, for less power, prestige and money, and have the 'government' pay for it."

"Mm hmmm." There wasn't much to say. Bishwanath understood the problem. Jason understood the problem. The idiots couldn't, wouldn't, and weren't here.

"Other factions, of course, expect the opposite, to show that I do not play favorites. All expect handouts for their groups, again paid by some mythical government that has bottomless pockets from some source of revenue not in existence. The only relevant source of income in this nation was black market percentages. That is now gone. If we can come to some agreement with our two neighbors, we can exploit the asteroids. They are far enough outsystem to make them easy to transport. Of course, that requires a stable nation here first."

"Bootstrapping," Jason commented. "Check."

"Blast you and your unconventional strategy," Bishwanath said. A moment later, both of them lacked queens. "Or is that a strategy?"

"It is," Jason admitted. "Though it's for lower grade players, most of whom don't play well without a queen—they rely on it. So by swapping I force a more tactical game I can play better."

"Astute," Bishwanath admitted.

A few minutes and several moves later he said, "I thought you were also offering that as a gaming metaphor for something I should do in politics. But if you are, I cannot see what it is I am to do."

Jason laughed, heartily but softly. "No, sir. No ulterior motive. I have opinions on politics, but if I had any aptitude or real interest, I'd work for BuState at the very least, not as a mercenary bodyguard."

"Ah, BuState," Bishwanath said.

"Aggravating?"

Bishwanath seemed evasive. Finally, he said, "How well do you get along with Mister deWitt?"

"Well enough," Jason offered. "I think he's former military. Honest, straight shooter in a nest of snakes. Decent guy, but stuck in a job with starry-eyed idiots."

"Yes, I agree." Bishwanath moved a piece and sighed. "Check. Apart from him, they all know what's best for me, and can quote historical examples. When I point out that every such example is a nation that either survived on charity from some major power, or fell into endless civil war, like Indonesia in the twenty-first, or Liberia or Iraq before they were absorbed, they get rude, as if they're doing me some favor."

He breathed deeply, obviously angry, and said, "*I* am doing *them* the favor. They have a list of wants and needs to be accomplished. I am willing to give them at least half of what they ask for. Instead my goals for my country are ignored, or worse, treated with smug contempt."

This was how well the man played chess when exhausted, angry, and focused elsewhere, Jason thought. He could see his defeat in about four moves. Bishwanath wasn't even looking at the board, really. He was giving his attention to Jason and the conversation.

That attention was a distraction. Strong personality. Still, while the game was a challenge, hearing his host and employer out, as well as shamelessly gathering that intel, was more important. He blocked the attack with a pawn and spoke.

"I've never liked the hubris, I guess it's called, that these guys show. If they're so smart, why are they bureaucrats and not leaders? Washington, Franklin, both Elizabeths, William, Carl Gustav, Caesar, Mao, Pitt, Ghandi, Shaka . . . whether heads of state or statesmen, we recall them and their works. No one remembers a SecState or a Deputy Chief of Economic Development Counseling or whatever."

"And yet every one of them believes himself or herself to be my superior," Bishwanath said, holding a rook and gesturing. "Even deWitt. He is informative and educated, but he does make assumptions on how I will deal with an issue. In his case, he's been here long enough to have some picture. Usually, he's not far off, but he presumes to proceed. I can't blame him; it was like that until I was brought in a few weeks ago. In some ways he has more experience than I do. But I am the President. I am not the warrior you or your comrades are, but I have fought. I am no Marcus Tani, no Simon Bolivar, no Winston Churchill. I seek to run a nation that has somewhat less resources and assets than Atlanta or San Diego, but I do seek to run it, and I have experience with these people and this planet. These . . . desk-sitters . . . would tell me how to do the job, with nothing to support their theories than older theories." He placed the rook down carefully and said, "Checkmate."

It had taken two moves. Wow. The man was cagey.

"I'm not sure what I can offer, sir," Jason said. "I'm just a mechanically inclined grunt who got lucky. A high-gravity environment lets me keep fit, and I've done executive protection because it was available and I was good at it. I have opinions, as I said. I can't offer any useful insights."

Bishwanath was carefully putting the chess set away.

"I appreciate being able to vent to an outsider," he said. "And

I wish the other nonexpert outsiders shared your modesty. We must play again sometime."

"Certainly, sir. I or Bart are awake most nights, and Elke plays, too. She's likely better at problem solving."

"I'll keep that in mind. Thank you."

"Supply run," Jason said the next morning. Alex was at the morning chitchat, leaving him in charge.

"Where are you going?" Aramis asked from his computer. He had a list of sundries and luxuries he could use filled.

"Someone is going on post."

"Someone?" he asked to confirm. "Hell, send me."

"I also," Bart said. He'd been watching the wall and doing push-ups from boredom. The local dialect had to be even harder for him, not being a first language speaker of English.

"Military Exchange and then some stuff from Operations Store. I have a purchase order number and a corporate card. We're allowed two hundred each discretionary, after that it comes out of our pay. Got the list for team goods. Everyone scrawl down what you need."

"Suits," Aramis agreed, grinning.

Elke looked over. She was hunched up in a chair almost cuddling her screen. "I have a few things." She scrawled hastily and handed over a note page. Her printing looked like that of a machine. Very precise, very fast. Made sense, if she handled explosives.

"Sidearms, carbines, and grenades only. No heavies. Take the Pimpmobile," Jason ordered. That was the oldest Caddy in the vehicle barn, and looked the least presidential. "Stay in contact. Scramble Seven."

"Seven," Aramis agreed and set his radio accordingly. Body armor, casual local tunic to blend in better, even though his skin was lighter than the locals, especially in this weird orange light. Phone, sidearm, magazines, a handheld with maps and codes. Lists, cash, cards, corporate ID, all the basics he wore every day, adjusted for a civilian mission.

Bart was ready, and Aramis couldn't wait to get out of the palace.

Once out the rear gate and past the Bodyguards, who were stand-ing alert and conducting actual perimeter patrols, he gunned the engine and headed into the maze to the north, making several turns to evade ID. There was still a risk, but leaving the front meant going through the plaza and the heavily trafficked areas where being made and pursued were much more likely. After a couple of minutes, he deemed it safe to find a main road, using the onboard map.

It was always good to get on post, where most of the people were from Earth, a good number from America, and even those from elsewhere were part of the military team. Of course, a lot of them no longer considered him to be part of that team. The stigma of being freelance. Though he wasn't really free. To get an assignment like this meant working for the UN government, and the same regulations as applied to the military applied to him.

He pulled up to the gate and had his ID ready. He slowed as directed by the signs and the MPs and tried to be as accommodating as possible, professional to professional. He wove through the barricade slowly.

Window down, he eased up to the shack and said, "Anderson, Weil, Ripple Creek, Palace Detail."

The MP was younger than he was, and nervous under his professional demeanor. It showed. "Okay, sir. Can you get out of the vehicle for an inspection? And you'll need to sign those weapons in. Sidearms only for nonmilitary personnel."

"I'm Reserve," Aramis said quickly, pulling out that ID.

The MP was suddenly even more serious. "Not when on contract you're not, and I wouldn't show that around. You know it's a violation for soldiers to go contract."

"I'm inactive," he lied/admitted. "But can't you grant us the courtesy? We're at the palace, not some visiting advisor's guards."

"Sorry. Rule is all nonmilitary check anything larger than a pistol."

"No," Bart said softly.

Aramis wasn't even considering that. Something about it just made him refuse.

"Sorry, we'll have to stow them at the palace and come back. I can't turn company weapons over to noncompany personnel."

"It's a real pain to let a vehicle get out of here," the troop complained. "Can't you just do it? They'll be right here and tagged."

The debate was minor, stupid, and getting out of hand. All the MPs had to do was move a small barricade, since the entrance was designed so vehicles could be channeled in or out.

"No, I don't have that authority, sorry," he said, and prepared to wait.

Grumbling, the soldier and his buddy from the other side

closed the gates, then lifted and moved the barricade by hand so Aramis could drive through and back out through the maze to the highway.

"What do we do?" Bart asked as they turned onto the route. He seemed as agitated.

"Hold on," Aramis said, smiling. He keyed the radio. "Playwright, can you call your actors and tell them we need a favor, over?"

"Aramis, what do you need, over?"

"I need a better route. There were some roadblocks. Ones we couldn't argue with, over." He couldn't actually say what the problem was, even scrambled, in this environment.

"Stand by, over."

"Standing by, over." He kept driving, watching for blocks or threats. They were one vehicle, not a convoy, after all.

"Aramis, use Gate Four, over."

"Gate Four. Understood, out."

"That's just south of here," Bart commented.

"And guarded by Marines." Yeah, it sucked to admit that the Corps would treat them better, even with him being a Reservist.

Gate Four was set up the same way, but was guarded by four Marines. They looked at the IDs, checked the vehicle's palace transponder, ran around with sensors, and waved them through. The whole process took about fifteen seconds.

"All this to shop for groceries," Bart groused, leaning back with a hand on the integrally molded roll bar just above his head.

That part went easily enough. There were a few looks for the civilian vehicle and a few more for their garb. They'd left the carbines well hidden in footwells, but were carrying grenades that weren't on any inventory.

They didn't really need the extra hardware on base, but they weren't trusting the weapons, with disabled safeties and that were black market, around anyone who might follow up on the issue, and they certainly weren't traveling around town with just sidearms, especially with the violence escalating. At that, the rocket launcher under the seat bench had never been mentioned to anyone.

They shopped off the list, paid and signed the contractor voucher—which was also used by food service, transport, engineer, and other contractors—loaded up, and left. A thirty-minute errand with two thirty-minute, ten-kilometer round trips and a thirty-minute detour.

"What now?" Bart asked.

"Playwright, this is Aramis, over," he called while grinning at Bart.

"Go ahead, over."

"I'd like to shop in the town market, over."

There was a pause. "Go ahead. Keep location visible, stick to open areas, over."

"Understood, out."

"Extra weapons?" Bart asked.

"Weapons, maybe . . . souvenirs. Possible intel. All kinds of stuff." That, and he wanted to say he'd seen something of the planet other than cars and official places. He was entitled to an hour of vacation.

He planned to be cautious. No doubt, he and Bart could kick the asses of any twenty locals. There weren't twenty, though. There were thousands, and the end result of an argument would still mean they were dead. In civilian clothes, they weren't too remarkable. There weren't a great many offworlders, but enough that they were respected for the money they brought in. He shuffled bills and silver around into four different pockets and handed some to Bart.

"Don't want a strike to clean us out," he commented.

"Right. What are we buying?"

"Anything useful or interesting."

He parked in an abandoned lot with a dozen other vehicles in it, ranging from hulks to other modern contractor type trucks and cars. Good sign. They got out and started a tour of the booths and stalls.

Clothes, fabric, local food he didn't dare touch, tattoos, sex . . . all kinds of stuff, but not what he was looking for. Chintzy handicrafts . . . maybe that carved stone cat for his mother's collection. Nice choice, and cheap. He haggled the carver down out of manners and drew out a single bill and a coin, which simple act garnered the attention of every vendor and beggar within sight. Bart put on an expression that on his big German frame promised a brutal graunching to anyone who tried to horn in, and they moved on.

"Jackpot!" Aramis grinned. "Fucking sweet."

It was a bladesmith's stall of iron rods and canvas, with decorative souvenir butter knives in elaborate wooden stands, letter openers, axes, shears . . . and knives big enough to fight with, tomahawks, and other sundry tools. He carefully lifted one, examined the metal and the work. Not bad at all.

"I want seven of these," Aramis said, pointing at forty centimeters of big-bellied knife atop a thick leather sheath, probably elk or buffalo hide. "And seven of those tomahawks."

The vendor's eyes grew wide in his dusty, sooty face. "Sebn?" he asked. He was wiry but healthy looking. Besides the exercise, he was well fed. Likely because he had a skill set that was much in demand.

"Whatever you have to fit the bill. My friends and I need them."

"Yar, sho. That be fife choppy ax, two these beard ax, close I have." He held up a bigger, broader but thinner axe. "Sebn knifes gon clean me out."

"How much?" Aramis asked, flashing a hint of silver.

That made the man freak. He started waving his hands in front of him.

"No you bring that here! I'm'n honest merchent. Cash. UN cash."

"No problem," Aramis agreed, slipped the coin back, and drew bills. In only a few minutes they settled on ten marks each, M140 total. No licensing, no tax, and about one-tenth what he'd pay on Earth for anything close to that quality. The local was ecstatic with what had to be a week's income or more for him, and his family was certainly going to keep eating. The UN cash implied he'd be buying black market imports to supplement the local gruel. He shook hands effusively and insisted on a hug. Aramis was caught off guard, and the man had to feel the bulges of hardware under his tunic, but he said nothing, just gave a friendly wink.

"We'll tell our friends," Aramis offered. He meant it. Though what restrictions the Army had on such weapons was unclear. Still, there were other contractors.

"We're being followed," Bart said as they reached the car.

"Threat?"

"I don't think so yet." They got in and sat ready for a meeting.

A man approached, uniformed and tall. Off world. He nodded and gave a half salute.

Aramis nodded back. He didn't recognize the gear but he didn't look like a threat. Some kind of security hire.

The man stepped closer and said, "You're RC, yes?"

"Maybe," Aramis admitted as Bart closed his door.

"Sergeant Fife. ES Associates," the older man said, offering a hand. "I'm trying to locate some gear."

The guy was in black slacks and white shirt with patch and badge, overvest with radio and pouches. Aramis shook his hand and sat back enough to be comfortable, and so he could reach a sidearm.

"Okay, what kind of gear?"

"I need to sign out a couple of carbines, some flechette canisters and AP grenade mags for my team," Fife said. "Anything will help."

"Who are you with, exactly?" Borrow weapons. Not likely.

"I'm with a contractor tac team assigned to City Center."

"The mall?"

"Yeah, the mall." His expression seemed as serious as his buzzed hair.

"You want carbines and grenades?" Aramis could barely believe he was hearing this.

"Did I stutter? The lockdown has hurt my deliveries. I'm short on gear I need for my job. The Army's useless. I figured you might be able to help."

"What are you guarding in a shopping center that takes grenades?" Bart asked, sounding amazed.

Fife drew himself up. "It's not just a shopping center. It's a major threat point for terrorism. You'd be amazed what goes on there. Kidnappings, some of them VIPs, black market gang deals. Assault and rape in the bathrooms."

"I can believe that," Bart said. "It is the 'mall tac team' concept I am having trouble with." He was smirking.

Fife got belligerent. "Go ahead, laugh, asshole. You have that luxury. Who do you think's going to respond if you're in trouble there? The police? Have you seen the police around here? The store security or any of the corp crowd? They'd not only wet their pants, they're terrified of a lawsuit or counterstrike. It's up to me and my team to keep order and peace. With the collapse of this society and the decay of morality this world is getting more and more dangerous daily."

"Wow. I don't know what to say," Aramis said. Diplomacy was essential when dealing with a potential loon. He was pretty sure this was a loon, but he wanted to be sure.

"Yeah, it's a pretty heavy job. I mean, I get paid for it, but you can imagine the responsibility."

"I'm just trying to figure out how you use this stuff amongst crowds of shoppers," Bart said.

"If we're discreet, no one notices. We have electric carts to cut response time, and two marksmen for backup. But it can get hairy fast. I'm wearing double plates in the armor"—he rapped his chest—"in case of multiple eight millimeter rifle strikes."

"'Multiple eight millimeter,'" Aramis echoed.

"Yeah, that's what I said."

There was no restraining it. He started to snicker, Bart joined, and in moments they were gasping with laughter.

Aramis choked through the laughing, "Dude, that's one hell of a story . . . but I'm sorry, I can't give out corp-owned HE and weapons to another agency without it being approved . . . and definitely not from RC to mall security."

"Yeah. I guessed as much. Thanks, assholes." He turned to leave. Over his shoulder he offered, "Just remember, I'll back you up when you need it, because that's what professionals do. I don't need your attitude."

"Sorry we can't help you," Aramis said as he closed the door.

Aramis stared at Bart, Bart stared back, and then they were sagging against the seats laughing.

"Oh, man, that's just bizarre . . ."

"Double plated armor for a *mall*?" Bart asked. "That is the same mall I'm thinking, yes?"

"Only one type of mall around here, yup. Question is, is he just a loon, or is he trying to black market?"

"Dunno, but a fucking rent-a-cop, as you say. *Gott.*"

"How do we even write that one up?" Aramis asked.

"I wouldn't. We won't be believed."

"You're telling me. I'll call the boss, let's head back."

Horace checked over his supplies. He'd used a few on escort, a few more for minor injuries the team had acquired here and there, working and exercising, and quite a few additional on staff and guests of the palace. Technically, that wasn't allowed, but people needed help and no one had been inclined to complain. Certainly not either Mister deWitt nor Alex, and what anyone else thought wasn't really relevant.

He barely noticed when Aramis and Bart returned. Aramis was as excited as he usually was, and relayed a loud after-action to Alex. It jarred Horace from his concentration when Aramis slapped a package down next to him. He twitched slightly.

"Thank you. Is that everything off the list?" he said as he looked up.

"And then some." Aramis was grinning.

So Horace looked. The top of the box was covered with a rough-forged tomahawk with a vicious spike on the back, and a large bowie or panga style knife with a horn hilt.

"Impressive," he grinned. "You realize that file-finished carbon steel is a haven for toxins and bacteria that can turn a simple wound into a festering infirmity?"

"Really?"

"Yes. Most excellent!" he grinned and laughed loudly. The infection wouldn't matter to anyone he treated at once, and if he wasn't treating them, that meant the wound was one he'd rather did get contaminated.

Underneath were replacement dressings and medications as requested. He saved and closed his list and neatly piled all the gear so he could resume shortly. He'd received a gift, and that meant being sociable in return.

Elke looked at her slightly smaller blade and axe and smiled with twinkling eyes and a heave of her chest that had to be melodramatic . . . although she might have similar feelings to Horace, with his rituals for treatment. It was hard to say. She laid them back down and pointed at her screen.

"Oh, terrible news," Elke said. "I am in tears."

"What?" "Oh?" "Something wrong?"

She read from her screen and said, "Someone held a Mass Market Electronic Advertising Convention."

"Er . . . spammers?" Bart asked as he translated.

"Five thousand spammers in one convention hall," she said.

"Damn, and no one hit it." Jason sounded disgusted.

"Yes, actually. Someone fed nerve agent through the ducts and apparently killed over three hundred. More than a thousand are hospitalized."

"The tragedy being not enough died?" Alex asked.

"They should have called me," she said. Were those sobs real or an act? "I could have offered a hundred kilos, strategically placed with fragments."

"Hell, I'd do it with a ball bat," Aramis said. "Not efficient, but satisfying to see faces mushed."

"Damn. I wonder if that idea will catch on? People harass,

assault, and occasionally kill one . . . but mass murder. I like it. I would love to be on that jury," Jason said.

Horace asked, "To ensure the guy walks?"

Jason was grinning. "Absolutely. A god among men. A hero for our times. Anything that kills spammers . . ."

Alex interrupted with, "Anything of interest about here?"

"Yes, it's a forgotten war. Why are our troops on Mtali when they're needed here?" She even sounded sarcastic.

"There are no troops here?" Bart was still finding sarcasm awkward at times.

"Allegedly not."

Aramis was tense. "Man, right after the spammers, can we organize one for reporters?"

"Stand in line," Jason said.

"Just be sure I am called," Horace said. "I will be very happy to provide medical support."

That his statement ended the conversation was perhaps the most fun of the day.

CHAPTER THIRTEEN

A week passed with nothing but routine. They escorted Bish-wanath to other industrial and commercial events, some in near-bombed out sectors of the city. Everyone was tense, expecting trouble that never came. There was a Council meeting, and several Earth and other off-world investors came to the palace to meet with Bishwanath in the large drawing room. There were a couple of press conferences, with the President insisting on giving his own answers, not allowing words to be put in his mouth, and lots of late nights where he drew up plans and consulted by phone.

The only real break in the routine was the supply run.

First, a shipment arrived from Corporate. With Massa's help, they had authorization for proper rockets, a Viper light cannon that made Aramis drool, and ammo. The crate contained far too many capacitors, rations, and similar sundries.

"So those are your trade goods," Alex said.

"Yup," Jason said. "I figure a trade with Mister Dhe will create goodwill towards men and peace on Salin. That, and I'll get a better look at his goons."

"Makes sense, but be careful." Alex was a great manager, but he'd had far too civilized an upbringing, Jason thought. Even with his spotted past, he was too clean and straightforward. Of course, that could be in reaction to his spotted past.

"Aramis, let's go deal."

"Roger," Aramis said, grabbed a vest and carbine and was ready to roll. He scooped up a belt carrier of launcher grenades as he came.

Once out of the palace, the trip was straightforward. Dhe's territory was near the industrial section to the east. That was a safe route as long as one stuck to main roads. Jason barreled along, Boblight slightly bright because of an ongoing flare storm. The local life was all hiding, including the cute birdiles. The Earth imported life barely noticed.

Judging from the wandering, working, lazing people, few of them were even aware of the solar storm. He realized it was a good thing that the flares weren't dangerous, or most of this bunch would die. Although, that wouldn't be much of a loss. The difference between the settlers here and other places like Novaja Rossia and, well, Grainne was vast.

He drove into the parking lot of Dhe's office, which was a block building. He counted thirteen cars in the lot, varying from ruggedly functional to gorgeous. Strictly from a point of view of connections, Dhe might have been a "better" choice for the BuState people. He wondered what had arisen to prevent that. He was corrupt, connected, and a bastard, just the type they liked.

The guards at the door were no match, but they'd have backup and it was a long way back. He decided to humor them.

"Leave all weapons in the car," he told Aramis. "They won't steal them while we're here, and we won't be fighting."

"I . . . will comply," Aramis said, looking bothered.

"That means the second pistol, too," he grinned. "Yeah, I know about that," he said to Aramis's expression. Aramis sighed and slid the pocket pistol out from his pants and under the seat. While he did, Jason checked his own pocket for an item. Yes, it was there. A multi-frequency scanning imager, a fancy name for a camera that could shoot through fabric and around corners.

They each carried a box and walked up to the door.

"Whatchu need?" the apparent senior of the guards asked. The red and blue uniform still looked bizarre, but it was clear this bunch did at least know which end of a rifle to pick up.

"We have stuff to trade, figured you were the best people to trade with," Jason said.

"Damn true."

An hour and a bit later, they left, toting some local wastepaper, a few marks, and a handful of silver.

"Sucky price," Aramis commented as they climbed in and geared up. He seemed relaxed now.

"The idea wasn't to make money," Jason said.

"Oh, I know. And Dhe's no threat militarily."

"How do you figure?" he asked. He'd already reached the same conclusion, but it was good to have agreement.

Aramis wrinkled his brow as he spoke. "None of them have any notion of tactics or strategy. They're a halfway disciplined but untrained mob. They obviously don't have enough gear if they were buying that stuff, even if they thought they were getting a great deal."

"Correct. Any threat he poses is political. I don't believe he's capable of actual military force."

"Hell, he's a 'progressive.' They tend to wet their pants around weapons," Aramis said, rolling his eyes in disgust.

"Usually, but not always and a lot of that is Earth culture, especially Western. Elsewhere, they'll shoot in a second if they think it will avoid an election they can't win."

Once back, Jason wrote up his findings for Alex, who was delighted that he had photos.

"They didn't even scan," he said. "Quick look, lousy pat, and didn't check the pockets, so the camo didn't even matter. That's his HQ."

"Damn, it looks like a couple of banquet tables with a fliptop and satellite set."

"That's what it is," Jason agreed.

"Primitives."

Then it was back to the routine, but even routine was tiring, with pretrip mapping, weapons checks, commo, exercise daily, and updates on threats that Alex brought daily from his second briefing with White and Weilhung. The team was paid not only to stop attacks on Bishwanath, but to prevent them when possible.

Everyone knew there would be another attack. This was a nation at war, and high-end mercenaries hadn't been hired because of their image, which was a poor one to most people. Of course, when the attack did come, it was a political nightmare as well as, in Jason's terminology, a "tactical balls-up."

Another long convoy, Alex thought. At least they had air transport for most of it. The drive would have been ten hours each way, far down the coast.

It was amazing, he reflected, how routine something involving imminent danger could become. The convoy consisted of four civilian limousines, a loyal Celadon Army unit, specially cleared and reinforced with a number of UN Army soldiers and some Recon troops, ready to displace or take down the locals. The soldiers were mounted on local vehicles, mostly small diesel utility trucks. The Recon troops had their light, air-mobile armored cars. Rahul drove the second limo containing his boss, with Elke, Shaman, and Jason. Aramis, Alex, and Bart were in the third slot with Bart driving. The first and last limos were pure decoys. They had overhead cover, in the form of two vertols. This area had been described as "Hot," with three major factions duking it out for control. One sided with labor, one with the owners, and one with a group that wanted to annex the entire region and attach it to the one south, to reduce the drain on travel and acquire more government handouts.

They geared up, loaded up, and off they went, the President reviewing his speaking notes for a regional council meeting. These were farmers and orchard owners and their workers, with the usual management versus labor problem compounded by not having any real market for their goods. The hope was that they could be brought into a convoy co-op to transport the fruit to the capital.

How sad a nation was that such issues required a president's presence, he thought.

It was routine if tense. No convoy was quite like any other, but there was a standard feel to them. Having the military up front did help—armored vehicles had a way of clearing the road of gawkers and slowpokes. They also hindered—it was hard not to know who this was, with a convoy of limos and military vehicles. The occupant was obviously at least a mayor, governor, or senator, and these vehicles were fairly distinctive. There were a finite number of models and specifics. At Jason's suggestion, all the government vehicles had removed their number plates to make ID harder, but it wasn't too difficult for someone to make Bishwanath as the President. No other VIP was in this area, certainly not so protected.

Nor were any protected quite like this. In lieu of a carbine, Elke had her shotgun, which was shorter ranged but devastating for crowds. Aramis had the Viper cannon, which laid down smaller bursts than a machine gun, but with correspondingly greater damage. It fired a 15mm rocket-assisted projectile that would punch through anything optimistically called "armor" on this rock, and most of their so-called "hard cover," too. Aramis had joked that he could make a called shot to the Islets of Langerhans.

So they watched their sectors from the vehicles and clutched at weapons, low and out of sight. They tried not to overreact to excited teenagers and sometimes adults, to people drugged or crazy who reacted bizarrely. They didn't care particularly if someone got killed for being stupid. Elke's comment had been, "Chlorine for the gene pool," but it wouldn't do to attract the resultant attention if it wasn't necessary.

"Vehicle coming in!" Aramis shouted next to him. "Oh, shit, he's not stopping!"

"Understood," Alex said. He didn't turn to look. He had his sector, and it was a large one, being the entire left side behind Bart who was driving.

"I see the man," Bart agreed.

"*Brace!*" Aramis shouted as Jason said, "Confirmed thre—"

Bart braked hard as all the vehicles reacted.

"Strike, lead limo, right front," he said.

"Check right front," Alex agreed. Everything took on a slow-motion clarity.

"Vehicle to left rear on collision course with tailing limo," Jason said.

That was within the overlap of Alex's sector. He glanced back. Big truck, right through a crowd of civilians, limbs flailing as they were tossed like dolls.

"Both directions at once, I'm calling it deliberate. Mics hot. Elke, Shaman, stand by. Aramis, call it." He'd seen it, he had a better field of view, so it was up to him to call it. Alex was comfortable with that. The kid did know his stuff.

"Stay in vehicle and break," Aramis said. A tough call, but the other choice was to sit and fight against an enemy that had planned an ambush and executed it. That enemy couldn't beat the combined forces . . . and didn't need to. A well-placed rocket or mortar round into the President's limo would end it.

Jason said, "Impact, left rear limo."

And the convoy was cut.

These were professionals. The crashed vehicles had not inflicted much in the way of casualties, but were clearly designed to stall everyone in place, which was the one thing that could never be allowed to happen.

"Bart, Aramis, find us an exit. Mama, we're going to split up."

"Are you sure?" Weilhung asked from the front.

"Several directions, confuse this issue. Do it now!" Dammit, this was no time for a debate, an argument over jurisdiction, or a pissing contest. "Bart, Rahul, split us now. Rahul leads."

"Roger." "Check."

Then they were roaring.

Intellectually, Alex knew the vehicles had that kind of power. Multistage dual turbines with positive displacement rotors, assorted intercoolers, aftercoolers, reheat and variable venturis could take a tremendous amount of fuel and very efficiently convert it to tremendous torque. It just wasn't something one generally did in a luxoboat. He'd had no idea what it felt like to accelerate in one of these things. It was like a jet dragster. Bart had to be draining the capacitor bank, too, feeding the juice to the brake coils backward, because the car was pulling Gs. He fell back against the seat hard enough to wrench his shoulder.

"Son of a bitch!" he muttered in annoyance and awe.

Aramis popped the sky roof and stood on the seat, legs spread for balance. Jason handed up the Viper, and there was a reassuring *clack* as he dropped the safety. That was the perfect position for the kid, Alex figured. He could waste anything he wanted in a messy fashion and no one was likely to object. This was where the youthful exuberance came in.

The ride got rough. They were on curb, then riding over carts, the oversized wheels throwing debris and splatting vegetables against the side. The odor started entering, and it wasn't a pleasant one. Most of that produce had been overripe.

Bart closed up to ride perhaps a half meter off the bumper of the Presidential limousine. That made the two vehicles effectively one for defensive purposes, allowing the EPs on front and rear to swing to the side. So far, the only response was panicking, running locals, but that could, even would, change. Two of the armored vehicles charged ahead. One from the rear pulled up alongside the rear limo and poured fire into the attacking vehicle there. Whether or not the threat was intentional, the occupants of that vehicle were now dead and splattered.

They went through the crowd and carts, through some tattered and ragged building awnings, and a cafeteria's tables, followed by two slams as the vehicles crashed in the close quarters, then they were in an intersection and turning left. Rahul was a decently competent combat driver, among his other talents, and it was good to have him along.

"We're split," Weilhung said. "Want to pick a meeting spot?"

"Meet at Joe's," Alex said.

There was a pause. "Confirm . . . Joe's?"

"Joe's."

There was another, longer pause. "Understood. Update us soonest."

It had taken a bit. There was no Joe's. Alex didn't feel like broadcasting a plan at the moment, even on scrambled radios. He was still formulating the plan, and didn't want to give bad information or anything that could be used against them. Likewise, it was never a bad idea to confuse the enemy.

Three sections of convoy were going in three directions, and would attempt to regroup. Everyone knew the President's section had gone left. The Army could call AF for satellite tracking and catch back up. The locals probably couldn't. There was nothing to indicate they had that level of technology, but Alex was increasingly suspicious. There were lots of off-planet groups taking an interest in things.

And now they had two limos and only small arms to get back through the city with.

"I vote for revehicling," he said.

"Concur," said Jason, with Bart a moment behind.

"But we need to stay in here for now. Where should I go?" Bart asked.

"Ultimately back to the airfield. As to route, I'm not sure. Best guess. We need to let Rahul lead for a while. He's more familiar with things."

"Can we trust him?" Aramis asked vocally, shouting down through the roof.

"Mic off," he said in warning as he thumbed the button. "That's a damned good question. I assume we have to, and the President does. Hard for us to argue, and we have no evidence he's not on our side."

"Just that three attacks have happened since he joined us," Aramis said, ducking his head in. "Call me paranoid."

"The attacks are increasing in frequency and threat level. I think it's coincidence."

"Could be. Keep it in mind."

"Yeah. Mic on. Rahul, you lead, get us back to the airport by any route, try to avoid concentrations.

"Yes, sir!" came the reply.

"How's fuel?" Alex asked.

"Fine. I think we'll be okay if we can keep moving," Bart said, laconic even in the midst of battle. "Aramis, you keep the route clear. I don't want us to have to stop."

"How serious about that are you?"

"Mic off. Kill anyone who might cause us to stop. Is that plain enough?" Bart's voice was clear and slow.

"Sweeet." The kid sounded reassured rather than pleased. Good. He even glanced down at Alex for confirmation. Alex nodded. Not stopping was essential. Enough people could roll a limo, or block it in with chocks and then beat it or fire it.

"Bad route," Bart said tersely. Alex looked ahead.

"Fuck." There was nothing else to say.

Ahead was a fuel tanker, with some kind of petro or methane derivative that was combustible, even explosive, and they were going to pass it.

"I'd like to keep our distance from that, if we can," Alex said. "Rahul, we want to guide past that tanker, or parallel it, something, ASAP."

"Understood. I'll stay back for now."

"I agree," Bart said, and changed lanes while braking. "I don't believe it will be a problem, but why take chances?"

"Yeah." Alex didn't want to admit he was nervous. Sure, the odds were slim, but enough slim odds eventually came up to a good probability. Murphy said that this was the moment it would cut loose.

They passed what had been the local conference center. That moment was *the* moment, and the tanker just disappeared, replaced by a huge fireball laced with black, oily smoke; a massive, crushing blow; a deafening, stomach-churning boom; and a heat front that was painful through the sides of the car.

The collision curtains deployed, Aramis dropped inside and cursed, the vehicle bounced and came down hard enough to jar spines from coccyx to atlas. The engine stuttered from that shock wave. The short convoy slewed to a halt.

"Holy *shit!*" Jason said.

"Damn. You called that one right," Aramis said. He slapped at his hair, patted himself, checking for damage. The kid was always smart after the shit hit the fan. Get him to think ahead and he'd go from operator to team leader. He was also bleeding from both lips. Likely he'd bashed his face on the roof as he came down. His skin was flushing red from heat damage.

Bart accelerated and drove *into* the receding and rising fireball that was mushrooming out and spreading above, darkening the sky. Oily, burning streams were raining down, but the road was moderately clear, with vehicles blown off, or stalled from various aftermaths of the detonation.

"I don't think a second one will go off at this time, so let us get through," he said. Something crunched and the vehicle bucked and rose, dropped and dragged. Wheels screamed. Thick, fluffy soot, some of it still glowing red, fell through the open roof.

"I have clear sky," Rahul said. "Watch for threats."

Aramis shook himself then rose back up to man the gun that was leaning against the roof lip. He swung it out and scraping could be heard on the plastic and metal of the canopy top.

"Think it was on purpose?" Alex asked. He assumed it was. The timing was too cute.

Bababababababang! Automatic fire lashed out and raked the right side, starring windows but not penetrating. Aramis swung over and cut loose with a return burst from the Viper that made shit explode. Bart accelerated, Rahul said, "I do," and Alex grinned and cussed.

In the lead vehicle, Elke leaned out a window and fired grenades, and tossed what could only be small mines into the gutter. Jason was out the top with a machine gun and laid down . . . well, not indiscriminate fire. He aimed well, but he didn't seem too worried about collateral damage. Above, Aramis took that as a cue and added to it. They chewed apart some ratty storefront that had definite military gear set up in a clear space.

"Playwright, this is Calico actual, over," said a female voice, Captain Berit Lyngstad, a blonde Norwegian paratrooper who was running one of the reinforced local platoons.

"Go ahead, Calico, over," he said over the clatter of guns.

"Stand by for backup. Indigenous unit to your right, one block, over."

Whatever had happened, this area was way past hot.

"They can best stay where they are to cover the flank, over," Alex said.

"They're trying to link up to reinforce the convoy, over."

That wasn't what he wanted to hear. However, his jurisdiction ended outside the limos. He could direct them anywhere Bishwanath wanted. He couldn't control the military. Bishwanath could, but it would screw things up worse to even try that.

"Understood, over," he said. Things couldn't get that much worse, he thought, as they growled over debris, bouncing only slightly in the massive vehicle.

Lyngstad spoke again. "Playwright, Snow White informs us the enemy has commo, over." Captain L. was definitely easy to understand and calm under fire. Pity the bitch only had bad news.

Then Aramis poured fire down the cross street as Bart tried to run faster.

"Those are good guys, dammit!" Bart said. At least on paper.

Alex was all set to make an apologetic ass-covering comment when Aramis said, "Mic off. One: cover your ass. Two: get paid first."

"Hold fire," he said instead. Blast it, the kid was right, but the timing and phrasing sucked. At least he'd killed his mic.

Aramis looked down and said, "Boss, you didn't want them along. I didn't kill any, dinged a few vehicles at most. Now they're not along. Ream me later."

"How does our route look?" he asked, just as Captain L. cut back in.

"Playwright, please control your fire. Friendlies, say again, friendlies, over." She had iron control, he had to give her that. Why weren't there more like her?

"Confirm friendlies," he said. "ID problem, now resolved, over." Yeah, she'd believe that.

But they hadn't planned on the collapsed building blocking the street.

"That was not on the map this morning," Bart said, looking from the wreckage to the dash. "And is not . . . wait, it's updating. From our input."

"Well, I'm glad we can provide recon for everyone else," Jason muttered aloud. Both drivers forced their vehicles around in hard, traction-breaking turns.

The hostiles didn't seem to be entirely interested in the cornered President, though there was some sniper fire.

Then there was mortar fire and more sniper fire.

"It would be good to have more than the single fighter overhead, and one transport," Alex said.

"Playwright, this is Calico. Be advised incoming fire is not targeting you. You are discreet if you can break out, over."

"Understood, over." Yeah, the fight was going on regardless, they just happened to be here. Which still sucked. They were boxed in, valuable bystanders in the middle of a war, ripe to be anyone's hostages, targets, or punching bags.

Aramis fired another heavy burst back at some shooter and fire erupted from a window. Jason pulled a rocket out and put an exclamation on the burst that took out a section of wall for massive overkill, which made a point that would hopefully be taken.

"Boss, I recommend moving up here, over," Jason said.

"Good idea," Alex said, and reached through the hatch to the trunk. Get all the hardware out and use it now. Clear an area around them and wait for backup.

Bart took weapons like firewood, kicked open the door and ran as Aramis fired bursts of suppressive fire. Alex followed with three rockets and two dump guns. Then he and Jason provided suppression for Aramis. That put everyone in one vehicle, for better protection of the President and better outgoing fire.

They hunkered down. The vehicle wasn't a great redoubt, but it was armored.

"Suggestions on retreat?" Alex asked as he shot at another threat. It was just some punk, but a threat if ignored.

"Recon," Elke said, and leaned out with her shotgun. She fired four shots in four high arcs to the cardinal points, her body bent at odd angles out the window, then handed a cord to Alex. He plugged it into his computer and opened the video.

The slugs she fired had cameras aboard. Their resolution wasn't great, but they were for battlefield recon, not glamour shots.

"I don't see anywhere not filling up with hostiles," Alex said. "Bad. Hope they get here quick."

"Arriving," Calico said. "We took a wrong turn, over."

The punctuation was a roar of noise on a psyops speaker, followed by pops of some kind of nonlethal gas.

"Ah, shit," Bart said. "Close the vehicle?"

"Yeah, all we can manage. Fucking morons."

They scrabbled back and rolled the windows. With seven in back, the limo was fairly tight. Bart crawled up front to get the engine going. The ignition wasn't responding to Rahul's attempts. The turbine might have inhaled something during the debris-throwing chase.

"Shit gas," Elke reported. "Full bore incapacitance agent."

"Calico, we do not have filters, over," Alex said. He was amazed how calm he sounded.

"Why not? Dammit, you're supposed to have filters at all times! Over." Lyngstad sounded panicky now.

"Well, we're supposed to have a lot of things at all times, but there's this image you want us to maintain!" Alex snapped. "Don't fucking worry about it, just deal with it fast, over."

"Roger, Playwright. As fast as we can. I have called for vertical, over."

"Yeah, great. Out."

The engine didn't start, but the capacitor bank had enough juice to close vents and the roof.

"Are we to be affected?" Bishwanath asked. He was a fantastic principal. Did as he was told, stayed out of the way. At least it wasn't their screwup.

"Yes, sir. As soon as that gas enters, we're going to be spewing from every orifice, hallucinating, and twitching. It's messy and undignified, but not long-term harmful. But they'll have to carry us out and either deliver an antidote or wait for it to wear off."

"Thank you," he said. No sarcasm, just understanding of the facts.

"Getting some whiffs," Elke said. "Not bad yet, but rising nausea."

"Better than outside," Shaman said. "Look at that." He pointed.

The crowds half a block away had disappeared at a hint, but the few who'd missed the warnings were convulsing heavily, anything from twitches and shakes to staggering and dancing. Then they started vomiting, snotting, drooling. Stained clothes indicated sphincters cutting loose.

"The good news is the threat is now gone ohhhh erp!" Aramis said. His face bore the panicked look of someone who knows he's about to be sick. Violently sick.

"Here it comes," Alex said. "Calico, it's hitting us, you're in charge of recovery. Thanks for clearing the areurllph!" and he was vomiting, spewing, guts alternately clamping tight with cramps and then jerking. Fear reflex hit, and he could see Elke whimpering, head in hands, curled up tight on the floor. Jason was kneeling over the seat and clutching at it for support as the car rolled over, tossing Alex sideways . . . or was that disorientation from the gas? No, the car was . . . no it wasn't, couldn't be, but the President was falling atop him and . . .

"Mister Marlow?" he heard through a fuzzy purple jelly that surrounded him.

"Agent," he said automatically. The goo cleared. It was all hallucinogenic.

"Are you recovering?"

A military medic was over him, and his vision was returning. His pulse hammered in his ears . . . no, he was aboard a lifter and that was the engine hum.

"I think so," he replied muzzily. He was lying in a puddle of something slimy . . . he wasn't going to think about that. Even though it was intentional and chemically induced, it was embarrassing.

"We'll be landing at the palace in a few moments."

He finally was able to focus on the helmeted face in front of him. "How's the President?" he asked.

"You don't need to worry about him," came the confident reply with a head shake. He waited a moment for further comment. Nothing.

It might have been the recovery drugs, the gas, or the cumulative stress, but he reached up, clutched the soldier's flight suit by the front, and yanked.

"Listen," he glanced at the collar, now in focus, "sergeant first class, I am the senior fucking Agent in Charge of the President's personal detail. He *is* something for me to worry about and you will goddamned well give me a sitrep or there will be worse shit than the puddle I'm sitting in to clean up!"

The sergeant's arms came up defensively but not violently. They ran strength against strength, and even sick and doped, Alex was stronger.

"Easy, sir," the man acquiesced. He was old enough under his helmet that he likely wouldn't make an issue of it, but Alex didn't care.

"The President is fine, recovering with the rest of you. He's over there," and the medic pointed with his half-free forearm. "We'll escort you all in on landing."

"That's all I wanted," Alex said, took a look to confirm it was the President, and sagged back, exhausted. The gas had taken a lot out of him. Literally. He snarled to himself.

An hour later, everyone had showered, after a humiliating trip through the palace dripping shit, sweat, and puke from their clothes. Bishwanath had his staff come and get the team's clothes and gear, and it was back, clean, scrubbed, sterilized, and folded.

"I swear," Aramis said, "I am so pissed." Everyone ignored the obvious pun.

"It's more than that," Alex said. "It's the assumption that they can play without consulting with me. If we take fire and you see it"—he pointed at Aramis—"you're low man around here . . ."

"But I take charge until it's under control and hand it back over," Aramis replied.

"Right. The guy on the spot stays in charge until properly relieved. No one smart jumps into the middle of a firefight and gives orders without a sitrep, unless things are a total balls-up. I thought we had things largely contained."

Jason wasn't as nearly as distraught at the others. "I got to try that shit in training for Grainne's forces," he said. "But it's still disgusting."

Elke came down the short passage from the shower with her hips wrapped in a towel. She was topless but clutching a support shirt.

"Especially dangerous if I have detonator controls in hand," she said with a raised eyebrow. "You might point that out to them."

Alex was at once taken by the scene. First of all, fantastic tits. Modestly sized, perfectly shaped. Push-ups did amazing things for the woman. Second, Bart had scarcely noticed, merely a glance. He was also from Europe with its casual attitudes, and had been security for several female celebrities and performers. He had to have seen a lot. Shaman was a doctor. Jason came from a socially relaxed culture with hot weather that encouraged little clothing. But Aramis was stunned. Only for a moment, and the kid got it under control fast, but he definitely wasn't used to the idea. Between the shave he needed and the tousled hair were a pair of eyes as big as saucers.

She had her shirt on in moments and wandered off to get pants. "If I'd had something live," she called from her room, door open, "I could have twitched. Mention that to them, please," she reiterated.

"Will do."

He wasn't going to snicker at Aramis for trying to sneak a peek past the door frame. He'd been without sex at least as long and would love a glimpse of the rest of her, but it wasn't professional and he had more control. Aramis would just have to learn.

There was a knock at the door, then Bishwanath walked in. Elke returned, dressed.

"I apologize for barging in. I am somewhat unhappy with the performance earlier."

"Yes, sir," Alex said. He was afraid of this. "It went bad after the convoy broke up, and . . ."

"It was spectacular, Agent Marlow. Right up until the Army tried to take control of a situation you had in hand and caused me to befoul myself. This is all over the news, and is a staggering blow in this culture. The public humiliation . . ." He stood there tight-lipped and irate.

"I came to apologize to you," he said, taking them all in with his gaze. "It is unconscionable that you should be treated this way. I will be speaking to the Army's people and making a few things clear."

"Sir, we are clean, glad of your hospitality in getting our stuff cleaned, and they did keep you alive. I am not unhappy with some minor trouble for us, though I do see how it's a severe problem in your position, but we're used to being grubby."

"You would like to be kept out of it," Bishwanath observed.

"If you need us, we're there. Feel free to use the leverage, but we don't need a claim on our behalf, though you're kind to offer."

"Very well, but on my behalf, I am about to flay someone." His expression made Alex wonder if he meant it literally. Considering some of the fighting that had taken place in the past, he just might.

"Need an escort, sir?" Aramis offered.

"It would be prudent?"

"Yeah. Sir," Alex said. Sure, the kid could go along and watch. So could someone who could report back. "Jason, go with him."

"At once."

Both men grabbed their clean gear and fell in behind the President as he left. The man almost left heat ripples in the air. He was *pissed*.

As soon as the door closed, Alex said, "Well, that fucks things up."

"Yes. For whom?" Shaman asked.

"Everyone," Alex said. "Everyone."

CHAPTER FOURTEEN

"You'd think those morons would get the hint," leMieure bitched to Weygandt about the contractors. The colonel wondered why he'd been singled out for such attention. Maybe it was considered an honor.

"I don't know that they're paid to take hints, sir. They seem to value courage and teamwork above all else." He tried to make it obvious he was working, watching his screens, raising the audio a bit . . .

"Yeah, yeah. And if I'd known that bitch might have had a bomb in her hands, I'd have timed it better, if you know what I mean."

Weygandt's neck hairs bristled. He was a soldier, a lawyer, and a human being, and that statement was pushing all professional, legal, and moral envelopes. He was glad he was secretly recording this. That couldn't be admitted as evidence in court, but it might save his ass if there was a court-martial or even just a Mission Effectiveness Inspection.

"Maybe they need orders directly," he suggested diplomatically.

The fat bastard leaned on a shelf and smeared it with sweat. Why did he always have to come here? Was it from his vid and sensie days, he required an audience?

"The 'President' is officially their employer, through his office. Officially, we can only advise. It has to be that way so it at least looks like he's in charge. The budget isn't through my office or I'd cut them. It's through MilBu with a rider and I can't touch it."

Weygandt pondered. How best to phrase this?

"That doesn't mean they can't be given orders," he said. "Just that we have to find a way to get those orders issued by their office, or the President. He might be, um, persuaded with the right leverage. I'm sure we can find a way to lean on Ripple Creek. When were they last audited?"

"For taxes? I have no idea." Of course the scumbucket didn't.

He checked off on his fingers. "Taxes, compliance with ISO, compliance with military standards they contract to, and to relevant military regulations . . . no one is ever perfectly in compliance."

"I could kiss you," the fat man said, grinning gleefully.

Good God, please don't even joke about that, Weygandt shuddered. Instead, he said, "Let's just agree that we can resolve the contractor problem and have professional soldiers take over."

"Who will do as I order, yes."

Well, we'll see about that later. I may have some bad news for you, Weygandt smiled inside. If he played this right, he could take care of both at the same time.

The door opened and Bishwanath came in, escorted by two of his goons.

Holy shit.

"Who works for who here?" the President asked.

"Um . . . sir?" Weygandt said when leMieure didn't. LeMieure was in shock and cowering back toward the wall.

"Who is in charge here?" he repeated, louder and more forcefully. His guards stayed behind him and didn't seem disposed to interfere. This had to be due to the events earlier, and they actually were in goon role, looking ready to shoot anyone he asked them to.

Weygandt had a pistol. He knew leMieure had nothing.

"That would depend on the situation, sir," he replied. "If you can tell me what—"

He was cut off as Bishwanath shouted, "*I am in charge here!* This is my nation, my palace, my plan. Those of you advising me are speaking for me in ways and places you should not, and making the situation worse. And you—" He turned to leMieure, who tried to brace against the onslaught but failed. "—are a fat, meddlesome *idiot*! You do not speak for me, and from now on I will contradict and denounce the statements you make on my behalf. If the press wants conflict, I will by God give it to them, and I will have you arrested and shot!"

Weygandt silently begged leMieure not to be stupid enough

to admit any of the things he'd discussed in front of this man. Weygandt had already witnessed too many discussions he'd rather be able to deny. He also didn't want leMieure to raise the issue that the President wasn't really in charge. He wasn't, of course, but if he thought he was being pressed he might just have people shot. That wouldn't be legal, but wouldn't matter to corpses.

Luckily, Bishwanath stormed back out with a door slam that shook the air.

After a moment Weygandt said, "I think we need to increase the Recon presence down here."

"Yes," leMieure agreed, trying not to blubber, the coward. "I will feel safer with that madman at a distance."

Weygandt hadn't been thinking of leMieure's safety at all. The man fit perfectly the snide definition of a buddy: someone larger and slower who could soak up a lot of fire.

We are definitely earning our pay, Alex thought.

It had been someone's bright idea to build a shopping mall. He couldn't imagine Simoncorp thought it was a smart idea; maybe they needed a tax write-off. Finance was beyond him. In any case, a hotel, a mall, a small park, and some other trappings were built, and there was an attempt at creating tourism in the works. So far, it was only high-level execs of the companies in question taking advantage of the tourism opportunities in this wasteland, as well as a few politicians with their entourages, and annoying clueless celebrities.

Ironically, most of them were guarded by Ripple Creek or other contractors. Alex had already recognized a couple, and Jason and Shaman pointed out a few more.

There wasn't much time, though. The mall was atrociously designed as far as security, with a huge patio between vehicle apron and front door, under a huge, vaulting concrete archway that almost begged for explosives to knock it down on hapless victims. Elke concurred and said so.

"Boom and crash. What were they thinking?"

It was a broad, open area. This entrance was VIPs and their guards only, and all guards had to be from a select list of contractors, to maintain the President's safety. General public entrances were guarded by Bodyguards backed up by soldiers. That also presented a possible hazard.

Besides that, the celebrities and press made it hard to do

anything. Despite jokes about "expendable cover," which were not going to be made over the radio, the PR damage of hurting any of them was an EP nightmare.

With the team in close and handpicked Bodyguards out from there, handpicked by Major Weilhung, whom Alex did trust for that, they moved across the decorative bricks and to the reserved entrance of tall, crystal polymer that looked like glass but was stronger and less likely to shatter.

Inside wasn't a receiving line, but rather a choreographed group of little gaggles for the benefit of the roving cameras. Tables and chairs sat in a garden type arrangement with a small fountain and potted plants.

"Lots of stuff for us to use as cover," Aramis said softly.

"Doesn't look much like the 'video mapping simulation' we were shown," Jason said. He didn't sound surprised.

"I can't offer any explosive," Elke said. "Too much fragile clutter." She'd also expressed a very vocal and Czech objection to not having her shotgun.

Shaman said, "But if anyone else does, the fragmentation effects will be brutal."

"We throw ourselves on the Dishwasher and pray," Bart offered snidely. "Not much else will work."

A number of annoying airhead celebrities who wanted to be socially relevant—and keep their names visible for future contracts—were here. Seamus Plume, who could be counted on to appear anywhere there was "trouble." His current and previous and likely again girlfriend Messalina. Francia Pikes, allegedly a virgin teenager wearing *that* outfit . . . she was a virgin if there was money in it. Rumor and photos said the three of them as a trio and here they were side by side. There was that obnoxious and hideous Vienna Marriott, wearing troweled-on makeup and looking like a hooker. She used her family's fortune to try to make herself a star. She was, in the sense that you could download her escapades with everything but the mule for a few cents.

Given that, it felt pretty good to be guarding even a small-time president. Alex saw Kyle and Wade with others he didn't know guarding the brats. He gave the barest hint of a nod, which they returned.

The only good thing was that with this many professionals in the place, any attack would be stupid.

There was a very pretty fountain in the atrium, with three levels of balconies and transparent elevators on two sides. All parties had decided that VIPs would remain on ground level for the duration, with one or two lesser targets going up to a private reception in a third-level club after the official activities.

It was telling. The cameras took in the President briefly, and a small number of reporters came over for a sound bite, but most of the attention was on the Earth celebrities, who were interviewed at length for their political take, as if they had one that mattered. Granted, Bishwanath didn't have any of the fancy degrees the "professionals" had, but he *had* run a district and a major tribe. Real world experience counted, having portrayed a leader in a sensie at some point did not.

The fountain had three rotating arcs in a sequenced program and was probably quite pretty. There wasn't time for that now, though. The area matched reasonably well with the map they'd been given and the walk-through he'd done, though quite a few other things had been moved. That was always the danger when money wasn't an issue and the architect showed up to dictate to the engineers.

It actually made sense as a PR circus. The press could use the celebs to generate interest for tourism, the President was there for the official part without dominating it or drawing attention to himself.

It also gave lots of bodies to hide behind in an emergency. Not that he'd say so in public, or that it wouldn't be a disaster if so, but it was always an option to keep their principal alive.

The speeches turned into more interviews, with clusters of cameras around the speaker. They were ongoing, with the interviewers rotating and drifting as suited their needs and moods. Alex watched that none of them got too close, none got between Bishwanath and the exit, and that none were armed. That latter was hard, as all the commo gear they carried interfered with his scanners. He had Jason and Elke backing him up on that.

One of the reporters actually tried to talk to Elke, who stared through him as if he didn't exist until he gave up and moved on with a scowl.

Yes, it was a fine event from a PR point of view, and the general manager was getting some camera time. Of course, that disgusting leMieure he'd been lucky enough to avoid so far was, too. His two henchmen didn't look much like guards, nor like assistants of any kind. More like "moral support" or "yes men." Both were young and slim, which suggested the rumors about Mister leMieure were true. Apart from that presence, the rest did make sense as promotion. There were pure tourist nations. The UK made a lot that way. So did Bali, Macau, and Sulawan, most of the Caribbean states, Sharjah . . . it wasn't a bad concept. There was no way this place would ever be a power, but it could achieve self-sufficiency rather than being a poorly subsidized excuse for crime syndicates.

In any large group, there are a number of stupid people. With a charismatic leader, or time to stew and swap ideas, or arousal by outside agents, those stupid people can be prevailed upon to do things stupider than their collective stupidity. Alex realized that afterward.

In short, a firefight started. He realized that at once.

At the first burst, he took care of business, to wit: putting Bishwanath down. He and Jason and Bart formed a second perimeter, pushed some people aside, including Vienna's stunned form, skirt crawling up as she ran, and not at all sexy. Her own guards tackled her and dragged her aside.

Bishwanath had learned and went limp as three EPs dragged him between a large potted fern and a pillar, Bart and Shaman behind him and backs to him, carbines coming out from cases and pistols going back under coats. The local variety of fern closed up as it was touched, whipping into a little ball as if even it wanted away from the shooting. Elke crouched in front of him, behind his umbrella, with her reinforced case up as additional cover. That case wasn't quite ballistic armor, but it was enough to stop fragments. Bishwanath had his extra armor on and hunkered down small. The Bodyguard crowded in around, flinching and shouting and uncoordinated, but brave. That set alarm bells off in Alex's mind. One of them could be an assassin with this as a diversion, and it might be done well enough no one could blame said killer.

That first burst was followed with the unadulterated roar of a full machine gun in a real caliber, and some light explosions. Smoke started wafting.

Then more explosions started on another side.

Time to move the Bodyguards. "Grays, please secure a perimeter at ten meters!" he shouted and gestured, feeling very exposed standing up in just soft armor and no headgear in the midst of real combat.

"All right, we're retreating," he said into radio. It was too loud and echoey for voice alone. "Call for any available transport up to the door. Captain Nugent, this is Playwright, I need these da— other VIPs pulled to safety without them blocking Dishwasher. Can you assist in routing, please, over." It wasn't a request. Recon were professional enough to know that he was the guy on the bubble.

And it was the worst place possible for a fight. Civilians everywhere, lots of breakable stuff, reporters with cameras, like some farcical sensie. Someone was already trying to get close with a camera. Alex almost shot them, because doing a low crawl with a camera, monitor, and antennae made them look like a missile crew or such.

"Is someone actually starting a fight in a mall?" Elke asked, mirroring his thoughts.

"Behind the pillar," Aramis shouted and gestured. "Dishwasher against it, backs in."

"Good enough," Alex shouted agreement. "Shitty, but good enough." Right now they needed any kind of cover before moving for one of the stores, most likely.

"Roger, Playwright," Nugent agreed. "APC in three minutes, over."

"Warn me at six zero seconds, over."

"Roger. Be advised my unit is busy and cannot assist, over." Good man. Blast on the availability, but they were likely trying to secure the exit and cut off more incursions.

The team maneuvered to get Bishwanath to the far side of the pillar, where they could run straight for the door. Still scanning, Alex ducked down himself. The screams were louder than some of the fire, and there was now outgoing fire doing damage to stores. Small fires were erupting from tracer and a few grenades. Damned Army. He didn't fault them. They were doing what soldiers should do . . . which was the wrong thing for this situation.

Although, he conceded as another massive burst and the bang of a rocket shook the upper balcony of the atrium, it might be a good idea in this case.

One of the Bodyguards prodded the camera crew with his toe and gestured. They argued until his weapon swung, and then skittered away. Well, they were local and not Alex's problem. He smiled a bit. If they needed documentation, Elke had been wearing her "glasses" the whole time. Intel quality only, not PR, but it would set the facts straight... if anyone cared.

The massive number of civilians meant the good guys were very limited in their fields of fire, and the attackers knew it. Suppressing fire was trashing the place, which might have been the desired outcome of the attack, and not hitting anything of tactical importance.

Still, he saw flitting figures now. Not as professional as Recon or EPD, but professional enough to stand and fight. That was rare around here.

"I swear that one looks like one of Dhe's guards," Elke said.

"I don't see it, but save it," Alex said.

"Roger."

The easiest way to spot the action was to look for screams of running civilians. Someone was definitely trying to pin down the exits, because the crowd kept running in toward the middle. That was a clanging bomb warning.

"Captain Nugent, Playwright, we may need containment, over."

"Understood. Ninety seconds on APC. Main doors are not secure, over."

"Roger, over."

Alex saw a bona fide squad of somebody across the atrium and down the hall. They were shooting, and the crowd was dispersing in a frenzied Brownian movement, bumping and colliding like some comedy, sprawling and then crawling. Their uniform was cobbled together, neither Army nor Bodyguard. There were still too many civilians, and four fucking camera crews pointed this way. The military solution was to attack. Alex couldn't do that. The Bodyguard were spread out, and he wanted them in the retreat, too.

A grenade exploded in the fountain, creating a cloud of mist. With that added to the smoke and some kind of gas, likely tear gas, a substantial fog tickled the back of Alex's throat.

"Get Dishwasher masked," he ordered. He wasn't going to gear up himself yet, but maybe soon. Certainly it was time to start retreating out the door, too. Out some door.

"Grays, please fall back to our position plus five meters. Argonaut, move the Dishwasher out to the curb for pickup. Detour left."

"Roger," Jason said, as the various units moved into their next positions. Gray-uniformed Bodyguards stood up too visibly, but moved with discipline, a few Recon around the edges sought position and targets, other EPDs moved screaming, panicked spoiled celebrities behind cover in stores, seeking emergency exits, and a unit in white shirts and peaked caps arrived on electric carts.

Who the hell were they?

The team shuffled out, moving faster, a porcupine of weapons with a masked man in the middle, now at a zigzag jog.

The carts whined across between the belligerents. Five men in white shirts with shoulder patches rolled out and took positions behind the buggies with carbines and grenade launchers. In seconds, a cloud of smoke and retch gas was blowing from one cart toward the gang, propelled by a ducted fan. One of the arrivals turned and looked at the Ripple Creek team.

"This is Lizard Forty-Five," he said into a shoulder mounted horn. "Continue your retreat and watch the emergency exits. I have one man in each for surveillance."

Aramis shouted, "I do not fucking *believe* this!"

Lizard 45 heard him and replied, "Hah! You laughed at me. Guess I called this one right, eh?" he shouted, then turned and duckwalked with his carbine at the ready. He pointed and gestured, and two of the mall guards dove low and slithered for cover behind another plant. He fired a burst, and the other two advanced. Overhead came the crack of a large bore rifle.

"Marksman, two floors up," Shaman said.

"Retreat," Alex said, pointing at a clothing store. "Elke, Bart on lead. Aramis left, Shaman with Dishwasher. Jason and me on right and rear. Move."

"Sir," everyone chorused and rose as the firefight behind them shifted to a new front.

They whipped through the store, nodded, and made polite noises at the manager ducked under the service counter, and Alex led the way out the back door into a service hallway in seconds. Then he was back on radio.

"We could use that extraction, over."

"Waiting, left of the road, over."

"Right out this wall," he muttered, staring at the concrete. "And exits are fifty meters either way."

"One exit," said Elke, as she moved forward and slapped a handful of something against the wall, followed by another one lower down.

"Elke, I don't—" he said as he dove back into the store. She slipped in just as the heavy door closed, only to bounce off its hinges as a *SLAM* announced an explosion.

"We have an exit," she shouted and led the way through, slipping a remote back into her pocket.

An exit indeed. The store's fireproof door fell off its frame with a muted bang, and there was a gaping hole of reinforcing rods and shredded polymer and concrete in the wall, big enough to walk through.

Aramis was having a ball. Shooting, explosions, the whackjob mall ninja, they were carrying the President to safety and generally doing what they'd been hired to do. It felt good. He eased around the fractured edge of the hole and looked for threats. It was clear, apart from a roiling cloud of dust and smoke from Elke's blast. No, she wasn't bad, he grudgingly admitted. Knew her stuff and kept cool. Behind them, the shooting in the mall was fading.

Behind him, Bart said, "APC twenty meters. Move."

He saw movement in the haze, and shifted into a stance for immediate threats. Whatever it was . . .

"Whatthefuck?" he shouted. The smoke cleared. Giant ugly bird.

"It's a goddammed ginmar thing," he said.

The beast was obviously close kin to an ostrich. It looked at him with dull, stupid eyes. He tried to make a shooing motion, and it pecked his arm.

"Goddam!" he yelled, and poked it with the barrel of his carbine.

At that point it went berserk, squawking and batting with heavy wings and kicking wildly. It really was uncoordinated, and only got him one clipping smack with a wing. It turned in a circle, ruffled its posterior feathers, and let loose a wet rumble. A splash erupted that struck the ground and splattered halfway up his calves, as the stupid bird faded back into the dust of its passing.

Furious, he fired a shot and was rewarded with another squawk, this one loud and indignant. He slipped backward, following the huddle toward the APC.

Then the damned thing was back, farting and kicking and thrashing in the grit. It was fast enough he couldn't get a good shot, and annoying enough that wanted the thing dead, but it somehow never managed to connect to him with anything. He blocked with his weapon and kept moving, moving, then they were backing up the ramp.

The thing flapped away and didn't return, but its presence had certainly been putrid. He took a seat at the rear of the bench and as Bart dialed the ramp up, he looked around to see if anyone was laughing.

"Gross, eh?" Jason asked from across, panting for breath and caked with dust and sweat on his skin, powdered gray on his suit, which was shredded in several places. He bled from a couple, where he'd caught the rebar in the wall. Shaman was applying bandages and disinfectant.

"Yeah, kinda." Kinda. He felt hugely embarrassed. What a contemptible fucking bird.

"Kinda? Son, I'm halfway to puking from the smell of that disgusting fat chicken. If you're only *kinda* grossed, you're a better man than me." Jason didn't seem to notice the treatment of his shoulder.

"I can see why no one likes them," Elke said.

Attention moved back to Bishwanath, who looked fairly clean and just a bit ruffled.

"I thank you," he said. "I am not sure what that was all about, but I am in your debt again. I am unharmed and somewhat invigorated, if annoyed at why *the infrastructure of my country keeps getting torn down by these bastards!*"

"I wish we could offer help on that, sir," Alex said. "But I don't know who to ask, unless Mister deWitt knows."

"I know," Bishwanath replied, head in hands, looking tired. "We shall just carry on."

There was an awkward silence for a moment, while everyone tried to find another subject.

Alex finally asked, "Aramis, who was that back there in the mall? You seemed to recognize him."

"Uh, it's hard to explain, Alex. I'd rather not, in fact." He was flushing crimson, possibly from exertion, but it was definitely at least partly embarrassment. This was not a great day after all.

Bart added, "Let us just say it's a mall world after all."

Aramis cackled at the joke. Bart had done it in English, too.

"What?" Alex was really confused now.

Bart said, "That was about our response, *ja*. You don't want to know. Trust me."

"Okay. I'm guessing you met up with some other contractors."

"Close enough."

That was all they would say. Aramis was grateful for that fact. He was going to need to burn these pants when he got to the palace, and shower in bleach. Explaining about a mall tactical team didn't appeal.

CHAPTER FIFTEEN

Well, the news is full of it this evening," Bart said.

"It's my experience the news is always full of it," Jason said. It took Bart a moment to get the joke, but yes, that was true.

"On the positive side," Jason said, "the worst they are saying about us is that we 'gracelessly dragged the President to safety while doing substantial damage to a store and the outside of the mall, see attached picture.'"

"Who's taking the flak?" Alex asked, pulling the channel up on his fliptop.

"Factions," Bart said. "They do not attempt to say which faction or why. I believe they just want the banners and like the word."

"That's their audience," Jason said. "Anything beyond a sound bite is too tough to figure out. Recall that this war started because 'the SecGen has shipping interests.' Yes, rather than start a trade route or embezzle some funds, he started a war no one likes against people who blow up ships, threaten starports, and offer to toss KE weapons at cities, just to get rich."

"Eh, that's why I don't bother," Aramis said.

"That is how we stay aware of our jobs and possible next contracts," Shaman said.

"I'm going to take a nap," Jason said. "I'll cover tonight. If you need any help with weapons, leave them tagged on the rack. Later." He limped slightly from the dings he'd taken.

Bart was experienced enough to have some grasp of politics. There was no money on this planet for itself, only for its use as a transshipment point. There were bound to be lots of people who liked it as such, and didn't want it to change.

Aramis came through from the bathroom, cleaned up and in casual clothes. He still looked angry.

"I had to toss the pants. Couldn't get them clean of the stain."

"We'll want to avoid those things," Elke said. "But the locals get upset if you shoot them."

"They don't seem to do anything with them," Bart said, wondering.

"No, they're useless and annoying, but are seen as a sort of disgusting entertainment, and people pity them."

"Strange."

They'd eaten a snack before the event, but since it had been brought to a halt, none of them had had dinner. That was just as well. The team's dinner would have been field rations eaten cold in rotation, hiding in a back room out of sight. This way, they got a proper meal Bishwanath had brought up from the kitchen, with salad, sandwiches, soup, and some stew and light desserts.

Bart was glad he was not in charge. Every one of these events caused Alex to sit in the corner grumbling as he typed and dictated an after-action review. One at a time they reported their findings, and Elke downloaded her photos and vid.

When it was Bart's turn, he gave a terse rundown of hearing the fire, watching the crowd's reaction while moving the President to safety, and the disengagement and withdrawal.

Alex asked, "Okay, so who were those mall ninjas?"

"Mall ninjas?" he asked back.

"You know who I mean."

"Honestly, boss, we spoke to them, they wanted weapons, we said no. We thought they were some kind of nuts. They seemed to be well armed."

"Better than some of the alleged pros. I wonder how Simon-corp arranged that," Alex mused. "Well, not my problem." He ran a hand through his sweaty hair. "But I'm certainly tired of the bookkeeping."

"You should clean up and rest," Bart said. "You started early this morning. I'm awake now, Jason will be up later, we'll call Aramis if we need relief."

"Yeah. Good idea."

Bishwanath stayed up late quite often. He also found himself spending more time with his real security detail. They were all very bright people who took a sincere interest in him as their charge. Not at all the mercenaries they were made out to be. And apart from some comments by young Mister Anderson, they were quite reticent about the scorn heaped on them.

Although, he'd noticed, if you watched carefully, you could see the tension. That reached a crescendo when the news came on. While it was easy to be secure in oneself, a little professional recognition was nice once in a while, and like he, they were not getting it. That also might explain why he found their company pleasant—shared misery.

Their schedule was hard to parse. Jason Vaughn, from a substantially longer day cycle, slept in odd shifts and kept odd hours. Alex was on the local day as dictated by Bishwanath's schedule. The others varied.

Tonight, his company was Bart Weil, who was very reticent and quiet. His English wasn't quite as good as Elke's, and he seemed to be more private even than she. He didn't play chess well, but had a keen mind for other puzzles and for building fascinating structures out of cardboard, toothpicks, small boxes, and even ammunition rounds. Some of his mindless doodles were enough to make the eyes water. He understood illusion and misdirection quite well, and he was a good card player.

But after a day like today . . .

"Mister Weil, would you mind terribly if we practice some more this evening? I don't want to disturb anyone, but I need to work out some anger."

"Certainly, sir," Bart agreed. "It is always a good idea if you don't overdo it."

So he spent an hour in his apartment, running through drills on cover and concealment, donning extra armor, and how to move under fire. Then, Bart showed him in detail what he could do in his apartment.

"I would hide right under that chair," Bart said, indicating a wickerwork piece. "It doesn't look large enough, but will hide you for several seconds while we respond. Never under the bed. It is too obvious and will be shot first. That dresser will probably stop some pistol rounds, and if you are armored will help provide additional barrier protection."

"Yes, I see. What of the closet?" he pointed.

Bart opened the door and looked. Among the robes, suits, casual clothes, shoes . . . it was as big as the first house Bishwanath had lived in.

"I would move all the way back and under one of the stands. But that is only good for a few seconds. Obviously, your best bet is to run into our rooms. In an emergency or if you feel threatened, by all means come right in to any room, shouting your name as you do."

"I don't think it will get that bad," Bishwanath said. *Dear God, I hope not!* "But if I need to I will. I owe you the courtesy for all you have done."

"We will try to make sure it doesn't come to that, sir." Weil grinned. "This is just a worst case scenario."

Sweating and tired, he felt much better. He had a few aches, but that came from not being twenty anymore. He envied the team their fitness. With the diet and culture in Celadon, even the most muscular couldn't hope to be on par, and certainly not once over thirty Earth years old, like Vaughn and Marlow.

"Do you feel better, sir?" Weil asked.

"Yes," he replied. "Yes, I do. Also more confident and relaxed. If I could shoot a few things myself once in a while . . ."

"Sir, I haven't actually shot anyone yet, and hardly any suppressing fire."

Bishwanath stopped for a moment and thought. No, no he hadn't. He was used to thinking of firefights where hundreds of rounds were fired, and eventually the odds caught up with someone. He'd also thought that as trained professionals, they should have a higher rate of hits. In fact, they'd hardly ever fired their weapons.

It was something to consider. Having fought didn't necessarily equate to skill or knowledge of anything other than the fear and intensity one felt.

"It must be frustrating to be locked into your role," Weil offered as they walked back into the parlor.

"It is very frustrating," Bishwanath agreed. "I'm flexible on development, as long as we have something. I'm even willing to give Dhe and his cronies—Ton, Mer, and Stein—more than an equal share of development. They may be corrupt, but they do want to make their people happy.

"It seems that was a mistake," he said, sighing and taking a seat on the couch. "They don't want to share. They're willing to attack each other, and possibly themselves, in order to create strife they can blame on each other, and me. The aggravating thing is I can't just have the National Army exterminate them."

"No, that would be very immoral." Weil sat facing the door. Always.

"It also wouldn't work. Their local forces are better than anything I can bring to bear. The BuState people call it 'warlordism,' but that's not quite correct. They're above being warlords, but are certainly feudalistic, greedy, and fascist." He was cooling down at last. Yet Bart was hardly mussed.

Bart was intrigued and flattered to be talking to a president. Bishwanath was far more educational and satisfying than music stars. In this case, the principal was smarter and better educated than he, rather than the other way around.

"Can you place them in positions where they take the blame for failure?" It seemed reasonable and moral to use their own techniques against them. He went to get a drink from the kitchen, and Bishwanath replied as he did so.

"I would, but they are masters of deception. If something goes wrong at their end, it's my fault for hindering them. If it goes wrong here, that's also my fault. With off-planet media supporting them, I am damned no matter what I do. Accept UN help, I'm a puppet. Refuse it, I'm selfish and egotistical.

"Not only must they succeed, others must also fail. So they fight each other, and ally together only to stab at me."

Bart pondered for a moment and said, "Perhaps you are lucky in that you know none of them will attempt to play you from behind." He handed over a glass of apple juice.

Bishwanath chuckled. "There is that. I can assume they are all threats. And thank you."

Bart wondered if the man was being too nice. If the locals respected bastards, then be a bastard. Kill a few here, jail a few there. King stork, as the parable went. While not a good thing, it might be better than the childish fighting now. After all, it was what Bishwanath's opponents were doing.

He didn't think it was the kind of thing he could offer, though, nor was it his place.

"Have you taken your medication tonight, sir?" he asked instead.

"Yes, I have," Bishwanath replied. "And I am grateful that you treat it as quietly as you do, all of you and Rahul."

"We are happy to help, sir," he said. "We would not want you to get ill or worse under our protection."

"Oh, I wouldn't worry, Mister Weil," Bishwanath replied. "No doubt my opponents would blame that on me, too."

They both laughed heartily, and then Bart realized something.

"But the press would claim it had been our fault. They'd be fighting between themselves to decide which story gave them more dirt: self-caused death at your end, or incompetence or dishonesty at ours."

It was a dark, dark joke, but the potential truth made it hysterical.

A door opened, and Jason stuck his head through. "I'm awake. Care to fill me in on the humor?"

CHAPTER SIXTEEN

Four fucking weeks, Aramis thought.

Four weeks of psychotic, on-edge fear and insanity, with attacks all over. Most had been incompetent and foiled far away from the President's entourage. The Army had done its job and caught a good number of factional operations with its patrols.

But some had gotten through close enough for both the team and Recon to have to hit it. Violence was growing elsewhere.

Every morning, Bishwanath and Alex, with Jason sometimes, were tied up in meetings. Alex was on the phone with District quite often now. This was an independent command, but their supplies and payroll came through District.

The good news was that Corporate had managed to get another shipment of weapons in and they were coming up from Receiving now. Jason almost giggled at the stuff being laid out.

Looking at that again: Jason *was* giggling. Some of the firepower was . . . impressive. There were missiles, sensors, extra ammo, a brand new machine gun, another tonne of explosive for Elke, and a Medusa. How the hell anyone had managed to get a Medusa, and get it sent here, was one hell of a question. Aramis had only read about them in news releases and speculation, but that massive, clunky thing couldn't be anything else.

"What the hell are we going to destroy with that?" he asked.

"Anything that gets in our fucking way," Jason said. He looked his age, and very cynical. With all that experience, the man knew his weapons and knew what to ask for.

"What can I do to help?" Aramis asked quietly.

"Ah, Grasshopper. I will show you the Force," Jason grinned. "Help me tear down and set the defaults on the Medusa."

"This thing is just outrageous, and would make the press wet their pants if they knew about it," he commented, grabbing a toolbox.

"That was the criterion in the promotional video that made me decide to get it."

The smile on his face was not a friendly one.

Alex looked over and said, "Dammit, why do we have more explosives?"

"We need more," Elke said as she dove in like a kid at Christmas.

"You know, Plan B doesn't have to automatically be twice as much explosive as Plan A."

"Of course not," she said. "Inverse cube law calls for eight times as much."

She smiled a sweet, cute smile that belied her deadly nature.

"Can I marry or adopt you?" Jason asked. Before she could respond with more than a slightly offended grin, he said, "Forget marriage. You'd have to be junior wife and that's not your style."

Everyone laughed at that image.

There was a small problem with the Medusa.

"I think this thing is designed for someone in a powered skeleton," Aramis said as it was laid out. The thing was *huge*.

"Yeah, fifty kilos loaded," Jason said, "and fairly bulky. I expect Bart can carry it for a while, and we only have it for emergencies, and," he admitted, "I wanted to play while we had some taxpayer money to experiment with."

"Is that backpack full of just ammo?" Bart asked as he came over, having heard his name. The others were gathering around, too.

"Don't scratch the flo— oh, to hell with it, we've already ruined things," Alex said.

"There are four carbine barrels." Jason pointed. "Actually long pistol barrels, on individually gimbaled necks, fed at three rounds per second. This is the grenade launcher firing one round per second. This protrusion is the sensor. You can adjust it for whitelist—everyone is friendly unless designated, blacklist—everyone defaults to enemy, or just pick targets by eye and build a database as you go. At full rate of fire it lasts about two minutes, but field tests show an average hit probability of ninety-two percent against targets in the open, even those taking evasive maneuvers. So that's fourteen hundred and thirty-five hits, plus any collateral damage from grenade frag. It's mostly an APERS weapon but does have fifteen antiarmor grenades and ten incendiaries." Everyone had gathered around before he was done talking. Even Rahul had come through.

"I want to have sex with it," Bart said. "And by 'sex' I mean 'kill lots of people.'"

"Just so you know how well designed it is," Jason added, grinning at the joke, "the capacitors last *ten* minutes at full rate."

That was good, Aramis thought. "Do we have a charger?" he asked.

"And a spare capacitor, too. Let's try a dry test. Bart, would you?"

Bart grinned a huge grin and hefted the backpack ensemble up with a flex of muscle.

Aramis helped fasten lateral straps and shift it as Jason plugged connections and adjusted sensors, then slipped on the headband with its visor.

"Now, with no ammo on board, press the Test button."

Bart nodded, took one joystick control in each hand, and turned carefully. Even with his mass and slightly lower than his normal G, the thing was a chore.

Jason referenced the user info on the included scrollpad. "Using the selector at left, designate Aramis as a threat."

"Why does it always have to be me?" Aramis laughed nervously.

"I have done so," Bart said.

"Now release, turn around, and freeze program."

"Check."

"Now, everyone stand over here," Jason said. The group nervously complied, standing in one rank across the floor. Jason looked things over, nodded, and read again. "Select All Weapons and then unfreeze."

There was a sudden snapping sound, and the necks snaked around like the mythical Medusa it was named after. Aramis looked straight into five barrels. He gulped. Each of them had a perfect point of aim, it seemed from here. No one else was targeted. There were sighs and shifting. Bart turned his back and the necks swiveled to keep Aramis bore-sighted.

"Now select All Threats."

The snapping sound repeated and each barrel sought a different target. A collective stiffening jerk swept across them.

"Deselect Elke by eye."

One barrel shifted and doubled up on Rahul, who was the largest present.

"Oh, thank you," he said looking shocked and amused behind his graying beard, as Bart turned around again and the barrels stayed oriented.

"We're done," Jason grinned.

"Perhaps, but I want to do it again," Bart grinned. "When do we get to use it?"

"Only in a last-ditch scenario," Alex said. "Sorry."

"I will pray for you," Rahul offered.

"I will help set it up," Aramis said. Yes, this was going to be a fun day after all.

"We've had a number of attacks," deWitt said as the morning meeting started.

"We have," Alex agreed. "And I want to credit the Army and AF for providing good intel and good reactions. I'd also like the attacks to stop."

"There is a large amount of unrest in this sector," Weygandt said, looking slightly defiant. "Which is what a great many people predicted about the President. He's seen as weak, as a sellout, and as biased. Sorry, sir."

Bishwanath said, "I am aware of that perception. It is not helped by constant undermining of my position by certain elements."

"You mean leMieure," deWitt said, "and I agree. But I can't talk to him, you have to do it."

"I've tried. Not only is it unpleasant to breathe the same air as he, he acts as if I am ignorant and unschooled. The arrogance is appalling."

"'Conceit,' please, sir," Weilhung said.

"Major?" Bishwanath looked puzzled.

"Conceit is bragging of traits one would like to possess. Arrogance is when you can back it up. Agent Marlow and I are arrogant, and brush each other over it. LeMieure is less than that."

"And that is all we can say on this," Weygandt said, looking uncomfortable.

"Indeed," said Bishwanath. "I will handle the politics. Tell me what I need to know of the military matters."

"I want to know why the escalation," Alex demanded. "We've

gone from random fire to dedicated, then from attacking the President's political position through nearby infrastructure, to military attacks. It takes time to set these things up. It takes money and brains. It takes intel, and that means someone from off planet with access to our commo."

White said, "I agree, but there are no physical leaks to my commo. At all."

"Not my people," Weilhung said. "I guarantee it."

"Do you?" Alex asked. He didn't mean to sound confrontational, but there it was.

"I do," Weilhung said, eyes cold. "I have even made occasional checks with false intel, to set up ambushes where I had another team waiting to smash it. Nothing."

"Fair enough, I believe you." That was good thinking.

DeWitt shrugged as everyone looked at him. "You have my assurance, for what it's worth, but I only speak for me and three processors under me. There are a lot of people in BuState, and a lot of them have the schedules of events. That leaves only getting the intel of which route . . . and there aren't that many routes."

Weygandt said, "Of course, you know with my background I wouldn't dare." It sounded weaselly, but it was true. The man was a lawyer and knew exactly how bad it would be for his military and future civil careers. He'd be sacrificed in a second and burned.

Alex speculated the leak was leMieure . . . but even that wasn't sure. The man was disgusting, but no tactical thinker. He might be part of it, almost certainly was, and untouchable. He, however, was not smart enough to have any firsthand knowledge of anything going down. Beyond that was the seething morass of civilian management of Army, AF, BuState, Commerce, several local factions with off-planet interests . . . nothing anyone here could do anything about, and something that would take an independent auditor weeks or months to dig up.

"It's definitely making the news, being used against SecGen, against the Army, against you," he said, indicating Alex. "Hell, against everyone."

"Is the press doing it?" Alex asked, and conversation stopped.

Finally, Weygandt said, "No."

"No?"

The man sipped his coffee and shook his head. "No, the press are . . . not helpful. But their whole MO is to stand back and stir through people's images, then glean more ratings. If they had a leak, they'd be publicizing the fact and scooping each other. That's how they think. They're just not that subtle. But it might be a good idea for Major Weilhung to help me clear my own office," he said with some embarrassment.

"I'll arrange a scan, too," White said.

"I agree the press would not do so," Bishwanath said. "They are even friendly to me personally. I am, after all, ratings for them. They would not attempt to prevent or inform anyone of such an event, though."

"So we carry on as we have," Alex said. He felt tired. "If anyone has any ideas, can we agree to share them all around? We have our issues with each other, but it would be nice to get the job done. We can fight over credit later. It's safer than fighting over blame."

"I agree," Weilhung said with a nod.

"Yes." "Sure." "You know I have been." "Point."

They were all in agreement.

But I'm still not telling you where the explosives are hidden, Alex thought. Not until this was over.

Another day, another escort, Horace thought. The routine ones were not troublesome, merely work with a low-level threat all around. That was the justification for half their pay, he figured. The other half of the pay was for the ninety seconds here and there where the entire world was trying to kill them.

He hoped this return trip would avoid one of those sessions, but it wasn't guaranteed at this point. The loitering crowds were increasing, and there'd been a few tossed rocks as they left in the morning.

"The plaza is bad," Alex said.

"Yes, they really don't look happy out there," Horace replied, squinting. He wasn't looking out a window. He had a camera view from the palace relayed through to Alex's computer.

"Increasing riots and protests," Elke said. "And all of it focused here."

"The President has offered them a scapegoat," Bart said.

"I really recommend finding another way back," Aramis said. He looked nervous, and wasn't joking around. In fact, he was carefully checking over some of the weapons.

"Nope, it's on," Alex said. "Just have to drive through the crowd without killing anyone. The press will be watching. They love crowd scenes."

"Can we use tear gas to clear a route?" Jason asked.

"I agree with that," Horace said. "Better to make them cry than run over them."

"I'll ask," Alex said. He didn't look happy. He might need some stress medication, since drink and sex were not options.

"Can we divert and air evac?" Jason asked.

"Trying," Alex said with a bit more strain evident. He had a lot of people demanding answers, including someone on the phone. "Yes. Thank you, sir, and fuck them very much." He clicked his phone off and sighed. "BuState refuses to cough up for air support. The military won't do it *unless* we are in a fight. I had Massa check with our people and other contractors. Nothing. There isn't enough air support on this planet, because the government doesn't want to 'escalate the intensity' of the conflict."

"So we have to drive in?" Aramis asked, sounding disgusted.

"Yup. I did ask for tear gas. Weilhung agrees with me," he said. "DeWitt does not, for perception reasons, but agrees it's a logical choice on our part. Higher up, leMieure has accused us of germ warfare and terrorism, without seeming clear on what those words mean."

"So we aren't doing it?" Aramis asked.

"We are doing it," Alex nodded. "It took a call to a general, but we're doing it."

"Excellent."

"I, too, wonder at the repercussions," Horace sighed. "Mobs don't react well to much of anything, and we can't shoot them all."

"I believe that is the fundamental issue we face," Elke said. Though she didn't seem to have her usual wit about the statement. She was stroking her riot gun. She seemed to expect to use it.

All convoy drivers called and cleared, and the vehicles moved out in close order, a bare two meters apart. Once in the plaza proper, they closed up to a meter. Progress was slow.

People crowded in close as they drove by. Ahead, the relayed camera images showed the Marines, Norwegians, and Indian troops at the gate having a hard time keeping control.

There were definitely cameras on them, and the crowd was not nice. Nor was it organized, but it seemed to be an entity of its own. As people crushed up against the cars, others moved in front until the convoy slowed to a stop. Rioters beat and rocked the massively armored limos, spray painted them, which would just hose off the molecular-painted surface, tossed rocks, screamed epithets, and raised misspelled banners. Everyone clutched at weapons and prepared to fight if the vehicles were breached. Nothing seen so far was even close to a serious threat, but it wasn't impossible that there was a rocket launcher out there . . . and a limo was not a tank.

They crept forward a bit more, almost touching bumpers, while the crowd milled about in a psychologically driven Brownian motion, depending on anger, ego, or machismo.

Then a loud hiss and a roiling transparent mist of gas caused screams of panic. A large bubble opened in the crowd and they tried to advance.

And stopped.

"Mama, this is Playwright, what's the problem, over?" Alex asked.

"Bodies in the road," Weilhung replied. "Got to wait for them to move. We can't run them over . . . over."

"Understood, over. Shit."

It wasn't unpredictable. People on foot could be pushed aside by slow pressure. Even a moderate speed would cause injury, but they'd clear the route. Once the vehicles stopped, there was no practical or moral way to drive over the gasping gas victims. The convoy was effectively stopped a mere five hundred meters from the palace. No one had anticipated the crowd being that tight.

Horace realized he was going to be administering a lot of aid before this was over.

"What do we do?" Jason asked. "Sit and wait? Drive on? Call for the Army?"

"Stand by. Conference," Alex said.

He conferred by encrypted phone for security. Meanwhile, Horace watched the crowd gather its small wits and great anger and swarm back in. They were close to each vehicle and beat on them like drums. The limo rocked with pounding noises, and Alex had to shout, and demand that the other speakers shout, even with the soundproofing and armor. Bishwanath was silent, motionless apart from a quiver, and wide-eyed.

Then flaming fuel was dumped on the hood.

A quick whoosh from the vehicle's engine fire suppression system stopped that, but it was only an indicator of how much worse things were going to be.

They sat for eighteen minutes by Horace's watch, sweat dripping despite the air-conditioning, watching the crowd close in. Some had even licked the glass obscenely. Now several were urinating on the car. Horace decided there was a strong danger of brutality and rape if the cars were breached, and it wouldn't just be Elke.

This wasn't a simple riot. It was a massive uprising. There weren't that many firearms in this immediate area, but there were thrown rocks, sticks, spears of wood or pipe with machined metal heads, flails made from plumbing pipe joints and chain, shields of plywood and sheet metal . . . it looked like something from a medieval documentary.

The Recon troops atop their vehicles were nervous. This was something they were trained for, but at present lacked the equipment for. The Hate Truck couldn't handle more than a couple of hundred at most, and there were *thousands* of rebels here. Even if they emptied their weapons, there'd still be over a thousand, assuming perfect accuracy.

"There are no nearby units," Alex said, sounding amazed and disgusted. "Between the uprising out west, the battle in the north side, and some attacks on the base, no one can get here in the next thirty minutes."

"How inconvenient," Horace said. "Do we think it's accidental?"

"Weilhung does," Alex sighed. "He said no schedule was changed. He thinks and I agree that it's a combination of piss poor planning, a fear of doing anything to the poor people, and plain old apathy."

The radio spoke, "We're going after gunmen and major threats. You're in charge of the kitchen. Confirm."

"Roger, Mama, good luck." He looked around. "We retreat toward the palace. On foot and through obstacles if needed."

"Roger that."

He looked at Horace and Jason while dialing the others in on air. Then he faced Bishwanath. "Sir, we're going to pop smoke—gas—again. We're going to dismount, after it's thinned out but probably before it's all gone, so we're going masked. Then we're going back to the palace with you in the middle. Would you like a weapon?"

Bishwanath shook his head. "I would greatly appreciate one, but if it comes down to that, history will treat me badly enough as it is."

"That's an interesting choice, sir," Jason said. He didn't push the issue. Horace wasn't going to call him an idealistic bloody idiot, but the thought did come to mind.

"I'm waiting for the right position in the crowd, based on what Recon shows of the route back the way we came. Also, they're going to toss gas back along that line. Recon will also dismount and act as support and decoys."

"Roger." "Understood."

Bishwanath nodded and said, "Thank you for your efforts." He sounded very fatalistic.

"We're not dead yet, sir," Alex said with a grin. He didn't look up from the screen, though, where he was monitoring movement.

Horace checked his kit and shouldered it, and checked his weapons. He grabbed a spare magazine for his off hand to speed reloads, and set everything down while he donned his protective mask. Those would hinder visibility and breathing, thus increasing the likelihood of casualties. Casualties on their side. There were definitely going to be casualties on the other side.

With everyone ready, it came down to waiting again. This time, it was much shorter. In only forty-five seconds, Alex said, "On three."

Gas whooshed out and sent the crowd leaping back in a crush into itself, as he said, "One."

"Two," and Horace clutched the door handle, foot up and ready to kick, then . . .

"Three."

He pulled and kicked, leaned out and dumped one of the cheap H&Ks into the ground, moving the burst toward the crowd but around downed rioters, who were clutching at faces and throats and strangling on saliva. No need to add to the body count.

He drew Bishwanath out as Jason bounded over the top and jumped down next to them with a grunt. Then Alex was with them and the others from the front limo, with Rahul. Rahul wore military body armor, a submachine gun, and a huge grin inside his mask.

"It is time for some payback," he said.

The gas shells were still bursting along the road, clearing a corridor for them to advance. They started at once, not waiting for the Recon element.

He realized in seconds that the mask was going to make him one of the casualties. He simply couldn't draw enough air in. With the crowd back and disoriented, he reached up and loosened a chin strap until he could feel cool air blowing past his chin. He'd open his jaw to block the flow if he caught a whiff of gas, and this was only an irritant, not full-blown incapacitating agent.

Aramis was scared. There was a very real possibility of being ripped to pieces, literally. That wasn't glamorous and would be very painful. They were on their own, with the Recon unit forming up behind them to make its own advance.

He, Bart, and Elke were advancing from their limo, with Rahul bounding alongside, a broad man who'd make a broad bullet stop. He seemed decent.

"Shoulder to shoulder assholes," Jason said on air, apparently not caring if he was heard. "Makes targeting easy."

"Yeah, I figure anyone in this mix is a hostile," Alex said.

Needing to say something, Aramis said, "Let's hope they figure that out."

"I'll keep them distracted," Elke said.

"Elke, if you're handling demo, can I get the shotgun?" Aramis asked. He wanted a bigger gun, dammit.

"Sure," she agreed. "Standard shot, frag, breacher, and recon loads are in the cassette."

"Got it," he said, taking it as she unslung it. "More firepower now, and maybe we'll need less later."

The mob retreated slightly, forming a ring around the line of gas and daring each other, shouting, building to a frenzy. Soon they'd attack, and if there was no way through or backup, it would get really ugly.

They made a hundred meters, the gas effect and the threat of death working to keep the riot back. Once in a while, a wiggling victim on the ground would try to tackle one of them and earn a vicious but professional kick. Most of the crowd was male, mostly younger, almost all underfed. One on one, even ten on one, no problem. Aramis moved at a moderate jog at this pace, which was frustratingly slow; he wanted to sprint, but their speed was predicated by the capabilities of their principal. Elke carefully tossed bombs that were definitely loud, all concussion. Anyone within a few meters jerked and shied from her toys.

Aramis shot past the head of someone who was getting too aggressive with his club waving. The shotgun beat his shoulder, and he idly wondered what the heavy shot would do when it fell from the sky? Likely less than a carbine round would.

He'd have to watch his ammo. The shotgun cassette held twenty, and Elke would not want it left behind. She was very enamored of it.

He'd gotten used to Boblight, but with gas and the mask, it looked quite a bit more orange. It wasn't close to red, but it seemed to indicate a bloodiness anyway. Weird. His mental state couldn't be helping. He made sure he wasn't tunneling; his vision was clear.

Calm, he urged himself.

They thumped over the ground, eating up distance. While their footwear looked like classy dress shoes from a distance, they were very agile military boots underneath. Those were one of the expenses they had to cover out of pocket, but it was well worth it. After this, however, they were all going to be scuffed and ugly. Jason already had marred his with blood. Aramis's mind hit him again, wondering about suing the asshole who dared bleed on his expensive shoes. It was a cruel but entertaining thought.

The bubbles were eerie. Chanting, screaming people throwing stuff, most of it falling short, though he did have to dodge a brickbat or two, and then this safe zone with just a few on the ground, now slowly recovering and standing. One rose not too far ahead, and Aramis leaned over, thrust out his fist and bashed the shotgun butt into his face. Down he went again.

But the bubbles were collapsing quickly, and they were nearing maximum range that those shells could reach. The vehicle crews should be bailing out now, hopefully, and would be en route as a mass formation.

Whose worthless fucking idea had it been to dispense with air cover and support elements? It was as if they wanted Bishwanath dead.

Did they?

Then they were approaching the wall, because the gate was blocked. Not only was there the entry control barricade the military had, there was that crowd of rioters. Alex led the way straight to the wall, but the safe zone was getting smaller. Rapidly. Elke kept tossing explosives, but there was a practical limit being reached.

The bodies were moving in, some topless, some in work clothes, a guy who almost made a really good-looking girl wearing a dress, which meant Aramis was going to have to scrub his brain out again.

Jason and Bart pulled out canisters of tear gas, but even the military grade stuff they carried was good for no more than twenty full shots.

"Think I can open a hole if I have a few seconds," Elke said.

Bart said, "I've got the grenade launcher, too."

"How about it, boss?" Aramis asked Alex.

"Yeah, good idea. Elke, blow a channel, and we'll hold on the far side."

Elke dodged under Bart's arm and got ready to throw another downsized grenade. She hated that. This called for shaped charges and frag to shred people into a state of fear, but they had to be nice. She didn't like the mask and the exertion was rough.

Someone shot far too close to her. She tracked the shot, identified the man, and pulled a premade device off her harness. Leaning back, she pitched it like a baseball. The device was a plastic missile with fins to stabilize it and it corkscrewed in to a perfect impact on his chest, where it blew bloody gobbets out the back.

Now *that* was sexy, she thought.

"What the hell was that?" Aramis shouted next to her.

"Father Christmas brought him bullets for Christmas," she said. "He brought *me* Composition G."

"I swear, Elke," Aramis returned as he fired another slug and she tossed her next flash charge, "you like that stuff far too much. Do you make dildos out of it?"

"No, it's too soft and oily, and toxic," she said to annoy him, admitting she had considered it once. "Or I wouldn't need men."

Aramis moved in front of her and kept shooting. She was glad of it. He was eager to use the shotgun, and it was visible and loud. That was the primary thing. Not bodies. Fear. She drew a breaching charge from her ruck, pinned it on the wall where it would do the most good and shifted sideways. There was no good place for cover, and this was going to hurt.

"We need a few meters lateral so they can blow," she said.

Aramis shouted, "Elke, all I've got is the recon rounds. Do we need recon? Can I use them as slugs?"

Leaning back, she said, "They'll work as slugs. Not quite as much impact, but they'll be fine against unarmored skinnies." She bent to skate a flat pack under the crowd's feet where it would cause some nasty lacerations.

"Roger," he said.

"And move!" Alex ordered.

Up, light suppressing fire all around, skip forward. Ensure the rear, which was now their left side, stayed back so they weren't squashed. Dammit, a good series of real blasts and bursts would have sent the survivors running.

"*Fire in the—*" Elke said, with the *hole* drowned by the detonation. The thick wall collapsed into a heap that wasn't much easier to cross. It had been built to take explosive. Alex and Jason raised their grenade launchers and shot into the pile. Two clattering booms, a substantial slump of rubble, and the hole was crossable.

Turn and run, with Aramis shooting right past her shoulder. Bishwanath was urged through the hole by Bart and Rahul. All looked a bit stunned. Bart and Rahul must have been up close and protecting the President with their armor and bulk . . . and Rahul had the umbrella opened. Smart man. He tossed it at someone, who clutched at it as some kind of trophy, waving it madly.

Aramis must have hit someone center mass. Her glasses lit up with the ghost image from the slug's camera. She saw a gawpy mess in thermal, with pulsing waves that had to be an internal organ of some description. The image overlaid the real scene in front of her.

"Oh, I did not need to see that," she said, shaking off nausea and wiping her hand over the switch that cut imagery.

Then they were through and into the palace grounds.

Skinnies were pouring over the wall, disregarding the wire. Nor did the voltage seem to bother them. They were pouring in several places . . . bad. Very bad.

"Into the hutch!" Alex shouted, pointing at a maintenance shed with a lovely, carved façade and neat landscaping.

Bart shoved Bishwanath in and they fanned out to protect it. Alex screamed to Weilhung.

"Dammit, we're in this location, mark. Lethal force is essential, and that's for you. We're already using it! I need a path to the building or a squad on my location now with support weapons. Move! Over."

Elke shot one with her pistol. There weren't a lot advancing yet. They did respect the weapons the team held, but they were growing in number. It was easy, she reflected, for those in the rear to be brave with the lives of those in front. And hurled rocks were always unafraid. She dodged a brick torn from the wall.

Alex felt panic. He locked it down and carried on. They wouldn't die. Lots of ammo, deadly force authorized, adequate defensive position with backup en route. All cool, except for those two guys running in tossing rocks and dodging, acting as if they'd faced troops before. He raised his carbine to shoot.

He heard the ear-stabbing scream of a small motorcycle being revved.

No, not a motorcycle. Bishwanath burst out of the utility building with a fifty-centimeter chain saw, screaming threats and profanities in three languages.

For a moment, Alex thought he was the target and his guts clenched, bowels trying to empty themselves.

Then the President was past him and caught one of the mob across the chin with the zinging metal blade. The resultant scream was louder than the small engine, and blood and bone splashed for a second as the victim dropped, kicking, crying, blubbering, and thrashing in convulsions.

With that, the rest of the toughs disappeared, sprinting to do credit to Olympic athletes, weapons abandoned behind them.

Alex was shaking, shuddering, and couldn't speak. He pointed at the gyrating casualty and Shaman stepped forward. He glanced Bishwanath over, nodded, and proceeded to the bloody mess.

Bishwanath was greasy and dusty but unhurt. He switched off the saw and placed it down. The capacitor latch was loose. He'd had to force the old one out for a fresh one, Alex saw.

"Chain saw?" Alex asked, trying to sound relaxed. *Holy shit. A fucking chain saw!*

"It was that or a pickax. This took longer, but I decided the delay was worth the psychological effect." His voice was muffled by the mask. He raised his hands as Elke patted him down for wounds.

"Indeed." There wasn't much more to say, and the screams weren't getting quieter. Generally, you didn't want the principal to try to help. Best if they just went limp and let you move them as needed. In this case, however, the help had been quite useful and clearly thought out.

The victim shrieked and screamed, but lost consciousness quickly. Shaman shook mystical powders into the air and chanted something. So far, all he'd done for treatment was to pour alcohol onto the wound. Or maybe it was peroxide—it foamed, and burbled up pink with spots of oil. That had to be one of the more gruesome wounds Alex had ever seen. Flesh was ripped and shiny white, fresh-cut bone exposed. Teeth, too.

"Aramis, stay here, deliver the prisoner to Weilhung when done. Bart, Jason, get the door. Elke, we're taking Dishwasher inside." They moved at once, up the hill, over the rock garden that had been one of the reasons for taking cover, because it would have been a pain to tackle, and then across the cleared green grass. "Unmask," he ordered, and gratefully tore the rubber octopus off his face. It was greased with sweat.

They entered the building as a rotating mechanism of pointed weapons with Bishwanath as the hub. Everyone took a deep breath.

"Okay, we're going to have regular soldiers here now, as we should have," Alex said.

"Yes, we must," Bishwanath agreed. "Though I fear the insult it offers, as valid as it is, will make things worse."

"It can't get much worse than this, sir," Alex said. "But I am seriously fucking impressed, pardon my language. That was awesome thinking, and fast, and just what we needed."

"Yes. Will the man survive?"

"Huh?" It took Alex a moment to decipher that. "Uh, if he can be saved, Shaman will do it. He didn't look to have suffered any life-threatening wounds. You missed the subclavian and carotid arteries and it didn't look as if you got the lungs. What I saw was just horrifyingly messy, disfiguring, and painful for weeks on end."

"That is unfortunate," Bishwanath sighed, looking sad.

"Sir, no offense, but he tried to kill you, and not even man to man. He brought five thousand of his cowardly friends with him because he couldn't do the job alone. He's just a punk from a mob."

"Yes, and I will gain much credit for fighting as I did in some groups, and be reviled as unmanly in others. A good treatment for him is diplomatic."

"If he can be saved, Shaman will save him. He just won't be gentle about it. You can ensure he gets . . . sir, are you okay?" He suddenly interrupted himself because Bishwanath was shaking like a rattle. Heart?

"Stress," Bishwanath nodded. "Weak, faint." He was pouring sweat and looking pallorous.

Elke and Jason each grabbed an arm, raised it, and started running, Bishwanath's toes barely brushing the ground. Alex passed them to get the door, only to be beaten by Rahul. The man was bearlike but fast.

"White, anyone with AF, I need help now! Recon, medic, anyone!" He shouted as well as transmitted, because he believed it was stress. He also knew it might not be, and had to be handled at once.

Up the elevator, as Jason slapped a sensor on Bishwanath's neck. The fat little black case matched the supplemental earbud he clapped to his ear.

"Pulse rapid but strong, breath shallow and fast, blood pressure high," he reported aloud. "Getting heart . . . rapid, fluttery."

"Fluttery's bad?"

"Can be. Isn't always. Consistent with stress and shock."

"Arriving," Elke said.

The door opened and they ran, as two AF personnel came down the hall the other way at a steep sprint. One was Sergeant Buckley, but he didn't recognize the other. Buckley had a medkit, half open and was already reaching into it.

Elke stretched out and coded the door with a swipe, kicked it open as the latch clicked, and led the way to the couch. She ran around the back, Jason twisted under Bishwanath's shoulders as Alex lifted his legs. Elke reached over from the back, grabbed his suit and split it, buttons popping, then ripped his shirt. The sheen of sweat could be seen on the skin here, along with a variety of scars. Yes, this man had been in other fights.

But those were years past, and this was now. He wasn't young, was taking a physical and emotional beating, and might be dying.

They were out of the way before Buckley could say anything.

He slipped between them, skidded to his knees and slapped his own earbud in and sensor on Bishwanath in one motion.

Horace demanded an update as soon as he heard. The punk on the grass had suffered no life-threatening injury, though he would have gruesome scar tissue inside and out of his mouth, with some loss of jaw function. His gums were a torn mess. Truly, it was disturbing.

"And what of the President?" he asked again as he entered the room.

"Hyperventilation," Buckley said, standing to face him. "He was breathing hard, and taking the mask off dramatically increased available oxygen. Especially as the partial pressure here is a little higher than either Earth or the high-altitude district he comes from. He'll be fine."

"Excellent," he nodded. "You will understand that I will confirm your diagnosis?"

Buckley grinned. "Of course. Rahul found him a mild sedative and I approved it. He is awake but resting."

Things had to be bad if Alex authorized a drink, Bart thought. Though two good shots did make him feel a little more relaxed. For now, the grounds were crawling with soldiers, while an engineer unit threw up a berm and some defensive positions. The wall was being reinforced, too, and the voltage increased from an annoying level to one that was lethal with the current involved. The military hadn't been hard to convince. BuState was, as always, the peaceninnies who prevented things from proceeding.

"Everyone ready?" Alex asked, indicating their computers. Bart sighed, as did the rest. Lethal force had been used, and now they had to do the paperwork. Rounds fired, hits made, warning shots . . . Elke's video from the time they hit the gate on departure was running on the wall, edited to chop out the time waiting in the car. Time ticks showed when gas was first used, when they debarked the vehicles, and her POV moving back to the palace, with occasional sweeps to take in the others. That, and radio records plus audio would allow reconstruction of the events. It was necessary, but not something Bart cherished after a fight with a mob.

It took two hours and one more grudgingly authorized drink

to come up with a review that would be satisfactory to BuState, Army, and Corporate. Luckily, he had shot only one man at the shed, and none on the way in. He wondered if he'd be criticized more for the probably lethal hit, or for the forty-seven rounds of cover fire he had expended. At this point he didn't care.

"The next week is cancelled," Alex told them after they'd all rolled through and gotten the info swaps they needed. "All events are moved here. We will be doing boring-ass guard duty outside his apartment door and standing behind him at the conference table downstairs."

"That actually sounds good," Aramis commented.

Bart wasn't so sure. Safe got boring in a hurry. He knew that from backstage work.

"We'll kick it over in the morning," Alex said. "For now, great job of protection, everyone is healthy, and it's time to sleep."

"I will cover first shift," Bart volunteered.

"Thanks," Alex acknowledged. "Take your time in the morning."

"I will." He needed to stay up for now. There was a lot to think about.

CHAPTER SEVENTEEN

Nice of those contract assholes to kill protestors," leMieure bitched.

Weygandt almost laughed. He figured their mistake was in not killing a lot more. Which was the problem with having BuState lay down wimpy regulations. Real soldiers would have handled it faster. The Recon unit, with all its weapons, had not been molested to speak of. They'd killed a few, but that was also charged off to the contractors for stirring the pot. On the whole, it kept getting better for the Army with this fat clown trying to run things. That would be the case until he started getting soldiers killed. Then he'd have to go. Weygandt had his own emergency procedures for that.

That he refused to meet with troops, whom he referred to as "those filthy dropouts and macho-laden fools," or contractors, whom he didn't deign to gift with an epithet, said lots. A presidential appointment didn't make him anything other than a glory-seeking suck-up.

A dangerous one. Who was still ranting.

"I don't suppose anyone has thought of treating these people like human beings, with respect and dignity."

Bishwanath's been doing that, Weygandt sneered silently. *Look what it's getting him.*

"The problem is, I can't pull their contract. Not yet."

That was interesting. So the man was tied by authority or necessity he wasn't admitting. However . . .

"What can I do to assist with that?" It wasn't that he hated the contractors personally, but they were in the way, played fast and loose, and the conflict between BuState and Mil would be much easier with them gone.

"I need reports that show them for what they are," leMieure said with a grin. "Every bent rule, illicit purchase, foul insult, everything. You were supposed to help with that."

"The information is coming." Weygandt smiled. Everyone always had a stack of violations, if you cared to list them. The problem was finding anyone to waste the time on bullshit. If this man liked the taste of bullshit, Weygandt would serve him a feast.

"I do not believe we are going to try this again," Aramis muttered.

"I do," Jason snickered. "And I have to hand it to you, sir," he said to the President. "You've got guts."

Bishwanath shrugged. "I do what I must. If I hide, then I have lost any hope of accomplishing my task."

Everyone was speaking into headsets. This trip was being made in an armored car. Bishwanath had acceded to the need, and even that fat asshole from BuState had approved. Of course, he claimed credit for it, even though it had been deWitt who'd promoted it.

It was obvious though, Alex realized, that the plan was to make the team redundant. They were in a military vehicle, surrounded by military personnel. Most of them were not trained to do EP, but that was a fine point most people wouldn't recognize. The next step would be to put Recon troops in suits and have them replace the team. He hated to fight against a rational idea, but he was in the process of doing so. He was on the phone with District Agent in Charge Massa.

"We do have our own armored transport. I'll be getting it there ASAP. You made the right call, but we've got to get on it quickly, or our whole justification disappears." It was odd, hearing a voice clearly in one ear and engine rumble in the other.

"Right," Alex replied, "image versus reality, with image managed by BuState, the press, and the military."

"We knew from the beginning this would happen. Put on the best show you can. You say the President does believe in us?"

"Absolutely, sir. All the way," Alex said.

"Roger. I'll work that angle. Also that we cut soldiers loose to be soldiers, not guards. Cady is promoting the BuCommerce mission she has. Apparently, the Army hadn't considered it would have to guard playboy investors, but seems to think that will lead to more chicks. I'm sure the investors are playing that angle, but they'll never deliver women to anyone below general rank."

"Yes, sir. I think they want to hog it all. If we were contracted through MilBu, it might not be so bad."

"But we'd be stuck using their doctrine. Thwack, ugh, hit hard with hammer. Even Recon suffers from that." Massa sounded a bit derogatory, but who could blame him? And he'd been Recon.

"That they do, sir. Anything specific for this run? We're getting close now."

"Keep close in, and try to exercise more solitary protection."

"Yeah." Alex grimaced. Don't call for backup. Prove you could do it alone. That wasn't a great idea operationally.

"Yeah, I know," Massa said, reading his tone. "Look, you work that end, I'll work this end. I think we'll hold onto the lower echelon contracts regardless."

"Roger. Got to get to work. Later."

"Out."

"Three minutes. Look sharp," he said. There was a clatter of weapons checks. He faced Bishwanath and said, "We're going to stick around as long you need us, sir."

"Glad to hear it," Bishwanath replied. "I like the professional and nonmilitary presence you offer."

"We try." *And we'll keep trying. We* are *civilians. Of a sort.*

The vehicle was pulling up in front of the rebuilt National Building. Bishwanath was going to address the council in its home space, which was big news. That meant it was likely going to be disrupted. Alex had everyone in hard armor, no matter how bulky, because they might have to throw themselves in front of any threats inside.

"Arriving," the driver said.

"Roger. Everyone stand by."

They vibrated to a stop and Jason grasped the latch. At Alex's nod, he opened the gate and let the hydraulics run it down. He didn't realize how hot it had been until he felt the breeze outside. They were all soaked with sweat.

They formed a block with Bishwanath in the middle and strode down the rough-textured ramp, standing up as they exited and giving him just enough clear space to wave. There was a cordon set, and a red carpet laid out for this occasion. Several councilmen were on the steps applauding, being seen, including Mister Dhe, who looked almost sober and regretting it.

"Go," Alex ordered, and they stepped forward and into the street.

An explosion rocked the air.

And the ground.

Jason and Bart hugged the President, shielding him front and back from any fragments. Aramis and Shaman maneuvered the huddle toward the ramp. Elke and Alex shifted around to keep the area clear, and backed in last, after the other five. A gale whipped through the streets, and drove dust into tiny bullets that stung and bit Alex's skin. The crowd disappeared shrieking, while the video crews turned their cameras toward the source of the blast, past the front of the APC.

As Alex closed the door, trash and litter roiled past in a wave. The armor clanked reassuringly into place.

The heavy armored vehicle was shaking.

"Holy shit, that was a blast. Elke?"

"There." She plugged in, zipped up her computer, and scanned the image on her screen from the vehicle's panorama. She pointed. "Building coming down."

"Fuck. I take it that's from a volunteer demolition agency?" Aramis asked.

"It's nothing I know about," Alex admitted. The building turned into a collapsing pillar of debris under a veil of smoke and dust.

"Back to the palace," Alex told the driver. "We're not going anywhere until it's safer. Shaman?"

"He's fine," Shaman nodded. "Sir, you're fine," he said.

"Yes, thank you." Bishwanath was pale, almost ashen. "I agree. I'll go back for now." He paused for a moment. "If you don't mind, I'd appreciate some company in my apartment for the time being."

He was admitting to being scared, and it was hard to blame him. The explosion had been beyond anything they'd ever felt and it had been *close*. Bomb? Missile? No way to tell yet.

Alex got on the phone. He had to dial power up enough he should have been able to reach orbit in order to get hold of a nearby antenna. *Must be a lot of metal in the air, or static from the dust*, he thought.

"Playwright here. I want to know what happened when you can. I understand military takes priority, but I have the President here. Yes, he seems fine." The conversation was largely straightforward, but it was aggravating. There was a procedure to follow, and he was on the list, but he had to wait his turn.

Then he called back to Massa.

"Explosion, big one, just nearby. One important note: Dhe and others were there. They're not the martyr type. So some outside agency was doing this."

"Makes sense. I'll start digging. Well done."

"We'll be at the palace. No one is taking this man anywhere for now. That's per me." He was very firm. Between shock, fear, and professionalism, he was not in a mood to argue.

"I'll back you up." And it was great to have a boss with similar experience and feelings.

Since Cady was on planet, maybe she had something, he thought, and called.

"Cady." Fuzzy reception still. Odd.

"Jace, Alex here. The shit just hit the fan."

"Oh?"

"I was hoping you had some rumors for me." Cady was in charge of the team guarding the BuCommerce facility and all the CEOs that went with it. She should have intel if anyone did.

"Only obscene stuff about leMieure and his assistants," she giggled.

"Whatever went off here was big. Several hundred kilos or more. It took out a building. Any rumors on stuff coming in?"

The young woman snickered. "Alex, stuff comes in here by the freighter load. I can easily get you drugs, caviar, food, diamonds, women . . . men . . . sheep . . . anything except weapons, armor, or field gear. Can you be more specific?"

"I'm afraid I can't," Alex admitted. "Please keep an ear out?"

"Sure will. Hey, did you know 'infantry' is not a perverse form of adultery? And now I know."

"Cute," he grinned. Bad joke. He'd heard rumors about Cady that were rather explicit, but she lent class to them. "Take care. Marlow out."

"Cady out."

They got back inside the palace in a hurry and cleared the vehicle in pairs, rolled through the military cordon, and shifted to inside posture, carbines slung and pistols out, as they moved upstairs to Bishwanath's apartment flanked by Recon troops. It didn't seem like a drill this time. It seemed real.

Bishwanath was shaking when they got there. Alex found it easier. He had to face the prospect of catching something. Bishwanath had to realize that every incident was intended to make him dead. Enough of that would make anyone gibber.

Alex said, "In pairs, four hours, Bishwanath's apartment. Second pair sleeps on the floor, armed. Third pair down in here, but awake. Cycle Rahul in on that, and Mister President, You Will Wear A Gun."

"Sir," they chorused.

"I do appreciate it, Agent Marlow," Bishwanath said, flushing now. "But I'm not sure it's really necessary. It was just an old man's fear."

"Sir," Alex said, facing him. "It's tactically easier for us to be here, and it makes us feel better about our jobs. We'll stay close unless . . . until the situation changes. It's no bother. Really. You're a good principal and we're well paid."

"I'll do as you say," he agreed.

His phone buzzed and he keyed it, had already said, "Marlow," before he realized he had a call.

"Marlow, this is deWitt, and I've got Massa at District on conference."

"Hello," said Massa.

"What can I help with, sir?" he said to both of them. Shit, this had to be big.

"I need Sykora on the line in private at once."

"Er, yes, sir," he said, then turned and snapped, "Elke! Dial in now!"

She fumbled with a phone, looking worried. "Sykora," she said.

"Marlow, disconnect please, and secure."

"Er, check." He clicked off. Wow. Something was going down.

Elke was saying, "I can. You'll have to talk to Marlow to clear it. Yes, sir." She turned back. "Marlow, dial back in."

He clicked for connection, waited, and said, "Marlow."

"We're borrowing Sykora. Maybe twenty-four hours. Hopefully not more. We need her expertise in explosives."

"Er, yes, sir." He didn't have much choice, but was being informed as a courtesy.

She was already packed as he disconnected, with her BOB— bail-out bag, containing all her professional gear. She wore only her pistol as a weapon, but did take extra body armor. Her explosives became a neat pile in the corner, along with assorted sundries she apparently figured not to need.

"Elke, what the hell?" Alex asked as he held up a condom. There were hundreds of them in her bag. Male condoms, female, dental dams. She wasn't a nun, but she couldn't be *that* active. "Trade goods?"

"For waterproofing caps, capacitors, and charges," she replied, looking slightly flustered.

"Oh." Yes, that made perfect sense, and was likely cheaper, more flexible, and more discreet than many other methods.

"I may not answer the radio. I'll be back when we're done looking at the explosion site," she tossed over her ear as she strode through the door. That was the only mention made of what she was being called for.

Jason and Bart were on guard in the President's apartment in full gear and armed with everything except rocket launchers. Rahul and Shaman were bedding down on the couch. Alex and Aramis were in the parlor, and Elke had gone prospecting. Meantime, Alex wanted more military and more contractors around the area.

Massa was eager. "I'll see if I can promote a courtesy supplemental force. Dockery's team is available, and they're long-range shooters. They can take position against possible mortar or rocket attack."

"Right, sounds good. *Stand by, please*," he said, because something just occurred to him. He coded another number.

A voice answered, "Aerospace Force Information Assets, Palace, Sergeant Arensberg." He knew the name. One of White's opposites.

"Sergeant Arensberg, Agent in Charge Marlow. I need to know how secure we are against missile fire here."

"We're fine, sir," was the reply.

"You're sure?"

"Absolutely. We have a cone of satellite intel, a command-and-control bird, and we've got a disruption bubble overhead. The only reason your phone can reach outside is because of the antenna I've got set up at the back gate."

"Thank you," he said, much relieved. The information might not be true and might not be adequate, but from his knowledge, that meant they were doing everything they thought was effective. He'd check with Jason, though.

"You're welcome, and we appreciate the inquiry."

Dammit, those AF types were so nice. What the hell game were they playing?

He got little sleep, and Jason took his shift on guard. He wondered if he should get one of the surgically implanted phones that some execs had. This one was starting to make his ear canal itch.

He'd barely got to sleep when something happened at the door. He sprang up from the couch and jogged past Aramis and Jason to see what was up.

It was Elke. She looked exhausted and wrung out.

"You okay?" Jason asked as she came through.

"Yeah. Long day."

"Can you talk about it?" Aramis asked.

"A little," she said. "I don't see how they can keep it secret." She was stowing her bag and talking loudly to be heard.

"Keep what secret?"

"That explosion last night." And she was soaked with sweat and dust.

"Yes?" he coaxed.

"Nuke."

"Say *what*?" "*Holy SHIT!*" "You're serious?"

"Someone came up with a gravity triggered gun type compression weapon," she said.

There was silence, and then Jason asked, "Is that even possible?"

"Absolutely," she said. "They have an old fission reactor in Kaporta. It is reliable, doesn't put out as much energy as fusion, but it is simple. It is designed for enrichment for building shipboard power units, too. Someone was taking bits of HEU—enriched uranium. They are digging to find out how much now."

"I thought that stuff was accounted for?"

"Yes, but if a ship contracts a packet and doesn't use it, where does it go? That's one of the problems with private corporate craft."

"Which every second-rate nation has now, to prove they're players," Alex said.

"But how does a gravity triggered bomb work?" Shaman asked.

"Device," she corrected automatically. "Forty kilograms of HEU with a ten-centimeter tungsten carbide reflector milled at a local machine shop. If it can be assembled faster than forty-eight milliseconds, it has a better than fifty percent chance of reaching critical state. In this gravity, a five- to six-meter drop would give it a good go. Fission would be suboptimal and incomplete, but potentially greater than ten kilotonnes yield. A very dirty device. Perhaps two percent efficient, and the rest highly radioactive fallout."

"Forty kilos?" Bart sounded pained. "That's a lot of *Gott-*damned metal."

"Several loads, yes," she nodded. "They're trying to figure out who's been ordering it and not using it."

"But is that what we heard yesterday?" Jason asked. "Big, but not possibly big enough for a nuke."

"Right," she said with a nod. "It didn't achieve proper fission. Partly because they tried too hard. They added explosive to the gun to propel the assembly, and encased it in a building with enough concrete to shield it from detection. But the shot was a near-failure. The conventional detonation wave tumbled the upper hemisphere, and it struck at an angle and sheared. They got neutron emission, and it went critical but not supercritical. Add that to a lack of gas injection or implosion or any other nice thing like additional tamper and it fizzled."

"Technical crap aside, what yield?" Alex asked.

"We estimate about three hundred tonnes," she said. She looked straight at him.

"Thr— so they got a third of a kilotonne by doing everything wrong?" That was a pretty spectacular failure.

"Yes. The good news is, we don't believe they have enough material to try again soon. Most of the material is still in that building. It was shot down into a subbasement and scattered underground. Though some of it is contaminating the rubble that was thrown."

"Is there bad news?"

"It's in the press," she said with a downturned lip, pointing at the screen where "Breaking News" flashed. "And it can and will happen again. A slightly better design in a truck by the palace would have vaporized us."

Bishwanath finally spoke. "If you feel unsafe and wish to cancel our contract, I will completely understand. Taking fire in transit and during an attack where backup is expected is one thing.

Sitting with me on a nuclear weapon you can't do anything about is another."

There was brief silence and stares, then Jason shrugged for the rest and said, "Dead is dead. Bullet at long range, explosive up close, nuke across the street. There aren't any good ways of going."

"That's very brave and philosophical of you," Bishwanath said. "But we are speaking of a nuclear weapon."

"We'll stay," Aramis said. He looked very subdued and unsure, but his determination was clear. "A nuke isn't as bad as some other things."

Bart was on duty in the President's apartment waiting for his partner. Elke cleaned up and came right back on shift. He wasn't sure he blamed her. He couldn't sleep now, and he hadn't been dealing with a nuke. Not directly.

She nodded and finished gearing up. She didn't look feminine once clammed in and in a helmet. She did look deadly, though, with her shotgun slung.

"Elke, demolitions is your job, but how do you know about nukes?" he asked softly. Bishwanath was actually dozing at last.

"I was trained as a nuclear qualified munitions disposal technician," she said.

"Impressive," Bart said. "It strikes me that you should do something that pays better than just EP."

"I do get paid better than EP," she said.

"Oh."

Everyone had just assumed she was one more blaster in a field that had one for every twenty to fifty regular operators. They got a small bonus for the skill, and another for each "event" they dealt with, either setting or disposing of explosives. If Elke was a nuke, she had to be making a fortune.

Of course, for that money, all she had to do was crawl into a hole with some illiterate amateur's attempt at a nuclear device and assess or remove it as called for.

Maybe that wasn't such a great contract after all.

CHAPTER EIGHTEEN

Alex took over guard the next day, after he had crashed for ten hours. He felt guilty about it, but he'd needed it after hours of prep, dealing with a nuke, hours of conference and more maneuvering.

He'd just started to grab his armor when his phone buzzed.

"Marlow."

"Get in a private location for this discussion," Massa said.

"Stand by," he agreed, and left the room. Elke raised an eyebrow at him. He raised one back. This was an interesting occurrence. If by *interesting*, of course, one meant "probably dangerous."

"I'm secure," he said, once he was in his empty room with a security oscillator up. The gear on the desk and his baggage on the floor were the only signs of occupancy. The room was neat and decorative and he was afraid of disturbing anything.

"Please state for the record," deWitt said. Alex hadn't realized this was another conference call.

"Sure. Agent in Charge Alex Marlow, Ripple Creek Security Detail assigned to President Bishwanath, confirming a secure and scrambled connection for this conversation."

"Agent Marlow, we have a situation none of us like," Massa said formally.

"That's putting it mildly."

"You've noticed, of course, the escalation in force, from skirmishes to frontal attacks to outright mobs and now a more potent device."

"Yes, I heard about the device." If they weren't going to say *nuke* even here, he wasn't either.

"This has caused us to have a change in strategy," Massa said.

"I don't like where this is going." He was getting agitated now. They weren't just giving him orders. They were laying a lot of background. That was ass-covering.

DeWitt said, "We're pulling out and regrouping. We'll try again with a different candidate."

There were several ways to take that. None of them were good.

"Sir, I respectfully disagree."

He was cut off. DeWitt said, "Marlow, I respect your opinion. The problem is, the people calling the shots don't. They're four or five echelons up. I've got my orders, and you've got yours. You'll need to commit this to memory and not record. Ready?"

"No, sir, but I'll remember what you say. Go ahead."

Alex made notes anyway. He had a code unlikely to be broken, and unlikely to be looked for, the way he wrote it. He'd burn them later. He also recorded on a second circuit Jason had rigged up and attached through the mic jack. He wanted a record of this bullshit. They could pull his contract, but no way was he going to take any blame, or let anyone under him take any crap.

Thirty seconds later he broke his pen. It was rated for combat use, but he was gripping, pressing, crushing it in outright rage.

He said nothing until it was all done, then replied with, "Understood, sir."

DeWitt said, "Marlow, I wish I could do something. There is not a fucking thing I can do about this. I can't even get drunk over it."

"Doesn't help me at this end, sir."

"I know. If I had anything to offer, I would."

"Do you know a diplomatic way to tell them to eat shit and die, sir?"

"It would give me a warm feeling and nothing else. Sorry."

Disconnecting, Alex swore. He went on for several seconds, very ungrammatically, obscene, profane, and stuttering. This was not only unconscionable, it was . . . he didn't have words strong enough.

He walked back in to the common room and looked evenly around at everyone. They weren't going to believe this. He wasn't sure he did himself. He closed his door behind him, as if that would close him off from the conversation he'd just had.

"The President is dead," he said.

"Say again?" Jason asked.

"The President is dead," he repeated. "It went out on the news this morning. 'Died during renewed violence near the palace.'"

"He looks very much alive from here," Bart said, looking at Bishwanath.

"Only an illusion."

Aramis asked, "So what the fuck does that mean? Sorry, sir." He nodded at the President.

Bishwanath didn't say anything. He just looked tired.

"It means our contract is cancelled and we're being pulled out. BuState is working on a new concept to implement later. The Army is going to pacify the capital again."

"But there's a discrepancy between alive and dead," Shaman said. "How is that resolved?"

"I spoke to Mister deWitt. He had no information but agrees with the discrepancy. He's as pissed as we are. However, I gather that the plan is that Bishwanath *will* have died in the fighting, one way or another."

"Like that, eh?" Aramis asked.

"Like that," Alex nodded. "Major Weilhung has already been pulled, and his troops are trickling out in squads. That leaves the regular palace guards and us."

Bishwanath saw everyone looking at him and finally responded. One could only handle so many shocks, and he'd had plenty.

"Gentlemen, lady, I am sorry to have been a burden for you. You have my thanks for your exemplary and, ah, *creative* service, and I wish I could properly credit you as you deserve. Do please take my thanks . . ." He stood and offered a hand to Alex.

Alex didn't take it.

"While on contract, we have a noncompetition agreement with Ripple Creek. Currently, the six of us are off contract. As the presidential detail is no longer a RC contract, there is no competition. Would you, Mister Bishwanath, like to hire us on an interim basis to protect your person?" There was just the faintest trace of smile on his lips.

Elke and Aramis both snickered and exchanged looks. They'd come somewhat to terms, and common enemies have a way of building bonds. Bart was still reticent but cracks could be seen in the façade. Shaman chuckled deeply. Jason stifled a smile by looking away.

Bishwanath said, "I'm afraid I have no assets with which to pay you." He was smiling now, too, though his eyes were watery.

"So we'll just have to get you to where there are assets."

"Then I accept."

Alex stuck out his hand. "It is a pleasure to assist you, sir. Again."

The door opened, and Rahul came in. He held still, apparently unafraid, as six EPs holstered and slung weapons, after determining he wasn't a threat.

"I apologize but I bring bad news," he said.

"New bad news, or an update on existing bad news?" Jason asked. To the puzzled expression he said, "Never mind, what's the news?"

"The guards are leaving. Not all, but many. They are returning to their homes. They were told they would not be paid further."

"Who said that?" Bishwanath shouted. "Dammit, who said that? *I* am President and I take care of my staff! They will be paid as they deserve, and . . ." He trailed off. His face had the empty look of overpowering rage and sadness.

It struck a chord with his Alex, and from expressions, the rest. They'd all been military. They were all professionals. Certainly, the money was important, but beyond that was trust and integrity. You didn't call someone on their word without reason, and you didn't abandon your own, your mission, or your buddies for anything.

"Bad news from outside, too," Aramis said.

"What is next?" Bishwanath asked. He sounded beyond surprise.

"An angry mob with torches to see you, sir," he said and pointed.

As Bishwanath moved to look, Alex placed a hand on his shoulder and said, "Come on, sir. We have to relocate at once, and decide on a course of action. You also need to stay away from windows."

He had no idea what that course might be.

But you didn't abandon your word or your mission—or your buddy—for anything.

He brainstormed aloud. "First, we get out. Now. Grab weapons, explosives, any cash, barter goods like booze and jewelry if they're small. Whatever we can carry. Wear basic gear, carry two bags, be prepared to toss them somewhere discreet to avoid looking like we're scramming."

He didn't need to tell them to move. They were stripping the room as he started.

"Mister Bishwanath, we'll need you to help carry gear and try to look like one of us."

"Absolutely," he agreed, some color returning to his face. "May I pack a personal bag?"

"I'd really recommend not going back in your apartment, and I plan for us to leave in about three minutes. I'll have two bags for you. Jason, you're about the same size, hand him any spare gear."

"Roger. Sir, take this." Jason helped him don a vest with food and water. There was some extra ammo onboard, but Bishwanath was basically a bearer in camouflage. He had some combat experience, Alex knew, but not how extensive or how well trained. Still, anything he could carry might help.

People were zipping bags, the weapons locker was much depleted, and others were standing ready. Bart came back from the windows and observation. Jason had the rest of the weapons in pieces ready to be destroyed, with key trigger group components to scatter outside.

"Not good, boss," Bart said. Alex walked over.

It only took a few moments to ascertain the palace was surrounded by factional firefights and mobs. That trouble had been building all day, but the Army had been ordered to pull back and it was increasing.

"We are going to have to fight our way out." Bart said. "Long odds."

"What heavy gear do we have?" Alex thought aloud. "Explosives, three machine guns, an auto launcher, ten rockets..."

"The problem is," Jason said, "heavy gear for us is light for an army or a mob."

"We have the Medusa," Bart commented.

"That we do," Alex agreed. "Psychological effect. Okay..." He stared into space then continued.

"Aramis first. You're point and trip. Bart second with the Medusa to throw down fire. Mister Bishwanath will be escorted by Elke and myself...and Rahul, of course. Shaman and Jason bring up the rear. Comments?"

"If I'm to be discreet, please call me Bal," Bishwanath said quietly. He sounded scared, but he also sounded determined. From president to refugee in one phone call.

"Noted, Bal. Anyone else?"

"Sounds workable. How many vehicles?" Jason asked.

"I'd say two. It's discreet and gives us a backup."

"I concur," Bart said.

"Elke, how much boom do we have?"

"I have boom," she grinned. "Throwable, droppable, delay, remote, and some mines. I'll make more as we drive. If you can load it, I can get two hundred kilos right now. If you want to strip our emplaced stuff from down the hall, I can get another five hundred."

"Start with the two hundred," Alex said. She nodded and ran out at a double-time. "Rahul, can you perhaps get us a cart or dolly on this floor? And of course, you haven't seen the President, and are very agitated if someone asks."

"So he's not here either. This is most disturbing," Rahul muttered as he turned and slipped out.

Bishwanath said, "Young lady . . ." and she paused. ". . . Elke, am I to understand you have *half a tonne* of explosives mining my palace?"

"No, sir," she said, and he seemed to relax. "I have half a tonne in this wing. Total amount throughout the palace is one thousand, one hundred, twenty-three point seven kilos." With that, she turned and strode briskly out the door.

As she left he muttered, "I'm not sure if the exact amount reassures or scares me."

"Elke's like that," Jason said. Then he grinned. "God, I love her."

"You realize we must get through the palace and not get stopped?" Bart said.

"Yeah, that could be a problem all by itself. We don't want to fight any of our theoretically own forces." He had no idea what to do if they got caught, and he needed to. Dammit, time was short.

Alex's phone rang. He jerked, swore, fumbled it, and said, "Marlow."

"This is White. I'm coming down."

"Uh, Tech White, now is really a bad time, if you don't mind."

"Of course it's a bad time. That's why I'm coming down."

He wanted to reply but she'd gone.

"White's coming down. Everyone act casual," he said. "Bal, hide in Elke's room, please."

"Yes, sir," he said, taking orders at once in a way that surprised Alex. The man was good. Dammit, this was not only unfair, it was contemptible.

Everyone dove onto chairs and grabbed entertainment. Their timing was good. There was a knock at the door and Tech White came in. She had three men with her. A quick glance showed them to be Security Techs, in full gear with carbines and vests stuffed with ammo: Technical Sergeant Buckley, one specialist sergeant and one Tech 1. They looked nervous.

She looked around, and Alex's blood pressure spiked. He started sweating.

Calm. Calm. If they've been monitoring, nothing we can do except maneuver or fight. If not, we can bluff, as long as you look calm.

White was dressed in battle gear, too, including helmet with visor up, all quite new and hardly worn. She carried a standard rifle slung on her shoulder.

"Well, where is he?" she asked, looking around. He hoped she didn't see the microtremors on the team, who were ready to take his orders either way.

"Who?" he asked back, stalling.

She stared straight at him with an expression that would freeze lava.

"Do not tell me that the Great Operators are not prepared to help Mister Bishwanath. You're just going to leave him here? If you're not packed in six minutes, you're getting left behind."

He stared for just a moment. No, it couldn't be a setup, he decided. Too complex.

"Bal, come on out. Everyone gear up. We're rolling."

Tension defused, they exploded into action. Shaman grabbed Bishwanath, everyone started shouldering the gear they already had, and at a gesture from Alex, Bart handed over extra ammo to the STs. There was no point in leaving any behind.

"What do you have?" he asked White. She was young and not as well trained tactically, but she was obviously plugged in on intel.

"I hope you're not surprised that I can still monitor your commo," she said, taking more stuff herself. She was quite laden.

"Okay, continue." He'd known she had a back door. Who else had heard it?

"It doesn't take much to figure out what your encrypted call said, when the Recon pukes suddenly start being evasive, refusing to talk to me, don't know where the President is, have to clear the building, et cetera. They're bailing on him, yes?"

"Yes."

"I asked about escort. They invoked orders and procedure and did it badly. They know they're pussies, but they won't argue the point with their bosses. Just when I was starting to think the Army actually had some people who were good for more than breaking things." She looked disgusted. "Fuckers."

He'd never heard her swear.

"Can't really blame them on that," he said. "It would be Weil-hung's ass. His bosses are assholes."

"Bull. He can fake it. Shuffle people around, help clear the palace and the mob, damage cameras in the fighting. Right?"

Her three escorts weren't saying anything, but had the door covered. Occasional glances were all they gave to the debate.

"It's not quite that simple," Alex said. "But yes, they could."

"There's an Aerospace Force convoy coming through in a couple of hours. We're joining up with them. I reported fighting, invoked bailout procedures, and am implementing them. Obviously, any allied force is welcome to come with us. *I* have not been given any orders through my chain to abandon Mister Bishwanath. Of course, I've never been given orders to do more than coordinate with our forces." She looked a bit nervous about it, but clearly determined.

"Welcome," he said. "And thanks."

Bishwanath was too stunned to say anything. He'd lost his nation, his home, all his own people, and was now dependent for survival on mercenaries and renegade troops who regarded him as more worthy than their own orders or lives. He was still getting used to the idea that people could fight for more than their own group. These people respected him for himself, not for who he represented, and were going to risk their lives to take him to safety.

He managed a nod, and a "Thank you," and kept breathing so he'd stay responsive. His heart didn't like this, and his guts were churning. The stress was far beyond that of politics or combat.

"Can you handle a weapon?" Marlow asked.

"Not nearly so well as you can," he replied. "But I can operate one, yes."

"Hand him a carbine. Elke, how's it going?" Alex asked as she came back into the room.

"You want flames, boom, or discretion?" she asked, stacking all their computers and portables. She was going to destroy them. Tens of thousands of dollars of personal possessions they were going to destroy to keep secure. That equipment could run a major business here, but he was more important to them even than it was.

Bishwanath determined that if he did get out of this, his own life was forfeit. He could never repay a life debt. Especially as none of them had hesitated. The seven people who knew him slightly and the four he'd seen only in passing were throwing their belongings away and risking their lives and careers.

"Why?" he tried to ask.

Bart looked over at him for a moment, then said, "Because the people who play power games live for convenience instead of doing the job right. That is why they always make it bad."

The answer wasn't to the question he'd asked, but the corollary was there. These men, and woman, were more than mercenaries. Possibly no one could have their level of training without a regard for their own honor. They'd gladly kill people for money, but they were very selective about which people. Then, Miss . . . Tech White, and her three personnel were risking criminal charges and military misconduct even if they succeeded.

"Thank you all," was all he could say. He had to sit down. Too many shocks in one day.

Alex saw Bishwanath sit somewhat hard. The man was a bit pale and shaking, which was probably nerves but could also be medical. He flicked his eyes and Shaman stepped over that way with a nod.

Eyes were starting to drift that way, so he took control by saying, "What's our plan, and where is your convoy?"

"The convoy isn't coming directly to the palace. It's going to swing past—" She paused for a moderate explosion outside. "—about three kilometers from here, on the Esplanade of the Nations."

"Pisser they won't drive in to get you, eh?" Alex said. He realized it was bad phrasing as soon as he did.

She turned. "They have other intel and listening posts, a detachment at one of the lift ports and at the embassy, and a couple elsewhere. Are you suggesting the four of us in a minicar could not meet up with them through that rabble?" she indicated the window.

"And that answers the next question," Alex said. "One vehicle. Got another?"

"We do not, and any staff car would be a target," she said. "Also, the guards are securing those."

"What is your official bailout?" he asked.

"I slagged the intel and computers, told the other shifts not to come in here and to meet there, called, and reported. I have five thousand in UN marks and gold, and the four of us and one armed two-seat minicar. That is the bailout plan." She gave a curt nod. She was obviously a scared young lady, but she was going to carry out her duty regardless, and didn't seem bothered at the idea of killing anyone in her way. Untrained, maybe, but she could be counted on, if Alex made his guess.

"That's it?" he asked.

"That is the third bailout plan, per the manual," she said. "We already went through A and B and figured they were no good. But the manual does cover this so I'm sticking with it for now. It says to assist allied military, Bureau, and contract personnel if possible. Since I have not been ordered to do anything shitty, I'm on clear ground."

"But one minicar," he said. That was a staff vehicle, not a tactical vehicle.

"Right. I can't take you all. I could take the President."

"Call him Bal. And the problem is, I can't let him go detached. I'm in a serious bind if I do, contract or no."

"I understand." Yes. She understood. She wasn't going to budge.

"Can you detach your men to me and let me put mine with you?" he asked.

"Negative," Buckley said. He'd been silent if attentive until now. "Our transport, our assets, and we have to escort Tech White until she is secure, or prevent capture of the intelligence assets she has."

"Prevent . . ." Alex stared at her. Holy shit. Did that mean . . . ?

Yes, it did. The NCO didn't look happy, but he too looked determined to carry out his orders.

"So we travel together," she said. "You'll have to travel separately, though we can cover you if it does not interfere with our mission. That's pushing the regs, but I don't give a damn."

Alex nodded. "Bart, go down and get us transport. Jason, go with him. One at least, two if you can. Fast, goddamit, be fast."

"Sir," they said, and moved.

White and her escorts left. "I'll stay in touch by phone," she said on the way out.

Everything always took longer than planned. Alex had said three minutes. White had said six. Fifteen minutes later, they were still gathering gear. Elke made three trips back grunting under piles of explosive. Rahul returned with a cart and some personal valuables that could prove useful. Bart and Jason admitted there was nothing nondescript that fit their needs for transport. Most of the vehicles had been taken by palace staff. "We risk it in a Mercedes limo or we go on foot," Bart reported. "I like Mercedes, but here I think it would be an attraction."

"Damned straight," Jason agreed. "We're safer on foot. Blend into the mob."

"I concur," Alex said, reluctantly. He remembered last week's convoy. Damn. So how to get to the real convoy, the one with the weapons and free-fire orders . . .

Weilhung finally called. "Marlow, I know you got the same orders I did. I know it sucks. Where is Bishwanath?"

"I have no idea, Major. Haven't seen him since I got called away for that phone call. Nor his assistant. I gather he figured what was going on and split back to his people."

"Don't bullshit me, *contractor*. Where is he?"

"Major, if I knew exactly where he was at this moment"—Alex was carefully facing away from the group and didn't know Bishwanath's exact location—"I'd tell you. There's a very good chance he's still in the palace. But I was ordered to stop guarding the President, and pulled. So I'm not guarding him. Look somewhere else." *I'm guarding Balaji Bishwanath who is not the President. So it's all true.*

"Maybe I better come up and take a look myself," Weilhung said. His tone made it obvious he meant to come up in force.

"If you insist, just call from outside and knock. We're getting pretty antsy waiting for transport."

"Yeah, I'm sure. You haven't even called for transport yet."

Well, that was an interesting admission, Alex thought.

"I have plans for transport," he said agreeably. "Thanks for asking. So I don't need to take your offer." The offer hadn't been made. Shit. Weilhung had been a straight shooter and a decent guy, but he did have to follow his orders and he did have to protect his own ass, literally and politically. Now they were certainly not allies, even if not quite enemies yet.

"I'll be up shortly."

As the carrier dropped, Alex checked his own phone was off and said, "Well, that just fucking sucks. How fast can we move?"

"Not too fast. There are firefights on the palace grounds now," Jason said.

"Really? Excellent. Elke, can you make them a door, right now?"

She turned to her computer, plugged in her phone. She checked to make sure he was serious, tapped in a password, a filename, another password, and hit Return. There was a sharp bang from two floors down.

"Awesome. Can you still collapse the staircase?"

"Not as effectively, but yes." She tapped in a bit more and the floor shook with the next report.

And the phone rang.

"Marlow."

"You cocksucking bastard, I am going to fucking deal with you," Weilhung said. He was careful enough not to make an actual threat, but he was pissed.

"Major, now is not the time. The palace is taking fire and we've had two explosions in this wing. You might want to consider evacing now and not worry about us. We'll be fine."

"Yeah. You're a son of a bitch, Marlow. You have been a constant pain in my ass from the word go, and I wanted to get along. You've got your wish. You're on your own. I can't and won't risk any of my men to check up on you."

"Is that all?" Alex asked.

"Almost. Good luck."

Carrier dropped.

So, Weilhung was not going to be an active hostile. That didn't mean he might not decide to apprehend Bishwanath if he saw him. Noted.

The phone rang again. "Snow White here," she said. "How are you, Streambed?" White and Creek. Good.

"We're fine. Go ahead."

"We heard explosions. Are you able to make rendezvous?"

"We should be. The explosions were outgoing. The local guards seem to be putting up a fight." It was an absolute lie and piece of misdirection to anyone listening.

"Do you have transport?"

"The basic kind," he said. Did she...?

"We're secure on this channel. We're on foot, too," she said. "Someone chopped the locks on our vehicle and took it."

If there was one skill the locals seemed to possess, it was bypassing locks through brute force.

"It's only a couple of klicks. Are we going together?"

"We're in the basement heading up," she said. "Come down and meet us at the Informal Entrance?" she asked.

"Agreed," he said. "We'll be there."

He closed the phone, checked radio, and got acknowledgment back from everyone.

"We're on foot," he said. "Rope for rappelling, one ruck each, one carried personal bag you may have to abandon. Marching order as given, break out the Medusa. Jason..."

"No drones, the network could be compromised or hacked."

"Yes. We're risking it with these." He tapped his earbud. "I don't see an alternative, though."

Since White had admitted being able to crack their encryption, that meant any video they had might not be secure. It wouldn't do to have potential hostiles locate their principal by their own gear.

Alex started shuffling cash, split it into six stacks with a handful of bullion. "Everybody take one," he said. "We can pool it again later, but in case we don't all make it, the survivors need assets."

"We will make it," Bart said. He sounded confident.

"I think so too," Alex said with a grin. "Take the money."

Aramis and Bart pried open the crate next to the arms locker and brought out the Medusa. As combat equipment went, it was bulky, cantankerous, and horribly inefficient, which was why the military didn't use it. Of course, it was also intimidating, loud, and put out a lot of fire, which is why it was perfect for a mob.

Bart donned the headset, shrugged into the harness, and started tugging at straps. Aramis plugged and wired everything in until Bart nodded.

"I am good," he said. He looked like some mad scientist with a helmet wired into his brain, wearing bizarre spectacles and carrying a footlocker on his back. The Medusa needed a large operator. Also, it took practice, as became apparent when a weapon popped out above his shoulder while he was setting recognition protocols.

Everyone ducked, but it withdrew.

"Sorry," he said with a slight expression of embarrassment. "Getting used to it. Let's go."

Alex nodded. "Aramis, move."

Elke lit an incendiary above the pile of computers and other gear. The bright jet started scorching straight down through them, and would continue through the puddle of plastic until it hit the table and carpet, setting them on fire.

CHAPTER NINETEEN

Aramis wasn't thrilled at being point, and really ticked about the reference to "autonomous mobile biological mine clearing device, single use," that Jason made. Still, it was his job and he was suited for it. He just determined that he would be such a badass on point they had to credit him. Aramis had reluctantly left the bulky Viper behind for the mere firepower of a carbine. Damn, he wanted to take that bitch, but it was too bulky and too massive for this. Bart was the support fire.

Of course, being good would mean he'd be stuck on this detail. If he failed, either he'd be dead, or not trusted for anything more complex, and stuck on this detail.

"Goddamit, I am not the plucky comic relief," he muttered.

"But you do it so well," Bart commented.

Bart was strapped into the Medusa. Even on him the bastard looked huge. The sensor eyes poked over his shoulders and around his visored head. The straps met across his chest and pulled even at his shoulders. The man was a carved chunk of granite, and the device was a strain. It made him that much larger and the quarters tighter.

"Everyone ready?" Alex asked from behind. A chorus of "Ready" came back on air.

"Good," he continued. "Jason, please go over the carbine with Bal and check his gear. Bal, follow along with us. If one of us points you somewhere, move and expect that we will catch up. Remember, I want you just to point that weapon to your right and spray if we do. We're going to waste some ammo to make a lot of noise and get through the crowd. Then we can use finesse."

"I understand." He nodded and looked a mix of agitated and eager.

"Ready, and go."

No one noticeably moved. Aramis waited that interminable half second as pressure built behind him, then the goose on his ass told him they were ready.

"Go!" he snapped and shoved the door.

He swung right, that being the shorter section of passage. Nothing. Bart had the left. Nothing. There were sounds of looting and vandalism elsewhere, and shooting in long bursts from locals, and short, controlled bursts from the military. There were no sides anymore. Anyone with any brains was vacating, and anyone stupid was fighting for personal gain.

"Elevator is working!" Jason said. He was still unscrewing the control panel and prepared to take control if there was a problem, and Elke had a hand in a pocket of her vest that indicated she was prepared to blow a hole in the floor so they could rappel. She grunted and heaved for breath with the extra explosives, her regular gear and her share of Bart's gear he couldn't carry with the Medusa.

"You okay there, Elke?" Aramis asked.

He really was trying to be concerned, but she looked at his face and snarled.

"I can carry it. Get on with your job," she snapped. Her face was hard.

"Easy, and will do." No need to fight. Then he thought that *easy* might come across wrong. Fuckit. He'd do his job, she'd do hers. She'd been good enough so far.

The power failed, leaving them in near darkness.

"Elevator is not working," Jason said needlessly. He had an H&K, a slung carbine, some archaic relic he must mean to use as a dump gun, and a rocket launcher. Aramis didn't say anything, but he didn't need a reiteration of the danger. His pulse went through the roof and nausea tickled at him. He slipped down his goggles, but even thermal only showed the immediate bodies, looking ghostly and ethereal.

"All right, we go through the palace," Alex said. "Could mean some rappelling. What does the map look like?" Alex clattered

under a carbine, two Bushies to dump and a pair of pistols. Even
Shaman had extra weapons.

Elke sounded icily calm as she projected a dull green map on
the wall from her camera. He found that irritating.

She said, "With the stairwell down, they will be funneled in
both directions. We should retreat toward the rear, north on
this floor. That will be of less interest to the looters. To reach
the Informal we will have to go back through the left center of
the building."

"Aramis, lead the way rear, we'll reconsider as we go. I prefer
to avoid the vehicles. Bound to be surrounded early."

"Concur," Jason said. "Might have to proceed on foot."

Aramis tensed up. That was one thing with a hefty paycheck to
offset things, or some kind of government sanction. Even if the
reasons weren't great, you knew you had some moral support. But
this now was a fight for survival, and they didn't have any friends.
He had his pulse under control, sort of, maybe 130 a minute now,
and the tunnel vision was gone. He figured that was from training.
The nausea and sweats were still there, though, and worse.

So he stepped back out of the elevator and along the hall. The
grand stairway was still venting dust, and the crowd below could be
heard smashing and stealing, breaking, tearing, and throwing.

That was the part that ticked him off the most. Much of the
décor didn't appeal to him at all, but he recognized it for its historical and artistic value. Stealing it would make sense, for people
with no money or no food. Though there weren't many outlets to
sell it. Destroying it . . . Scat-flinging monkeys behaved better.

It was pitch black, and there was little thermal. He took careful, flat steps, skating forward. He fumbled and clicked on an
IR diode just as someone else did, and they had plenty of light
for them. Bishwanath was silent, allowing himself to be led, and
a glance showed him to be radiating tremendous heat, flushed
with panic reaction.

That someone else was as shaken as he, was reassuring to Aramis, and he got some additional semblance of control.

Turn right, down the long corridor that led back. The initial
security assessment had led to choosing a smaller apartment and
office for Bishwanath. Back here was the official residence for the
President, which was open and broad.

No damage yet, no indication of anyone present. On the other hand, the Recon guys were the best the Army had, and there was every possibility they were setting up an ambush that would kill them all. Plucky comic relief? No, he was point, to trip said ambush while the rest pulled Bishwanath back. Lowest ranking, least trained individual. That was him.

Fuck, it sucked.

There were noises, but telling the rustle of gear behind apart from the clash and thud below or the potential faint sounds of impending death from an assault team nearby was impossible. His earbuds couldn't resolve anything like that, and his own senses hadn't had time to learn it all yet. Still, the rest of the team were behind him, so the front was his only concern.

They passed into the broad, open plain of the Presentation Room. The soft earth tones were all harsh green in this artificial glow, fuzzy and dark toward the edges, the pool of vision fading into a black nothingness. No heat sources, no obvious threats. A line of brightness flooded from under the doors ahead.

They skittered along, silent apart from breathing and the swish of gear on fabric.

Aramis's pulse hammered at the sight of heat distortion, but it was just that—heat, rising from somewhere below.

The door was heavy wood, double, a lovely piece of carving. None of that showed in this enhancement.

He flipped up his goggles as he reached the door, felt the team stack behind him, then turned the handle gently, just enough to let pressure off. He used his foot as a pressure guide, waiting to feel the slip where the latch released just a little . . . there.

He pulled it open and was through, hearing it slam against the frame behind, the seven of them boiling through.

Nothing.

He realized it was likely there would be nothing on this floor. He was stressing over the initial stages, before contact was even made. Cursing himself, he led the way on.

Through the official suites, now largely bare or abandoned to dust, to a back service stairwell that led down to servants' quarters on the third floor.

Those stairs were narrow, tight, and had small landings. Aramis was first, and an effective shield for the rest of them—he filled the space almost completely. Behind him, Bart swore in German. The man was large enough it had to be awkward, and more so in gear.

Then they were on the ground floor.

"Standing by on doors," Jason said. These were the inside doors to the large gallery that was the reception area for the Informal.

"Go," said Alex.

"Opening."

The doors slid open and five muzzles poked out. Bart lurked back with the Medusa, and Bishwanath was in the middle for safety. There were figures at a distance, but no one nearby worth worrying about. Ahead was the large hole Elke had just blown in the wall. No one was coming in that way. Yet.

"Risk exiting there?" Alex asked. "Or out back and go around?"

"Shorter is better," Aramis said. "I vote for speed."

"I do," Bart said.

Alex looked around, met Aramis's eyes again, and said, "Go, Aramis."

He did. Straight ahead at a lope, weapon at high ready, fake to the right, and kick off to the left through the gap.

The crowd outside wasn't stacked deep. They were milling about, aimlessly, drunk and stoned and largely just there for the sheeplike feeling of being part of something. There were still dust and haze from Elke's blast, and the people here seemed reluctant to push the issue until things settled more. The dozen shredded bodies right outside might have had something to do with that. There were a handful of people sitting on the broad patio, snoozing, talking, eating, and they were perfect targets, but the goal right now was to move. Aramis cleared them in a leap and panned around. There was Bart, the rest, and a confused-looking, scattered crowd.

He ran as straight as possible, individuals unconsciously moving out of his way. He dodged around clusters and groups, all of whom stared in surprise. So far, no one had made any hostile moves. Most of this crowd didn't intend direct violence.

Behind him, there was some surprise at Bart's appearance, though few realized exactly what he carried, other than a large weapon. Behind him was the entourage guarding Bal.

A glance indicated there was nothing bigger than a rifle in sight. There could be a few small support weapons in windows, but on the whole, not bad. The explosions were from the occasional badly aimed rocket, cars driving by and dropping packs, or, of all things, a group of guys crimping caps to commercial blasting blocks with their *teeth* and throwing them. Insane. Inefficient.

He still didn't have a target, which was good. Outside it was hazy but bright, and the mob was spread out but large. Their small cluster was not noticeable, but would be sooner or later.

They had less than twenty-five minutes for three kilometers. That was a respectable run, with Bal who was fit, but medicated and not young, and with all the gear, especially the monster Bart was carrying, and for Elke, who was, face it, female and smaller in the upper body. She could pass Corporate standards for fitness, yes. Aramis was able to destroy the standards.

Screw that. He was busy dodging lazy bodies, milling freaks, trying hard not to breathe. The haze of pot and other drugs was only part of it. Under that, these fuckers *stank*. Sweat, decay. Shit. These people needed running water so they could bathe.

"Crowd moving!" sounded in his headset, from Jason, as carbine fire sounded to right and rear.

Here we go . . .

Bart was straining but happy. Loads sucked when they were just cargo. When it was this much firepower it wasn't too bad.

He heard the call from Jason, and the burst. A glance that way showed the threat to be behind. He wasn't about to turn unless he was needed. Behind them was good. Eventually, that would be a problem, but for now, it could be ignored. These savages could not shoot well enough to matter. He had the Medusa live but his finger on the freeze button.

The exchange turned into a short trade of fire, quickly left behind, but it drew attention. Ahead, people were looking toward them. Likely none of them would recognize Bish— Bal, but they'd see a group that was a challenge and want to fight. A typical tribal response. They'd back off once beaten, but that would draw more attention to heavier armed groups.

His shoulders wrenched in pain. At some point, he'd have to abandon this bitch. Meantime, he wanted to use it, because otherwise it was annoying encumbrance to no gain. Besides, it was firepower and he could use it indiscriminately.

He shouldn't have worried. Up ahead, they'd been seen. Whether they were perceived as Army, contractor, faction, or challenge was irrelevant. Shouts and points and frenzied dancing presaged a swarm heading their way. Aramis was already on it.

"Threat at front-front right!" he shouted. Bart heard him in his ears and phones both, and the short burst fired at the closest member of the party, though "closest" was still fifty meters, but closing at a run each way.

Bart sighted the group through the viewfinder, zoomed in close enough to avoid most civilians, and let loose. Medusa selected a frag grenade, whipped the barrel over his shoulder, and fired. He heard a bang and a hole appeared in the crowd.

The ersatz squad closed up, providing interlocking fire in all directions. The carbines split among each side and rear, allowing the Medusa's firepower up front now.

The rear was still mostly secure. So far. No reports, no fire, nothing triggering the rear sensors on the Medusa. He concentrated on the front, peripherally aware of the sides.

It wasn't a straight running collision. Both sides waded through a crowd, and that crowd was starting to sense a threat. That made them a hindrance. There was a technical term for that in executive protection. *Soft cover.* You couldn't have any qualms about using stupid locals as sandbags. At least there were a lot of them if it came to that.

Aramis slowed to almost a walk, and Bart almost ran over him.

"What are you . . ." he started to snap, but realized the reason at once. Empty cartridge cases from old-fashioned cased bullets. Thousands of them. No, likely millions. The shooting had been going on here on the edge of the plaza for days, and the ground was littered in low spots by the rolling cases. They were mostly from Kalashnikovs, a few from Bushmasters. You knew the enemy by what he used, and these people used the cheapest, most inaccurate, and in some cases crap weapons they could get hold of. It was surreal to see this many cartridges, though.

"Shuffle, slip hazard!" he said, warning the others, who would be closing on the point fast. He saw a man raising a rifle to shoot. He was in the "pose" stance, showing him to be a man for his friends. The stance was horribly inaccurate and he was unlikely to hit them, but a lesson had to be delivered and Bart wasn't taking the chance on bad luck. He pointed a finger from his waist, and the Medusa extended one snaking neck with a barrel and shot. The single bullet was dead center of mass and almost blew the guy in two.

Bart eyed his nearest allies and made sure they were whitelisted. Aramis was not panicking. Bal wasn't his problem, as long as the man didn't accidentally shoot him in the back.

The kid had learned well. He obliqued across the incoming front, since he was already to their left, and began a firing retreat toward a group of burned out vehicles. They wouldn't be much cover, but would be concealment.

"Lateral left, supporting fire right, cover on vehicles," he said for everyone else's benefit. Bart backed him up. The sensors registered friendlies moving in behind. There was incoming fire, but it was hard to localize. The Medusa's sensors could backtrack shots down to 3mm, but the random motion of the crowd made determining which body was responsible harder. The shooters were hitting other parts of the mob, while only coming close to the team. For now, they were not a severe enough threat to waste ammo on, though that would change in a moment, sometime soon.

Males would generally be the threats, but that was made harder by the damned cross-dressers. They didn't have the Asian chic affected by transvestites on Earth currently. They were just bearded, manly men in skirts and dresses, and hats. *Gott*, what an array of hats these people had. He still had not got used to it, and likely would not. Having some "lady" charge up with knotty biceps holding a gun or a club was always freaky, and potentially lethal.

Threat! the Medusa flashed in his visor, and he turned, pointing, ready to unleash Thor's own thunderbolt. He dropped his hand at once.

It was the AF contingent, abandoning a light vehicle that had been hit by fire and by . . . actual *fire*, probably a Molotov cocktail. The smoke trail indicated they'd driven it from the direction of the palace garage. Quickly he punched up the threat circuit and let it read all four of them as friendlies.

It looked as if they'd been willing to let the team hang off the edges, but someone had decided the vehicle was a serious target on the way. Bart was glad they'd decided against vehicles themselves. The only vehicle that would work in this crowd was a tank.

In seconds, the four fell into formation. White ran up, offering him a dirty look, and shot at something as he turned his attention back to the fight.

Two things were obvious about White from the way she'd been moving. First, she had very little training beyond familiarization with personal weapons. Second, she was disciplined and professional. That latter was more than compensating for the former.

"I am in the cover and shooting, watch movement and retreat.

White, you must duck and roll right now!" The voice was Elke's, and the response was instant. Five EPs moved straight back while shooting, two of them hauling Bal. Three STs dropped low and kept station on White, who fell instantly to the ground, took but a moment to orient herself, and started rolling, carbine clutched close. She banged her chin and face on a roll, and took some bruises from debris, but did exactly what she should.

Discipline.

Then Elke, God bless her, made the world explode.

The first blast had to be from her grenade launcher. The sequential blasts following it led back across the plaza, and a couple erupted in the crowd. They were bright with metal powder and heavy on report and smoke. The crowd *stopped* for a moment, and that was enough for all personnel to dive into the pile of vehicles, which had been left crashed and abandoned on some marked road on the broad plaza. They weren't a solid line or ring of cover, just some artificial boulders to hide amongst. She must have left charges in her wake as they ran, and had triggered them now. The line of blasts looked like major fire from a vehicle-mounted weapon.

Marlow said, "Reload, rearm, check for casualties in turn. Bart, Aramis last."

Bart turned his back on the huddling, gasping group. Fatigue aside, they were in good order and all accounted for. Shaman checked Bal first, then others. Elke was busy rigging more explosives as fast as her dexterous fingers could move. The STs reloaded and were in conference with White.

"I'm hit," Anderson said in dead calm. Bart looked over, fearing something catastrophic, but it was a flap of forearm skin ripped loose by a bullet. Shaman slapped a field dressing over it and tied it.

White said, "Convoy delayed. Twenty minutes from now. Gives us some breathing room."

"Dammit, I don't want breathing room!" Vaughn snapped. "I want to get *through this mob!*"

"Right. Through the mob and hole up. We can't stay in the thick of this."

Bart didn't answer. A short squad of men with rifles was climbing atop a fountain and shooting in his direction. He selected and pointed and a grenade zeroed them in a matching fountain of fire supplemented by all four carbine barrels. The Medusa was god. The Medusa was also a heavy bitch and getting heavier, and wouldn't last forever on either ammo or capacitors. He concurred with Vaughn. They must get through fast. He took a glance to where Shaman was bandaging some nicks and scrapes. Patdowns were important. One could be injured and not know it. Luckily, the Medusa protected most of his back, and Shaman glanced over him, nodded, and kept moving.

A thought came to him and he said, "Anderson, can you carry Bal if he slows down?"

"What? Yeah," Anderson replied.

"Sir, I suggest we split and move. Anderson and I will take a direct, fast route to our destination with Bal, Snow White, and the . . . dwarfs. The rest can act as a fighter escort and flying squads."

There was a pause for a moment only. "Excellent. Everyone load back up and prepare to move."

"Roger," "Check," *click* came multiple acknowledgments.

"And move!"

It was none too soon. A section of the mob had decided those guys among the vehicles looked like interesting loot. Anderson shot off a burst, and two of the STs were alongside for support. One, Buckley, stayed with White and was directly behind.

As soon as they'd fired, the two men swarmed around a car and headed straight toward the far side, where a platform stuck out from the Esplanade for parades. Bal was next with Aramis close by him, ready to drop weapons and carry him if need be. Bart could provide enough support for both, and he was behind. One side benefit of this tactic: They moved at a slow lope to save Bal's lungs, which took a little strain off Bart. White was to his left and Buckley left of her. They almost bumped as they squeezed between the melted metal and plastic hulks of the vehicles.

Two men popped up in the crowd, sitting on the shoulders of others. Both waved toward Bart and shouldered rifles. No sooner had they done so than the Medusa flashed *Threat!* and snaked out two barrels over his shoulders. They spat twice each and that was the end of it. Another warning blinked and the heavy barrel rose to shoot at the building across the plaza on their right. The range was two hundred meters or more, Bart was running, but it fired two shots and stopped. The first round was antiarmor and punched a hole in the wall that blew out. The second was an incendiary that made the hole erupt in white flames.

"We will acquire a vehicle," Marlow said. "Good luck. Currently flanking to your right rear-rear, cover fire if you need it."

"Check," Bart said, and grinned. "Acquire" a vehicle. There were only two ways to acquire one, and he didn't see Marlow dipping into his pocket right now. He continued his thudding sprint through the crowd, not bothering to dodge any males. The Medusa cleared a swath for him, shooting anyone within ten meters as the tentacles waved and cracked.

Bishwanath felt alive! He knew he could die at any moment, but for the time being, his purpose was resolved. He had his side, loyal and willing, and everyone else was an enemy. That was crude, even atavistic and shallow, not to mention immature, but it took all the complications of debate and politics off his mind.

He was allowed kill legitimate targets to burn off rage at those who would figuratively sodomize him.

Oh, yes, he planned to stay alive. If living well was the best revenge, he intended to take it.

But he was gasping for breath. The trip through the palace, *his* palace that was now being looted and violated, then down the steps and across the plaza had been a marathon run as far as he was concerned. He'd been fit once, but no longer, and much exertion was involved.

That thought was tinged with disgust and shame. His people, and those of other tribes he'd hoped to bring forward, had maintained their position as peasants and savages, looting and smashing anything that suggested progress. It was almost as if they liked filth and squalor, and resented the suggestion that there was a better life.

All there was to do was to put on a good show. He was worried at first. Amid a crowd like this, with weapons everywhere, none of the professionals fired a shot. His experience screamed at him to fire a burst. One wanted to warn, scare, unnerve the enemy. Then, if one was good as opposed to merely brave, one could pick a target. But none of them fired. His finger fidgeted with the trigger before he forced himself to stop. This was a completely different way of fighting.

Through the grounds, through a hole in the wall. He'd cringed when Aramis and Bart had blown that gaping wound in his pride and property, but it made sense. Nor was it his palace now, and might not be ever again, but it was dispensable if he could get to safety and get a message out.

He had no idea how they'd navigated the wandering mob. Weed, liquor, other intoxicants filled the crowd and the air. Men milled aimlessly, shuffled, argued with one another, themselves, and the empty air. Occasional fights turned to brawls, as did minor brushes because someone's honor was offended. Then there were the actual gangs and tribal contingents, armed and colorful and looking to fight.

He should be shooting, damn it. He kept watching Alex for a signal that didn't come. The EPs and STs pointed their weapons occasionally, but did not fire, showing a level of control he found worthy of respect, because it matched the control he had to exercise when dealing with obnoxious elements whom he nevertheless needed favors from.

He was amazed at how far they got before being noticed, how long it took for that notice to turn to recognition of them as (mostly) foreign and armed, and how long it was before that recognition turned to any kind of response.

They were a kilometer into it, with Bishwanath's heart pounding in his chest and ears, adrenaline coursing in response to the exercise and the nearby gunfire, before any kind of activity was directed at them.

One of the STs fired a burst at a man who was pointing a shotgun generally in their direction. They kept running, ignoring the shrieks and shouts from the surrounding people.

The scattered cases underfoot were both amusingly ironic and embarrassing. That so much money could be spent on so much ammunition and used to so little effect ... versus this group of professionals that had fired almost never and scored almost every time. Aggression and weapons were necessary, but without discipline, the rest was meaningless. He knew that even against the Army, this team would prevail against substantial odds. That was a blow to Bishwanath's ego about his people and country, but it was a boost to his confidence in survival.

Being without communication was aggravating. He watched for direction changes, and accepted both Horace's and Jason's tugs at his arms for cues with minimal upset, though he hated being touched. His culture didn't touch if avoidable.

There would be balance from this. Abirami and his children,

left on Earth, thought him dead. His colleagues thought him either incompetent or a shill, or just a scapegoat to be tossed to the mob. That would be corrected. He would correct it.

Nearby fire cracked and he jerked back. He almost clutched the trigger and sprayed, but looked at Alex . . . nothing. The man was iron and ice. Inhuman by the standards of Bishwanath's raising.

Then Alex did fire, in short, accurate bursts. Bishwanath looked up and saw armed men, pointed in that direction, and emulated the leader.

Or tried to. The burst was comforting, and he held the trigger longer than the others, raking the sky. Flushing a darker red, he forced his fingers to move more deliberately, snapping and releasing the trigger. That got a burst. That's how it was done. That burst had far better effect than the longer one. Or he thought it did. There was reaction in the mob and a man fell. It might have been someone else's shot, but he knew he was becoming more effective.

He wished mightily for a radio to keep in touch, as the others had. He was in an information vacuum, unable to see or hear much, and with no intelligence from other sources.

The group was bunching up, which seemed to indicate they were about to change direction. Normally, they moved in an extended, open formation. He was correct, it seemed, when Horace and Jason pulled him to the left, toward a mix-up of wrecked cars where the rest of his guards were already hiding.

Aramis grabbed Bal by the upper arm and started running. He had his carbine slung for ease of carry, muzzle loose and pointed generally in the direction the last threats had been. Bart had the sides and back. Overlapping fire was from the STs, and White was on the other side of Bal.

With her along, Aramis could appreciate the difference in men and women under fire. Elke was almost as strong as a man. White was very much a girl and having trouble keeping up, but he grudgingly admitted she wasn't quitting, asking for a break or lagging. She coughed, and had obviously puked on herself earlier. The violence wasn't great, so it was probably exertion, especially considering her tired eyes. She managed by jogging fast with interspersed sprints to keep her pace up.

The STs were good. Well trained, no crap, good gear. He had

to admit the running comments about the Aerospace Force were proving false. They were as professional as he was, which was more than the Army. That was an embarrassing admission for its truth.

He buffeted a few people as they ran, and that AF sergeant was behind and to his right to help block. The other two were left and left rear. The movement was good and they had a decent amount of power, and having two maneuver units made for better response and safety. Every bump and bang made his arm scream and try to go numb. He wished it would. It hurt bad, and seeping blood stuck and made a mess as it congealed. He'd need proper treatment in a bit.

Bal gasped and staggered, but didn't stop moving. White stumbled but was still running. The rest were fine. They'd only come a few hundred meters, after all. Amazing how for most people, that was a strain or an impossibility.

He snapped back to the present, as it became necessary to elbow through the increasingly dense mob. He swapped his carbine to his left hand, snatched a stun grenade from his gear, and lobbed it high overhead. He watched it arc back down, spinning, and blow about ten meters ahead.

With screams, the crowd fled. Off to the left, Elke tossed something that crackled and popped. The combination left plenty of empty space to move in, and he hustled everyone forward.

The problem with a good, clear perimeter, he discovered, was that it encouraged those with weapons to move into it, and they could now clearly see a team, who were a group of armed men and women, certainly not locals, probably UN, moving toward them. That caused some to retreat and others to yawp in anger and glee and close.

Ah, shit.

CHAPTER TWENTY

The other team lit out at an oblique, then paralleled the President farther back. Elke had spent her break fabricating new charges, and had lots of them. Explosive was a wonderful tool. A few grams here and there simulated weapons fire, a few more scared anyone not familiar with them with the report and overpressure, and a little more was a legitimate weapon. So much more flexible than mere bullets.

Then there was the special round in her grenade launcher. She had three of them, and was planning to use one per reload. Tentative plan. Things might change.

There were fewer potential threats here but more bodies, and they were close to the rendezvous point.

She scattered a handful of pellets just as Alex said, "Elke, something, please?" And she grinned. Things worked better with everyone on the same page.

Behind them the cars chattered and banged. Chagrined, she said, "Oh, there's going to be activity at the cars. Sorry." She'd meant to say so sooner. She'd lost track of time. Yes, it had already been twenty-seven seconds.

This was like American football, dodging, weaving, and shifting. Jason was next to her, reliable. She liked him. She slipped left, he slipped right, elbowing against elements in the crowd to keep as much space as possible. You could either keep your distance or close. Here, close was better. There was no distance to keep.

But these locals were nicknamed "skinnies" for a reason. She could break them like twigs. A good shove or an elbow served to put most of them on the ground. She checked on that ground, too, watching for trip hazards. Besides the expended ammo, she saw debris and garbage, the occasional unconscious or dead body, cracks and fissures and blown holes. The surface could only be called paved by a very charitable stretch of the definition. Tufts of grass and weeds and some local stalky plant sprouted here and there, and it was worse as one got further away from the palace. Those buildings on the far side of the street had obviously been luxury offices and apartments. Now they were slum housing.

This place stank. The bodies were unwashed, as were the clothes. The smoke, rot, and decay plus the blowing chemical fumes in the humid air made it unpleasant to breathe. The air had been "fresher" inside the palace.

The crowd jostled back, but she kept dipping into her pockets and tossing out little gifts for them. That caused assorted small groups to mix up and clog any advance. The noise and flash was creating a riot *around* them, which was far better than them being in it. Of course, that meant it was slower going, having to divert around the clumps or push through.

It was all going well, until someone replied with explosive of their own.

A bang ripped the air, and people scattered. The blast had to be a couple of kilos solid in one shot; that tugged at her and shook the ground. Her earbuds squelched it, but she could feel it, and the sound was distinctive even when reduced.

Alex's voice crackled in her ears as the volume came back up. "We're falling behind. Attempt to regroup."

"Roger," she said, and nudged up against Jason. They swung out, backs to each other, and took a glance. Oh, *kurva drát*.

They'd been split by a running river of panicked people. Getting together would mean pausing in that flood or joining it, and being still targets meantime.

Jason said, "We should push on for transport and regroup. Keep live and updated. Concur?"

"Concur, dammit," Alex said. "We'll hold and perhaps be at our last location." *The cars.*

"Check," she agreed in turn. So it was her and Jason shouldering their way through the crowd, resorting to weapon butts and boots now, as well as elbows. She snapped out her baton and used it to jab and shock. The curses and convulsions that yielded would have been amusing under other circumstances. As it was, there were too many filthy people and too many filthy hands and too much bad breath mixed with the stink of the factories and the air.

But now they could move faster. More accurately, they could move as fast as she could. They weren't handicapped by Bal, or by group maneuvers, only by her speed, which Jason could easily match.

"Left," she said. "Let's get toward some cover."

"Left," Jason agreed as Alex said, "Disregard and forward." They were all stuck on the same frequency. Elke clicked off her transmitter with a swipe of her hand. She wanted to hear, but there was nothing to say at present.

They shoved through at a brisk run. Luckily, most of the crowd still had no idea what was going on. They were moving faster than any shouted rumors. At one time, the entire plaza had been surrounded by video screens. Those were still in place, but either physically broken, worn out in the guts or just nonfunctional. If they'd been live, they could possibly have shown what was going on.

"We have recon," Alex said. She twitched slightly and wondered what he meant, when a drone floated past her head. Balloon mounted. Then another. There were four balloons and three foam composite powered gliders that took to the air over the plaza and reported back to the AF specialist. He was funneling intel to Alex.

She turned back to her run. They could give the intel later. For now, she wanted cover to work from.

Her unconscious guess was astute. Every skinny with a weapon started shooting at the drones. Their accuracy was bad, but their volume of fire compensated sufficiently. The drones came down.

And the crowd was now rushing in toward the area they'd launched from. It was still a milling, uncoordinated group, mostly wanting to take a look, but it swelled and stirred and cut Elke and Jason off.

"Shit," she swore in English. That seemed to sum up the situation. Now it was time to get nasty.

She raised her weapon, made sure there were no kids directly ahead, and fired her special cartridge. She'd had a case base milled to take fifteen hunting rifle cartridges en bloc, and those were hand loaded with saboted projectiles that peeled into four subprojs as they left the tube. Sixty 5mm bullets cracked out at close to 1,500 meters per second, and tore a hole straight ahead, shredding several people into bloody hunks of meat. The second round was a normal canister load that ripped more bodies with flechettes and pellets, and the third was a standard HE that landed about where the gut-wrenching carnage stopped and blew the surrounding mass apart.

Reeling from the recoil of that first bastard, she dumped her magazine on auto and reloaded while striding, accelerating, reaching a power walk as fast as a strong jog that gave her the stability of a proper walk over the bodies and debris.

Behind her, Jason said, "Goddam, I picked the right buddy." She barely heard it; he'd muttered to himself, but she appreciated the thought.

It suddenly got easier to proceed. Granted, she'd probably committed murder or worse, not to mention the multiple violations of the Military Code of Justice she was answerable to as a contractor. Even if she argued out of the contract issue, conspiracy, murder, possession of illegal weapons . . . there had to be a list.

But knowing you were both condemned and *prdele* gave you a lot of leeway to violate the rest of the rules.

She tossed a larger charge, about fifty grams, out. The ongoing blasts and weapons fire caused the gap in the crowd to persist for now. Now she was barely a hundred meters from a building. Cover. Hard cover.

So the unit was in at least three teams now, which was becoming a problem. Individually, they could all be taken down. In pairs, they were marginal. She kept aware of Jason's location, and was glad of brushing elbows now and then. He was a friend, a compatriot, and the only backup she had at present.

The crowd was jostling again, and she tossed a flashbang at her feet. "Boom!" she shouted to Jason.

"Shiiit!" he replied, and hustled forward, dragging her by her forearm.

They shoved and elbowed through the crowd, and Elke remembered her baton. Jason already had his out and was zapping people as he went. Disgusted looks and threats followed behind them, but that was the point—behind them. They had to beat their way through one thick knot, but were then near the building and slipping along the side, past the edge of the growing crowd, though over the feet of those resting or unconscious against the wall.

Or dead, Elke discovered, stepping on a pair of bloated legs that squished and shed skin as she passed them.

A trash dumpster stood in front of them, a chunky barrel three meters tall that hadn't been emptied recently or even in months, who knew, and had piles of debris and rotten garbage around it. It was a perfect place for two mercs to squat amid boxes, filth, and the occasional pile of shit, and check weapons while sucking down water.

"Find transport," Jason gasped.

"Roger," she said. "We'll need to fight our way around the building to the front. Can you navigate back from here?"

"Yes," he said. "And Alex," *heave*, "knows where we are. Carry on."

"And we're up," she agreed, rising from between the crates that had hidden them for a few seconds. She slung her carbine and shifted to shotgun. The mass of both weapons was substantial, but worth it, and getting lighter as she burned off ammo. The felt weight increased faster than the actual mass drop, though.

The crowd had shifted and moved, and they were largely unrecognized. Certainly no one nearby triggered on them. They moved quickly, backs to the block wall and skipping along. Jason had his carbine tucked under his off arm, so it was barely visible. Elke's shotgun was not so discreet. On the other hand, it was a high enough tech piece that a lot of people didn't recognize it as a weapon intuitively.

The building wasn't large, but progress was slow. Looting was in progress, people passing goods out of windows. Elke saw computers, office supplies, chairs, desks, all largely useless to the illiterate masses, but that never mattered in these situations. What was important was to take from the haves, so they did. She grimaced in disgust. She was tempted to toss some charges into one of the windows, just as an evolutionary gesture. But it wasn't needed, she might—probably would—need the charges later, and it would draw attention they didn't need yet.

They ran past a loading dock, ignoring the theft in progress. Past some side entrances and portals, then they were around front and on a main street that five hundred meters to their right would intersect the convoy route.

Facing an actual military unit.

It wasn't UN or local. It was formed of civilian-clad men, likely all the same tribe, though it was hard to tell from the variety of dress.

But there were three squads with rifles, at least one machine gun per squad, and some rockets. She ducked.

So did Jason. All they could do was get low, skitter for some bushes, and cuddle underneath as the unit moved forward at an almost respectable march, into the roadway and toward the plaza.

"Close," Elke muttered as they passed. They were largely ignoring even armed men, as long as no shots were fired. The unit was obviously on a mission, but was it against the palace or some other faction?

"Alex knows," Jason reported. "They're nearing the rear of the building. Good if we can get transport in a hurry."

"Right, let's move," she said, but still paused until the native platoon was a few meters further away.

The immediate problem was that there were no cars on this street. Either it was closed with barricades, hopefully, and they'd find some a street over, or driving had become impossible and they wouldn't. The latter was not acceptable to their plans, so focus on the former.

Another advance got them to the next block. Traffic wasn't much better as far as vehicles, but there were fewer people, and more motion. Some were running toward the palace, with shouts about loot and vengeance. Others were sensibly running away. Another element simply ignored the happenings and sat, talking, playing, drinking.

Then they started taking fire.

"Shit!" Jason shouted as he threw himself prone.

"They saw we're Earthers," Elke said as she fired a burst in return. She'd been facing the fire. "Over there." She pointed.

And Jason was on his feet, because there was nowhere to take cover in the street. They zigzagged across an alley opening to a building with a nearby door. They stacked, her backward for defense, him forward, and he kicked.

The door was only wood and burst open. He fired a single shot straight ahead at nothing, turned left as Elke backed in and fanned right.

It was a flophouse, and the occupants scrambled for the rear.

"Going to be a delay on the vehicle," Jason shouted into his mic.

"We're still advancing, but it's getting tight," Alex replied. She heard it, too.

"We need to be moving," Elke said. "Only way to find transport."

"Yes, but let me take out that asshole, first," Jason said, pointing.

It really wasn't hard. They'd been targeted for being in the street, armed, and out of place. The would-be sniper was still sitting at the same window, occasionally taking a shot at someone or other. Jason's carbine wasn't competition accurate, even after his mods, but it didn't need to be. He lined up the shot, took a slow, measured breath, and squeezed. Half the *vŭl's* head peeled off in a splash of blood, and shards of the window—glass again—followed the body out of sight.

"Now we can go," he said.

There were two or three semiprofessional factions fighting their way in toward the palace, and various gangs and tribes forming a shifting pattern of allies and enemies. That did improve things in that a lot of innocent people were running around, creating distractions, acting as unintentional soft cover, and impeding progress.

"I'm going to shoot some recon," she said.

"Roger."

She slung weapons again, dialed the cassette for its two reconnaissance rounds, and raised the shotgun. One should go over that building to the next block, and one at an angle over that way. She felt two heavy thumps against her shoulder. The projectiles would work—and had worked, she recalled—as regular slugs, but were rather pricey for that, being pop-fin stabilized rockets with cameras. The resolution was adequate for this, but at several hundred meters per second, they caught only a few frames each.

Her glasses flashed. She didn't dare get out a fliptop in these conditions. The 10mm image on the glasses would have to do. She had six frames of each she could scroll through. Yes, there were quite a few cars. Of course, they'd have to find one either with a driver, or with its ignition already bypassed for easy starting. That happened a lot here since it was cheaper to do that than fix a damaged ignition lock.

"Over that way." She pointed. "Between those two buildings. Do you see the narrow alley?"

"I hate narrow alleys," Jason said. "But let's go."

"Argonaut to Playwright, we're about two blocks away and have located a taxi, over," he reported.

"Understood. Is my location on your map, over?"

"Stand by, over, break, Elke, got a marker on them on your glasses?"

She flipped a button to change views and said, "Yes."

"Affirmative, Playwright. Stand by for pickup, over."

"Don't take too long, out."

Most of the crowd didn't want to mess with anyone armed, and moved clear. Others didn't see them and could be slipped past. Only a few were disposed to trouble, but they could not be relied upon to be either logical or respectful.

No sooner had they entered the shadowy depths of the alley than did it become obvious some group thought them a convenient resupply. Jason sighed under his gasping breath.

The two of them were far better than any reasonable number of opponents, but quantity has a quality all its own. Some observer pegged them for their movement, weapons, or appearance, and fire started concentrating around them. Jason felt a bite against his ribs as his armor stiffened and went slack again. The shot had come from the door or the window to the left. He fired a burst in that direction and kept running. Which one wasn't relevant. Suppress and move. He heard Elke fire a blast from the grenade launcher. The result was another one of her horrifying meat grinders. He wasn't sure whom she hit, but blood splashed across his field of view.

They headed back out into daylight, but there was substantial attention on them now. They'd been made as either soldiers or some kind of contractor, and that made them a juicy target for kidnapping, abuse, or flat-out murder, so their gear could be plundered.

They were back onto a street, this one far less traveled, which was a good thing. On the other hand, without a crowd to hide in, they were far more visible to the ersatz unit now chasing them.

"Cover." He pointed, indicating a building front that was well bombed out but still looked structurally sound. She skipped ahead and entered a ragged hole in the brick face shotgun first. He dived for the hollow and took her back.

She announced, "Clear!" and turned.

"Company, and lots of it," he said. "Which way are those cars?"

"Left," she said.

"So let's move." The swarming threats had deduced their direction and were moving, too. Passing gunmen occasionally shot at them. At least the gunmen didn't have radio or any other signal method apart from shouting. They were coming, though, and at least one had made them and was pointing at them while shouting. He started shooting and they both dropped.

"Grab the spare cassette from my back!" Elke shouted.

Jason fumbled at her ruck, retrieved the drum, slapped her ass, and stretched it over her left shoulder. She reached up and grabbed it.

Jason dropped down and slapped her boot. She shimmied back and over him, intimately close even with rucks, gear, sweat, and incoming fire. There were clattering noises behind and a curse. Then she slapped his boot.

He fired a burst at yet another freak in the street, and shifted back into the crevice. He crawled over her, keeping clear of her muzzle, and she shouted, "Ten meters fast and cover me! Move!"

He glanced at the wall and didn't need to be told twice. *Holy shit!* He took the warning to heart and backed up fast.

He dumped his magazine at movement as she elevated and flew past him, like some magical elf in dusty combat gear. He counted three as he reloaded, eyes on the magazine. You couldn't shoot while reloading, and if you had someone to cover you, you didn't need to. Just reload as fast as possible and carry on.

Then he turned back to the street, as her voice burst from his radio.

"Now! Now! Covering!"

He turned to see her in a doorway, rimmed by concrete, and sprinted. She started firing, rounds within a meter of him, forcing threats back behind the alley corner. He passed her and took the next doorway, an alcove of sorts with a rolling door.

"*Fireinthehole!*" she shouted, and clicked a switch.

The cassette was designed so you could fire all twenty rounds at once, as a directional mine. But this one *erupted*. The blast snatched at his breath.

It had been pointed at an angle from the building's foundation, but left a divot in the ground and a hole in the wall as it blew. Whatever the bitch had loaded it with was just brutal. The sound was that of high explosive, but there was a lot of debris and fragments. A good amount of that was embedded in their pursuers. One torso lay legless in a pool of blood. Virtually every body on the street, still or writhing, was painted crimson, with skin peeling from shattered limbs.

That was all there was time to see as they backed around the next corner.

"Transport!" Jason shouted as he pointed his carbine at a car's driver. The man panicked and tried to accelerate. Jason shot through the windshield and killed him. He needed the vehicle, needed it now, and no lone male around here was enough to arouse sympathy.

He shifted around the bumper of the slowing car as Elke slip-stepped behind. Then they did a little dance step that ended with the body on the ground, Jason sitting on the driver's seat with warm blood against his hair and under his pants—the upper chest shot had splashed—and Elke pirouetting into the rear seat to cover 270 degrees in a moving arc.

"I'm leaving the windows for now," she said.

"Understood." He nailed the throttle and headed back for the rest. He honked at pedestrians and swerved around wreckage that included cars, trash, and the bodies Elke had left.

"Elke, what the hell was that?"

"I stuffed the empty space of the cassettes with Composition G and shotgun flechettes."

"Shit! What happens if someone shoots you?"

"Assumes a weapon energetic enough to penetrate cassette and my armor. As I'm not likely to care after that moment, I've never worried about that question."

"Elke, you're a fucking whackjob."

"Yes." He looked back at her, but she was scanning for threats as they bounced over bodies. That was it. Yes.

"Playwright, this is Argonaut, arriving in ninety seconds," he said into his radio.

"Roger, we're ready. What direction?"

"Blue." *South.*

"Confirm blue."

Driving through the crowd wasn't any safer. Enough bodies could stop a car, and his window was missing. He trusted Elke, and it was a good thing, because as he headed into the crowd, she shot right past his face, nailing someone who was trying to reach into the car and scrabble for the lock.

"Thanks." He was glad for earbuds and for the suppressed carbine. Her shotgun would have gone past the volume curve they were designed for and deafened him at that range. Not to mention the muzzle flash that would cause scorches.

"They are ahead and see us," she said, "and will clear an area loudly."

"Got it," he agreed. He wondered if the ammo could hold out, even on the Medusa.

There they were, up ahead, and they'd regrouped. That certainly made things easier. The crowd was thinner here, but a lot of people seemed to think the car was a taxi. They'd piled on the roof and tail. He dissuaded the ones on the hood by jolting the brakes to toss them off, while Elke pointed a gun and looked menacing. That mostly worked. Harmless passengers were great for concealment and to soak up any fire, but he had to be able to see.

He kept moving at a fast crawl, and people squeezed or jumped aside, beating on the car, cursing, occasionally raising a club. Someone raised a pistol and Elke shot him through the face.

Ahead, the team was in a huddle around a burned-out sandwich cart. Alex shouted something; it came over the earbuds but was too distorted to tell.

Bart understood it, however, and started shooting. He walked in a rapid circle, aiming his fire in a widening spiral that caused a huge hole to open. Aramis backed behind, picking targets near people's feet, and pointing at still forms for them to drag into the crowd. They seemed to be stunned, not dead.

Jason rolled through a thick cluster that had backed away from the fire, and into the clearing. That simple. Except there was no good way to get the doors open without the crowd trying to swarm in. They saw transport and they intended to exploit it.

"Aw, fuck this," he said, and dug into his pocket. He peeled off a couple of the larger bills and let them flutter into the foot well, then tossed the entire handful into a high arc.

"*Free money!*" he bellowed at the top of his lungs. "*Hundreds of marks!*"

It worked. Everyone on this side of the car swarmed toward the fluttering plastic slips. The downside was that the crowd on the other side swarmed over the car to get to it. But they were going over the low areas, not the high roof, which was still occupied. That reduced the torrent enough that Alex was able to get the door open.

Bodies piled in the back, far too crowded. This vehicle was made for four, not twelve. Once Aramis, Bal, and Shaman piled in the back, White wiggled into the hatch. Her three goons shooed people off the deck and sat on it. Bart jumped onto the hood, shaking the suspension and denting the plastic, but making a very good turret. That left the roof for Alex, because Rahul pulled open the passenger door and wiggled under Elke. He had a pistol he balanced on the door sill, as Jason ran all the windows down. Better they have easy fields of fire now.

"Window is stuck," Shaman said, followed by a splintering of the plastic. From the sound, he'd jammed something through it to crack the edge, and then pushed. "Good knife," he said laconically.

Bart dropped the Medusa on the ground next to the car, made clear eye contact with Jason, and said, "Run."

Jason gulped and nailed the throttle. Bart had just set the damned thing to autonomous function and a few seconds delay. They did *not* want to be around when it started shooting.

Someone fell underneath and screamed as Jason crunched over them, the car bumping, sticking, dragging, and the tires slipping on something wet and greasy—a body—before regaining traction and rolling. Inside, he cringed. Dammit, these poor bastards hadn't done anything to him. At the same time, it was their own fucking fault for not moving out of the way. He made a snappy comment of "Someone will have to give him a leg up." But he really hoped there wouldn't be any more incidents.

Behind them came the cacophonous roar of the Medusa seeking its own targets, powered necks sweeping around and shooting. The shooting got louder, because the crowd had swarmed it to try to loot it and had made themselves easy targets that muffled the noise at first. Once those bodies were down, it sought targets among those now fleeing. The necks twisted and swiveled and shot, while the grenade launcher neck tossed shells in high arcs to come down and blow frag into the mix. That would continue as long as the ammunition held out . . .

A moderate explosion slapped at them.

. . . and then it would self-destruct.

The windows were down or broken out now. The car definitely blended in better. Some people were trying to climb in, hang on, or take the vehicle. Jason kept his weapon on his right side, balanced over his left arm, and shot single shots whenever someone tried to climb the driver's side. So far, it had only been adult males trying to gain access, but females or children were fair

game at this point. What was the French term? *Sauve qui peut?*
Save what you can.

He stopped thinking because there were bodies ahead and someone climbed on the door. He shot, sounded the horn, shouted,
revved the engine, and kept driving. Bart shot into the ground
periodically to warn people away. Behind him, Elke cursed in
Czech, Rahul in some language he didn't recognize, and the rest
in English. Those knives and tomahawks were getting use now,
chopping and stabbing at groins, guts, fingers, and thighs of
anyone trying to stop or board the car. Bal had two stun batons
and was reaching out each side to help.

The crowd further back from the palace lightened, and he reached
a good speed. He wove a little, forcing pedestrians to dodge and
swear at him. They occasionally threw a rock or shot. He ignored
that. Bart had hooked his legs around the front pillar to gain a hold
while he shot right. Elke shot straight ahead right past Bart's spine,
with Rahul reinforcing the middle passenger side. Aramis stood
through a hole he'd hacked in the thin roof, offering support in all
directions even if he was exposed. Behind him, Jason wasn't sure
what was going on. He heard a lot of shooting and brawling. An
empty carbine flew out in two pieces, stripped by someone who
didn't need it anymore.

He grinned at the promotional video Corporate could make out
of this by enhancing Elke's recordings. *We only sent six operators.
It was only one war.*

"Man down, man down!" someone shouted. He didn't recognize
the voice but it was someone in this car.

Then four people shouted, "Man down!" in confirmation.

"Orders, Alex?" he shouted back. He slowed a little but didn't
stop. Two of the NCOs were hauling a limp mess back up the
rear deck.

"Sergeant Buckley is down, he's . . . dammit, keep driving."

Jason nailed it again. Behind him, White screamed curses and
emptied her weapon. Buckley was at least her compatriot if not
a friend, and he was dead.

"*I want all of you skinny little cocksucking illiterati to* die!" she
shrieked, punctuated by bursts that sounded very controlled.

Well, that was original. He had to wonder whom she was killing, because it certainly sounded as if she knew how to handle
a weapon. Her sobs were loud enough to hear over all that. She

was definitely having a stress reaction to close combat, not that he could blame her.

"Shaman, give her a hand," Alex said.

"Touch me with a trank and you die," she growled low and loud enough it sounded like an engine tone. Her voice was not at all feminine anymore. She stopped shooting. Her hyperventilating pants and sobs tapered off.

One of the other NCOs leaned down through the hole in the roof and yelled too loudly, so the earbuds muffled it, "Convoy is on Ammonia Avenue, has just passed this point. I advised them to keep rolling and we will pull into the rear."

"Roger," Jason nodded. "Alex, you concur?"

"Do it."

"On it." He revved up the archaic engine some more. Yes, he could see vehicles passing by down the street ahead. He took that route fast, and the outgoing fire volume increased, though it was strictly warning shots now.

The street they were on teed onto the Avenue. They weren't shot at from the convoy as he turned right behind it, though they were tracked by large caliber weapons, machine guns, and 15mm cannon, among others. The new ranking NCO made contact and they were expected as allied friendlies. There was some significant fire behind now, aimed at the convoy.

Jason was relieved. This group was professional to the nines. Good spacing on the vehicles, good supporting fields of fire. Some of them looked scared, and he could tell because they didn't have enclosed helmets, but they were still performing their mission.

Part of that, as he'd tried to tell people before, was that Aerospace had no "peacetime" mission. If you fucked up in a ship or in ground support, people always died, peacetime or war, and the costs were in the millions at least.

"I have not mentioned who our passengers are," the NCO said. "We are cleared to move in ahead of the rear convoy guard."

"Understood," Jason said, and slowly eased into position, nodding to the crew on the vehicle as he passed them: an angular, jagged-looking Cavalier armored car like that the Company had considered for use, which BuState had ruled "too military." There was little locally that could scratch one of those. It had a 15mm Viper cannon and a 6mm machine gun, and had been upgraded with two more machine guns and a mini rocket pod. Through the thick, armored ports, four Techs could be seen, and they were armed as well as equipped with commo gear. Add the two gunners on bubbles on top and it took a load off Jason.

"I do not *believe* we are doing this," Bart said. He could be the most conservative member of the team when things got weird.

"Neither do I, but I am impressed," Jason said. "These so-called fairies run a very professional convoy. Don't they, Aramis?"

The reply from Aramis was a mumble.

"What was that?"

"Yeah, they're good. Better than I expected. Better than the Army." He was flushing as he said it.

"Son, smaller forces are more selective, and almost always better. The training and the gadgets are never as important as the discipline. You should know that, serving here."

Aramis said nothing, but did give a single nod.

"What do we do when we reach the port here? Do we want to try to continue on?"

"Not with them. No way," Alex said, shaking his head. "B-metrics will stop us. Bahane is far more freelance and we can get a smuggling craft or stow away."

He confirmed his orders. "Jason, as they pull into the port, we'll wave off and keep driving. No one in the convoy proper should question us. By the time anyone thinks to, we'll be out of town."

"Understood." Jason nodded.

Incoming fire cracked and boomed. Yet one more harassing attack.

There were shouts and orders through the radios. Jason tromped the pedal to keep up with the accelerating vehicles around them. Outgoing fire chattered back, punctuated by two very loud bangs.

Bishwanath started sharply. Aramis said, "Whatdafuckwasthat?" He was watching rearward and didn't turn.

"Sounded like two Peltast missiles," Elke said. "Expensive."

"Looks like," Shaman agreed. "Someone has money to spend."

"Space Force has a bigger discretionary budget than the Army," Jason said. "That's why these vehicles look newer."

"Fucking Space Fairies have gear the Army should have," Aramis grumbled.

"Fucking Army can't unfuck itself long enough to get someone competent in charge of logistics," Jason grumbled back. "Or they'd have it."

White shifted and shouted down, "You seem glad enough of the support. Does it make you feel unmanly?"

"Stop." Alex said quietly. He was really getting tired of that debate. Jason had reason to be pissed, but he was overdoing it, though White could use any distraction after losing a friend. If she could be friends with someone whose job was to shoot her to avoid capture. They were all under stress and didn't need the argument. Off to the right, two dark, roiling mushroom clouds indicated the AF security had pegged something with fuel.

"The word is the Army has cleared out of the palace," White said, holding her headset. "They got out with no dead, some minor injuries."

"Oh, good," said Elke, and pulled out a phone. She had to wiggle atop Rahul, then squirm to get it where she could reach it.

She was punching numbers by hand as Alex asked, "Elke, who are you calling?"

"You said the palace was empty of friendlies."

"Elke, no, don't—"

Far to the right and behind, a muffled boom sounded, and a cloud of dust started rising. She giggled and sighed, her chest heaving again.

"Only nine hundred kilos and change, but it will do," she said.

"Scratch one mob," Aramis said, grinning.

"Also scratch one building someone is going to ask about." Alex sighed. Yes, killing freaks was good. Disposing of the explosives so no one else could use it was good . . .

Actually, given that last, she'd made the right choice. They were going to get blamed no matter what. Might as well cause some damage.

He wondered if he could stay out of prison, if he stayed alive through this. Maybe a local exile with Bishwanath was a good idea.

"We're not there. I used local purchase phones. There is nothing anyone can attach to me," she said.

The radio suddenly blared, "Jesus *Christ*, the palace just blew up!"

"Space Force is good with the satellite intel," Jason commented. "That's potentially bad if they start tracking us."

"We're moving onto another route," Jason said. "Detour through the industrial area."

Once again, there was incoming fire. At least one rocket shot through the convoy, although it didn't hit anything.

"I notice something," Bishwanath said.

"Yes, sir?" Alex replied at once.

"The attacks have occurred at each bend or corner we take on this route."

"Meaning someone leaked the route."

"It could be coincidence," the President said.

"It could be," Alex agreed. "I don't like coincidences." He reached for a radio.

The NCO said, "I'm supposed to relay a message that convoy commander is coming back to discuss some issues. We'll be stopping to perform convoy support and fueling in four kilometers."

They all locked eyes for a moment before forcing themselves back to their sectors.

"Discuss because they see the same threat? They suspect us? They want to change plans and have us peel out because we're drawing attention or don't want to be responsible?"

"I suggest we depart now," Bart said.

"Go," Alex said without pause. There was no good reason to stay here.

Jason goosed it, ducked around the vehicle ahead, and went straight while the convoy slowed to turn left.

"Tech White, Sergeants, we're going to have to leave you here and run our own evac. We greatly appreciate your help and it was a pleasure to assist."

White nodded, her face red and stained and lined with stress. "That's probably best. Good luck." She had a thousand-meter stare and wasn't tracking well. She'd done a hell of a job, though.

"And you."

Jason braked, the Security Techs jumped off the roof and assisted White out the rear. One of them grabbed Buckley's body, and he could now see the wound. It was a headshot from the side, just under his helmet lip. Ugly. The rear vehicle of the convoy slowed and prepared to board them. Once it was clear they'd be picked up, Jason nailed it again. Allies were an iffy thing around here.

Rahul opened his door, shimmied from under Elke, and stepped out.

"What's up?" Jason asked, puzzled.

"There are things I must do for my chief," the large man said cryptically. "I appreciate the ride to safety." He stepped to the back, leaned far in to hug his boss. "I will get things started for you, sir. Good luck."

"I owe you much, friend," Bal said. "Be well."

Then Rahul turned and jogged down the street to disappear into an alley.

Jason shrugged and kept driving.

CHAPTER TWENTY-ONE

An hour later, Aramis relaxed slightly. They were hidden in a hotel of sorts. It was a large addition built onto a house, with several suites. They stowed Bishwanath in a bedroom, with a strong drink for his nerves. He'd tried to refuse, and Alex insisted. Shaman claimed the bottle was "medicinal," and distributed a double shot each.

The house was in an outer area of the city, and was just a frame building with a moderate amount of wear from outside. Jason had slipped in and rented space for a reasonable rate plus bribe from a thrilled owner who assumed they were smugglers. Jason was good at such things, Aramis admitted. He wanted to learn more from him.

Now they had a few hours or a day or so before trouble would find them. That was enough to wash, rest, and regroup. Aramis used the time to check weapons and catch his breath from the chase. That had been an intense experience. Thrilling, even. *That* was a firefight, and serious EP work that would look great on a resume at some point, and he'd done a decent job, he thought, protecting their principal and literally carrying him to safety.

Some of the others were still stressed, though.

"Alex, you realize we're breaking all kinds of laws by doing this," Elke said. She hunched over, obviously nervous now. Her drink was untouched. She caressed her shotgun.

"Well, Elke, there are laws and then there are laws," Alex said. Aramis didn't blame her. She carried the stress well, though.

"I think we're cool," Aramis said. He sprawled on a couch and was comfy, dammit, even if it was musty and torn. "After all, if he's dead, we're not guarding him. We're just evacuating and taking some random civilian we felt sorry for out of harm's way. If he's alive, we've discovered an error in the system. Being incommunicado, we can't correct that error, so we have to handle it directly. Assuming we get out, no one can object . . . well, not officially." He finished his drink, crushed the cup, and bank-shot it into the corner designated for trash.

"Goddam, son," Jason said, "you are a major dormitory lawyer. I think there's hope for you yet." He was sitting by the window, eyes out. An opened bulb of beer was next to him, but he'd hardly touched it. The alcohol was more for bonding than use.

Bart was the exception. He'd produced beer, had one, and started on a second. The brawny German was true to his heritage. Beer wasn't just for breakfast anymore. It could be a snack.

"Let's look at easy options first," Alex said. "Book tickets and leave."

"They scan his face and stop him. If they're looking to eliminate him, they have to have planned for escape routes." Jason was cynical about such things, but usually correct.

"Worse if they identify us with him. He can't travel alone and accomplish anything." Elke said.

"Which rules out having Shaman scar him up a bit in the interim. Then there's b-metrics at the port," Aramis added. Shaman nodded. He was glad the President—Bal—wasn't here to discuss that idea.

"Option Two," Alex said, ending discussion of a dead idea, "hide somewhere quiet and pretend not to be who he is."

Bart said, "Accomplishes nothing but will keep him alive. Last resort. Or should that be first? It is not as if he can be in charge here anyway."

"Last resort. We need to get the money," Aramis said.

"You know, there's a name for people with that attitude," Elke said, voice tinged with annoyance.

He stared back. "Yeah. Corporate mercenary. It's in my contract. You cash your check, don't you?" He was going to twit her over this, dammit.

"Well, yes," she said with a shrug. "But there's also the playing with restraints and explosive in an unsafe fashion between nonconsenting adults. That's my part." Ah, her sense of humor was back. That was a good sign. Aramis also knew now it was a sense of humor. She wasn't quite as insane as she came across. Not quite. She really was human and not the bitch she pretended to be.

"Last resort," Alex agreed. "We'll keep him alive if we can, claim we got cut off if anyone IDs us. Keeps him alive, doesn't cost us anything additional. We'd prefer to get the money *and* get him out to blow this thing. Option Three it is. Take him out and make lots of noise so we can always find contracts. Though my guess is Corporate won't mind."

"Oh? Why not?" Aramis asked.

"Because it doesn't violate our contract on paper, as you noted," Shaman said.

Aramis muttered, "That was largely for reassurance."

Shaman drowned him out. "And it proves we can accomplish our mission without backup when shit hits the fan, as you say. Put those together, and they'll love the publicity."

"I think you're optimistic," Bart said. "Most of our contracts are with government, specifically BuState. They will not be happy."

Shaman nodded. "Good point . . . though they won't dare admit it and can't hold it against Corporate. That means we may get stuck with NoGo missions for a while." He wasn't worried, of course. His skill set would always sell somewhere.

"Hell, if we wanted to be safe, we wouldn't be in this job," Alex said. "So we do it, yes?"

"Yes."

"Sure."

"Does that mean I can use more explosive?"

"Elke, my incendiary love, you can use all the explosives we can find."

"Why, thank you. A gift beyond price, as we have almost none." She looked much more cheerful, though. Crazy.

"Hit the base," Aramis said impulsively, but he had an idea here.

"Say what?" Alex asked.

"Hit the base, load up a truck with gear. Drive it back out."

Jason said, "Sure, and they'll just let us waltz through the gate to do that? Using what authority?"

"This authority," he said, and pulled a holocard from his pocket, his reserve Army ID. "I need a uniform, get Elke a set of vid gear and civvies as a reporter. We beat up a truck, load you guys

as casualties, and bang our way through Entry Control screaming and crying. Hit the armory if we have to, or just schmooze
with Ordnance Logistics. Drive back out in a different vehicle
waving as we go."

"We'd be violating so many UN codes and Army regs I can't
even count," Jason said. He grinned. "Fucking awesome."

"I like it, too," Elke said.

"As a plan, that lacks a monstrous amount of planning, prep,
and coordination," Alex said.

"And that's a problem?" Aramis asked.

Shaman dryly said, "I rather think that's an advantage around
here. While it lacks the elegance of a drawn plan, it has a certain
raw appeal."

"Exactly," Alex said. "We'll tweak it as we go. Let's roll."

As they stood, Jason said, "Hey, Aramis, you've shaped up good.
I'm glad to work with you." He held a hand out.

Aramis took it and shook. "Uh, thanks." He seemed flustered
and unsure how to respond.

"Aramis?" Elke said. He turned, still shaking hands. "I'm impressed.
Really. Because I'm impressed, you can have this." She leaned forward and mashed her lips against his. There was a ghostly flutter
of tongue against his. Then she leaned back.

"And because I'm a sadist," she grinned, eyes vividly bright, "that's
all you're *ever* going to get."

Fuck me, that was . . . "You're a bitch, Elke," he said. "But I
promise you'll do more in my dreams tonight." He could still
feel her hands on his chin and . . . wow.

"I have every night," she said, "and in the shower and the head.
Are you going to call a fire mission on your chin?"

As he started flushing bright red, she punched him lightly in
the arm and started laughing. He was still having trouble with
that. She was a fine operator, but she was also decently hot when
you saw her out of a suit. That was bothersome, especially as she
was the only female around here who wasn't a disease vector or
likely to kill you. Well, maybe not the latter . . .

Bart interrupted the scene with, "Another issue to take care
of is getting Bal up to speed on weapons. He's rusty. By 'rusty' I
mean he never learned proper tactics. Brave, but unschooled."

"Just like the Skinnies?" Aramis asked.

Bart shook his head. "No, not that bad. He knows about cover, concealment, maneuver, and the need to work as a unit. It is not like he's a twenty-five-year-old child. He just never got taught the proper way to go about it."

"So what are you giving him?"

"Everything. Fire and maneuver, both advance and retreat under cover. Panic reaction. Room clearing."

"Do you think we'll need that?" Shaman asked. He looked bothered.

"No, but it is good training for handling weapons and follow- ing orders. He's a merc for the time being. He must move and act like one."

"True," Alex agreed. "As to assets, we've got the weapons we have, one shitty vehicle that we can't use much more, and a small amount of money we'll have to save for food and possible bribes. Though not much in the way of bribes. Once we hit Kaporta we'll need a lot of stealth, because we don't have the requisite levels of cash."

"Maybe I can help with that," Bishwanath said, standing in the doorway. Alex looked him over. He'd obviously had another couple of drinks. Good, he needed it.

"With what, si— Bal?"

The ex-president reached into an inside pocket and drew out a small but bulky sack. Alex had assumed the bulge was a weapon.

"I brought some additional funds," Bal said, as he stepped for- ward and dumped the contents on the bed. "Six ounces of gold, some jewelry and two watches, an uncounted wad of marks Rahul was able to grab, and some more miscellaneous stuff." He went through his pockets drawing out assorted chains, rings, bullion coins, and some more cash.

"Excellent," Alex said, looking impressed. "Well done, sir. That'll help. That will really help."

Bal nodded. "And if Rahul has made it to safety, he will deposit into a small account I keep under another name. There could be a few thousand there."

"Keeping in mind that transporting us anywhere is going to run in the thousands per movement, that's a great asset that we didn't have."

Aramis fondled one of the gold bars. "PAMP Suisse has such beautiful stampings," he said.

"Strikes," Jason corrected. "Coins and bullion are struck. Though I rather think the cash is better, being less noticeable. Bullion bars will not swap for even close to metal value down here, except maybe in barter."

Aramis realized he was correct.

"It's cash we didn't have before," Bart said.

"No." Jason shook his head. "It's *potential* cash we didn't have."

Shaman asked, "What's wrong with the exchange rate? We can visit any proper dealer or jeweler, once we clean up. I'm sure Elke can look appropriately professional."

"We cannot take any of that to a legit dealer," Jason said.

As people looked confused, Alex said, "Assay numbers."

"Oh, right."

Every bullion bar was coded with an assay number, attesting to its purity. Once scanned for confirmation, there'd be a file number in the bank. Most of it was Swiss or Canadian bullion, the finest available, and very discreet. But both PAMP and RCM records could be accessed by the UN with a warrant. They would have to go into black market circulation, at no more than seventy-five percent of actual market price, possibly fifty percent.

"Well, it's still a big help. Thanks, sir," Alex offered. "Anything we can get will be an asset. So let's talk about transport and weapons."

Weilhung was pissed. It didn't matter how many times a bureaucrat stuck his dick in a vise, he had to repeat the lesson with each new disaster to be certain that it was, in fact, a stupid idea and would hurt. He just wished he could do some of the cranking to apply that lesson.

This meeting was BuState and Army, and not only was it about a jurisdictional dispute, but issues close to conspiracy, misuse of authority, and even treason were being discussed. As the junior man present and a deniable asset as part of Recon, a cynical part of him was seeking some kind of deniability of his own, fast. He considered that deWitt was not a backstabber, Weygandt could be but hated BuState, but that fat bastard leMieure, present only on vid, thank God, was a self-serving pig.

"So we don't actually have a concrete location on Bishwanath, or his six hired thugs," Weygandt bitched.

DeWitt said, "That might be best. I was never happy with the concept of just denying the man. If they can get him somewhere quiet, he can just disappear quietly back into his tribe. If he reappears in a decade, or even a couple of years, it's not a big deal."

"I don't share your optimism," Weygandt said.

"Nor do we." Michel LeMieure was a disgusting, bloated toad. Seeing him on vid didn't do justice to the reality. What Weilhung knew of him was just as unpleasant. What was rumored about his personal habits was disgusting. It was also believable. There was that invoice for a crate of mayonnaise. That the man actually showed up to talk with soldiers and dirty himself said he was having serious misgivings about the stupid, morally corrupt plan he'd sent down. Good.

"If he shows up suddenly, it's not just a mistake," leMieure said. "We have to be very clear on this. Bishwanath disappears, dead in the fighting, so certain agendas can be aided."

He's going to be a martyr, endorsing Dhe and other scumbags from the grave, Weilhung thought. Well, that really wasn't his problem. However, he did have a problem with exterminating a man over political differences. Bishwanath had been a good man. Hopefully still was.

"Sir," he said, addressing Weygandt. "The Army cannot be party to an assassination. If you want to track him down and recover him, that we can do. Any 'accident' will be serious bad PR. We can't do it," he reiterated.

LeMieure cut in, "We'll use what we need to, Major. There's more at stake than any bullshit 'honor' or other military crap."

Weygandt looked stunned for a moment. "Ah, sir, I'm afraid I must concur with Weilhung on this. As senior legal officer for this operation, I—"

"I'm sorry, Colonel, I thought you followed *orders* in the military." LeMieure had a snarl to his fat, sweating visage.

"Absolutely," Weygandt said. "Get those orders from my chain of command, with valid exemptions to the existing Laws of War and the Geneva Conventions, and I'll follow them."

LeMieure stared at him, then at deWitt, who said, "Don't look at me, sir. Same applies to BuState. We don't have troops, we don't need the hassle, and I will not relay any orders to that effect."

"You can be relieved of your position, deWitt." LeMieure was frothing now.

"Have at it," deWitt said with a tight voice. "I'll be happy to comment on why. You may be the press's darling, but they'd love to take you down, too. Celebrity status doesn't protect you." DeWitt wasn't having any of it.

Weilhung kept quiet. This was turning very ugly very fast. Best he not be dragged in. There was nothing good that could happen to his career if these scumbags started fighting. DeWitt caught his eye, and the two of them obviously agreed.

"Do you even understand the problem here?" leMieure shouted. "We have announced the President is dead—"

"You have announced," Weygandt insisted.

"—and if he somehow survives we then have to put a good spin on it. He'll come out a hero."

"I warned you not to make assumptions about the effectiveness of a mob," Weygandt kept pushing.

LeMieure slammed his fists down on the desk below camera view. "You could have just fucking done the job yourselves and saved the hassle!"

"This military does not engage in assassination," Weygandt repeated, standing and getting face to face with the holo image. "I am not setting up any of our people to be your bitch after doing your dirty work."

Okay, this was getting interesting, Weilhung thought. Also very dangerous, and there was no way to sneak out.

On the other hand, he mused, Weygandt *did* have a level of courage under the bureaucrat.

LeMieure backed off, just a tad.

"That's not the plan," he said. "All I—we want, is for there to be an accident. Find the reneging bastard, make sure there's a mob nearby. The graphic video will make it popular and martyr him for the *right* reasons."

"Well, first we'd have to find him," Weygandt replied.

Then everyone in the room was looking at deWitt.

Eying the incoming fire, deWitt said, "The possibility exists, with enough resources. I'll need moving backup from Major Weilhung."

Then everyone was looking at him.

"If the assets are there, through AF intelligence, and our intelligence, and BuState," he admitted, trying to reswallow his guts, "it's possible we could locate him. That's as far as I can commit."

"Well, we appreciate your moral courage, Major," leMieure said with a sneer and gritted teeth.

Weilhung promised himself that the scumbag would pay for that comment at some point, somewhere.

CHAPTER TWENTY-TWO

The first problem was to acquire a functional military vehicle. Local troops were unlikely to offer one, or part with one. Nor were they likely to not notice one missing.

"I believe I have an idea," Bart said. He found the wall more comfortable than the abused furniture, and was sitting back against it.

"Is it a reliable one?"

"It has worked before," he grinned. "But will take a bit of money or theft."

"We're tight on money. What do you need?"

"I need a case of good beer and some schnapps."

"Nothing like armed robbery to add to the excitement. Any liquor store?"

"No, only a couple will have what we need. But it's safer than trying to fight our own allies."

"There is that." That was something they really hoped to avoid. "That should be within our budget. Spend the money."

"I had hoped for the robbery, too," he said.

"Spend the money," Marlow reiterated, looking half amused and half stern.

Bart couldn't blame him. You never knew with this crowd.

Shaman went out at Bart's direction, with very clear instructions on brands of beer. Belgians, Germans, and French were the main patrols in this area, and they would not be impressed by the ice cold goat piss Americans passed off as beer, or the urine-warm bitter rot the Brits offered. This would be a rough task as it was. Good beer was essential.

Actually, Bart reflected, good beer was essential to almost any human endeavor. At least in this one, he would get to drink on duty and it would be sanctioned.

Well, on unofficial duty. There was still that minor point of the regulations to deal with.

Shaman was the logical choice. Europeans and Americans from Earth would stand out too much. Bal was of course the closest racial type, but there were obvious reasons he could not be seen. That left Shaman's features as the closest to the local genotype, even if his skin was far too dark.

He came back shortly, with several large crates.

"I have the beer," he announced with a wide grin. "But it was expensive."

"How expensive?"

"Two hundred marks."

"Fuck me what?!" Vaughn near shouted.

"Imported, scarce, of no interest to the locals because of the price. I think it was there for months. Very dusty. Obviously just for tourists, especially as it was at a place called Celadon Imports."

"Ouch," Bart said. He'd considered keeping seven beers out for them, as a goodwill gesture, but with that much money disappearing, he'd better get results from it.

"I will need the vehicle," he said. "I had thought of taking Elke, but she is too distinctive. Vaughn, will you go with me?"

"Delighted," Vaughn agreed.

Bart had Vaughn drive, and navigated. There wasn't much to this step, really. Drive around, looking like some kind of contractors or hires, hoping to God they weren't entered into some recon drone by DNA or face, and look for appropriate troops.

Of course, the hard part was driving the worst *scheisse* "contractor truck" on the planet. With one window missing and well dented, it was fine for the locals but not nearly good enough for anyone under UN cover, but it would have to do. It was the best they'd been able to steal.

It wasn't hard to avoid most official vehicles; there weren't many. The trick was to only approach the right one so as not to be questioned. Also, to avoid any existing roadblocks and checkpoints.

Forty minutes later, wrung out and sweating, he found what he was looking for: One of the ubiquitous grumblies with UN overpainted on a Canadian base. Excellent. He was about to steal half of Canada's military mobility.

The three troops inside were Macedonian, which must have left their country defenseless. The joke got old quickly, but there were so many nations with token militaries, and all wanted to play. Canada's best bet was to accept the American offer of a confederation, and Macedonia should just stop pretending to dignity it couldn't afford and join the Federated Yugoslav State of Europe. In the meantime, there were these soldiers, and this beer, and this thing to be done.

"Harr!" he called out, waving.

The troops grinned and waved back, prepared to keep rolling on patrol. He gestured down with his palm and they came to a stop, cautious but attentive.

"Drive alongside," he said to Jason.

"Of course."

Once alongside, he said, "Lunchtime, *ja*?"

"About that," one of them replied. A sergeant. Good, no one too high ranking or experienced. Though they were all young and tough.

Bart held up a bulb of beer.

"Join us?"

"We're on duty."

"We, too! Want beer?"

"*Ja!*" the sergeant replied uncertainly.

He made a quick call on the radio, in English, giving coordinates and saying, "We will take lunch now."

That was a potential minor problem and meant moving up their timetable. But it might work out well.

The patrol followed them to a nearby park. It wasn't much of a park, but it did have shade and nonpaved surface. Bart was sure it couldn't be this easy.

Vaughn was a good actor. He was at once into lip smacking and grabbing a beer while driving. He made as if gulping it, but the bulb Bart got back was near full.

So he took one good swallow and passed it along to the sergeant as he climbed out of the vehicle. The bulb made the rounds as he grabbed two more from Vaughn, and then a couple of fresh apples and a block of cheese. Yes, this was expensive, but if it worked . . .

In ten minutes, all the soldiers were sitting under the shade of a tree with long oblong leaves in sheaves. They were working on a third beer each. A good start. The food disappeared steadily and Vaughn, the former engineer, regaled them with tales of some construction project somewhere else that had nothing to do with here and now while he picked at corklike tree bark. He occasionally tossed a piece to a nearby birdile that seemed to enjoy it.

"So I'm hanging on the side of the building, harnessed, but some idiot from the team next to us comes and borrows our ladder, leaving me hanging, and . . ."

Bart pushed one more beer on them for the road.

The story continued as he walked over to his burned out vehicle and fiddled with it. He only really cared about one thing: disabling it so it wouldn't show, and doing so unseen. Since it was a diesel, there weren't many options on that. He had to fake a fuel flow or a starter problem. One large screwdriver across the injector terminals and a flash that wouldn't be seen in daylight, and their transportation was kaput.

Which really left them no choice. They were committed to a theft.

He made a visual point of fiddling a bit more, then tried to start it and got nothing but a grinding sound.

To the looks he got, he shrugged and walked back, where Vaughn was saying, "But he'd left, so the ladder they had was too short by about a meter. I could barely reach it in my harness. Now, you know how safety personnel feel about nonstandard ways of doing things."

With everyone looking at him he said, "Our vehicle has failed. Is it possible you can drive us to our site?"

"Yes," the sergeant agreed. "Least we can do for your hospitality. Shall we depart?"

"Take the rest of the beer," Bart suggested. "It was paid for by the company."

There were cheers, and at a finger point, Vaughn grabbed the beer and joined the soldiers climbing into their vehicle. Bart went back to get their "tools" by which he meant "incapacitance grenade," which in this case was mercifully not one to release the bowels. It was still a very fast-acting hallucinogen, sedative, and reaction inhibitor. The problem being that Vaughn was in the vehicle with them.

Of course, the windows were open, which was not ideal, and the wind was from that direction . . .

As he walked alongside, one of the soldiers said, "Other side. We're full here."

"Thank you," he said. "Would you hold this?" as he popped the spoon, dropped it into the footwell, and took a deep breath.

The soldier shouted, bent over, and got a faceful of the vapor bursting from the grenade as Bart yanked his baton out of the tool bag, zapped the soldier in the seat behind him, and ducked fast, still holding his breath. Vaughn grabbed the driver and tried to pin him in his seat. Said driver fumbled for a gas mask while trying to hold his breath.

No shooting, Bart thought. That was good so far. He pointed the baton and fired, but the smoke grounded the plasma carrier the stun would ride on. He took a breath carefully, and waded in through the window, over an unconscious body.

Well, it was not a neat job, but shortly, all three were unconscious and stuffed in the back. Vaughn had been taken by surprise and was woozy, but alert enough to restrain the troops with cable ties.

"I swear, you could have warned me," he muttered. "I could have . . . could have . . . done somethinhng."

"Are they tied?" Bart asked as he climbed into the driver's seat.

"Yeah, tied and out. I should crash until we get back. Have to have Shamu give me an antidate." With that he fell over.

Not a perfect operation, Bart reflected as he shoved it in gear. They didn't have long to exploit the window. But they had a vehicle. Now for Step Two.

"On the way," he called on his radio. "Ready to load for the beer run. I need a wakeup call."

"Roger," was all he got. He hoped Marlow understood him.

Twenty minutes later, he pulled up behind the hotel.

"We must go right now," he said. "They will be missed within the hour."

Anderson and Marlow quickly unloaded bodies into the room. Shaman pulled out syringes and ensured they'd be out for hours. He took one glance and handed another to Elke, who slipped it to Vaughn quite professionally and shook him awake.

"Yeah, I'm up, bastards," he replied muzzily, coming back to the present.

Marlow tossed a bag of gear in as Anderson darted around to the front, already dressed in the best fitting of the uniforms. They were the new UNCAM camo pattern, which simplified things a lot, as his ID said he was U.S. military, not Macedonian.

Bart and Vaughn squeezed into pants and T-shirts with their own boots, as the vehicle started rolling. The kid could drive fast and eagerly. He wasn't as dangerous as the natives, but Bart did have to say, "We're not wearing restraints."

"Ah, right, sorry."

Though the shifting vehicle did cause their makeup to be sloppy, which was good. They wanted to look half dead.

"We'll meet at the far side, as planned," Bart said into his radio as he splashed on more "camouflage."

"Roger. Where's the old truck?" Alex asked. They hadn't discussed those details yet. No time.

"It was disabled and I was in a hurry." That seemed to be the most concise summary.

"Right. We'll steal another one. What's one more vehicle theft among friends?"

Back in the hotel, there was much action and preparation. Alex liked having a team who could all react to shifting situations quickly and intelligently. Now if he could just get certain elements, like Elke, to not measure success by the size of the cleanup bill . . .

"Are we just leaving the soldiers?" Bal asked.

"Yup. Right where they are. They'll either wake up and call, be found by the manager and woken, or rolled, or someone will try to track them with a recon drone." He went back to preps and was jolted back again when Bal asked again.

"But they'll be okay?"

"To be perfectly honest, I really don't give a shit, sir," Alex said. Really, the man was too nice and it was aggravating. To the stunned expression he said, "They were incautious, drinking on duty, didn't keep control of the situation and didn't even ask for ID. They're alive. That's more than the Skin— locals would have given them."

Bal nodded. He seemed to get it. Possibly he recalled that

BuState's original plan had been for him to be guarded by such, and there were still elements in the Assembly who complained about the cost of Ripple Creek.

Of course, he thought, they had good reason to, now.

Back to business. "Okay, we're meeting the others on the far side of the base. We need transport. Ideally, we'd buy one from a peasant or rent one. There are none for rent except inside the White Zone where we can't go and don't have time. They're too valuable for anyone to want to sell one."

"So you'll commandeer one," Bal acknowledged. "Mister Marlow, I may occasionally ask for elucidation, but I am in your hands. It's unlikely I'll object to your actions. So far, you've demonstrated wit, originality, flexibility, courage, and iron discipline. I trust your judgment."

"Thank you, sir," Alex said. Damn, that was real praise. Although things could have been better planned—more wit and less flexibility.

Aramis swerved on purpose, driving erratically. They had to believe he was panicking when he got there. He pushed the envelope of speed and recklessness until he saw a warning burst fired into the air, whereupon he braked abruptly. He drove with more apparent control, but still at a vigorous rate. The MPs were all jittery when he arrived.

"Let me see your *holy shit*, guy!" the one at the window exclaimed.

Aramis waved his ID card. "Quick, I'm Sergeant Anderson, Logistics. I've got to get them through."

"Will do. Wassen, check that side fast! Casualties."

"Hurry!" Elke said from under a helmet worn backward in torn clothes that made her look small and helpless without actually showing a lot of skin. A hint was all it took. She'd acquired a completely broken handheld video recorder and audio mic to add to the image. Her micro gear was running for record purposes. They still believed they might need the evidence at their court-martial.

"Please hurry," she blubbered. Her eyes were red from rubbing and weeping from a touch of tear gas. Just wiping a finger across the nozzle and her eyelids was enough. Aramis thought she was nuts, but hard-core. She was okay, for a woman. "Ohgodthey'rehurt!" she squealed.

In the back, Bart and Jason writhed and moaned, stuck with black gunk and tar that would look like shrapnel at a glance, and covered with a half liter of pig's blood. A couple of well-timed twitches added to it.

The MP said, "Roll, guy. Clinic's that wa—"

Aramis was already spitting gravel.

"Stand by, maneuvering," he said, and started taking turns. The idea was to head generally toward the clinic so no one would question it, make it possible they got lost so no one would panic for a few minutes, and slow down on the way so as to blend into existing traffic. Bart and Jason wiped off with rags and chemical towels to look no dirtier than troops fresh off patrol. Elke changed into uniform pants and T-shirt, showing a lot of skin that Aramis would like very much to appreciate, but dammit, work came first.

"I hope this works," she muttered.

"It will," he said. "Jackpot."

"What?" Bart asked.

Aramis pointed. "That building. Squad back from patrol, cleaning, showering, drinking. They aren't paying attention and there's a lot of weapons. They're probably cycling them back to the armory in loads."

"Good call," Jason said. "Distract them in front, load up in rear. Park over there behind that utility building." All the buildings were much the same: poured concrete blocks with slant roofs. Their military experience was all that let them quickly tell housing from utility buildings.

"Yes, but we'll also need to find explosive," Elke said. "I'll need that bottle of liquor now."

Bart handed it over.

The troops in question were cooking food—meat especially—over an improvised grill. Beer was present, and the few women were getting a lot of attention that officially couldn't lead anywhere but might, just might unofficially.

It was less than fifty meters from the open vehicle to the barracks. On a sunny day on post no one had any reason to expect serious security problems. Making up losses from one unit to another? Sure. Outright theft of major firepower? That wasn't a concern. Yet.

✧   ✧   ✧

Elke smiled as she walked by in a shirt too snug and an expression too loose. The man officially guarding the rack alongside the building stepped around the corner as she glinted at him.

At once, Bart and Jason were on the weapons like dogs on a downed antelope. Eight rocket launchers and two machine guns disappeared, along with belts of ammo and several mines. There were always people loading or unloading weapons, so they weren't noticed by anyone else. If the rack guard hadn't stopped them, it must be okay, so the occupants of the adjoining barracks said nothing. It was a fair day, slight haze under a noon Bob, and everyone off duty was enjoying it. She sought that guard and kept his eyes on her with a sway of her ass.

"Are you going to get off in a while?" she asked, deliberately meeting his eyes and not watching her comrades.

"Another hour," he said. "Have we met?" He stared back, fascinated.

"Hello, Lucy Rabino, over at Logistics," she said and offered a hand. Logistics was going to get a lot of inquiries from this event. "Are they going to save you some meat?"

"Bastards better," he said. He was grinning and still staring.

"Do you want me to ask? I'll make sure they do, if I can get a sausage out of it." She was throwing innuendos left and right, but there was no time for subtlety.

"Sure, please," he said. "Will there be any of that bottle left?"

"Oh, I expect so," she agreed. "I've hardly touched it yet."

"Thanks!" he said. "I appre— Come back here with my rifles, you cocksuckers!" he yelled as his glance caught the happenings behind him. He'd missed the first load. This was the second.

Bart turned, made a gesture, and laughed. The plan was to play it as a prank, and not let them worry until it was too late.

"Recon rules!" he shouted. "You can buy them back with beer!"

"Assholes!" the troop returned. Some of his buddies were heading over, but the rest were snickering and pointing. They thought it was a score of bragging points.

Meanwhile, Elke slipped back, grabbed a drum-fed grenade launcher and edged around the building behind the crowd. One man made to stop her, but she handed him the bottle as she walked by, and just kept walking. He eyed the bottle, eyed her, shrugged, and said nothing.

❖   ❖   ❖

Bart and Jason panted as they piled into the grumbly. They weren't young anymore, it had been a long day, and they'd grabbed an overload of hardware. Aramis nailed the throttle as soon as they were balanced more inside than out, and came out onto the street where Elke was at a sprint, grenade launcher at high port. She *threw* it at the open door where Jason was, who caught it awkwardly and hauled it into the back, while she dived into the passenger side through the window.

Her abused victim had a great view of her ass, framed by the window as the team drove off shouting obscenities.

"Back gate, fast," Jason said as he helped haul Elke in. He grabbed shoulder, breast unintentionally until she squawked, arm, and belt and got her fully inside. She tumbled from head down and ass up to sideways to right way and buckled in.

"Hand me that grenade launcher just in case," she said.

"In case of what, exactly?" Bart asked, but handed it over.

"If the gate is closed, we go through the fence," she said.

"We're going to die or go to jail for this," Jason said.

"That gives it some spice!" Aramis whooped. "Don't you feel alive?"

"Not as alive as I do after a good beer and a fine blow job," he said. "Sorry, Elke."

"No problem, I agree," she said.

"It's been less than three minutes. Think it's safe to go through the gate?"

"Change vehicles? Split up?" Bart suggested.

"Or just say FIDO," Jason said. "Fuck It. Drive On."

"Drive on it is," Aramis said.

They made it through three of the four weaving barricades on the exit before someone came running toward them shouting.

"Just smile and wave, boys," Jason said, and did so.

Then they were through.

Behind them, Security seemed unsure. A military vehicle with military personnel had run out the gate. They had military weapons. The report was that pranksters had taken hardware from another unit. They were outside now, and a firefight wasn't a good thing to have on the street. Then, they *were* military, and that wasn't a cool thing to start . . .

By then it was too late. Aramis took a corner, another, and a third, and slipped into a long line of traffic of which every tenth vehicle or so was military.

"So far, so good. Now we head back."

"And then we have to decide how to get out of here," Bart said. "We're still in hostile territory and have just abused our friends."

In ten minutes, a car behind blinked its lights twice. "We're here," Alex's voice came. "How's it look?"

"We're good if you are." Casual. The radio lingo was very casual. Anyone scanning the net should decide they were civilian workers.

"Follow us to dinner," Alex said, then pulled up and passed them. He and the others were in a much newer enclosed truck. Aramis was pretty sure it hadn't been purchased. It looked like another contractor vehicle. That made sense. Contractors hated reporting thefts, and the military gave them low priority anyway, as they were just basic transport, not military gear, and it was largely deemed an insurance issue.

He led along one of the main routes, with military vehicles going both ways. It took serious balls to drive a stolen vehicle with stolen weapons as a solo, not part of a convoy, and act as if everything was cool. It was working, though, and damn, was it a rush. Jason was chuckling, Bart quiet but smiling, and Elke snickering. They had a hard time keeping serious expressions, because they were so blatantly in trouble if they got caught.

Shortly, they pulled into another cheap motel, this one a long row of little boxes, the type of place where six men of various races and a woman would be taken as an illicit party, a criminal enterprise, or government agents making a woeful attempt at camouflage. They'd be watched by the locals, but they would not be reported, if Aramis guessed correctly.

The others swarmed his grumbly and looted it for everything removable in seconds: weapons, tools, first aid kit, and the second capacitor. Elke brought out empty packs and bedding that were used to camouflage the stuff for transfer into the room and the other vehicle.

Then Jason jumped into the grumbly with Aramis while Bart grabbed the new vehicle.

"Follow me."

In short order, they abandoned it in a seedy neighborhood and swapped to the new one. Aramis kept his hand on his pistol. It was that kind of neighborhood, all burned-out stores and houses converted to something else, with little going on save drinking. He figured the grumbly would be stolen or spare parts or ransomed back within the hour, and leave a confusing mess for anyone to decipher. Of course, an in-depth scan for DNA would identify the occupants. Bishwanath would not show, though, so it would be taken as simple theft by the team. Since they could legally travel through BuState or Mil, that would mark them as having gone criminal, likely over some black market stuff. He didn't envy Alex the job of explaining this afterward.

"Well, that would appear to be significant," Weilhung said to deWitt. Both were seated at terminals with a screen set up in front of them. Two intelligence troops and some contractor from BuState were helping sort through information.

"Money spent, military vehicle hijacked, and base raided for weapons. Certainly significant," deWitt agreed. "What do we make of it? You're the military expert."

Weilhung clouded for a moment then realized that deWitt meant it earnestly, not as a slam.

"Well, there are similarities between me and Marlow, but considerable differences, too. We're talking background, training, and current mission and assets. I see this going one of two ways. Either they're trying to set Bishwanath up somewhere with guns and money to be a local lord who won't be noticed. That means eventually he'll send for his family and we can track him that way. He's not the type to abandon them. Or else they're gearing up to find a way off planet."

"How likely are they to pull that off? I served decades ago," deWitt admitted, which was not too surprising—he had a good, professional attitude that smacked of soldier, but it was also rare for a bureaucrat to admit to getting hands dirty. That he said so was a mark of trust. "But I'm not as up to date on a lot of this gear as I'd like to be."

"There is no chance they can get any ship we control, which is anything leaving this continent," Weilhung stated as a fact. He was sure of that, because no matter what one thought of Aerospace Force, they did have very strong security measures around their ships.

"So you expect them to hide out here? Maybe set him up, then either go private locally, or scream for help and say they never saw him? Plead misunderstanding?"

"I'm not sure, sir," Weilhung said. "Neither option makes sense or is viable. They shot themselves in the ass as soon as they started this." It was true enough. He wasn't going to mention the other option. If those crazy fuckers really thought they could get across planet and hijack a ship there . . . well, they'd probably die in the attempt, but he'd grant them the professional courtesy of allowing it. You didn't rat out a troop who was doing something spectacular and likely to become a legend.

"Right," deWitt said. "So, let's assume they do plan to get off planet eventually, to some stash Bishwanath or his allies have. Because staying here does not make sense."

"I would agree, sir," he said.

"And let's assume they do want to hide him. Here, he has no assets. Off planet, he can hit his bank accounts and transfer holdings before the UN moves to freeze them. Being even a 'dead' head of state gives him some advantage there. He might lose half or more, but he can still be a comfortable exile, as opposed to dead."

"I can't fault him for wanting that. I'd guess his best bet is just to quietly disappear and never even hint that he's around. He's not young. Another thirty years and it won't matter, and he's old enough to be patient."

"So if I wanted to get off planet and knew everyone was looking for me," deWitt reasoned, "I'd find another way off planet. Something that didn't involve UN ships or military perimeters."

Damn, but the man was good.

"That . . . wouldn't seem any more viable than the other options," he cautioned, trying to dissuade enthusiasm for the plan.

"What are the chances of them deciding to head for Kaporta?"

He paused for a moment. "Sir, I'd never attempt it if I didn't have to. But if they think they have to . . . I can't say the odds are good."

"That's not what I asked."

Damn.

"They might. They've been crazy and resourceful so far." *And, God, I wish we had a thousand troops like them.* "It's unlikely, but feasible." *And I will do everything I can to convince BuState that it's the last thing they'll do.*

"I'm going to add it to the list, then," deWitt said.

His expression made it clear he didn't like doing so, either.

✧   ✧   ✧

In the hotel, the team held another strategy conference. Horace was exhausted from the events of the last day, and he hadn't even been part of the raid on base. The younger ones seemed possessed of limitless energy, but he knew they'd collapse soon enough.

"We're going to Grainne Colony," Alex said from the back wall where he could watch the door. "We can use the laissez-faire system to get us where we need where we can do it with cash and smooth talking, whereas on Earth we'd run into bureaucrats and guards, and even Elke doesn't have that much explosive."

"You shame me in public," she commented. "But are probably correct." She sat where the now stolen vid had once been. There were no local stations anymore, anyway. Around her were tens of disassembled grenades and rockets. The filler was mostly standard Smitherene with booster layers she sliced off. Horace cringed every time she scooped some into a small pan she was using to melt it and recast it into bricks and conical breaching charges. She also had a few kilos of Composition G salvaged from flex mines.

Jason picked up the brief. He and Alex had plotted this at length, at least ten minutes, while Horace and Aramis had moved gear into the room and secured it. Jason had also spent that time with Elke's help, destroying the transponder on the vehicle and trying to change enough signatures it wouldn't be found before parking it behind the row of shacks called the Plaza Hotel. That gave at least some measure of distance in case of attack, while keeping it within reach.

Jason also watched the front of the room, from the corner of the bed and wall. "So we need to get onto a shuttle into orbit. That can be done with money. Then we need to get hold of a gig and get to a Grainne-bound and Grainne-registry ship. We know the ship. We have a tight schedule or else we'll be left hanging and will probably be IDed by the UN Space Guard or Aerospace Force."

"How do we do that?" Horace asked. "Get aboard?" He was leery of this, not having worked in space much.

Jason answered. "There are gigs, floats, loaders, sleds, and such around tramps to load them. No one expects stowaways, and nothing armed can get up there from this hellhole, sorry, sir"—he nodded to Bal—"so we'll be assumed to be loading. It's common to go inside to unsuit and get relief. We just stow away until they're ready to button up. Then we do whatever we're going to do."

"Carrot and stick," Alex said when attention came back to him. "We'll need someone on the hatch, someone in the bridge, and the rest ready to provide force. From here out, Bal, you're a mercenary. If they don't know there's a VIP, they can't ask any questions."

Bishwanath nodded and said, "I still know how to use a weapon well enough. I could use more of your tactics to blend in better."

"Absolutely. Bart, teach him more."

"Of course. Whenever we have spare time."

"What's the end plan, then?" Aramis asked.

"I must make it clear I am still alive," Bal said while Horace watched carefully. He seemed much more present now that things were moving and they had distance from the palace. Horace had checked him over. The stress was not good on a man his age, but seemed to be under control. After coaxing, he'd agreed to a quarter dose of tranquilizer.

Bal continued, "If I can get that word out, it gives lie to everything going on here. Then we can negotiate."

Aramis said, "Any broadcast in this system would be squelched. We'd have to try to time it for a departing ship to carry it through." He was fidgeting, which was normal for him.

"And to a system other than Earth. They'll squelch it at their end."

"Any ship leaving here goes through Sol System," Shaman said.

"Yeah, I hadn't missed that point," Alex said. "So we have to go through Sol System and find somewhere else to put the word out, making it common enough knowledge that BuState can't deny it. That's why we decided on Grainne."

"It would be better if they try to," Horace said.

"Oh? How do you figure?" Alex asked.

"If it's increasingly public knowledge, with Bal making releases and statements, if they lie about it, it improves the response when they're caught because it's an obvious conspiracy to commit murder, stage a coup, control the smaller nations. The entire Colonial Alliance would be outraged, and smaller Earth nations."

"Right."

"But I fear it will be a hard task to get him out."

"Yes, yes it will. Worth the money?"

"No, but it is very much worth the man." Horace had dealt with several principals. They varied from annoying to a pleasure, incompetent to genius. Bal was tops in both categories. He might not be the right politician for the job, but he was very much the right *man* for the job. That BuState didn't see that was a scathing condemnation of this administration.

"So we just steal a ship?" he asked, hazy on this and wanting background.

"'Charter' is the term," Jason said.

"Charters take money," Bart said, "something we are short of."

"There is always barter," Bal put in.

"Barter for charter," Aramis laughed. "Accept my charter or I'll shoot."

"If we have to, yes," Jason said. "But I think I can be persuasive, if you all give me some room when I ask for it."

"Not a problem," Aramis said, sounding confident. "You lead, I'll provide the goon factor."

"I am the goon factor," Bart said, smiling. He was easily twice the mass of most men on this planet.

"Getting a ship means getting to the port first," Elke said from her perch. She was now using her bag as an armrest and cradling her shotgun while watching the melting explosive. The brief detour without it had clearly bothered her. "It is well guarded, as we discussed."

"We're not going to this port," Jason said.

Aramis looked interested now. "Are you serious that we *drive* to Bahane?"

"Who'd expect it?"

"No one," Horace said, "because there is the small matter of an ocean in the way, or a long detour on dirt roads through the subarctic."

"I don't anticipate any real problems until the sea," Alex said. "It's a discreet principal movement with a one-car convoy."

"Are you thinking of buying or renting transport as we go? Or commandeering?" Bishwanath asked.

"'Commandeer' is so formal," Elke said. "Now that we're closer, shall we just call it stealing?"

Bishwanath chuckled. "I am so very glad you are on my side, and I wonder how any of you stayed out of jail so long."

"Because we had official sanction and lots of guns," Jason said. "We still have half of that."

"Guns, explosive, and big brass balls," Elke said.

"So let's rest for a few hours. I want to roll as it turns dark," Alex said.

CHAPTER TWENTY-THREE

Bishwanath woke at dusk. He was groggy, but he did feel better. He'd survived a real firefight, a car chase, an infiltration, and theft in two days. If not for these professionals, he'd be most assuredly dead.

He recalled that when first presented with the budget for his security, he'd balked, but Mister deWitt had insisted that these were the professionals that anyone in his position needed for protection and image. He was not arguing with that anymore. They'd saved his life multiple times and were risking everything to secret him out. "Mercenary" was a foul insult, and the commentary in the press obscene. These people had the highest integrity and honor he'd ever encountered.

Of course, he reflected, that was what people were paying for, at the same time they sneered at it: loyalty that could be bought and kept, no matter what happened.

They hadn't fully accepted him as part of the group, and likely never would. He simply did not have their training or fitness. However, they were treating him less like a president and more like a normal man. That was partly cover and partly familiarity, he presumed.

He appreciated the humor, even if some of it was rough to his ears after so many months portraying the gentleman.

Shaman was sorting his medical gear and making lists, as he did often.

"We are running out of band-aids," he said. "Everyone will simply have to scrape their knuckles and limbs less."

"You heard the man," Jason said with mock sternness. "Get hurt less. That's an order."

Grinning, Shaman continued, "I will need something I can use as heavier trauma dressings. I can substitute feminine pads in an emergency. Elke, can I delicately ask if you have any?"

"Sorry, I use leeches," she said with a shake of her head, not even looking up from the pistol she was cleaning.

Bishwanath choked. Her delivery was deadpan, and no one else even twitched.

Bart said, "It would not hurt to have some stocking material we can use as either masks, bore snakes, or washing bags for small components."

Jason handed out food, mostly field rations with some candy. "There is water boiling over a fuel tab in the shower for heating," he said. "Don't move the stove. The fumes are going out the vent from there."

Bishwanath took his through to heat while the others kept packing. He had a pistol in a holster for close-in self defense, and nothing else to carry save a change of clothes. The shower stall made him shudder. Certainly, the palace had nice plumbing, but he'd grown up using a bucket and hose wedged over a door. This, however, was disgusting. Between native molds and Earth mildew, the "nonstick" surface was a rainbow of reds, blacks, blues, and greens. One of the team had wiped an area clean around where the small stove sat, but he wanted desperately not to touch the rest. This "hotel" wasn't even a flophouse. He'd rather go dirty than shower here. He tried to ignore the filth as his ration pack heated. There were self-heating rations available, but they bulked more than these, so they weren't common amongst infantry or bodyguards. Given a choice, he'd take the bulk at the moment.

"Eat fast, we roll in twenty minutes," Alex said. "Bal sits in the middle with Jason and Shaman flanking. Bart drives, I have shotgun. Elke and Aramis are tail gunners." He stuffed his own gear down even tighter and tossed out some of the rubbish that always accumulated in gear.

"I should ride shotgun," Aramis said. "It's the standard position for the plucky comic relief."

"You are not the plucky comic relief," Jason grinned.

Bishwanath sucked down the last of a package of beef stew—quite good, for a field ration, certainly better than goat jerky or pickled fish.

"I am ready," he said.

"Sit here until we are," Shaman said, indicating space on the bed. It was well worn, having been used by the two of them to sleep in. Jason and Elke had slept in the other one with everyone else on the floor and a rotating watch. The constant movement had prevented a solid six hours sleep, but the enforced rest and napping had helped. Bishwanath was alert enough to be nervous again. He wanted to move now. It seemed ages until they piled in.

That was a lesson in preparation. Alex stood next to the vehicle and said, "Go!" and they did.

Elke and Aramis strode straight out the door, climbed in with their bags as cushions and unlimbered weapons they'd wrapped in blankets. Shaman and Jason moved one ahead and one behind of Bishwanath, settled in, and started positioning small arms. Bart mounted up front as Alex locked the room door, leaving the old-style key card inside.

There was only one route going where they needed, and it had a certain level of military traffic on its five lanes. That traffic would decrease the further they traveled, but it was possible there would be checkpoints, too. From discussion, they were prepared to blast through or detour around as indicated. Bishwanath let himself slump back into the apathy and dullness he'd learned when young. Sometimes, it was the only way to stay sane on this world.

Alex wasn't thrilled with having one vehicle, although it was in great mechanical condition. He was paranoid that one breakdown was a hundred-percent mission kill, rather than fifty percent or less. He was also nervous that the vehicle might be IDed, transponder and locator signatures aside. On one hand, distance took them further from obvious recognition. On the other hand, the further they went in a good condition off-planet vehicle, the more obvious it would be. Fuel would also be a problem. Diesel fuel would work for a while, but it wasn't the best formula for a precision turbine, and would also crud things up eventually. Any debris in it would play hell with the fuel system, too.

They were adequately armed now, with a belt-fed grenade launcher, three machine guns with ammo including some Bart salvaged off the Medusa, plus their carbines with grenade launchers and pistols. Jason had been and was still busy disabling safety circuits, and several of the local weapons were needing ongoing percussive maintenance to keep things working. Elke had a few kilos of HE salvaged from the rockets, plus her shotgun with only two cassettes, the third cassette having been expended leaving the palace. The video of that was impressive. He'd had her burn a spare file on the one computer they still had, just in case the evidence would help them.

He kept watch out the window in the rapidly falling dusk. It was amazing how *big* a city could be when it was nothing but shit. Most of the continent wasn't terraformed, roads were few and mostly dirt tracks, so the population strung out along those few roads. When infrastructure and commerce collapsed, they moved closer and closer to the few functional centers. A historical example was Mexico DF, which at least had had electricity and some plumbing. This was a nightmare of filth.

"You know there are golf clubs back here?" Jason said, drawing one from the storage tube under the seat and along the turbine hump.

"You're kidding," Alex said, bringing his attention back inside.

"Nope. Not a full set, just two drivers, a wedge, and a putter, I think. I'm guessing. I don't play golf."

"Can we salvage them?" That was weird. He'd swiped this from sewage contractors, who apparently had more downtime than they admitted.

"Possible carbon fiber tube, molded grips, possible trade goods as is," Jason said.

"Then keep them for now."

"Traffic is building up," Bart said.

"Yes, I noticed that. Tail gunner?"

"There are a few vehicles, yes. Mostly trash," Elke said.

Trash was true. There were a dozen vehicles or so within a kilometer. Most were missing windows and were jury-rigged in various ways. Most were piled with cargo. One actually had cages of chickens atop, a donkey trailer behind, and kids hanging off the roof. God help them if they fell. Even after the beating so far, this vehicle stood out, dammit.

"Don't use lights," he ordered. A few moments later, he added, "Snarl up ahead," as an advisory. The road had been fused at one point but was broken rubble and dirt now, rutted and rough. Still, it was better than cross-country, which was why it got the traffic it did, which made it worse.

"Why the snarl?" Bart asked.

"I'm not sure. There's an intersection ahead of that market." He sighed. He was starting to hate local markets.

"I see the awnings and carts. I see cars. I see one empty corner lot full of people and three buildings," Bart offered as confirmation and as intel for those who couldn't see.

"Two-story shacks, not real buildings," Alex said.

"And traffic is stopped." Bart braked. They were three vehicles back in a four-wide jam against three-wide coming the other way, with vehicles stuck across. At least they could see the cause of the trouble now. Two ginmars were mating in the middle of the intersection. No one wanted to get too close, and Aramis's experience was probably a good reason why.

"That may be the most ridiculous and disgusting combination I have ever seen," Shaman offered, laughing.

"It certainly lacks dignity," Bart agreed.

"I'd hate to think how pissed off those things are if you interrupt them getting a piece," Aramis said. "If your car has broken windows, you're not likely to mess with them."

"Can you get us through here? I hate being stuck," Alex asked. That wasn't the right phrase for it. He wanted maneuvering room now. People were staring at the truck.

Then some were moving.

"I think we're about to get jacked," Elke said.

"I think you're right," Jason agreed.

Alex said, "I'll take Elke and cover the left. You take Aramis and cover the right. Bart drives escape if needed. Shaman, stay with Bal. Bal, do as Shaman says."

There were "roger" and "check" all around, and shuffling to move positions.

"Are we getting out, then?" Elke asked.

"If they get closer and we're still stopped, yes. We'll take the fight to them. Much safer for our principal."

"Terrain sucks," Aramis said. "Close quarters, cars, small buildings. Fire and maneuver. I see three potential hostiles on this side."

"Confirm three," Jason said. "Pistols and clubs."

"Four on this side, rifles and pistols," Elke said. "Fire and maneuver, because there's a potential mob. I think it's a case of entertainment and loot rather than grand theft. I will not be anyone's entertainment."

"Sure you will," Jason said. "Just drama, not comedy or romance."

Alex said, "Stand by," as Elke said, "This could be quite funny," and dropped her shotgun on its sling in exchange for one of the Bushy carbines. He looked approvingly and turned his attention back. Elke could take care of her job just fine.

The men were closing in on both sides, in practiced, darting movements. Two were in front of the car now, the others near the doors. Behind them was enough of a crowd to make the threat serious.

"Maneuvering, *BRACE!*" Bart said, and gunned the engine. The bumper squashed the two in front against the truck ahead of them, eliciting howls and horrifying expressions as the two men flopped across the hood, arms flailing in agony. Their legs were shattered, and survival unlikely from the trauma inflicted.

The car tilted and stopped, and Alex yelled, "Go!"

He and Elke kicked their doors and fired their dump guns. Two cacophonous, sustained bursts chewed at vehicles, storefronts, and the two immediate hostiles. The crowd started to pull back, with several people slapping at wounds.

Alex shifted to his primary carbine, and Elke raised the shotgun. If the sound of the carbine now abandoned in the footwell was impressive, the 15mm shotgun was a bolt from God with impressive muzzle flash.

BANGBANGBANG! Her three shots sounded like a burst of auto, and were followed by several sharp cracks of explosive and billowing smoke. She'd shot gas rounds.

Alex cursed, "Warn me before you pop smoke, dammit!" and picked point targets, skipping left, or forward on the vehicle, to keep clear of the cloud. He took a scan.

Bart darted his head around, watched all four unass from the car, then gunned the engine and pulled forward left. There was a tiny little trike there, petro powered, or possibly vegetable oil. The exhaust from it stank. It was small and he was able to intimidate the driver into backing up until he crashed into the vehicle behind, which left just enough space for Bart to rumble through the space, denting and gouging every vehicle in the area. That should scare and piss off a lot of people, Alex thought.

Jason and Aramis came out fast, Aramis slightly ahead. The kid burped off a burst that was probably effective, but also used up a lot of ammo against a pair of fairly tame targets. Jason held a golf club, and took a mighty swing.

"Forebrain!" he shouted, before burying the steel inside a skull with an egg-cracking splat. Letting it go, he raised his carbine and shot one neatly center mass, then again in the throat, and turned to place one round in the head of the other, who had taken a couple of rounds from Aramis's burst.

BAD joke, Alex winced.

If anyone survived or made a point of recording for study, they would notice that he didn't actually engage the sights. He point shot, plain and simple. Damn, the man was good.

Bart bashed through the intersection and blocked traffic. The four backed rapidly toward the vehicle, slip-steps and skips, looking like some macabre dance routine. Shaman and Bishwanath opened doors, and the four fell inside in heaps as Bart goosed it hard, turned left, and took an alternate route.

"Bal, goddamit, you stay well inside and *do not* expose yourself!" Alex shouted. Seeing his charge jerk back, he slowed down and said, "Sorry, sir, but without you we're just criminals or hired guns in the ass end of nowhere. You have to stay out of it. We sure can use the help, and appreciate your courage, but you are no use to us dead."

Bishwanath nodded. He likely didn't get chewed out very often. "You are correct. I apologize."

Alex wasn't enjoying the stress. At this point, they'd all committed enough crimes to be convicted of felony conspiracy to commit murder, grand theft, hypothetically kidnapping—though that wasn't likely to be stickable—arson, assorted weapon violations, insurrection or rebellion or both . . . They had no contract, no orders, and couldn't pretend they weren't able to get in contact. While he'd been ignoring his phone at first, and then pulled the capacitor because he knew he wouldn't like the messages that had to be filling it, not to mention how it could be used to track him, he couldn't claim he was unable to send a message through other means with a pocket full of cash and bullion and comm companies in every town.

"Okay, how do we arrange to avoid towns from now on?" he asked.

"You can't," Bal replied from behind him.

"Sir?" he asked, turning enough to make courtesy eye contact.

"The roads are few, so towns are on them. The roads connect mines, ports, large farming areas. Otherwise, no habitation except bush folk."

"Can we skirt the towns?" He turned his attention back to the road, which was dusty, bumpy, but nevertheless well-cleared from regular use.

"The outskirts will be pricier, less well-equipped, more on the lookout for interesting loot. Inside where the gangs and tribes are is fairly safe—status quo. The fringes are where the fighting is. Except for the capital which is the free-for-all arena, unfortunately." He sounded bitter.

"Right. So we're stuck going through towns as obvious offworlders and hoping not to be either made or taken down," Alex said.

"It gets worse," Bal said. "There is only the one port—Witrand— we can make use of to cross the Strait. Surface travel really limits our options." He seemed to be having second thoughts. It was too late for that.

"Yes, but we can change routes and hide on the ground. We don't have that option in the air," Alex said.

"Yes, the anonymity and space help, but sooner or later we run into a block."

"Sooner in the air," Alex reiterated.

Bald didn't reply. They listened to the bumps and spitting gravel and the tone of the engine. Diesels had an almost musical tone compared to turbines. This was a whine.

After a while, Alex added, "Sir, I know you're nervous, and there is no good answer to this. We'll just have to do what we can."

"It's worked so far, Alex. I hope it continues."

"So do I."

Vapor rose in the compartment. Something stank. Bad. Again. The food they'd been eating was loaded with unfamiliar spices, or were military rations, and both caused the intestines to hold chemical warfare drills.

"Goddam, who shit in their pants?" Bart asked. "It is worse than the aftermath of a sauerkraut and beer festival."

"Actually, that was me. I do apologize," Bishwanath said. He looked somewhat embarrassed.

"Ah, good one, sir," Aramis said, with Elke and Jason joining in. The joke played up to his position, and everyone laughed. Hell, if you couldn't stand the farts, you could get out and risk the weather or the bullets.

Bart drove.

He was good at it, with years of experience in both EP and now combat driving. He enjoyed it. That didn't mean it was fun to drive all night in a nation like this.

He had to fight highway hypnosis on the long straights between villages, while watching for overhead threats. He wasn't sure what he could do about them if he saw any, but he had to be aware. As dusk turned to near dark, he snapped his fingers and pointed, and Alex handed him night vision binox. Those gave him vision, and even color, but it was coarse and grainy even with enhancement. Add in little things like the seat not being quite right, and it turned into a chore rapidly.

It was his chore. He also wasn't keen on not being able to shoot generally. The driver had to control the vehicle, and if he had to shoot, things were really down the dump-filled toilet. He would find it reassuring to be able to shoot, though.

"How far?" he inquired.

Alex was snoozing, which he needed to do. The man kept long hours and was going to be making more decisions. Jason was right behind Bart and said, "Two hundred klicks to the port. How fast?"

"Forty, tops, so five hours."

"Aggravating." Jason sounded groggy.

"Yes, it is."

Conversation died again. Bishwanath slumped against Shaman and slept restlessly. Shaman was out hard. Aramis had the energy of youth, and Elke always seemed alert. He wasn't lonely, really, but it was quiet, which was disturbing in its own way.

The one advantage was that as dark as it was, any approaching vehicle would be easy to spot. So would habitations with lights. The hazy enhanced image gave Bart all the info he needed for what he was doing.

It was going to be a long night.

Jason woke aching. He'd had a long night, with intermittent sleep and wakefulness, a cold breeze from the AC vent on his face and left ear, tight confines making him sore all over, neck especially, and he was hot and sticky against the seat. The only way to keep cool with this many people was to crank the AC high, and that created zones of hot and cold. The windows had to stay closed as much as possible to keep out dust and to keep interference down. It was actually easier to hear inside with them closed, especially with mics placed on all sides.

There was a clear whiff of sea and signs of a port ahead. They were driving through the edge of a port town, which had to be Witrand.

"We're shipping from here?" he asked. It was a rhetorical question. Of course they were.

"Yeah," Alex said, barely awake himself, rumpled and mussed even in the casual stuff he was wearing. He needed a shave badly. After a quick rub, Jason realized he did, too. His hair was flat on one side. At least by growing it he looked closer to the local style of chop-it-off-when-it-gets-in-the-way.

"I will drive past the docks," Bart said. "Shout if you see something good."

"Don't get too close. I wouldn't bet on them not monitoring," Aramis suggested. "We've got at least one military vehicle to the rear."

"Coast Guard?"

"Naval Port Security."

"That's actually a good sign," Jason said. "We'll use them as a cover if we need to."

"Hard cover?" Aramis joked.

They drove for several minutes, getting a feel for the area. There had been a shipyard here, now shut down, the gantries and scaffolding all in disrepair and collapsing. There were kids playing and adults fishing in the ways. The fences along the docks were coated steel with concertina wire topping, no modern measures. There were breaks, gates, and cuts that rendered them largely useless. People wandered through drunk or high, selling fruit, parts, or themselves.

"I'd prefer to sell the vehicle as we leave," Alex said. "We can use the money."

"You'll never get what it's worth," Jason replied. "Not around here." There was little in the way of money or its results to be seen.

"It didn't cost us anything."

"Hehe. True." Still, this was largely a fishing town now, with a

few, very few actual packets and lighters taking cargo. Some of
the crews had obviously been living aboard their ships and were
becoming settled to fishing for food from their houseboats. Some
were being parted out to provide living money, tangible capital
being cannibalized in exchange for food.

"That's what we need, right there," Bart said. He pointed.

"Where?" Jason asked, and then said, "Oh, you beauty."

"Whatinhell is that?" Elke asked.

"Hoverwing." It was old and worn, but clearly functional. They
were very efficient, basically a ground effect skirt with a lifting
body above it. Once it came on the step, you could choose to
lift and cruise a few meters up, using the weight of air as support for the craft, and gaining efficiency because there was less
friction in air than on the surface.

"Ah," she said. "I recognize it now. I've never been near a body
of water that used them."

"Efficient, got the range, requires only a small crew. Just what
we need."

"Are we bribing them or hijacking again?"

"Yes."

"Jason, can you fly, float, pilot, whatever it's called, that thing
if need be?" Alex asked.

"Absolutely," he said. "It's a ground effect wing. Easier in some
respects than a flying wing." He hoped. There would be differences from thermal effects and certainly from ocean waves, but
he was confident he could sort it out.

"Port Security is taking an interest in us," Aramis said.

"Keep me advised," Alex said. Jason agreed. Not looking back
was a good idea. Everything was kosher as long as it appeared
kosher.

Bart turned in through a gate that had been cut into the fence,
creating a rough dirt road with puddles for access. Seagulls and
local birdiles flapped away as he entered. The smell came easily
into the vehicle now, salty, bitter, and tinged with rot.

"I should get the charter," Jason said. "Someone else hock the
vehicle. Remember to hide weapons."

"On it," Aramis said, and started bagging and wrapping stuff.
Elke helped. They kept things low and out of sight, though it
was possible a good sensor would pick them up anyway. Nothing
could be done about that.

"Disperse us as you drive, Bart. Aramis, out now and walk."

"Yes, sir." Bart pulled to the side of the track and Aramis slipped out the rear with a bag over his shoulder, looking as if he wanted work. A couple of scrawny men pulled at him. He shook them off firmly but not roughly.

Jason slipped his carbine into a bag and stowed a rocket. They'd want at least one weapon each. At this point, the stun batons were very optional, but Bal could continue to carry them. They also might be quite useful in the future.

"Bal, Shaman, Jason all get out at the ship."

"Understood," he said. "Bart, give us a full second stopped to get Bal out." He shouldered his loaded bag.

"Will do."

They pulled in front of the rickety dock, sunken pillars with metal and plastic railings installed in multiple generations. On the whole, he'd rather walk down the sand, which was an option here. The hovercraft were doing better business than the ships simply by making the loading task less arduous by pulling in close.

The car stopped, Jason lit out and pulled on Bal's arm as Shaman pushed. It took only a second for all three to be standing while Bart drove off, Shaman's angled arm slamming the door as the car moved past, splashing sand and grit.

"Hurry," Jason said, while moving at a purposeful walk. Running wouldn't be discreet.

There were crew aboard, he noted. That was good and bad. Stealing it wouldn't have been hard, and no crew would make that easier. Now they'd have to negotiate with limited funds.

Once eye contact was made, Jason waved. The man who must be captain from his hat and ragged but marked jacket waved back. Resisting the urge to shout, he led the others closer.

The captain was understandably nervous about three men with gear approaching, and they stopped a few meters back. Everyone kept quiet.

"We'd like to charter a trip for seven," Jason said. "We'll pay cash."

"Sho," the captain said with a professional smile. "I spec t'leave widin for-two hours."

Jason drew out a couple of bills and let them be seen. "We'd like to leave sooner." He saw Elke arriving from the next gate at a brisk walk and pointed her out. "Here's one of our party."

The captain turned and looked, then back quickly, distrustful. He had two men on top of the cabin section looking down, probably armed but with light stuff. They probably didn't know how to use them to any effect. However, the shooting would attract attention the team didn't need.

"Hunnerd mark each, minimum of fife," the captain said. "We leave tomorrow."

Aramis arrived, sweating in the humid salt-sea air. Ahead, Jason saw Bart and Alex at a brisk jog. Time to speed things up.

"Seven hundred it is," he agreed, peeling off marks. "Plus three hundred to leave now." He reached out and pressed the money against the chest of the captain, who took it.

The man was still reluctant. "I can fit more passengers," he argued.

"Yes, but we're in a hurry." Jason stuffed another hundred into the man's shirt pocket.

"And I need clearance from the harbormasta," he said.

"I think he doesn't want the hire," Elke said. "Take the money back."

"No, no, but we must wait," the man protested, arms out.

"Ordinarily, yes, but we are in a hurry," Shaman said. "There are only the seven of us. You can fit us."

"Yes, you'll fit, but . . ."

Jason slipped one more hundred over. This was about the limit of what he'd spend, and he hoped Alex had done well with the vehicle. He glanced at him as he arrived and got a nod.

Bart escalated by walking slowly toward the ramp, bag over shoulder. "Time is wasting," he said. Alex moved alongside with Bal between them. Good idea. Get him out of sight.

The captain was still stuttering, but his mate above was wide-eyed at the ongoing bribe. The other four crew varied from eager to cautious. This much money obviously indicated something was wrong. But there were only seven people.

"But . . ."

Jason turned with the others and started boarding. They made it up the swaying gangplank, an actual plank onto the boat and down into a cabin situated under the rakish command deck, whatever it was called on one of these things. There were couches and tables and a viewing window. The setup was comfortable enough, but made for crew, not passengers. Of course, everything was torn and worn from years of being overly packed to squeeze more money out of peasants who didn't care for even that luxury. This was definitely the right choice of boat.

As they sat, Alex gave him a look, with his eyes glancing up.

Can you pilot this?

He nodded very slightly. Yes, he could figure this out and it wouldn't take long. The only relevant question was fuel and range.

Out the hatch, Elke could be seen, as the captain jabbered away.

"But it's no problem," she was saying. "You do want our business, yes? We are all aboard."

The crew were definitely nervous. On the other hand, they did proceed to run through the checklist and start the engines. Jason kept an eye on his scanner for any encrypted signals.

"Anything?" Alex asked.

"Nothing. Though of course, they could be using a code I can't ID. Seems unlikely, but the potential does exist."

"Worried about it?"

"Nah," he said, hoping he sounded confident. "This is a tramp, they'll be glad of the money. We'll need to be sure of our position before liftoff, though."

"Plenty of money, I think we'll be fine. As long as we save enough for later."

"Yeah, don't blow it all on this. We still have to get off planet, out of system, and somewhere good. How did you do on the truck?"

"Ah, the truck," Alex sighed. "A good local deal."

"Why does that bother me?" he asked. There wasn't much money around here.

"I got two hundred cash, and a dozen head of cattle."

That was an interesting trade, he had to admit. "And the cattle are where?"

"We can't fit them, of course. But we do have the two hundred we didn't have before, plus the three hundred I took when I knocked the guy down. He gets some extra hardware in the trunk when he wakes up."

"That just sums this place up, doesn't it?"

"Yup," Alex agreed. "Yup, it does."

The crew cast off and they backed down the sand easily. The

hoverwing was currently in boat mode and bobbed lightly. The bobbing stabilized as the impellers came up and the plenum filled. Then they were bumping, battering over the harbor chop, building speed and clearance to a skittering skip.

The captain kept a running dialog with port control, and Jason and Bal sat nearby, acting interested in the controls while listening intently for any subterfuge. The man's accent was even thicker than those in the capital, barely English, choppy and fast. Jason kept a hand near his pistol and an eye on Bal, waiting for an indicator.

It took hours to clear the harbor, it felt, even though it was only a few minutes. The captain looked over at them once, saw the tension, and said, "We hafn eben lift yet. Stress he gon' kill you." His expression was suspicious and apprising.

Jason forced himself to chuckle and said, "Work-related, and I get seasick. I'm sure I'll relax when we lift. I like the air." He glanced out as the docks fell astern, leaving only the rocky protrusions of the harbor mouth ahead.

"Ah," the captain replied. He seemed somewhat mollified. "We lift in five mints."

"Then I'll relax in six," Jason said, and Bal chuckled to offer some support.

Everyone was true to their word. In five minutes, the wings dramatically extended out into a broad anhedral. The ducted propellers increased in speed to an angry whining buzz, and the ride became rough as the craft bounded then skipped over the waves. The striking water made a drumming sound that tapered off into occasional slaps and then they were airborne.

Stress flowed out of everyone, almost in sequence with the props feathering back to a level that held lift and speed most efficiently. Accent aside, the captain couldn't be stupid if he could control this behemoth. Even "lightly" loaded it was carrying a lot of cargo.

"Can I hope you keep yo guns away for de duration?"

There wasn't much to say to that.

"We do prefer to do things honestly with cash when we can," Jason said.

"Good," the captain replied. "I like that way, too. May I shake your han, Mista Prezdent?"

Bal stood, stepped forward, and shook. "I thank you for your support, Captain," he said.

"When did you recognize him?" Alex asked, curious and wanting intel.

"After I recnize de lady, who blow things up on de news."

"Ah." Yes, Elke could be distinctive. This was such a case. Better remember that.

"So, we want to make it to Bahane, Kaporta, and do it quietly," Alex said.

"Of course. But you can't go into harbo. Watch well, they do. Tough to bribe. One person maybe. Not seben."

"So we need to stop short of there," Jason said.

"Short and out of sight and radar," the captain said. "That mean using fuel. Gonna be tight."

"Too tight?"

"I don' care who you are. I won't wreck my ship."

"That's understandable," Alex said. He didn't say that he considered that as a possibility if necessary. Jason could read it.

The team and crew socialized just enough to lower the crackly electric tension in the air. The crew understood that the team were mercenaries. The captain didn't mention Bal to them, and if anyone else figured it out they didn't say so. Mercenaries clearly meant gray areas of the law. This ship and its crew had done their share of smuggling, so had some idea of the issues facing mercs trying to be discreet and tossing money around while armed. The team was on edge about Bal's identity, already made once. They faced thirty-six very tense hours of travel.

CHAPTER TWENTY-FOUR

Alex stood at the railing on the covered rear deck, watching the sea, listening to the draft. Partly he was trying to avoid nausea. He didn't handle water well until he had time to acclimate, and there wouldn't be enough time on this trip. The rest was old thoughts.

"Something wrong, Alex?" Shaman asked. He must have appeared jumpy.

"Oh, flashback is all."

He looked disturbed, and Alex immediately added, "No, not like that. Just a stray memory from another boat trip."

"Oh?"

"Yeah, the one that led to me resigning my commission in the Corps."

Shaman nodded. "Of course I had heard mention of that," he said. "And of course it's not the kind of thing one asks about."

Aramis said, "So, Alex, why did you decide to resign?"

The kid was great at just stepping on things, like a kitten jumping on the dinner table. Alex sighed. It was one of those things that you could be proud of, in an embarrassing way, and so off the wall no one ever believed it.

"The problem with Barbados."

"I didn't know the U.S. had a problem with Barbados." Aramis looked confused, as if he was flipping through his history.

Alex decided to save the kid some time. "It didn't until then."

"Oh."

"Now I am interested," Shaman said.

"Well, back when I was young and stupid," Alex explained, "I got mixed up in an issue. We were doing drug interdictions in the Caribbean, right after it started coalescing into the Pan Carib States, and a lot of them were micronations—this was right after Sulawan went independent the second time, and all kinds of little islands were following the lead. Some were still territories. Some were nations, some were already PCS. The drug growers were booming, because the trade deals made it impossible for small farmers to compete with the big fruit conglomerates. So ganja was big business, and most of the independents had only a patrol boat or so and couldn't stay on top of it.

"So, America being America sends the Marines."

"Something wrong with that?" Aramis asked.

"No, nothing wrong with that. This time it was the right thing to do. So we were down there, with harbor boats and SkateRay patrol boats, using lifters and ACVs to drop in on growers. We'd usually hold them and torch the crop. Occasionally, one would take a shot or two for honor's sake, then surrender. Only a couple wanted to die.

"Anyway, we had downtime—"

"That was the problem," Elke said.

"Yes, but it started with a keg of beer."

"Uh oh," said Shaman. "I see where that went."

"Right," he admitted. This was where it got painful. "We'd been down there about three months. Everything should have been good. We had support, regular supplies, friendly locals. Officially it was peacetime, so the guys could get drunk and laid. Everything was good."

"That made it worse?" Aramis asked.

"After the fact, yeah," Alex agreed. "We'd been working with the locals. They didn't have a military, just an official police force. We're talking a nation smaller than most second-string U.S. cities. Heck, smaller than some suburbs. Good bunch of people, but police, not military."

"Yeah, I dealt with them about that time," Jason said, leaning forward. "Built them a runway. Heard about some trouble but never knew what it was. They hushed it up."

"That had to be it," Alex agreed, and knocked his drink back. This took some bracing. The rotgut was definitely bracing.

"So," he said, "we were drinking, talking about capabilities. We had been training. Ship recognition, weapons, relative nation force sizes, and it just continued as we started drinking. Someone pointed out our hosts had only six very small patrol boats. They were all around fifteen meters. Another someone said, 'You know what? I bet we could take them.'"

"Oh, no," Bart said, chuckling.

Nodding, Alex continued, "Next thing I know we're conducting an amphibious assault of the Barbadan Security Force Armory. All their weapons were stored there, it was just up from the dock, so it was one oporder for the whole mission."

"'Mission,'" Elke repeated.

"Yes, we drew orders up. That is, I drew orders up," he admitted, flushing. "Of course, that attention to training detail may have been the thing that saved my ass from jail," he mused. Could it? He hadn't thought about it, had tried not to, but those orders had been submitted as evidence.

"You actually drew up orders for it?"

"I really did."

Even the captain was chuckling now. "So you have histry of hijacks, then?" he asked.

"It was one of those things you do when young and stupid," Alex said, looking at him. "This one was planned."

"So you took the armory?" Bart asked.

"Oh, yes, we took it, and held it. Didn't need to fire a shot. Everyone knew the score. It was a drunken prank, no harm done, and the locals were willing to consider it such if we backed off."

"So what happened?" from Aramis.

"We held it until dawn. The problems were exacerbated when some of the grunts decided to hold a native ritual in the administrator's office. That, and someone field-stripped all the local weapons and left them in a heap, with a sign on top offering a free jigsaw puzzle. All still on the fun side, but then our brass showed up. They took it personally."

"Brass do that," Jason said.

"And we held out," Alex continued. "Worst thing we could do. Tried to play them off against each other. Bad mistake to bring politics into it."

"What was the ending?" asked Bal, who was most amused and seemed happier than in days.

"The ambassador convinced us the Royal Marine response would be a tougher nut to crack," Alex said. "It was hard to argue with."

"Yeah."

"So, it was suggested, strongly, that we officers resign."

"Bastards," Bart said in humorous sympathy.

"Indeed."

There was silence for several minutes. There were few stories that could top that, or even be offered in the same vein.

"Wait!" Aramis said, objecting. "If you resigned in lieu of court-martial, how did you get into Ripple Creek? That's on the no-hire list, enforced, and no waivers allowed."

"Court-martial was never mentioned," Alex said, sighing. "The colonel said something to the effect of 'You disgraceful assholes will be out of my Corps within twenty-four hours or else.' None of us wanted to find out what 'or else' was. I resigned. Honorable letter on file, but no medals to show for it."

"You could theoretically go back?"

"I believe a letter was filed about the circumstances. They attached it to my honorable discharge. The code says my term was satisfactorily completed and I have no service obligation."

"That's an enlisted code, not an officer code," Jason said.

"Yeah, I kinda took that as a hint," Alex said.

"Never had anything like that," Jason admitted. "But I did drink too much tequila once and got sick."

"Doesn't everyone?" Aramis asked.

"Yes, but not everyone wakes up at oh nine hundred the next day in a park on the beach, twenty kilometers away from the bar . . . no phone, no wallet, no memory, and no bruises to explain it."

"Wow, seriously rolled." Elke said.

"You'd think so," he nodded. "The weirdest thing was that on my chest was this little statue of a Hindu god with a massive grin on its face."

"I call bullshit," Aramis said with a roll of his eyes. "Not buying it."

"Oh, I do," Elke said.

"Certainly," Bart offered in support. "Sailors often have strange experiences."

"We shall not discuss Africa in this context," Shaman offered with a deep chuckle.

"I tried for officer once," Bart said.

"What happened?" Elke asked. "You were senior petty officer, yes?"

"Yes. They rejected me for officer training when they found out my parents were married."

Bart was so serious, so reticent that the joke had great effect. Added to the stress they were all under, it was much appreciated as they laughed loudly.

Bob was sinking over the horizon, apparently into the water. Huge clouds towered up on either side, warning of a storm the next day. Those clouds were bright flames in the backlight, reflected in the shimmering water.

"Bob really is gorgeous when seen like this," Elke commented. "A big, orange ball bouncing on the waves."

"Bal, that's one thing we were never clear on," Aramis said. "Just why is the local star called 'Bob'?"

"Just as Elke said," Bal nodded.

"Hmmm?"

"Big Orange Ball."

There was silence for long seconds.

Bart finally said, "You must surely be joking."

"No, not at all," Bal insisted. "Look, it can't be the Sun. It can't be called by a catalog name. No one on Earth ever gave it a mythological name, because it can't be seen well enough to matter from twenty-one light-years. It was never even given any proper constellation name, and let's be honest: literacy is a rare commodity here. And it does have far more yellow to its spectrum than Sol."

"Big Orange Ball," Alex repeated.

"That's actually quite clever," Aramis admitted.

"So how long until we port?" Shaman asked. He hadn't said anything about Bob, but was chuckling.

"Late tomorrow," the captain said. They still hadn't asked his name and weren't going to. He hadn't asked theirs, though they'd been talking enough. Not good. Still, they had to unwind, the captain was in on this as a smuggler, and everyone who mattered knew who they were anyway and would twig once a hint was given.

"Even better, we'll have concealment."

"That was my plan, yes," Jason nodded. He looked over at the captain. "And you will be released, sir, and paid. We do apologize for the inconvenience."

"And I do hope we can count on your silence, under the circumstances?" Elke commented.

The captain stretched and sighed.

"Yes, I will be silent," he said. "As long as I am paid for both ways and no furder hassles."

"I see no reason for them," Alex said. "All our hosts have been such nice people."

Elke smiled and said, "Well, Alex, you get more respect with a kind word and five kilos of high explosive than you do with a snarl. You should have had demo support in Barbados."

It was eerie to look out at night. With the navigation lights and bright starlight illuminating the crests of waves, and some luminescent fish, they rode above a glowing blanket, occasionally jolted by a pressure gradient. The broad wings and heavy compression did make it a very smooth flight overall. They were at fifteen meters, just high enough to clear normal waves, but in danger for a storm.

"They'd land and drift if that happened," Bart said. "This is not a craft for a planet without good weather prediction."

"No, that would be bad," Elke agreed. She'd been at the window or the rear deck most of the trip, not looking queasy, but looking as if she was afraid she might be.

It was efficient, however. They were making a steady hundred kilometers per hour using less fuel than a boat and comfortably seated for breakfast, even if the rations were self-heating prepacks. The captain offered them, and it beat what they had.

The captain came up from below and relieved the second mate. He held a bulb of coffee and looked rested and awake. He glanced over the instruments, nodded, and said, "We make land tonight at dusk."

"Can you delay until dark?" Alex asked.

"If I dial back speed, sho," he said, sipping. "Need to save fuel."

"Do so. We want you to make port so no one is suspicious."

"Gonna wonda why I'm late," he shrugged.

"For another five hundred, I think you can make up a good story."

"I think so, too," he grinned, then raised his coffee in toast.

The day passed with them discreetly checking weapons and

gear. Ammo was in short supply, and it wasn't likely they could get more. He was always amazed at how many thousands of rounds one could burn through for suppression and distraction. Bart was at the chart table with a broad, hi-res image up, and pointed out features to the rest.

"With an air cushion vehicle, we could land on any stretch of beach. The problem being that most of the beaches along this coast are rough rock. This is a postglacial flooded plain, so there hasn't been time for any real beach to form. We have a choice of rocky bluffs, the harbor, or a sandy shelf beach all the way over here." He indicated on the map.

Alex looked at the screen. He looked more. He was familiar with sea charts as a Marine officer, but it had been a long time and he didn't see what he wanted to see.

"Okay," he said finally. "You're telling me we land in a harbor full of customs agents, or in the ass end of nowhere where it could be hours before any kind of transport comes along."

"If we could refuel, we could go further. There are strict limits on the range of this craft."

"And any regular boat would be even more limited."

"Yes, exactly," Bart said.

"So why can't we just fly up the rocky beaches?"

"Turbulence. Between land, water, rocks, temperature gradients, wind currents—"

"Yeah, I get the idea."

"We can land and port, or land and try to climb a beach and look for transport, seven armed people with no good explanation, hoping the first people we encounter are not Coastal Patrol."

"I suppose we should talk to our host some more."

"Yes, we should."

Jason sat at the controls getting the hang of this thing, with the captain at his elbow. Better altitude gave a smoother flight to a point, because the air stabilized from the wave motion below. At peak altitude, lift fell off. Once you learned to keep it in the zone, it wasn't bad at all.

That discovered, he engaged the autopilot and punched in direction and speed. They didn't have exact coordinates yet, so he just told it to fly generally for the port. They had a couple of hours, and at this range they'd be invisible against the sea.

The captain nudged him, and they joined the rest in the debate. Where to land?

"There is traffic on de coast road," the captain offered. "But not much. Small trucks. Some land trains."

"'Land trains'?" Shaman asked.

"Multiple trailers behind a powerful turbine tractor. They take their own fuel and supplies and don't stop between destinations," Aramis said. "They still use them in Australia."

Shaman said, "I don't see a faster way of traveling. We flag one down, it'll be suspicious, of course, and we try not to hurt anyone."

"The standard of living is higher over here, too," Alex said. "So bribes won't go as far." He noticed the extra body and said, "Captain, would you please join the crew? I don't wish to share this info."

The captain didn't look happy at all, but he did climb down the hatch after a hurt and suspicious look. Bart dogged the hatch and said, "Go ahead."

"I was going to say," Alex continued, "then we have to dismount well outside of town to avoid being pegged. We can't just drive into the spaceport."

"Why not? That would be faster. Less time for anyone to react," Aramis asked.

"Assuming we find a vehicle going there. If someone hauling us is reported missing, and they're seen, the *local* alarm gets raised sooner. We want the locals looking in the wrong place for a while and never thinking of the threat to the port."

"You're correct, of course."

"So how far out should we start?"

"I don't know that we can," Jason said. "The beaches are heavily bluffed and rocky. There's one area that's flat above the cliffs and low enough that this bird can reach it, and it means a tricky transition from wing lift to skirt, then back the other way without nose-diving and wrecking. The captain has to do that latter part."

"Once we're gone it's not our problem," Aramis said.

"It is if he crashes and is seen, or if he decides to cruise along behind us until we're seen." That coast looked ugly on the chart.

"There is that." Aramis looked embarrassed, but it wasn't a hard mistake to make.

"You advise against it, then?" Alex asked.

"I do," Jason admitted. "The captain's being truthful. Our best bet is to get into the harbor and sneak out from there." It wasn't getting any better.

"He said they watch," Bart put in.

"We're not going to look like refugees. We're going to look like crew. Elke and Bal are the only potential problems, although Bal speaks the language."

"I'd like to hang onto weapons for now," Alex said. "Can we manage that?"

"Small arms and batons, yes. I'm sure I can find a way." Jason wasn't quite sure which way yet, but there had to be something.

"We should send Bal through first," Aramis said.

"Yes," Bart agreed.

"That's a disturbing concept."

"I can manage the talk, as they say," Bal said, nodding. "I am a liability in a fight, so if I can get at least to the gate first, I am easier for you to extract. If I make it through, I am not a concern should you have to blow your way through."

"I agree," Elke said.

"Yes," Jason agreed. "Makes sense. We'll start with Bal, then whoever is most obvious, so it should get easier. What do we need? ID? Bribe? The proper look?"

"Bring the captain up," Alex said.

The captain seemed glad to help if only to assure they were off his ship sooner. "I give you clodes," he said. "You blend in, say your piece, and try to slip out widout papers. They may not ask if they're busy."

"We'll have to hope for that."

"Then let's land. I think the captain has earned a bonus," Alex said while Jason cringed. They were getting desperately low on operating cash and would need more.

The captain brought the lights back up and headed back into the pattern. As spread out as the craft were, it wasn't glaringly obvious they'd been dark. He slid to the south and picked up the beacon into the harbor. Gulls and birdiles flew in formation with them. It occurred to Jason that he hadn't seen much local life. Apart from a few reptilian forms, most of what he'd seen was Earth forms. Few lived on land here, and the chemistry difference seemed to have chased most locals far away from the invading humans.

Ports at night always looked surreal, with sea mist halos around lights, illuminated structures, boats, and black water. They settled, skittered, bumped, and slowed, then drove in on the cushion, bobbing slightly.

Everyone was tense, more so with weapons stowed in luggage. Aramis was good. He'd made it all look like typical sea bags and crew bags. Of course, if any of it was scanned or opened for a search, there would be trouble. To that end, he'd stowed weapons loaded so they could be grasped in a second. They just might be shooting their way out of this.

Jason considered that soberly. They were already guilty of multiple MCJ violations, local laws, UN civil laws, including conspiracy, murder, arson, grand theft, embezzlement, attempted kidnapping, not to mention weapons violations . . . it was a hell of a time to be a good guy.

The docks here were much more modern, with proper gantries and davits for unloading cargo onto conveyers and modular transporters. At the crew's direction, they fell to and helped sling a container each, then rode with it onto the conveyor. Bal was with Shaman for comfort and safety. Jason rather enjoyed the lift, and was sorry to jump down after unsnapping the hook. Back to the threat zone. He sighed.

He made sure each member of the crew got a slice of the captain's take. That was a security measure. If they'd all taken a modest bribe, they were not about to admit any impropriety. However, if the captain had kept it all, that could be likely.

It was bright enough under strong lights. A modern port never slept, and this was modern enough. Sharp shadows contrasted everything, but he could see most of the dock despite them. He could clearly see where the exit was, and off-duty shore details and some crew were heading that way. They joined the gaggle. Shift change was a good time to press through. Security would be busy and hopefully accommodating.

There was a line through the personnel gate. They had agreed to be close for mutual cover, even if it meant an act to pretend not to know each other. Luckily, few of the departing crews wanted to talk.

He felt the prickly alertness of the others, and that wasn't good. Bishwanath was first, then Shaman, he, Alex, Elke, Bart, and Aramis, in a clear run from oldest and most necessary to youngest and most expendable. Hopefully, though, they'd all make it. He stepped forward into the tube-lit tunnel past the checkpoint.

No such luck. They were inspecting bags and not at random. ID didn't seem to be an issue. Contraband was.

A tunnel. We're in a fucking tunnel, he thought. That created all kinds of problems.

On the other hand, it meant no threats from the side. He looked around for cameras, yes, there and there, and there had to be barricades . . . there. Now, did Elke have any explosive? Everything was supposed to be stowed, but he was betting she still had a hideout or two . . . because if she didn't they were all steak.

The line moved steadily, with an even ten inspectors checking bags mechanically. The way Aramis had wrapped things, they might not even notice, but the odds shrank with seven inspectors on the seven of them. He kept an eye out for cues and intel and prepared to start his own if need be.

Alex unzipped the rear of his bag. That was all he needed to know. He followed suit and noted the location of his baton's grip. He was glad they had those along, now.

He edged forward, eyes slowly sweeping. Everyone was ready, and something ugly was going to erupt any time now.

They shuffled forward and the inspectors grabbed the first three bags: Bal's, Shaman's, and his. He kept a calm outside while watching expressions. He already knew they were busted. The question was how much and in what fashion? He got the answer in about a second.

All three men twitched, one looking up at Shaman, the one with Bal reaching for his gun, and the one facing Jason reaching for what had to be an alarm.

The only good thing was that the reaction was simultaneous, a group response.

Bal was no slouch. He yanked a baton from under his coat and zapped his antagonist. Jason drew his from the bag as did Shaman, and the rest of the team swarmed forward for backup, all facing forward or sideways except Aramis, keeping the line behind at a distance it was too happy to keep. Shouts, yells, and clatters made the fight obvious, but they were surging forward past the inspection point.

Ahead, a gate slammed down, then another behind. It was obvious how the locals felt about such things; neither one had any safety interlocks and two people were almost punctured by the gate ends.

"Move!" Elke yelled, slipping flat against the wall and low, skittering sideways to the forward gate. She fumbled for something in her pack, and Jason cringed, because in this tunnel it was going to be deafening. None of them had hearing protection in. They wanted to be discreet, and the high-end filter earbuds were not what anyone in this port wore.

A tremendous boom echoed down the hall, but the gate was still standing. Then he realized Elke was still setting her charge. That had been gunfire. He turned to see one guard with a large pistol, just as Aramis raised his free hand and shot him through the face. Another cringe. They had hoped to avoid local casualties, but a goon in ballistic and shock armor necessitated an escalation, and he had fired first. Aramis staggered. He'd been hit.

"*Fireinthehole!*" Elke shouted, barely a moment before her detonation shook the walls and tore the grate in three places. Jason's head rang. She kicked at the residue while cursing before disappearing into a wave of explosion-churned dust filling the enclosed space. Jason took a deep breath, grabbed his bags, and *pushed* ahead of himself. He nudged Shaman and Bal, they all waddled forward with arms and batons out to feel.

Elke shouted, "Watch the baton, *vûl,*" and shimmied underneath to rise alongside Jason. She threw something else that popped and turned into a smoke screen.

They emerged from the tunnel into an open area still filled with dust that resolved as the vestibule to outside guarded by a single, surprised-looking man whose function was clearly to stop people entering the wrong way. Someone zapped him and he went down, then they were on the street in a dock area, industrial facilities giving way to bars, casinos, whorehouses, and assorted other crude entertainment. Jason saw pawnshops, repair ops . . . great places to hide. No one here would talk to a cop unless threatened, and likely the local union/mob conglomerate ran things. They just had to hope their casualty wasn't anyone who got a job through connections. Likely not. He was a low enough level flunky.

The problem was they were an obvious group. "String out," he ordered, not waiting for Alex, who was bringing up the rear. They made eye contact, he signaled the same in hand signs, and Alex nodded. Shortly, they were three small groups about ten meters apart, with Elke backing up Shaman with Bal. Bart moved up close to Jason and started talking.

Loudly he said, "Yes, a drink. That is what we need after a long day. I shall buy you a beer." Then softly he said, "All port towns look the same. Let me lead."

"Go." Follow the sailor to the beer.

The two of them moved briskly ahead and overtook the presidential detail. Behind, a massive response was brewing at the security point. They wanted to quit this area quickly.

Bart did seem to have a feel for the area. He led the way down an alley, where everyone was paranoid until they passed a guy leaning against the wall, pants down, and getting head from a hooker, who smiled and waved as they jogged past.

From the alley they crossed a street, still in separate groups, and followed a walkway past a construction zone. They were perhaps five hundred meters from the dock, but that distance had put a great many people and several turns between them. As long as they weren't being followed now, they were much safer.

Shortly they were gathered in a dark lot. They didn't stand out. Multiple small groups, some social, some gangs, were clustered here and there. Jason doubted any were as well armed as they, however. The ground had been paved at one time, was now largely gravel with grass and scrub poking through, mostly some local plant that was all spikes somewhat like a cactus.

Once gathered, Bal held still for his obligatory looking over. He bore it stoically. He was needed alive even more now.

"Me next," Aramis said. Jason was shocked when he looked at him. The man was pale, shaken, and had a stain seeping down his pants from under his jacket. The jacket had a ragged hole.

Shaman helped him slip to the ground as he winced and twitched. He ripped the coat open with a knife, sliced and peeled back the shirt and said, "Ballistic wound. I would say the guard shot too low and hit the counter. The projectile fragmented. It is not life-threatening, but will need further attention." Jason saw antiseptic, wound sealer, and a bandage going in, and a twisted chunk of something coming out. The wound was the kind one called a "scratch" later that was excruciating and debilitating at the time.

"Pity we can't broadcast from here," Aramis commented. He was gasping slightly. They all were, but he had more reason than the rest.

Jason said, "Right. With that same BuState running their operation here. Even if we broadcast it, it'll be suppressed. At most, a rumor gets out. Bal has to be in a clean system. That's not this one." It ticked him off, too. The bureaucrats could screw anything up.

"Fortunately, from here out we can solve many of our problems with money," Alex said. "So I require twenty-five percent back from everyone. We're going to be tossing bribes."

"We're getting low on that," Jason said.

"Which is part of why we smuggled the rocket launchers. Do you think you can sell them?"

"Of course I can sell them," Jason agreed. "The question is, how fast?

"I'd say soon. We are going to be tracked."

"Definitely," Elke said. "That explosive charge was from the base. A detailed examination will show it."

CHAPTER TWENTY-FIVE

The attack made the intel net before it made the news. Even though it was far too early, a war council was called over it. That meeting wasn't held in the palace; there was no palace anymore. Nor were the Aerospace techs along. They'd bailed out of the capital and back to the spaceport, "to keep evacuation secure for everyone." That showed a cunning Weilhung didn't like. You won a war by fighting, not fleeing, but AF seemed to think that's what the politicians would do. He was afraid they were right.

Fighting was general, if disorganized. BuState didn't want "unarmed" men shot, and the locals had learned that nonlethal weapons were, well, nonlethal. There was no reason not to attack, and the military didn't have facilities to detain thousands of rioters.

"That's pretty clear," deWitt said about the info scattered on charts and screens. He didn't sound happy about it. "Explosion at the Bahane port customs gate, with four to ten suspects running through, at least one female."

"I want to see the lab on the blast, but yes," Weilhung agreed. He couldn't believe they'd screwed up like that, but he was duty bound to nail them for it.

He would, however, be very sloppy about taking the President into custody, in case he wanted to run. He might let one contractor go with him as backup. The rest would have to take their chances in court, with Corporate to back them up.

To that end, Massa was along. "Can I reiterate the need for nonlethal force?"

LeMieure arrived late, with Chester Rawls, a "noted" cartoonist who specialized in childish art and shallow but extreme left politics. He was officially here as a commentator and peacemaker. If Weilhung had his guess, though, leMieure enjoyed a him before battle, and Rawls was the him. Their hotel was overrun and they'd be staying in the Civic Center until they bailed. Rawls looked at the uniforms and slunk to the corner.

LeMieure, as usual, had to open his mouth and put his asshole in it. "I'm sure, Mister Massa, that your precious team will not be killed unless they're even stupider than they've been so far."

The man really hated everyone, Weilhung realized. Perhaps he'd been abused growing up, or mocked for his corpulent grotesqueness, but something made him just hate anyone competent. How he'd turned a total lack of morals, talent, skill, or honesty into so much said a lot about a large segment of the population.

Massa looked ready to rip things apart. Weilhung cringed. Massa had been Recon, and had been very good. Some of the stuff Weilhung knew about, that leMieure never would, was hairy. Massa was not someone to antagonize, and he was a District Agent for Ripple Creek because he had that much experience with hairy stuff.

All he said, though, was, "Mister leMieure, my people have always caused the minimal loss of life possible, something you have attacked them for. If attacked with nonlethal weapons, there is a chance to bring everyone down peacefully, which I thought was your goal here. If they're attacked with lethal weapons, they will respond accordingly, and you will have at least fourteen casualties," at which his tone and volume increased, "because I double-guaran-goddamn-fucking-TEE you they will take out their opponents at better than one to one. If Sykora has time to rig charges, you could lose hundreds. Vaughn can outshoot anyone on any Olympic team or in any military unit anywhere, and they won't hesitate. There's a reason they are paid a thousand marks a day, and it's not for their statesmanship." He stopped, and still had a glare on his face that promised death.

LeMieure just did not get it. He faced Weilhung and said, "Is that something you're afraid of, Major? I thought you were soldiers in order to die."

Levelly, Weilhung replied, "If I must, but I prefer not to hasten the process. It's also hard on the families at home, as you have

noted in your works." He seethed inside. The hypocrisy, conde-
scension, and vitriol from this *thing* was beyond anything he had
words to describe his loathing for.

DeWitt said, "Sir, we need to keep in mind that they were con-
tracted through BuState. If things go really bad, we'll take the heat."
He intoned it so it was clear he was implying, "You'll take the heat."
Though it was likely that leMieure figured to pass the blame.

Document everything, Weilhung reminded himself. He was
recording this on a device too small to be found, and leMieure
was such an incompetent, and so distrustful of tech people, who
returned the favor, that there was no suppression on either audio
or electronics in here. He considered that if need be, he'd share
the info with deWitt to save his ass. He was a decent type. Massa
was doing his job, so that was possible, too. But there was no
way leMieure was getting this recording. The man was climbing
the ladder by fellating ahead and buggering behind, and if Major
Lee Weilhung could kick the legs out, he would.

"I'll load up and get ready to move. Colonel Weygandt has
already cleared the appropriate issues. If Mister deWitt will let
me know when confirmation comes through, I'll head personally
over," he said, while not saying, *to get away from you, slimeass,*
"and deal with it. In the meantime, I'll alert our element at Bahane
spaceport to expect an infiltration."

"We have one other item," he added. "Mister Anderson used
his reserve military ID to gain access to the base. It is in direct
violation of military regs and oath to serve in this capacity while
under military discipline."

Massa said nothing, and in fact it was impossible to tell if he
knew or cared or not. Weilhung expected leMieure to go bugfuck over the fact, but the ignorant sod didn't seem aware of the
relevance. That was a small mercy.

LeMieure said, "I have an important appointment. You'll have
to deal with this yourselves, as best you are able." With that, he
left, with Rawls scuttling along behind.

They all stared. Nothing was said until deWitt summed it up
with, "I'm glad it's Colonel Weygandt doing the reports on this
and not me."

"So, you've got our order to shut the starport down," Weilhung
said, hating it but realizing the necessity.

"Yes," deWitt said, not looking happy himself. "I sent that advice to LeMieure, who forwarded it when he was done with whatever he was doing at the time."

Weilhung thought that delay, no matter how short it was, might have been too much. He was of mixed feelings about that.

By daybreak, the team was near the spaceport. They were also dripping sweat, caked in dust, and generally not much to look at. They fit in well.

"I should move here when I retire," Bart said. "I can buy a Mercedes and four rocket launchers for less than a thousand marks." He meant it in humor. "And get two free machine guns."

"Hey, we were in a hurry both times," Vaughn said tiredly. "I only sold at twenty on the mark. Alex pretty much gave the car away."

"Yes, but it was an infinite return on your investment," Bal chuckled. "One can't complain about that."

"We can always complain," Anderson said. "That's what soldiers do, Bal." Though he hadn't said much about the laceration along his ribs, which had peeled skin down to the bone. Bart was impressed. Most people would have been on the ground from that. Anderson had run a couple of kilometers and rucked more, with straps running over the wound.

The trip had been a combination of cadging rides on trucks, walking, and running. They would need to clean up and rest before too long, but they also needed to hurry. Word was getting out about their escape.

They also had a professionally guarded spaceport in front of them, Bart reflected with disgust and approval. Even if they were safe in an abandoned storefront for now, one of several in the area, they would have to tackle the gate soon, before it was sealed against them.

"I see several ways in," Vaughn said. "The problem is that we don't want to come up out of the ditches or sewers or on the launch line for sabotage. We want to come up as passengers."

"We need to go through the front," Alex said, "then disappear into the crowd. The problem is buying tickets for cash."

"Are we sure they have our pictures?" Anderson asked.

"Are we sure they do not?" Elke replied. She was right, Bart realized.

"Do we want to try to sell the carbines and grenade launchers?" Vaughn asked.

Marlow shook his head. "I hate like hell wasting the asset, but there is no fucking way to get them aboard and we won't need more than pistols in space. The longer we hang around, the greater the risk of discovery."

"So we dump them." Vaughn sounded as if he was cutting a leg off. The man really liked guns. "I really wanted to take this AK with me." He held up the archaic weapon he'd lugged all this way.

"Leave them in here," Bart said. "It could be the former tenant will return and will have a gift to sell to restart his business. We can consider it a gift for breaking in."

"Makes sense. Out of sight, out of mind." Vaughn started slimming the bags down. The goal was to get to one carry-on each.

"Cut the mass way down," Marlow said. "If need be, we buy clothes and toiletries on the way. If need be, we share."

"I will share a toothbrush with Elke," Bart said. "But I will not wear her underwear."

"You assume I wear any," Elke grinned. "Though I prefer boxers with lots of room in front."

Marlow put down his pocket binox, carefully slipped them into the case, and handed them back.

"Abandon these, too," he said. Bart could tell it was painful. "It's mass we don't need. I'll recover the cost later."

If we do not wind up in jail, Bart thought.

Elke was actually hugging her shotgun and misty-eyed. "I must leave you now, Pierce," she said to it, and handed it slowly to Jason. She suddenly looked much less sure of herself.

Marlow picked up the outline. "Okay, we've got the gate and fence. We've got seven of us, one wounded. We need to distract the guards long enough to drive into the terminal, abandon the vehicle, then buy tickets without being seen."

"The last part is probably doable," Vaughn said. "Mesh over the face blurs features enough that an auto search won't find it."

That made sense, Bart thought.

"Are you sure?"

"Sure enough," Vaughn said. "I don't see that we have too many options."

"So that just leaves getting through the gate and inside," Bal said. "How do we propose to do that?"

"Well, Elke . . ." Anderson hinted, looking at her. Bart took a moment to figure it out. Oh.

"Yes?" she replied.

"You know. You could distract him."

" 'Distract him'?" she repeated.

"Yes, act sexy and interested. You know."

She rolled her eyes and sighed. "Oh, that'll never work. You watch too much vid."

It wasn't the cliché concept that had Bart wondering, but was her very manly, dirty, functional style of dress.

"He's male. It'll work."

Vaughn said, "I'm inclined to agree with that part, but I'm not sure it's a sound plan overall."

"Even if it works, it will take an hour of convo to get anywhere," she said.

"Five minutes," Anderson argued. "Act wide-eyed and interested. He's a soldier, you're press, you're fascinated by his killer instinct."

"Ah, is that what works on you?" she asked, eyes rolling again. She was starting to flush a little. She wasn't embarrassed by herself, Bart realized, but by how people reacted to her.

Anderson stuttered, then said, "It'll work. Get him clear and you can be a distraction behind. Heck, you could probably persuade two of them." He was clearly hurting. Every move of his ribs made him twitch. Shaman held up a painkiller, and he agreed to it with a wave and a nod.

"Oh, kinky," she said. "Fine. It's worth a try, but I have a bad feeling."

"Oh, go for it." He made shooing motions. "Give us a few minutes to get a cab."

She dropped her gear, picked the valise back up, and looped the camera strap around her neck. Wiping and slapping off as much dust as possible, she rose and strode straight into the street at a measured pace: fast enough to not be suspicious, slow enough not to appear a threat.

Getting a cab was easy. Several were leaving the port and it just took flagging one down. However, the driver looked at their appearance and balked.

Luckily, it took a minimal bribe to get him not to care. It was an axiom that people offering money didn't turn around and hijack you. At least, not if the money offered exceeded the maximum amount they knew you could carry. He obviously knew they were up to something, but the cabbie had likely seen far more unusual things so far. Bart believed they were about to raise that bar. He climbed in the passenger side while Bal, Shaman, and Marlow climbed in the rear.

Jason used the sensors he'd salvaged, and watched around the corner by microcam, lucky bastard. Aramis had to sneak a peek near ground level, but there was a hydrant that would cut most of his head from being visible. That also reduced his window, but that was a worthwhile trade. He ignored the flaming pain in his side. The painkiller was dropping it to a hot ache, anyway.

The guards did see Elke, and their eyes followed, but whether they were interested or just watching her as traffic was hard to say. She crossed the broad but lightly traveled street with her fake camera in hand, not quite in "use" but obviously her reason for being there.

Then she gave them a slight wave, nod, and smile.

The guards grinned back, showing lots of healthy teeth. They might have wiry, almost skeletal bodies, but their teeth were to be envied.

Elke sauntered up. What she really needed to do was sashay, though without overdoing it. Maybe she couldn't manage that. Or, he reflected, she may not have had any idea how to sashay at all.

The guards watched her approach and didn't make any serious attempt to stop her. They did keep hold of their weapons, and there were occasional hefts for reassurance. She wasn't a threat, but they certainly weren't going to just open the gate.

The question was, how corruptible were they? Most of this planet operated on bribes and payoffs, but there were always a few honest assholes screwing things up.

They were certainly happy to talk to her, and let her roll footage. So far, so good. Then she was commenting with a smile, and the men were posing with their weapons, hefting them and angling to show off muscle.

It did take a few minutes to soften them up. The problem was, they never moved far from their booth, no matter where she asked them to pose for photos. There was a clear limit on how long she could milk that.

"Guess we better start advancing," Aramis said.

"Yeah," Jason agreed. "We need to be there when something happens."

One at a time, Aramis first, they walked across the road trying to look at home. Aramis carried an empty box as a prop. If he could look like a delivery person or a scavenger, good.

He attracted a few looks from squatters, but his ragged coat and the box seemed to pass muster. He was left alone, and no type of alarm was sounded. He deliberately didn't look at his surroundings much, and not at Elke.

He sought more bushes and crawled in, once out of sight of the main road. He was surprised at how crappy the security really was. A good squad could blow through in seconds.

Of course, he noted, that would alert all kinds of people, and blow their cover. That wouldn't stop terrorists, but would stop stowaways and smugglers. Even that much was probably not from good planning, but that did not mean it wouldn't work against them.

Once in cover, he took a look for Elke. He was slightly closer and had a better angle here. There she was, and she'd run out of time.

Her cover as a reporter couldn't have lasted long, and then coming onto them had put her in a position of put up or shut up, or in this case, put out or shut up. They led her around the side of the building, and she was now in a position of assuming a position or starting a fight. He didn't need to be a rocket scientist to figure which one she'd choose.

Jason wandered over clutching what looked like a bottle in a bag, with his ruck hung by one strap so he looked like a wandering derelict. That look was marred by a recent shave, but improved by some dirt. A slight surreptitious wave got his attention, and Aramis indicated Elke's position and "fight soon."

Jason raised a hand and signed, "You go, I follow."

Back on his feet, Aramis started walking, with the box. One could get quite close to almost anything by acting nonchalant or spaced out. He tried for both, and now he could see how things were developing.

Elke had let one of the guards get her against the wall in a dark shady spot, legs spread. She was pulling at her shirt, but obviously couldn't go more than another few seconds without actually having sex. There were possibly reasons she'd go that far. He couldn't believe this was one of them. He fought against quickening his pace. That would screw things up worse if seen. He did wiggle his baton out of his coat and wedge it behind the box.

Then it all went to hell. The guard was eager, and tried to

clutch at her boobs and kiss her. She caught the incoming grab and twisted. She jackhammered her knee into his balls in a move so fast and balanced she had to have practiced, slam, slam, slam, slam. Despite his aching side, Aramis cringed. Damn.

The good news was both the guard and his buddy were busy. That meant just the one at the gatehouse was a problem. Their cab zipped in and slowed, braking in front of him, and Jason was closing, too.

Ten meters, Aramis thought. Close enough, but closer was better. He angled the baton behind the box and got ready to deploy it. If needed. Elke seemed to have both men under control, though it wouldn't be long before something blew the cover. Where was the cab now? There. They must be having fun trying to get the driver to arrive just at the right moment, he thought.

The decision was made when Jason said, "Now, kid." Aramis dropped the box at once, extended the baton at waist level, and point-shot. He was well within range for a good stun, and he had the power dialed up.

That was the moment when the fight turned to wrestling, and Elke got picked up and thrown. She blocked the charge perfectly, so she was unconscious when she hit the ground, and the second guard was unharmed and facing Aramis. Aramis swore, waited the half second for the baton to recharge while closing at a jog, and discharged it again.

Just as Elke recovered, jumped, and went for the guy. She wavered, stumbled, and fell, taking a fist in the eye more from accident than plan.

His swearing rose to a new crescendo. At that range, she'd be out for minutes instead of seconds. At that range, recharging was out of the question. They'd been told the baton cases were tough, and he gave it a real world test, braining the very confused guard, who collapsed over Elke, grinding her into the grass.

It was like a bad sensie.

He reached out and contact-zapped the one she'd kneed, who was recovering slowly but still wrapped around his crotch. Then he zapped the one twitching atop Elke, and grabbed him under the arms to heave him out of the way.

Elke's shirt was ripped, and yes, those were very nice boobs, and he grabbed her arm to heave her into a firefighter's carry, his rib screaming at him. He rose carefully, turned, and jogged around the building, baton ready in case there was a fight still ongoing—unlikely, but today had not been a good day.

He saw feet stretched out, and then a torso, and Jason standing over the body. A moment later, he reached inside and slapped the switch for the gate, as Bal opened the door and Aramis shoved Elke's form onto the seat. Alex propped her upright, Jason jumped in the bed and reached a hand down for Aramis, and as soon as he was in, Jason slapped the cab and Bart took off. The driver seemed to be sitting shaking in the rear. His eyes were hugely wide and terrified.

Elke woke up and was ticked. "I tode you *kozoks* it wouldn' work! *Kurva drát*," she slurred. "He wanted to take me to the guard shack so his friend could watch!"

Aramis flushed. Watching Elke struck him as a pretty good idea. Watching her with another guy . . . no. He couldn't say why that was the first thought he had under the circumstances.

Recovering, she said, "Hand me my bag." It was behind him in the stack, luckily on the right, so he grabbed it, pulled and twisted it out of the pile, turned around, and said, "Erk!"

She was naked and wiping her face down with a bleached towel from Jason. Aramis tried not to stare as she grabbed a blouse from the top of her kit, wiggled into it with some very interesting stretches and contortions, and got fastened. Slacks followed as she arched into them.

So *that* was what Elke looked like.

Damn. That was a story to tell over beers at some point.

Jason had already cleaned up, and the others were taking turns, except Bart who was driving. Jason reached around from behind to help Bart clean his face and neck. Aramis grabbed the towel and swiped at his armpits to kill bacteria, staying above the glued and bandaged gash. His shirt was unbuttoned and it came off at a tug, then Alex helped him slip into a new one. By the time they pulled onto the drop off area for the port, everyone was presentable, even if Bart was still wiggling into pants.

"So, we're inside the zone and safer, in that anything in the zone is considered to be cleared. Any ID check will be cursory," Alex said, "except that we've triggered somebody's alarms. At the same time, they're looking for threats, which is not us now. Stand by."

Alex pulled out his phone, inserted the capacitor, and punched a number manually. When he got an answer he said, "No, I don't want to talk to the officer in charge, I want to talk to the

NCO who knows what's going on. Yes, it's me. I have twenty seconds and have to be discreet. Can you give me a distraction, and I mean a big one, *right now* in your area? You need to be overrun by skinnies, dire wolves, aliens, Elvis, and Godzilla. Just make a whole bunch of noise. Yes, I know the risk. I'm calling in the favor for the naked chick in the flotation vest, swim fins, and duct tape. Yeah, I would. Thanks. Out." He turned and said, "Cady says hi," while pulling the capacitor again.

"I want to hear that story," Elke said.

"I am sworn to secrecy, but we have some distraction."

Aramis pondered while they traveled. He hadn't really expected to go this far. He intellectually had known what he was agreeing to with this bailout. But to actually go this far, and shoot the guard he'd shot the night before, was really pushing the envelope. He didn't think he could be mindwiped; it would be hard to get a jury sympathetic to chanting gangs and cops. Still, the risk was there, and life in prison was a given. Hell, he'd just started living. He'd damned near died, too, he recalled, his side seizing up again.

A lesser but valid threat was that they'd squeak out in court, broke, booted, and with no credibility. That would mean scut jobs, or else going back to school for credentials in something that didn't require high levels of responsibility.

The alternative was to attempt to write memoirs and produce a documentary. It was even possible that fat bastard leMieure would be interested in it. That would actually be a good thing, because if Aramis was going to be nailed for something, he wanted it to be for smearing that piece of dog shit across the concrete personally.

He realized the rest were looking at him, and that he was grinning.

Once at the terminal they piled out of the cab, immediately split into three groups again, and Aramis wound up with Jason. Bart shoved money at the driver and said, "Take this vehicle and get lost for the day." The driver nodded as if he had a spring in his neck, climbed in, and zoomed off.

Aramis and Jason were far enough from the others to appear unrelated, but close enough to offer backup. They milled around looking for security threats and schedules.

"There's the tramp flight to Grainne I marked," Jason said quietly as he scanned the departure screen. "Its departure is moved up. We need to board a shuttle now."

"Want to suggest a method of getting aboard?" Aramis asked. He had no idea what to do about this.

"I advise against stowing away at this end. Strongly. I think we're going to have to go up and get aboard while they're loading cargo. That gives us about twenty hours. Kinda tight."

"And once we do that?" Alex asked, wandering by.

"Then we negotiate."

"Guns or money?"

"Both."

Off to the side, Bart walked up to a man, squatted down next to his chair, and started talking. There was some disagreement, some anger, but in a few moments the man stood. Some exchange took place and Bart returned.

"I told him to disappear for the morning, to catch a later flight with a different ticket," he offered quietly.

"You're saying that a lot."

"It works," Bart grinned down from his two-meter height. Around here he was not just large, he was a monster. That also made him visible.

There was always a security issue with bribing someone, and that is that they stay bribed. The additional risk here was that it was possible the people whose seats they had were needed or expected. The kind of person who'd skip a flight and let their identity be assumed was either careless, criminal, questionably honest, or likely to turn in a report as soon as they'd made the cash go away.

Jason led the way over to an automated ticket booth that did have a face scanner. It took him only a few moments to slip a stocking mask on, punch buttons, grab a ticket, and unmask as soon as the screen blanked. Aramis followed, feeling obvious and stupid with the mesh over his face. The machine took his cash, but he was all too glad to get done and look unobtrusive again. He was in pain as he sat down, but once he did so he found a position that wasn't too bad.

"I must try to draw cash," Bal put in from the seat next to Aramis. "If Rahul was able to arrange it, I have some waiting I can draw in a moderate sum. Please let me know so I can make that very close to our departure."

"That would be now," Jason said, and rose to escort him.

For Aramis, there was nothing to do but wait for departure.

CHAPTER TWENTY-SIX

The flight was not full, but it was not run by a local enterprise, so there was no concern about squeezing every penny out. Bal trembled in nervousness though he wouldn't admit it. His nation had abandoned him. The comments around him were frustrating and saddening. Kaporta was ten times the nation Celadon was, and his friends still regarded it as a primitive backwater to be exploited.

At no point, however, had they treated him as less than a man or a leader. They were risking their lives for him, likely to no avail. BuState would call him a criminal and jail him at best, mock him and humiliate him into obscurity at worst.

He realized his own violent experiences in life were very shallow in a certain context. Within the last forty-two hours, this group had killed, stolen, burned, lied, and abused authority to get him to safety. Two had been lightly injured, and Aramis had taken a moderate wound right through armor designed to stop it. He had no doubt there were people in his clan and in the Bodyguard who would kill to protect him. He couldn't imagine anyone save Rahul would go as far as his mercenaries, and he'd known Rahul for fifty years.

He worried again about Abirami. As far as she would know within a few hours, he was dead. If he managed to find exile, she might meet up with him in a year or more. There was a possibility that with enough liquid assets and off-planet resources he could create new identities for her and the children. He could be a normal person.

For her, he'd do that. For himself, he'd almost rather be dead, because it was too ignominious to consider. But she and the children deserved whatever he could offer, even if it was only obscurity.

The worst part was that leMieure would not be called to account. The risk to Bishwanath's family was too great. His love for them exceeded his hatred for that thing. That was unjust but unavoidable.

As far as this extraction, he was along for the ride only, able to offer nothing except the trinkets he'd already donated for the coffers, and the money Rahul had just made available. He'd planned for that because it was impossible to survive in this culture without hidden assets. One never put all one's cards out, or wasted so much as a pawn without advantage. Resources were scarce. He was also elated that his friend and assistant was alive and hidden. That was a load off his shoulders for his own safety, since Rahul in hiding would never talk, and for Rahul's.

These people casually tossed away resources he'd kill to have. Part of that was necessity, but part of it was cultural. They did so because they could. It might be a tough decision at times, as with Alex and his fine binoculars, or Jason with a weapon, but they could make that decision. Just the quandary was more than most people here, Bishwanath included, could rationally entertain.

It was one more example of why nothing BuState did was going to work.

He smiled at that. If thinking about work would keep his mind off mundane, life-threatening issues, then he should go over his cabinet and budget again.

He felt the craft move, then roll. Lifting . . . and that was good, but they were not clear and wouldn't be while in this system. Every flight was by definition scheduled and monitored, and there were limited routes and ships available.

It was ten interminable minutes to atmospheric ceiling, and the draft of cold air from the vents didn't help to stop him from sweating.

Then the rockets kicked in, tossing them into orbit. Chemical rockets, and even if they were hydrogen-fluorine with some kind of expansion mass fed in, they were old-fashioned, violent, and loud. The rawness reminded him of the home he was leaving and might never see again.

The physical and psychological stress of it reduced the other stress for a time. Around him, he could peripherally see the others sweating and gripping their couches. The gees were maintaining, and there was this sensation of speed from the engine thrust.

Weilhung didn't think anyone here knew what they were doing. He was fine with that for now.

DeWitt had given up trying to talk sense to his boss, and it was hard to blame him. He was reduced to pissing on the resultant fires and pretending to be unavailable. He could do that because his boss was an idiot. Weilhung had Weygandt, who still thought he was running this op, as if he ever had in any capacity save signing papers, and a general who wanted results at a higher level, who was at least willing to pay to relocate the Recon element. Weygandt was no idiot, though.

Of course, Weygandt was tied up trying to prove an "attack" north of here, against a Ripple Creek element that handled security for the BuCommerce operation, was fake and a cover for Marlow. Of course it was fake. Sure it would end their contract if proven. Of course everything, up to and including everything had to be dropped in case some billionaire, his wench, or deputy catch a stray round. At the same time, not only would the billionaires back their bodyguards, it wasn't critical to follow up now. What was critical was catching Marlow, who had to be in orbit by now.

Weilhung wanted to wait on moving. If he made a move and it was wrong, it was his ass. Everyone would make sure of that. If, however, he just took their advice and orders after those were down in memory on a spare chip, he could point fingers himself. That it was a necessary way to run things didn't make it any less revolting.

I'm becoming a political officer, he thought.

There had been some trouble at Bahane starport: guards disabled and reports of some unusual activity, and BANG! had come that "attack" on BuCommerce. Once that had been sorted out with massive amounts of response by Aerospace, Army, Marines, Europe, China, and Ripple Creek, the important fact trickled through the intel net.

The starport's equipment was too outdated to have proper records, but it seemed to Weilhung that someone in a hurry would have lifted already and be in Highpoint Station looking for transit outsystem. He'd pegged three ships as probables, and was prepared to move after one of them with a bit more intel. He'd made quiet inquiries through AF for that, though it was a shame he couldn't ask Tech White. She could certainly have found out all he needed to know. He was equally sure she wouldn't tell him. He couldn't accuse her of any wrongdoing. AF played its own game here, as everyone else. She wasn't in his chain of command. The Army's assets were far more focused on the ground than in space, which hindered him.

But if he got the reports he wanted, he'd move to intercept and take the credit himself. He didn't see it as ladder-climbing. He saw it as getting someone competent into a position to do something. He could get rid of a lot of idiots lower down and shake things up, if he could curry favor from a political deed. It might be unpleasant, but it was useful. Marlow was an ex-Marine and his people all former military. They were not playing this game, they were the cause of a good part of the trouble, and they were expendable. He'd push for cells instead of graves, but they were not going to make him the fool.

Twenty minutes later he had the intel he wanted. Very interesting. There were several things Marlow could be planning in the Iota Persei system—Grainne. There were only a couple that would matter and he didn't believe the subtle ones fitted with Marlow's profile, and certainly not with Anderson's or Sykora's. Now to get assets there fast and give them a face-to-face.

Debarking was not a problem, though Horace had expected it might be. Certainly the word was out by now. On the other hand, they might be making an extensive search of the port. Nothing happened, though. The crew in the scuffed tube were there simply to help people who were awkward in micro G. None of them were cops.

The baggage center was quite modern. That had to be the doing of Trans Global, and all for PR. The baggage was in a cage in the center of the bubble. The waiting areas and docking gantries were arrayed around the middle, with services in the micro-G hub.

To get luggage, one waved a baggage tag over the scanner, it located the bag floating in the mix, and sent a drone crawling around the cage to retrieve and deliver it. The problem was, there were limited stations, so it took several minutes to get everyone geared. Alex got jumpier and looked ready to abandon some bags to save time, if he hadn't been worried about unclaimed bags with pistols in them.

There was only one bar/café. That was not going to make things easy. They sought a corner of one of the waiting areas and huddled briefly in a corner of it. Horace kept a close eye on Bal for any reactions to the boost and the micro G, but he seemed fine, just very remote. The ongoing stress wasn't killing him as it would a lesser man, but it was certainly taking a toll. The man's face was lined and stiff and he was shaking slightly. He of all of them was likely to be seen as suspicious.

"Bal, as your friend," he said, "you really must take these so you blend in better." He held up two trank pills and prepared to be ignored or rejected.

Bal took them with a nod this time. Apparently, he realized the effect the stress was having on him.

Jason said, "We need to get into the crew area. The bad news is that there aren't many people assigned here for any duration. The good part is that all ships have some crew, there are contract stevedores and the station staff. We need seven suits our size and to sedate the sources. We also need to wait until we know there isn't time to react without delaying the ship—"

"Which ship is it?" Alex asked.

"Ah, sorry. *GCS George*. A nine-thousand-tonne tramp, crew should be about eight. They transport foodstuffs out and a very few luxury goods in, though it wouldn't surprise me if they had other stops on a circuit. I think it's roomy enough, but we need to wait until they're almost ready to button up. That they've moved up a slot means primary cargo is loaded."

"So when do we need to move?" Bart asked.

"I will attempt to find out. Alex, see if you can find a site on how to wear vac suits. We're going to need to."

"I have done so," Elke nodded, "in training."

"So have I. Standard training for all Grainnean troops." That was an interesting revelation, Horace thought.

"How are you, Aramis?" he asked. Hopefully, low G was helping, because there was little more Horace could do for now.

"The painkiller helps, and there's less gravity. I'll last a while." He grinned a forced grin but was holding out.

"Good. We may be able to use sick bay aboard the ship."

He certainly hoped so. Bal was the primary patient. Aramis's wound wasn't likely life threatening, but was ugly. Everyone else was recovering from the scrapes, dings, cuts, and bruises they'd acquired over the last few days.

Jason wandered off to draw intel from somewhere. Alex plugged into the local net with a false ID. Luckily, that was something Company computers were programmed to do for obvious reasons of security.

Horace was nervous himself. This had gone from an escort mission to a wartime bailout that was technically outside the contract even if it had still been in force, to assorted thefts and murders, and now to an attempted escape through vacuum. He didn't cherish what might happen next—hang on the outside of a ship for concealment? This was past any experience he had. Space travel was becoming more common, but that meant inside ships. EVAs were quite limited. Elke had possibly done some, and Jason made it sound as if he had.

Horace was going to monitor Bal carefully for this. He slid over to the other couch.

"How are you holding up, Bal?" he asked in his most solicitous bedside manner.

Bal twitched and looked up from whatever thoughts were keeping him sane. Likely, his family.

"Well enough," he said. "I am scared, of course." He put on a brave grin but it didn't help. "Even this habitat"—he indicated the arching space "above" them—"is intimidating, but I have ultimate trust in you."

"Good," Horace smiled. *I wish I did.* "I am going to watch you closely, and adjust a dose of tranquilizer to keep you calm enough for safety, but responsive enough in case of rapid event changes."

"Yes, I understand. I'll deal with it, as much as I hate medications."

"Medications are often overused," Horace agreed to his charge's position. "But in some cases, such as this, are quite beneficial. We will be past this soon."

"I hope so," Bal said, his body language and tight posture indicating he didn't emotionally believe that.

Horace didn't either, but in a case like this there was no point in quitting.

Jason returned shortly.

"I don't have much," he admitted, taking Alex's computer and slapping a memory stick onto the pad. "They're still loading, and I was able to get a general hull layout of this class. There's a personnel lock in the hold here, which we can use." He indicated on the deck plan.

"Won't they notice it opening?" Shaman asked.

"No," Elke said, then stopped. "Sorry, didn't mean to interrupt."

Jason continued, "It is traditional to leave that unsecured so loading crew can make use of facilities, unsuit to rest, and get to shelter in an emergency. I doubt they'll bother logging every use. They might notice a few more cycles than normal, but they won't generally look at that log until later, by which time we'll have done what we need to."

"We're short on time, though," Shaman said.

"Yes, we need to move."

"Lead on," Alex said with a gesture.

Alex was uncomfortable. He had too little knowledge and too little control of this situation. He trusted Jason completely, but he wanted more experience in this area to make him relax, and he wasn't going to get it.

Part of the stress was Bal, who was critical but untrained. It would be nice if they could set things up and then send for him, but that was not an option. The man had to come along. He was bright enough, and fit enough for a civilian, but there was a measure of mental durability and confidence that came from hard training. That was why he was the noticeable one right now. Not because he was weak, far from it, but his strength came from years of leadership and dispute in an honor culture, not from dedicated combat and training. He had a different presentation.

The inner door from the station to the maintenance area was unlocked. The outer door was locked as required, but it hadn't taken Jason long to code it open. Alex watched and learned. The man knew quite a bit about his technical matters. They were here between shifts and there shouldn't be anyone coming out, nor was there. Bal was still breathing fast, pulse hammering visibly and a potential risk to discovery.

Jason motioned them in. They were in a modified assault formation and swam through the open door fast. The micro G was disorienting, but no one had gotten sick yet. Bal didn't need as much help as Alex had feared, which was good. Bart brought up the rear and closed the lock.

Obviously, no one relevant was present if Jason had cleared them in. Ideally, there would be suits for all just waiting from off-duty personnel. Worst case, they'd have to stalk and sedate or kill people. The reality was halfway in between.

They were in a locker room, smelling of sweat and astringent. Lockers, overhead and bulkhead rails and stanchions. Some litter floating here and there, small scraps of paper, a loose pen, and one soft space shoe. The padding on the bulkheads was scuffed and worn. This was the working part of the station and looked it.

Jason had already half geared up in a suit left hanging on a locker when Alex looked back. Elke found one about her size and started getting fitted. There was one far too large for Bal, but they stuffed him in to get him aboard first. That was an ongoing point. If Bal succeeded, it was hoped the rest of them would be recovered later, so they were somewhat mission expendable. The manner in which they were expendable had changed, but the ethics and tactics remained.

The suited pair stuffed the rest of them into lockers. Jason took it calmly enough. Alex was not particularly claustrophobic and the lockers were large enough and with forced air to help ventilate and disinfect the contents. That didn't reduce the worry about what would happen if someone opened the door and saw him there.

Nothing happened for long minutes, twenty-three by his watch. Eventually, he heard voices and the clatter of lockers. He stiffened as the one adjoining on the right slammed open and gear moved around. He heard a voice say, "Dammit, we'll need to look at the file again. Someone lifted Marvin's suit."

"Are you sure it was lifted? I thought he was reporting in early."

"Nope, he just called from the barracks. I get tired of these pranks. Isn't it always John who pulls that crap?"

"Could be. We'll check when we get downstairs."

Shit, that was going to screw things, Alex realized. As soon as they saw people gearing up, things would slap down with a terrorism warning.

However, that revealed that the area wasn't under live or autonomous surveillance. That made sense. Suits could not easily be smuggled into the civilian craft, and any station staff or ship crew would be easy to mark. Alex tried to decide if now was a good time to go for surprise when that exact thing happened.

As soon as he heard the slam and grunt of a fight starting, he came out, as did the rest. Jason and Elke were fighting hindered by their suits, but Bart was fully capable and strong, even if lacking experience in micro G. Aramis was injured but still had training and the element of surprise. They wrestled the two men to the bulkheads amid shouts that stopped quickly. The four bodies flailed around, Bart's opponent flopping like a fish and then suddenly still from a brutally effective choke hold. Aramis clutched his opponent in a viselike grip until Elke swam in and clenched at the throat.

"Tape," Alex said. Shaman dug some out of a locker and they peeled strips and bound the two. Shaman and Alex donned those suits. The process was simple enough; strip, wiggle into the body of the suit, press the front closed, being sure the gasket fit around your groin so you didn't get vacuum damage, fasten the neckpiece, and hold onto the helmet. Clothes went into a bag, which went into an artificial cloth cover alongside the oxy bottle.

"How long do these bottles last?" he asked. The one on his suit looked rather small.

"Several hours at full charge. Half or better is required for this duty. We should be fine on a tenth," Jason said. Alex checked the gauge, which showed seventy percent and a bit. Good.

Alex wasn't going to tell his two younger agents that if more suits weren't found soon, they were going to fly back down and be sacrificial lambs. Actually, that would provide a damned good distraction, with them misleading everyone as to where the rest had gone. He considered it briefly, but they were useful and would be so again. He preferred to keep everyone together.

Their two victims woke up in a panic. Bart looked at them as they were stuffed into separate lockers, promising, "You are not to be hurt unless you come out. If we wanted people dead we would have killed you already."

One of them nodded briskly, seeming to grasp the logic. His gag was several layers of tape right around his head, not a simple strip that could be poked away with the tongue, as on vid. Elke was thorough. But he panicked again as Shaman whipped out an injector.

"We still need suits for us," Bart said.

"Yeah, this could be a problem," Alex said. He knew they were both professional enough to take the news and do their jobs, but it was not an order he was going to enjoy. *You guys wait in the military's stockade for the rest of us. If all goes well, we'll get you in a month or so.* He didn't see any nicer way to phrase it, or any way around it.

Aramis saved Alex from that tough decision by showing up with two more suits from locker rummaging. Bart was going to be hellaciously squeezed into one, but they would all be dressed. That was a weight off his shoulders. They had to hurry, though.

"You okay, kid?" he asked Aramis after looking at his face. The man was sweating and wincing in pain now.

"It's a bit rough, but I'll deal," Aramis replied, sounding strained. "Really, get me out of here. Please."

That admission was scary. Aramis acted like a superman, and generally managed to pull it off. Confessing that he was having trouble meant his condition was serious.

"We have less than an hour," Jason said. "They will button up at thirty minutes till. We must move now." Even his laconic demeanor was stressed. He twitched in agitation.

"Jason's in charge until we're aboard," Alex said. Hell, he might as well be in charge from now on, with Alex providing oversight. This was Jason's domain and they were going to his system.

"The lock's that way," Aramis pointed.

"The cargo lock is this way," Jason said with a wave. "Mush, manual labor."

Alex grabbed a stanchion and then a rail. He was going to have to pull himself along.

"Five-minute lesson," Jason said. "Clip onto a padeye when I do, using a safety line. Swap lines before disconnecting. There will be a safety tech around somewhere, and even if he doesn't ID us, he'll see the violation. Then we have to stuff him, too. Move carefully, follow my lead or Elke's until we're inside. Absolute bare minimum life-or-death radio chatter. Let's go."

"That is less than five minutes," Bart smiled.

"It's the summary of the outline of the course précis," Jason said. "Let's go."

They hauled themselves along the rail set for that purpose. The access was a long docking passage that could likely receive long tubes or canisters. There had to be some purpose to it, but Alex wasn't sure what. The airlock ahead was big enough for all of them and more. It was clearly designed for shifts. The question was, would anyone notice them?

Jason led them around to a smaller side lock for station maintenance. He spent a few minutes inside the panel disabling the warnings and safeties, as Alex sweated. At any moment, someone could find their last victims, track the tickets, find some other way of locating them. Speed helped, but eventually they were going to bottleneck—as they were now, with one ship to carry them at least twenty days.

He hefted his bag again. After the last round, it contained two changes of clothes, one pistol and a knife, some tradable valuables, a few toiletries, and a fliptop computer. If they had to lighten the load any more, he was going to be naked with a toothpick.

They started cycling through, Jason first, indicating Elke would go last. That made sense. Jason could haggle or coordinate as needed, Elke had enough experience to pull backup. The rest of them were babes in the woods.

This was the longest Alex had ever been exposed to micro G, but his stomach and ears felt fine so far. He only recalled having trouble previously while watching movement and floating. So it was the contrast that was the problem, not the lack of gravity itself.

He was third into the lock. Again, Jason was being quite shrewd. He had medical training, they needed Bal, Alex was the boss, the rest were expendable. This was the order it had to be. Good man, good men all, excepting Elke who was a good woman to have along in a fight. He hoped she had some small amount of explosives left. They just might need it.

Then he cycled through inside a small compartment with a pressure gauge, two peepholes, and not much else. The pressure shifted, the door popped open, and he stared out.

Jason waved him to move and grab a stanchion. He did so, then reached down to fasten a line. He tried to avoid looking up because there was no up, no walls, nothing. The skin of the station curved away into infinity.

Elke was twitchy. Every minute, more of the team cycled through. Every minute, she was more alone in a station full of potential hostiles. Explosives were not an option and hers were packed, along with her pistol. The potential threat didn't bother her; it was the inability to do anything should she be attacked. As it was, her only option was to surrender and be jailed. She wasn't claustrophobic nor did she fear confinement per se, but the concept of being helpless to someone else's whim was not attractive. Not at all.

Then she was out, in open space. It was pretty! That slim, white cylinder had to be their destination, just a few meters around the station hull and a couple of hundred meters out the loading gantry. She followed the others, still feeling like a bug on a plate because this was not how the regular crew would reach the ship.

Apparently, though, they were taken for a maintenance detail, made more believable by Bart carrying a chunk of plating Jason had found stashed near the lock. Since everyone outside carried a bag with tools, gear, or personals, without a close inspection they were fine.

The gantry was just like the one she trained on for assorted terror threats. They loaded gear on a flat sled and then latched on following Jason's lead, with her helping Bal, Bart, and Shaman get linked, then she brought up the rear again. The mechanism whisked them out between two containerized loads and some netted small packages in rounded metal crates against high G.

The frame of the gantry wasn't actually white, but was polished titanium alloy in bright Boblight. Paint was not needed and would require labor better used elsewhere. That was space for you. Harsh and unforgiving even on the eyes.

They seemed to sit still as the cagework moved past them in a sedate procession, the thick pipes floating around them and drifting aft. At the far end, they entered "dark" shadow of the ship's hold, only to find it light again inside. The contrast between Boblight and artificial had created that illusion. The bright gas and plasma spots gave good clarity marred by very sharp shadows.

Elke had never worked in a hold. She'd trained on one space-ship for micro-G safing and dearming procedures. There typically weren't any serious terrorist acts in space. Sensors were quite good, so were remote removal drones, and the last ditch defense was to blow the compartment in question if you knew about an attack. The odds of having a device where a technician could respond, with enough time to matter, were near zero. She recalled her micro-G maneuvers, though.

She took her lead off Jason, who was unloading their sled first, transferring their crated gear to a net near the inner personnel hatch. He'd done this before, obviously. Bart was a bit clumsy, Alex decently composed, but Shaman and Bishwanath were near useless. Aramis was managing, but only through iron control. The kid did have good kinesthetics, fortunately. They had to look at least passingly professional to pull this off.

She listened to ongoing chatter. Channel One was nothing but crew and handlers, terse and professional. Channel Two had friendly banter and rude jokes. Morale was high around here, with the crew chief shouting and cursing his loaders and some of them throwing it right back.

She waved unobtrusively, her body shielding the gesture from others. It took three waves before Alex noticed.

What? His expression said through the helmet, barely visible.

She nodded and pointed, flailed her arms in front and feigned panic. Then she pointed at the crew hatch. *Get them inside!* It was the best she could manage at a distance.

Alex nodded with his whole torso and turned away. She kept an eye out as she moved containers. There was no real reason for anyone to question a new person on the crew, especially as there were several crews and the ship's contingent, too. Too many new faces would trigger suspicions. They needed to move fast.

Alex got face to face with Jason and talked through helmet conduction. There was some pointing and gesturing, then Jason dragged out a card and wrote something on it. Alex took the card, swam away, and snagged both Shaman and Bal. A few minutes later, they were near the crew lock in deep shadow behind a block of crates. When next she had a chance to glance that way, they were gone.

As she backed away from one container that was being locked down, someone tapped her on the shoulder.

Resisting the urge to scream, flail, or otherwise react, she turned slowly and saw Jason. He grabbed her by the shoulders, bumped helmets, and spoke loudly through the conducting material.

"Take Bart and go inside. Here's a rough map. Alex should be waiting. I'll bring up the rear with Aramis." He held up a card.

"Roger," she agreed, and took the directions.

"Bart's waiting." With that, Jason swam away to resume working.

Now, if only no one noticed that the large number of strangers had disappeared.

She advanced by the expedient of following an incoming container all the way forward, being towed along as it was cranked in. Once it reached the rear, she drew herself to the rails to dog it down. One of the real stevedores was alongside.

He called on a private channel. "You're new?"

"New on this crew. Done it a few times before," she replied. Literally true.

"Good. Can always use experienced help."

"Yeah," she agreed noncommittally. She wanted the conversation over. Every exchange increased the risk of discovery.

The guy did move away. Probably he was a shift leader or such. He hadn't asked anything that indicated he was suspicious. She moved behind the container, ostensibly to check the dogs there. That put her in deep shadow and closest to the crew hatch. She could see Bart, barely, a suit in shadow.

Another container clanged into place, with the noise transmitting as vibration. She clicked the switch that disconnected her line from the "overhead" rail and let it rewind. Then she waited patiently for a third, then a fourth container to lock in. That put the workers far enough away she judged it safe to move straight back, the row of cargo as cover, until she reached the bulkhead. That put her on open space, but still mostly concealed. The trick to staying hidden was to know what the opponent could see, not what you could see.

She crawled along the bulkhead by padeyes, trying not to be too hasty. There were lots of reasons for someone to be moving this way, and speed would indicate an emergency. Best to take time.

Bart was waiting, also patiently. He smiled and extended a hand to pull her in close; the corner he was in was just big enough for two. They were in an amusing parody of a romantic cuddle, his suited arms around her to minimize profile. That also destroyed their human outlines, making them a dark blob.

Two more cargo cans slammed in, monstrous blocks bringing black shadow, as if the ship was chewing them with giant metal teeth. The loaders moved over, ready to start the next row, and Elke felt herself lifted as Bart shoved with his feet. They both pushed off and tumbled, him using one arm to hold her, she using one leg, and the two of them nudged themselves into the cycled lock, sitting open for them.

Part of her wondered about warning signals in the bridge, telling of the lock working. On the other hand, nothing had happened so far that she knew. She dogged the hatch, punched for cycle, and grabbed a stanchion. There was no telling. Perhaps the ship's company was busy helping. Perhaps they were handling duties belowdecks. They could have left the warning signal off so loaders could use facilities to rest and clean up. Or they might be so sloppy they didn't care.

There was no one waiting when the hatch opened. Once through, she dogged it again, carefully, in case it was inspected. Bart moved ahead with the directions, and when she turned, he pointed at a hatch. He knocked softly, and it opened as she arrived.

"Get in, quick," Alex said, grabbing both of them in hand and using his feet for leverage. In moments they were inside and he closed the hatch behind them.

"So far, so good," Alex said. "Two groups came through to use the latrines and eat. Seems the ship isn't secured against that. Likely too much hassle to sign them in and out."

"Good. Glad it worked to our advantage," Bart said. "I saw them enter. Saw some of them leave."

"Yes, some are still in the galley," Alex agreed. "They take rotating lunches. So we're good. So far."

"Need to get stowed though," Jason said from behind him, where he was hanging on a shelf. "If they're even half-assed, there'll be a prelaunch safety check of anything loose. Like this."

Elke looked at where he was pointing, and around the compartment. From the bedding, tools, caretaker supplies, and spare parts he deduced it was ship's storage. Not something occupied, but it would be visited often, and might even be so before launch.

"Yes, let's burrow in," she said.

Climbing in micro G was easy. They were shortly ensconced in assorted nests, out of plain sight, potential camera view, and any cursory body heat sensors. Multifrequency radar would find them in seconds, but it wasn't likely a cargo ship would use such inside.

CHAPTER TWENTY-SEVEN

S ure we're safe here?" Aramis asked.

Jason whispered, "Safer if you quit talking."

Aramis nodded. The ship's sensors could potentially pick up their life signs, if anyone thought to look. He knew his wound was causing him problems physical and mental. It had oozed a lot in vacuum, and his entire side was now sticky. The pain and tightness made his left arm near useless, every movement sending fire from thigh to neck. He was developing a pounding headache from the wound, micro-G blood shifting, and muscle tension. He was not going to say a word yet, however, because he did not want to be left behind. He knew he was expendable, but he still could be useful and nothing was going to make him miss out on this.

He hoped they boosted soon, though, because he needed medical treatment and was getting nauseous from the pain.

He looked over and saw Alex scribbling on paper, quickly, quietly, and forcing himself to be neat. The man had always had atrocious handwriting. Elke and Jason were the only ones good at it. Both had to spend a lot of time making notes by hand for their jobs. Everyone else was dependent upon technology. Aramis had hardly hand written since primary school. He considered that that should be a skill added to the Company course. He'd note that if . . . dammit, *when*, he got back.

The light was minimal, but almost enough to read by. Aramis read the note as it came past in turn. No, Alex's penmanship was not world class.

"Standing by for boost phase. Will make an assault on flight deck, but (some word he could not read) to avoid any casualties. Pool cash again, give to S. Let me talk. V, can you pilot?"

Jason had ticked "Yes" next to the question, Elke had scrawled under her name. He passed the note on to Bart, and unzipped his suit to get to the pocket containing the cash. This back and forth was annoying, but necessary.

Jason sketched out a map and directions as everyone handed their cash to Elke, who stuffed it into a laundry sack. That sack wasn't impressively big, but some of the contents were gold and palladium, with bundles of bills mixed in. He wasn't sure how much Bal had drawn and he didn't need to know, but it was certainly enough to help.

Sign language followed.

Alex: *Jason will lead.*

Jason: *Weapons holstered. There will be no sudden attack. Wear suits against wind.* Meaning depressurization.

Elke: *Carry batons?*

Jason: *Yes.*

Shaman: *I will stay with Bal, and Bart. Right after point.*

Jason: *Concur.*

Aramis asked: *Am I point again?*

Jason: *Yes, until we reach HQ.* Meaning the flight deck. Bridge. Whatever.

Nods all around.

Aramis found it easy enough to breathe despite his side. The compartment was meant for inside cargo, so was still pressurized even if it wasn't really meant for human occupation. He saw temperature controls, but they were deactivated. That's why Jason had chosen this one. It was somewhat cool, and body heat wasn't going to raise it enough, between the volume involved and the airflow. There was nothing to do but sit and shiver slightly, waiting what might be hours for preflight to finish and a departure number to be issued. Discomfort and risk, and getting caught now would get all of them well-dead in space and Bishwanath likely "dead during the rescue," with them blamed.

But Aramis did get it. You didn't fuck over people this way. He was exceedingly pissed, and a bit frightened, about the situation. Okay, scared shitless. Jail and death were not good futures. Fighting skinnies was one thing. This was something else entirely, but he'd follow through. Fuck BuState.

They all stayed quiet, contemplating their own thoughts, as Jason carefully felt his way through the racks and found hiding places. Each of them had a good field of view of the hatchway, and some kind of insulation, whether fabric, padding, or laminate.

Aramis was ensconced in puffed plastic bubble wrap, the thick kind with ten-centimeter bubbles, peeled from between two boxes. His feet jammed the boxes tight against the shelf so they wouldn't shift, and his right shoulder was painfully against the rear upright, but that did make his left a bit more comfortable, while straining the right side of his neck to match. With a bag of coveralls in front of him, he was hard to see. Jason was directly behind the door, wrapped in a sack, and they met eyes and stared. Not good, not bad, just mesmerized and meditating.

The occasional indecipherable chatter on the PA was now replaced with, "All hands, report and stand by to secure for boost."

Critical juncture. Would they inspect with scans? Cameras? In person?

A few moments later, thumping and voices outside presaged the hatch being cranked open.

"Supplemental storage, check," said a voice.

"Check," said another.

Aramis didn't even see a head poke in. The crew were conducting a routine inspection for anything blatantly obvious; hull breach, structural damage, that sort of thing.

It got quiet again, but the background noise contained whirs and clicks now. When clanking noises started, he twitched slightly. Jason just nodded from his position, and waved a signal to the others. A snap and a rumble, and gravity started to return with a certain amount of unnatural vibration.

Jason rose carefully and signaled. Aramis rolled carefully out of his hide, raising his legs, twisting and lowering to the deck. Gravity built, but didn't seem to get above about .5G. Actually, it was boost, thrust, whatever, but it felt like gravity and made things easier. He had a floor now.

Shortly, they were stacked up to the side as Jason undogged and opened the hatch. They flowed through and to a ladder, then started up.

Aramis was halfway onto a step when Shaman grabbed him. He looked back to see signed, *Bal slow on ladder.*

Right. The man wasn't in as good a shape. Well, neither was Aramis at present. He could legitimately take a slow pace, not injure himself, and still be fast enough to keep the group together. He nodded and started climbing.

There were three deck rings between their cubby and the flight deck, bridge, whatever. The climbing was hard, because it had to be quiet, and the G field was unfamiliar. It made sense to have Aramis in front, even injured. He could scoot ahead quietly, stop at the next deck ring, watch for crew, then move across the opening to the next ladder. He just hoped no one noticed that he climbed with one arm, and that he had both weapons slung for that same arm.

Of course, the gut-wrenching fear was someone coming straight up or straight down. There was no way to explain a group of seven armed stowaways on the ladder, and the safety hatches at each deck were a sober reminder that they could be blocked in, sealed off, and the tube evacuated. Or they could just be held in a tube for ten days or so, then taken out filthy and half starved by Aerospace Force STs.

Enough of that. This was a commercial craft operating in a secure area, and no one had acted like they expected trouble so far. Initial boost was the safest time to be making this approach, so now was the time to do it.

And while he was musing, he'd led the way to the top. Two meters of corrugated decking separated the top of the ladder from the hatch to the bridge. Once stacked, they swarmed up and forward, and he grabbed the lock.

It wasn't necessary to hit as a unit, they hoped, and it was necessary to get across the space fast in case they were seen. One man opening the hatch wasn't too out of place. Seven would be. So he undogged it as the rest slipped up behind him, Alex guarding the rear, then pushing past to be up front. The latch came free, Alex nodded, and he pulled it open.

Deep breath, Alex thought and did, focusing.

Then the hatch popped out.

"Hi, we're hijacking your ship," Alex said as he stepped into the cabin. He only had a pistol. On the other hand, the crew had nothing. Bart and Aramis crawled through behind him.

"Excuse me?" one of the officers said. He moved toward an alarm button and Bart zapped him. The man tripped on his console and was sprawled in a moment, flat on the deck.

"We're hijacking your ship. Do you want to live or die?" He waggled the pistol.

A sturdy blonde woman at the far side, presumably the captain, raised her hands and gestured for calm. The two others, both women, complied, but kept looking from her to Alex and back. Their comrade groaned and started coming around. That was good. Killing anyone would screw the deal. The team spread out to cover all angles, though there wasn't much here. Alex noted large screens all around the hemisphere, control consoles with both wired and wireless connections that were modular and could be shifted around to the couches. There were lights focused on these couches and indirect illumination of moderate intensity elsewhere.

The woman said, "I am Captain Schlenker. Do you expect to get away with this, Mister . . . ?"

"Smith will do," he said. "Yes, I expect to get away with it. For three reasons." He let that hang.

"Yes?" she prompted.

"One, there's no need for violence. We just need a ride. Two, that ride is to Grainne, where you're heading right now. And three . . ." He waved a hand behind him, Elke stepped out, and dumped a bag of UN marks and bullion over the deck.

"We plan to pay you to continue with your flight and just keep silent."

After a moment's silence spent staring at the drifting pile, Schlenker said, "That is the most fucked-up method of hijacking I've ever heard of."

"We get that a lot," Alex grinned. "Do we have a deal?"

"We have a deal not to start trouble or scream for the military while you explain what's going on," she said.

"Done."

Everyone relaxed. It was obvious "Smith" and his cronies could cause a lot of trouble. However, declining to do so indicated . . . something other than piracy.

"Still, I require that everyone stand over there," he gestured. "And you come here so I can explain this quietly, Captain."

She didn't look thrilled, but complied. He couldn't blame her.

Cash on the deck was not cash in the bank, and nothing legal was going on. He stopped her at arm's length and handed her a sheet of actual paper, with the outline printed on it. Roughly, it said they were escorting a contractor, escaped from what amounted to indenture in Kaporta with their medieval laws on labor, and needed to get him beyond extradition range.

Shaman was with the President in the back of the group, keeping him somewhat hidden. The captain looked at them, reread the paper, and said, "And how do we do this, Mister Smith?"

"Simple," he said. "Two of my people stay up here all the time. No one does anything stupid, or mentions it belowdecks or on radio. We aren't wanting to hurt anyone, but we are determined to get there, and quietly. No one tries to talk to us and reason with us about how hard it will be to debark. That's our problem. We'll give you fifteen thousand now, mixed gold, palladium, and cash, and the balance upon arrival."

"Balance?"

"Hundred thousand total. If all goes well, our charge will give you an additional amount."

"And I take your word on that?"

Alex looked at Jason. "Pilot, show them the course to Grainne."

Jason nodded, handed his pistol to Aramis, strode over to a station, and began punching in coordinates, boost rates, and fuel expenditures for the jump point.

"You have a safety margin of eleven point three eight percent," he said as he worked.

"Eleven point four, but I get your meaning," Schlenker said. "You don't need us." She didn't seem scared.

"Not at all," Alex said. "Just a ride."

"If you're so decent, what's to stop us from making a scene?"

"If we're so decent, you don't need to. If we're not, you're risking escalation from bribery to piracy. I leave the call to you, but we are determined to get there. Pilot."

Jason said, "We'll debark at Jump Point One as passengers, and be out of your hair. We obviously know our way around a port. Since it's Grainne, we'll just declare ourselves and walk off. You don't need to declare the cash, except maybe to your company. That's between you and them. If it helps, we can not reference your ship. No trouble with Grainnean soldiers, no trouble with Station Ceileidh security. Our people meet us. You'll have your cash, and if the rest of our travels go well, you'll have the bonus for being gracious hosts."

"Tell me honestly why you're doing this," she insisted, eyes hard.

"Let's say we had a mixup with the UN over our contract, and don't want to debate the situation. They wanted a peaceful resolution, and we don't do that well." It was a believable story, and had happened before.

She nodded. "Fair enough. As long as you do it well here."

"I think we'll get along fine," Alex said. "Pilot, you and Babs will stay here for first shift. We need a safe stateroom for the trip."

"Our staterooms hold four," Captain Schlenker said.

"We'll be fine with seven in one, since two will be here at all times. That gives us five in one stateroom."

"You value your privacy and don't want to be split up," she said. Well, no one expected a captain to be stupid.

"We are professionals at arms, Captain. I advise against testing us. Really."

He hoped she'd take that advice.

Nodding, she said, "Mister Radaman, please show our guests to the stateroom." She turned and said, "We have one unused stateroom, one deck down. That will have to do, unless you'd rather displace me or some of the crew."

"That will be fine," he agreed. "We will retire there now."

Elke and Jason looked at each other and around, as they were left with the four crew on duty. Captain Schlenker glanced at them from time to time, but generally stuck to her console. An older redhead recovered the loot from the deck and counted it. She looked to be decently shaped even inside her coverall. He acquired her name from conversation. Gina, deputy captain and astrogator. She got called below a few minutes later.

"They need me in sick bay," she said on her way, not really asking permission, but assuming. "I'm a trained nurse, too."

"Who's hurt?" he asked suspiciously.

"One of yours." Her eyes were flinty.

Alex called right at that moment, doubling the surprise. The two of them stayed in contact, not trusting the crew even after a bribe. The ship was close to port and could easily divert. He'd made a point of keeping a close eye on navigation, just in case.

The combination of all those factors triggered his alertness to a level close to "fight."

"Yes?" he replied at once on radio.

"Kiddo is in sick bay. He was worse off than he let on, the dumb shit."

"Fuck. Will he be okay?" The kid was annoying but good. He didn't want to lose him. He gestured to Gina, who nodded acknowledgment and slipped through the hatch.

"Hoping so. While it looks nasty it shouldn't be life threatening."

"Keep me informed, please. Gina is on her way."

"Of course, and thanks for confirming. Out."

Jason pondered that. So far, that was the worst wound they'd suffered, but far worse was possible at any time. He felt himself getting old fast.

Thirty minutes later, Schlenker said, "We are increasing to one standard G boost," over the intercom and net. She looked at Jason as she said it.

"Understood," he acknowledged.

Thrust increased and then steadied. After checking her console, she secured from it, rose and headed aft.

"Going below," she said.

"See you next shift," he agreed. After she left, he commented to Elke, "Four hours to go."

Elke said softly, "I expect we'll change before that, without notice. No need for them to know our schedule. I also expect regular support visits."

"Undoubtedly," he replied. "Alex is good at schedules. I'm sure it'll be fine."

Sure enough, they were relieved two hours and seventeen minutes early by Shaman and Bart. That was a pair to intimidate anyone.

"Everything has been cleared," Bart leaned close and informed him quietly. "The reason you have not had a rest break was because a tour of the ship was necessary. The supplemental transmitters in Engineering have been disabled. The crew is not happy, but believes we mean what we say. Boss is patrolling with Bal to make him look normal."

"Good," he replied. "How's Ar— the kid?"

Shaman said, "Muscle damage, nerve damage, hemorrhage, muscle and bone, but he'll survive. His condition has made the crew somewhat nervous, as it was clearly the result of a firefight. They know we have inflicted casualties." He looked a little worried himself. Elke had a neutral expression that he'd learned meant she was worried, too.

"Well, at least they know we're serious," he shrugged. "And I'm glad he's going to heal. Back we go."

It was going to be a long fourteen days, he thought. Eight days of hard boosting until they reached Jump Point One, the only jump point this system had so far, and then six more days across Sol System, braving serious danger, to jump to Grainne, where they could freely and safely broadcast that Bishwanath was still alive. They still didn't know if that would matter once they did, but there were places to get lost in the Iota Persei system where people with skills could survive well paid and discreetly. As long as they got there . . .

The stateroom was about what he expected. The others seemed to have expected something more glamorous. It was a typical stateroom, with two stacks of two bunks with G harnesses rolled against the bulkhead, lockers under the bottom bunks, and enough space to stand between them. One end had a fold-down dining table/desk, a heating unit/refrigerator combo, and a door into a restroom with a shower, lavatory, and a toilet that pulled up from the deck on a lever. The door was a polarizing clear polymer.

Alex and Bal returned with an update on Aramis.

Alex said, "He's resting, lightly tractioned, and full of painkillers with healing goop plastered on his side. It'll take some time to heal. Also, the wound was getting aggravated to the point where hospitalization was essential. He will not be fully functional before we arrive. Gina and Shaman are with him."

"Damn," Jason said for everyone. Well, at least he would survive.

"I am going to go insane in here," Alex said to no one in particular, looking around at the tight quarters.

"Going to?" Jason asked.

"Plenty of room outside. Should I make you a door?" Elke snickered.

"Elke, please don't even joke about that," Alex said. "Sucks, but we'll manage. No one shooting at us, at least. Oh, yes, the captain was pissed," he continued, facing Jason again.

"Oh?" He had a pretty good idea why.

"Yes. There was no problem when I demanded her weapons.

She had one pistol and one shotgun, handed them over with no real protest, so I doubt anyone else is armed. She complained that the transmitter in her quarters was an emergency backup. I explained that her knowing it had been disabled was a violation of our truce, and reduced the final ticket by ten thousand marks."

"Harsh, but fair." He'd wondered at the money they were tossing out on faith that someone else would pay it. Granted, a verbal contract wasn't binding in Grainne courts, unless agreed upon and recorded. But a verbal under duress, with money on the deck . . . a Citizen Judge would want to find in favor of it. So they were running on hope that Corporate would cough up the money, or that Bishwanath would regain enough stature to call on either national or even personal assets to pay them.

At least, as trained security professionals, even if they were charged and lost, they could likely get good indenture contracts. *Heck, I could charge it against my pension if I have to*, Jason thought.

Shaman came in looking cheerful.

"He will be fine, though recovery will take some time," he said. "I gave him a special ritual just to see the expression on his face. He cussed at me."

"Yes!" Jason grinned and they all chuckled in relief.

Apparently paralleling Jason's earlier thoughts, Shaman said, "I believe I may be out of the contract security business after we resolve this. There are better ways to make the money I will owe."

"Depends on how Corporate treats us," Alex said. "If they come through, I'll charge it off as bad negotiations."

"I do appreciate it," Bal said. "No matter what happens, you have my eternal thanks. I wish your employer and my alleged ally was as honest and professional."

"Yeah, I think BuState is the heavy here." Jason was only vague on how things worked at that level, but it seemed reasonable that *if* Bishwanath got out, a lot of people's dicks would be in vises. Which was why the pursuit had been so rough so far.

He shrugged inwardly. If it worked out, he'd have enough money to see him through four or five years. If not, he'd be in jail being adjusted. There really wasn't anything to be done about it at this point.

✧　　✧　　✧

Weilhung was glad to be on-site himself. He had Weygandt on radio down below, which meant this was strictly a military matter at the moment. He aimed to keep it that way.

The station chief, named Lewis, was a no-nonsense type that Weilhung knew he'd work well with. Lewis had the details all laid out.

First, the video. Yes, that was the six of them and Bishwanath. Well done, he had to admit. Across a continent, an ocean, into orbit, aboard a ship. He had them pegged, though, and he was going to take them down. How that turned out depended on how they wanted to play.

"Okay, Chief, what else do you have?"

Lewis was lean, lined, bald, and brusque. "I've already interviewed both of our victims," he said. "I'm sure their story is legit. The perpetrators were seen outside, but were not distinctive enough for anyone to check in detail. You know how it is, sir." He adjusted his glasses and nodded. "You tell them to question anything suspicious and they still get complacent."

"It happens," Weilhung agreed. Things always did. Marlow had exploited that multiple times. So had Weilhung, on occasion. "We're sure of the ship?" he asked.

"We are, sir," Lewis agreed with a nod. "That was the only ship to leave in that time frame. The next freighter departing is in four hours if you want to search it. The passenger flight to Earth doesn't leave for three days, and I've ordered them to scan every face going in. I also made sure it was empty first."

"Really. How did you manage that?" Weygandt asked after a brief light-speed delay.

"I ordered them to depressurize slowly to half pressure, then come back up, then down to thirty percent, then cycle back up and down to vacuum. No one with any brains would stick around for the second cycle. As a plus, it took care of my certification for pests and quarantine."

That was creative, Weilhung thought, grinning inside.

"Excellent. While I know you're a private corporation, Chief, I'd appreciate some discretion on this matter for now," Weygandt said.

"You don't want the press leaking about the individuals in question, or about potential destinations," Lewis said.

Damn, this was too easy.

"That's it. We'd also like to avoid diplomatic issues," Weilhung hinted.

"I won't talk to BuState if you will run interference. I'll just send them your way."

"I suppose that's me," Weygandt said, looking unhappy. "Yes, I'll take care of it. And you, Major?"

"I have things to do here, sir," he said, "if the Chief can give me more info."

"Tell me what you need."

An hour later, Weilhung called his best operators, starting with Captain Nugent.

"So, we're gearing for space, sir?" Nugent asked.

"Bring it," he agreed. "But I plan to let them get into Sol space first. Just because we're better doesn't mean I don't want the edge."

"'If you ain't cheating, you ain't fighting,'" Nugent agreed. "Gear for spaceside and ground. Are we taking them alive?"

"If possible, by all means. If not, we want overkill."

"I'll pack. We can board in an hour."

"An hour it is. Out." Marlow was pretty damned good, but when it came down to it, he was a contract bodyguard. Weilhung was Recon. There was no competition.

CHAPTER TWENTY-EIGHT

Military service is described by the cliché of "months of mindless tedium punctuated by moments of sheer terror." That wasn't always accurate, Horace thought, and wasn't exclusive to the military. The trip out of system was long and tedious, and also sheer terror. He expected to have that stress until they docked in Grainne's system. He dared not take a trank himself. He needed to be fit for his guard watch and for medical support. He couldn't let anyone else touch Bal if there was a medical emergency. That was less an issue of trust than responsibility. If the man died under someone else's care...

He hoped they could relax once they arrived at Grainne. Once done, hands shook, they were free to travel as they wished. Colonies were much laxer than either UN nations or protectorates, and Grainne's founding corporation had very a laissez-faire–minded board. Unless the team injured someone insystem, it was unlikely any assets would be put toward tracking them down and extraditing them. That was safety, of a sort, while they screamed for help and backup.

Of course, to get there, they had to go through Sol System unchallenged.

In the meantime, he needed food and sleep.

It was eight long days of guard duty and boredom, crammed into the tiny stateroom. The announced Jump was a moment of exciting dreariness. *Halfway, and no interception. Yet,* Alex thought.

And if you wanted added frustration, he thought, Elke was a meter away, behind a translucent door, naked and showering. She was exceptionally professional under the circumstances and made sure she was fully dressed at all times. While it wouldn't have been a problem to walk around naked if necessary, the distraction would have been there, this not being the middle of a fight but still a crucially dangerous situation. The matter hadn't been discussed. She wore clothes, they tried to reciprocate out of courtesy.

"All hands, jump in thirty minutes," came the warning.

Alex dropped down the ladder and entered the cabin, after being relieved by Aramis, who was functional but still shaky. He looked around and pointed at Horace.

"Can you dope us to recover faster from Jump shock?"

"I can inject you with a stimulant that will keep you alert, but it will be rough."

"Rough is good. You, me, Bart. Jason is already there. I want four on watch and ready to react. I wouldn't put it past this captain to try to phase through weirdly so we get shaken up more."

Shaman smirked. "That actually isn't possible, merely a vid trick, but the base concern is legitimate," he said. He pulled out his kit and grabbed four tips. He was already wearing his small kit and pistol.

"Ready," he said.

Back out, and Schlenker was coming out of her cabin, directly across the passage. The vacant one they occupied was close to hers for security reasons. Ironically, that now worked to their advantage.

As they arrived, the crew were clearly surprised and a bit annoyed. That might be at the mistrust or the crowding—there was not a tremendous amount of room available in the small chamber, and four mercs plus four crew meant a large arc of spectators—but it also could be that they'd had something planned. After Alex's punitive fine, the crew seemed to feel the intent was to beat them down to a free ride. Maintaining order while keeping that an unused threat was becoming a problem. At least the crew had the deposit and knew *it* was honest. There was a bottom limit, though, below which the share of the loot would drop below the normal trip salary these people earned and make them much more eager to dispute the situation.

"Attention all hands, Jump in fifteen minutes!" Gina announced. She looked younger than her decades but certainly had the experience. She'd done a good job on Aramis. She'd agreed to play chess, too. He could see the board without getting too close, the hour or so a day their schedules crossed, and the few minutes of that one of them wasn't occupied.

He could feel the drug kicking in. Shaman had been first, as he always would for such a case, so he could gauge the amount. He very surreptitiously got each of the others in turn, while they rotated around to mask the event. He'd commented once that it was ironic that healthy people with good veins were easier to work on than actual casualties who needed it.

The side effects of the stim were faint nausea, a slight pulse-pounding in the head, and sweats. Luckily, both stress and Jump shock had the same symptoms, so no one noticed as the time ticked down.

"Thirty, correcting, thirty-one, thirty . . ." Gina called off. He let himself be part tourist, watching the maneuver from a great perspective, while keeping the rest of himself alert for trouble.

The few final seconds were tense from anticipation. No one Alex knew had ever claimed to enjoy Jump shock. He let himself go limp, because that worked best for him. Aramis was so stiff he trembled. Before he could examine the others they

Jumped.

Blurry, double-vision, nausea, and a wave of heat and itch from nerves badly abused swept over him, but he was still awake. Most of the crew twitched in their couches. Darwin the engineer was first to recover, looked up as he reached for controls, and got tight-lipped seeing all four hijackers alert and watching him. He slowed his movements and resumed normal operations.

"I need to call and conduct flight ops with Sol Jump Point Four," Gina said, matter-of-factly and very professionally.

"Continue," Jason said. "We want this flight to go well."

"Thank you," she said and keyed her circuit. "Jump Point Control, this is *GCS George* advising you of our arrival, time attached. The usual courtesy update to Jump Point conditions is attached. Last Salin broadcasts transmitting and updating at one-thousand-to-one rate. Our itinerary continues through to Jump Point Six to Grainne. Live response requested, priority routine, waiting, out."

It was seconds only before a male voice replied, "*George*, this is Arrival Control, your itinerary and flight path approved, attachments received, thanks for the contact. Stand by for news. Out."

Alex looked at Jason and indicated. With a nod, the man rose and they both headed below.

Once through the hatch, he asked, "Was that commo legit?"

"I have no idea," Jason said, meeting his eyes. "Oh, it sounds legit. I can't imagine they don't update like that. But no, I can't promise you there's no embedded code screaming to come and get us."

"Six more days, right?" Alex asked tiredly. It just never got better.

"Six days."

Horace didn't mind being crammed into the bed too much. At least it was a bed. Actually, it was quite comfortable. While the quarters were small, the roommates were courteous in the extreme, and quiet. Considering the open sky, bushes, rat-infested thatched cottages, or any number of other places he'd slept, it was choice.

"Four kings. Pay up."

"Christ, I'm dying here," he heard.

He rolled toward the middle, blinked, and looked.

Poker game. Jason, Aramis, Elke, and Bal. They were playing for . . .

"How many is that?" Jason asked, dropping between the bunks into forward leaning rest position.

"One sixty."

"Right."

Push-ups. They were gambling for push-ups in half G.

Despite his complaints, Jason knocked out a hundred sixty push-ups straight through with barely a pause at one-thirty-five. His form was excellent, though he was starting to shake at the end. He wondered how many previous sets had they all done?

He rose, groaning, and Elke dropped. She strained starting around eighty, but she did make it.

Bal said, "I shall not shame you with the attempt. Add it to my tab I still hope to pay."

"Bored, are we?" Horace asked.

"Hey, it's something to do, and we get some exercise, and we don't go bugfuck," Aramis said, as Elke just shrugged.

It did make sense, and summed up the situation so perfectly.

They were warriors, willing to fight against extreme odds. Sitting in a cell hoping for safety was out of character for them.

"I hope you are not doing push-ups, Aramis?" Horace said while looking over the boy's bandaged side and slung arm.

"I'm doing leg lifts," he said, looking frustrated. "I'll have to recuperate and work back up to push-ups and such." Indeed he would. There was a chunk of flesh missing from his side that was healing up for now and would have to be regrown later. At first it had looked like a scratch, but the damage had been almost deep enough to puncture a lung. It was a good lesson about wounds, not that it was needed with this group.

They were well into Sol System and heading back out. Horace found it ironic to be traveling so close to Earth and not stop. All of them save Jason had looked wistfully out the port, even though they never got close enough for Earth to be more than a dot. Even Jason had taken a glimpse or two, though that might have been just to pass the time.

Horace wasn't clear on the physics of modern space drives. He knew that energetic H-F chemical and certain nuclear-heated engines were used from surface to orbit, and that intrasystem cargo usually used ion drives that were steadily gaining in efficiency. The ships that drove to the Jump Points and through, however, used their energy not as reaction mass, but to travel lines of force in space itself. That process got more efficient further out from gravitational fields such as stars, but took substantial energy to generate the fields needed regardless of where. So once at a good clip, there was no need to boost as they were traveling at a speed appropriate for a Jump and fast enough not to waste much in the way of resources in flight. Much of the trip was in micro G, with only occasional thrust corrections. The ship was spun for centrifugal gravity, so it wasn't as awkward as it had been at times near the Jumps Points.

On the sixth morning ship's time, sitting after waking up, he commented to Elke, "I know we are not more at risk based on distance to Earth, but I feel relieved at being only a few hours out."

Alex sprawled above, ostensibly trying to sleep, though the man was not getting enough and Horace had cut him off from chemical assistance.

"It's normal human reaction," he said. "The unseen is less of a threat, which is actually stupid when you get down to it, but our hindbrains aren't that smart." He didn't open his eyes, which Horace took to mean he really was trying to sleep. He raised a finger to his lips and Elke nodded.

Bart was on shift with Aramis, and it was hard not to dope off. It had to be harder for Aramis with his injury and drugs. Their attention had to be on the crew, so talking to keep occupied was contraindicated. They could take turns interacting with the crew from a safe distance, but the crew had duties of their own.

Schlenker was matter-of-fact and treated them with a professional contempt. Gina was a little frosty but nice enough. That the team had all been perfect ladies and gentlemen, not offering any impropriety, had to help the situation. Gina seemed very much set on manners. Darwin, ship's engineer, didn't interact with anyone much, sticking to his controls here and below. Third Officer Radaman clearly didn't like them. He was the potential threat to watch.

Bart quivered alert, because the crew were all looking back and forth, agitated themselves and discussing something through their mics.

"What is happening?" he demanded.

Schlenker looked up and said, "We are being challenged by a Space Patrol vessel. What do you want us to do?" She was defiant, dropping the problem in his lap with obvious satisfaction.

"Boss, get up here now," Bart said into his mic. "Please put it on speaker," he said.

She touched a control and he heard, ". . . you are ordered to cut thrust and stand down. This is advice of our intent to perform a safety inspection."

Schlenker eyed Bart, saw that there was no budging, and did nothing yet. Good.

Because Bart also had no idea what to do.

Alex slammed through the hatch, pistol drawn, and put it away as soon as he saw things were still under control.

"What's up?" he asked.

"Heave-to order from Space Patrol," Schlenker informed him.

"What if we don't?"

She sighed. "Potentially, they shoot us, though I doubt they will actually waste a missile but they may beam us and wipe out the electronics. Practically, they'll relay a message on the next ship through with a summons, which I'll have to obey next time I come here. I doubt Grainne will do anything, but I'll be out of business and my investors will have to take a bite."

"That's all?" Alex asked. "Okay, run."

"It'd take a death threat to make me do that, Mister Smith."

"Consider it done." Bart twitched inside, in humor and horror. He'd learned not to call bluff with Alex in poker. Alex didn't bluff. He didn't even pause as he drew his pistol again.

Schlenker, to give her credit, didn't flinch. She sat up in her couch and challenged him.

"Mister Smith," she said, slowly, "I'm aware you can fly without me. I'm hoping you have some kind of common sense to go with your tactical brilliance, and some humanity, too. We're not getting out of this without a fight. I'd prefer not to be in the crossfire, or my crew. If you want to actually hijack us and put us on a boat, Space Patrol can rescue us, and you can have the ship. I hate like hell doing it, but at least I'm absolved of some of the guilt. I can say you overpowered me."

Seconds ticked by as the rest of the team trickled in, in pairs. The silence stretched out.

"*GCS George*, this is Space Patrol cutter *Sark*, repeating our instruction to cut boost and stand down for safety inspection." The voice on the far end didn't sound in good humor.

Jason climbed over to a console and grabbed a headset from Gina, who now looked suitably scared, with something like a *frigaten* outside and armed hijackers inside. She let him take it.

"*Sark*, this is *George*, Second Officer speaking. Ironically, we're having a control problem at this moment. I guess we're going to have trouble with the inspection, but we're probably going to be glad you're along. Please give us a moment to bypass some code and wire, and we'll cut boost."

To the eyes on him he said, "Well, we *are* having a control problem. Who's in charge?"

It was a valid question.

The expressions ran from amusement to annoyance to utter despair. Bart was somewhat amused, but this was too tense for much humor.

Bal stepped forward and said, "Ma'am, let me be honest with you. I'm Balaji Bishwanath."

Schlenker jerked and said, "Wait, I know that name."

"Yes, I was President of Celadon. I shall not go into the machinations here, but these are my contract bodyguard, who decided they would remove me from the mob before I was made to fit a press release. If I can get to Grainne, there is a chance I can get the word out, which will mean a great many ramifications. But I will offer all my assets not spoken for as collateral, which are enough to pay for this ship. I think. Barely."

Bart thought the man was hedging his bet too much. This ship likely cost a substantial chunk of the value of Celadon's entire economy. Not that it was that pricey a ship, but a few million was enough. Nor was there any guarantee of reaching his assets . . . or did he have some stashed in a numbered account?

Schlenker stared at him for long seconds. Finally, she said, "So these nutcases agreed to disobey orders, shoot through a mob, hijack ships, threaten, intimidate, lie to civil authority, stow away, and smuggle you into another system, hoping their asses would be covered at the far end?"

"So it seems."

"You guys are Ripple Creek contractors," she said.

"I guess we have to admit that," Alex said.

"You have a hell of a reputation," she said. Her jaw moved as if she was chewing.

She continued, "And you must be one hell of a man, Mister President, if they'll abandon that kind of money to save your ass."

She turned to a console, and said over her shoulder to Jason, "Pilot dude, whatever your name is, you feed them more bullshit. Everyone else grab onto something. This ship is rated for three Gs, but I've never tried more than two and change. Now's the time."

She sat down, fastened a harness, and started fingering controls.

"Because it looks like my only option for keeping my ship. You understand I am not happy about this." Her expression was icy.

Bart said, "None of us are, Captain. I have a list of people who must be spoken to at some point." Oh, yes, he did.

"You speak," she replied, eyes on her screen, jaw tight. "I'll be swinging a bat. Boost in fifteen seconds," she advised.

Jason was amazing in his ability to throw *scheisse*. He had the headset on, and replied back to something with, "*Sark*, this is *George*, we are preparing to test thrust controls. Thirty seconds." He physically clicked off the connection, and cackled.

"That should make them guess," he said.

"On five," Schlenker advised.

Bart sat down, the last to do so, found a nearby stanchion, and gripped it hard.

He had expected the thrust to kick, but it eased in over a second or two, and he could certainly feel the pressure. He shifted to get a better grip on his pistol, which was resting on his thigh. It hadn't escaped him that this might be an excuse for space-trained crew to attempt to overpower them.

He didn't think the Patrol ship really had a chance of catching them if they chose not to be caught. The volume, trajectories, and movements involved seemed to make it a losing proposition. Still, there were beams, akin to the stun settings on their batons, that could disable a ship by scrambling it. A missile wasn't likely, but if this had come about because they suspected Bishwanath was aboard, it wasn't hard to arrange an "accident." There was no guarantee, after all, that the ship in question wasn't an actual warship, not a patrol boat.

Acceleration steadied out at what he agreed felt between two and three times standard. Jason sat at a console himself, entering data, or flying, or something related to the ship. Elke and Alex were guarding everyone from that side, and the rest were providing backup from this side. He actually believed the crew were assisting in the escape, laws be damned.

Vaughn stared at his watch, counted seconds, and then transmitted, "*Sark*, this is *George*. Mayday mayday mayday! We've got a runaway phase and control failure. Will have to physically secure fuel feed and will need recovery. Trajectory will exceed safe maneuvering margin." He sounded scared. Bart wasn't sure at once that it was an act. The man was good.

A few seconds later they heard the reply, "*George*, this is *Sark*. Understood, and standing by to assist. Please ensure you are not on trajectory for Jump Point. Trajectory for Jump Point will be considered fleeing pursuit and a hostile act. Confirm."

"*Sark*, this is *George*. I'll do my damnedest but we've got serious power issues here. I've lost some guidance and navigation, as well as engine control. It's going to be ugly."

As he cut transmission, Schlenker said, "Gina, jog the thrust. I'm going to twist the trajectory. Stand by for maneuvers." She nodded back to Jason's gesture. He hadn't needed to tell her what to do, she'd deduced it.

It might be a civilian ship, Bart thought, but the captain knew what she was about and the crew were disciplined.

Motion in three directions, some here, some there. Thrust shifting, never below two G, sometimes close to three. It was an unpleasant, disorienting ride.

Which *still* could be used as a distraction to overpower them, Bart thought. He might be paranoid, but at this point, it was still the team against everyone. He forced his guts to clamp down and kept close eye on the crew and the hatch.

Schlenker finished programming, looked up and looked around, and said, "The side benefit of this distraction is that it works as evasive maneuvers. For a while."

Gina said, "*Sark* is bearing on a new course."

"I was afraid of that," Schlenker replied.

"What is the danger here?" Bart asked. He wasn't clear on what was going on now.

"The Jump Point," Schlenker said. "They're trying to get a missile into it. That will transfer through and lock down the Point, and we'll be stuck while it resets. That gives them more time to organize a closer-in barricade, and stop all traffic until they have us."

"Have they fired?" Alex asked.

"Not yet. I expect they will. At that point, we're going for broke. No evasion."

Jason asked, "Is that doable? What if they beam us, will your astronautics survive?"

"Likely burn out," Schlenker confirmed. "But we should be set for jump by then. If not, we're all going to be in jail shortly thereafter."

"You could still just blame us," Alex said. "Our pilot is at the controls."

"Yeah, I could. It'd be pretty crappy to deny I helped though, wouldn't it? And how would I get any credit later for admitting I lost the ship? Better jailed for smuggling than in disgrace for being hijacked." She shrugged without looking up from her screen.

Bart wasn't the only one looking confused, and a bit impressed.

Jason looked around and said, "Colonial attitude. We didn't move there to be nice to the UN."

And that was enough. Bart eased his pistol back and holstered it slowly in the high, shifting G.

"I've got a launch," Gina said tensely.

"Effective?" Jason asked, then said, "Sorry, not my place."

Schlenker said, "It's okay. Gina?"

"No way to be sure yet," Gina replied. "Depends on the acceleration, need a few seconds to . . . can't tell yet. Could be either way."

"What margin?"

"Thirty seconds. So fifty-fifty we make it."

"Full power," Schlenker snapped at once. G rose to where breathing was awkward. Bart's neck felt as if he was doing lifts with weight, the tendons standing out.

He wondered why that had not been done sooner, barring the evasive burns. That question was answered when Schlenker continued, "How's the drive holding up?"

"Juggling that too, ma'am," Darwin said. "We should make it with a few seconds to spare. We'll need to shut down and cool down as soon as we Jump."

"If we Jump," Jason added.

"We're Jumping," she insisted. "Might get beat up, but we're Jumping."

Gina said, "Twenty-second window on the missile. Still fifty percent probability of intercept." The nearest screen, Darwin's, showed intersecting lines that meant little to Bart.

"Cutting maneuvering, I'm going to drive it in," Schlenker said.

"We'll be oblique, need more delta V on the far side," Jason commented.

"Yup, but we get a fraction more power now. Jumping in twenty-seven seconds. Darwin, I'll need you ready to switch manually."

Bart wasn't looking forward to this. He reacted badly to Jumps, and under boost was going to make it worse.

"We're gaining against the missile!" Gina shouted. "Sixty percent in our favor and climbing."

"Expect them to beam us," Vaughn said. "We're not out yet."

Sweating. This was like a really stiff workout, just from gravity. Or maybe it was fear.

Yes, that was it. This was a battle, just not face to face, a starship was similar to a surface vessel. He recalled fire support exercises that had felt like this. Only this time, fire was also incoming, and real.

"We're in!" Gina yelled. "Barely, but we are ahead."

Schlenker said, "They can still—"

Right then was when the charge hit them.

It was far less dramatic than expected. Displays pinpointed, lights flickered, and the drive stuttered. The tingle was pretty severe, burning and jolting, but it only lasted a moment.

Then they hit the Jump Point and translated.

Ja, it was a Jump. Bart felt split, in two places at once, and disoriented, looking down, and then he was bursting with fresh sweat and half vomiting.

Schlenker's strained voice cut through the haze. "We're through. Darwin, shut down thrust and then reset everything. All hands, damage control. Get us working again. Gina, commo, call Star Guard and tell them we're having technicals, not failure, no assistance needed."

A few moments later, thrust stopped and micro G took over. Bart grabbed for the stanchion again to hold himself in place, and breathed deeply to steady his nerves and stomach.

Schlenker looked up from her couch, commanded them with a gaze of leadership, and said, "You fuckers owe me."

Alex straightened from his place on the deck and said, "Yes, we do." He rose and held out a hand, then worked his way around the deck. The relief turned into a group greeting with lots of grins. This would be over soon. Everyone looked wrung out, as if finishing a really good PT session. It wasn't likely to become the new weight loss fad, though.

The crew were efficient. Power came back, control came back, Gina resumed her couch and reported that Star Guard was holding off. He gathered that was significant, even though they'd committed no violations here yet. At least he didn't think so. They weren't offering threats at the moment. Catching Jason's eye, he asked, "What's with the Star Guard?"

"Ah, paramilitary rescue. Space Patrols are like surface Coast Guards. They're obligated to provide aid. Star Guard is part of the military. They can charge fees or demand a percentage as salvage. You don't call them if you don't have to. Besides, we'd stand out."

"So what now?"

"Now," Schlenker said, "we warp into the station. Nitpicky navigation and thrust, as close as we can get before we start paying for station control. We dock. You give me the money you agreed to, valid assurance on the rest, and then . . ."

She took a breath and finished, "You get the fuck off my ship and never come back. Oh yes, and whoever you know had better start vouching or I've made my last trip to Sol System."

"That will take about ten to twelve days," Alex said.

" 'Ten to twelve days,' " she repeated. "Because?"

"Well, Mister Bishwanath is officially dead."

"I see," she said. "That wasn't a part of the news I'd picked up on. So not only is he wanted, he's also . . . not wanted."

"Exactly."

"And you intend to address this."

"Once we can reach broadcast facilities, yes."

"I think I should stop listening now. You will give me those assurances now or I'm going to turn into a first class bitch the second you're off the ship. Unless you intend to hijack it now, without enough fuel to go anywhere."

"We do have some negotiating to do, don't we?" Alex said.

"Yes. Yes we do." She ran a hand through her sweaty hair and stared at him in challenge.

Bart cut in long enough to ask, "Permission to go below."

It was hysterically funny to his fatigued but relieved brain that both Alex and Schlenker simultaneously replied, "Granted."

CHAPTER TWENTY-NINE

Are we sure they're heading down?" Captain Nugent asked.

"We're pretty sure now," Weilhung agreed. "They are in the Grainne system. I can't imagine they'll stay in a station. If they leave, we will nail any ship as it goes through a Jump. I believe they could only make the one jump and chose that on purpose." His office wasn't as comfortable as the former palace, but it was certainly more secure, and even more so with AF STs guarding the gates and facilities. Listening to them whine about working with the Army was icing on the cake.

The problem now was that everything Marlow did involved cash and he couldn't simply call up files or compel assistance. Nor did Weilhung have much in the way of immediate threats to use for coercion against accessories. Grainne was sticky about extradition. They liked to rant about their colonial rights and invoke the American colonies. Although, he admitted, he did respect the fact they didn't play lapdog, but it was a pain in his ass at the present time.

On the other hand, it was the one colonial government that didn't try to stop individual entry. His call had a platoon go through on private passports and ID, unquestioned, though doubtless, the chartered luxoboat had drawn attention. Attention was fine, as long as no one could prove the matter.

"Then where, is the question," Nugent said. His tendency to think out loud could be annoying. He was methodical and cautious, and some people mistook that for slow. Weilhung had not made that mistake when he met Nugent as a lieutenant, and did not make it now. The man had a very keen, deductive mind. You just had to give him time to work.

"Bishwanath would have been more comfortable on Salin," Nugent said. "He would have had better support from his own people. He would have known where to hide. So he is not going there to hide."

"Correct. Whatever he's doing there, I don't expect him to stay there. He may lie low for a while, send for assets, and then relocate. We're watching his family on Earth, and looking for bank transfers coming in. I should say, BuState is, through Justice."

They'd been through this every day for the last week. All they could do was keep rehashing it with each day's added facts brought in.

It was a damned shame they couldn't collar Schlenker or her crew. The problems being that compelling them to speak would mean an international incident, it was entirely likely she knew nothing, and subtle inquiries to that effect, which were ongoing, had to be very subtle because word could also travel back the other way. Still, the word through her company was that bribes had been offered. If she didn't get a balance soon, she might be agreeable. In the meantime, neither her ship nor the two co-owned by the same investor could enter UN space. The Colonial Alliance was considering coming onboard with that, as a show of solidarity with Earth's nations. Of course, if Earth's nations had been able to make individual decisions, things would be a lot different and, ironically, the damned Colonials would be less concerned about their positions. All of that was a show of independence to slap Earth with.

On a side note, Weilhung wondered what would happen when all these systems started declaring independence and becoming rightful nations, but not on Earth. That would certainly make things like this tougher, with more than one "real" planetary system.

"You know, Johnny," he said, "I am so glad I don't have to listen to Fatfuck whine about how unfair it is we can't just extradite. I got to watch deWitt explain to him the whole dreary process to get someone out of this system. That was choice."

"I hear you, boss. I'll stick to military issues."

It was more than a dreary process. Prove Schlenker was a willing accomplice to Marlow in front of a Grainnean judge. Ask them to hold an inquest here to determine extradition. If that was proven, then ask for that extradition. In the meantime, she was under no legal obligation to attend and could not be restrained. Bastards.

Back to the matter at hand.

"We need to look at what facilities are there that aren't on Salin," he said.

"Besides everything, boss?" Nugent grinned and leaned back in his chair. His hair was just long enough to leave untanned spots on his forehead, even above the helmet line. Under those lines, his eyes rolled and his mouth twisted. "Military force isn't relevant. The courts are favorable, so that's one, but it won't keep him safe. He doesn't know that we can't kill him. He knows it is possible others could. He is not more discreet; he drew attention to himself going there. There is more of a banking sector. There is greater political pull than Salin, obviously. There is not as much as Novaja Rossia or Caledonia. There are better assets for publicity . . ." Nugent stopped.

"Publicity."

"He wants it known he's alive." Nugent placed his hands on the table and looked forward now.

That had to be it. The Colonials handled their own media. It could easily be stopped in Sol System, but stopping it going from system to system was virtually impossible.

"First we have to send a message to every UN media corp to keep silent on this. They'll invoke free speech, so . . . no, fuck that," Weilhung decided. "LeMieure wants to handle the political end, send him a message, he can deal with that shit. We do our job, he does his."

"That could mean Bishwanath will have time to get away."

"I really don't have a problem with that. He's supposed to be dead, let's call him dead. Marlow owes us, though. He owes us big. We focus on them. If we get Bishwanath, fine. If not, we can't be nailed for not finding a corpse."

"What do we do, then?"

"Do? You and I do nothing, Johnny. We send a team closer to the fight and take the credit for leadership. First Platoon's already through and in Grainne space."

"That's not as fulfilling," Nugent said.

"No, but it is as effective."

❖   ❖   ❖

Almost done, Elke thought. *Almost done, and everyone alive. Beat to hell, angry from dealing with* zkurvený *idiots, but alive.*

It was pretty clear that half the crew were fine with the assurances, and the other half expected to get screwed over. They didn't seem to doubt the money existed. They figured Alex was tricky enough to make it not happen. There were mere hours before docking and the tension was rising on a curve.

So they kept watch. Four on, two off, Bishwanath confined to quarters where he was protected by at least three people and numerous devices, with a space suit on and O2 ready in case of a breach. There was no love lost here. Amazing. They'd been friends right after surviving the boarding threat and the Jump, and now they were back to a troubled détente.

It was odd to be "sitting" watch while floating in micro G, but that was the term in English. She sat watch quietly, unobtrusively, blending into the scenery. Growing up, she'd hated her slim size and self-effacing manner. Although, she couldn't have hated it too much, she reflected, as she'd never done anything about that image. On the other hand, once in the National Force, she'd recognized it as an asset and cultivated it. People never noticed her. She was just the nerd in the back.

She ran explosive calculations to stay awake. How much and what shape for a bridge abutment? What about a reinforced wall? A titalloy vault door? Another part of her brain planned for contingencies on landing, which left part of her forebrain to watch the goings-on as the crew navigated and maneuvered. No threatening gestures, just business as usual.

She barely paid attention until she heard Radaman say, "*Harap ganti pakai Bahasa, saya ada informasi untuk disambungkan.*"

She snapped alert, kicked the bulkhead behind her, and stopped two meters back from the mate. She was close enough to kill him, too far for him to reach. "You will not switch to Bahasa Indonesia and you do not have information to relay," she said with a viperlike tone. "You can conduct all this in English, just as I do. Now, you will tell the controller a dirty joke in Bahasa, and switch immediately back to English. I know enough to follow that. If you say something I don't follow, we will immediately have what might be called a 'situation.' Do you understand?"

"Yes. Ma'am." The man was totally cowed.

"You will do everything in English until we reach our

destination. Unless you would like to use Czech, German, Spanish, or French?"

"Um, no."

"Good choice."

She kept her eyes on him as she kicked her way back across the bridge.

There was no need, as she saw it, to mention a demolition contract she'd had supporting engineers in the Sulawan Shoals as they built an artificial island. Her Bahasa was atrocious, but it wasn't a complex language and she recognized enough to grasp the gist. Since TanCorp out of Sulawan had been the primary developer of Grainne, it was convenient. Jason likely was passable at it, so he should switch to another shift. In fact, it might be necessary to have everyone on shift on arrival, she considered.

Jason wanted to feel relieved. He still felt impending disaster was possible.

The last few tense minutes before docking trickled down, with the whole team in the crew cabin next to the forward lock. The captain had the bridge, and she was definitely on their side to cover her own ass. She'd chewed Radaman but good over his attempt to slip notice out. That could only create more tension, but they were leaving the vessel so it wasn't their problem.

They sat on worn couches, unstrapped but padded. Any maneuvers at this point should be tiny burps, not blasts. Support was needed; crash protection was not. They each had a bag alongside, ready to grab and go. The airlock was there, inviting and tantalizing, and foreboding with the chance of hostiles beyond, which the crew had not been told about. Jason reminded the others, "You realize we still have a fight once we get there, and legal snarls." He kept his eyes on the hatch as he spoke. The chance of a military force breaking in on them was increasingly small, but he wouldn't feel safe until they were well clear of this ship. Then, of course, it would start again with the next leg of the journey.

Alex asked, "Yeah, I gathered that. How's that going to work? If there's no local laws, what are we doing wrong?"

Jason shook his head fractionally. "No, there are laws. The laws cover disputes. Basically, the government has no position on your actions, but if someone else does, they can demand a resolution. If we shoot up a studio, you bet they'll demand a resolution. At the very least we'll have to replace any equipment we destroy. If we kill anyone, even reporters, we're looking at literal millions in damages and years indentured to pay the debt off. Do not damage anything we don't absolutely have to, or someone will fucking own us."

"Isn't there anything about extenuating circumstances?" Aramis asked.

"Nope. No one is making us shoot. We could negotiate peacefully." Jason pulled at his collar. It was hot in here with all these bodies. Airflow was minimized during docking.

Alex chuckled. "Not going to happen. We're busting into their show. That's the only way we can get a big enough splash without them locking the broadcast. It's either that, or try to bull our way in the front without being stopped, or going underground."

Aramis nodded in Bal's direction. "I guess we minimize damage and try to get Corporate to pay for it. Or if Mister Bishwanath pulls this off, he'll cover for us."

Jason said, "Meantime, we could be indentured labor. Anything from mowing grass to shoveling manure."

"Will anyone be shooting at us?" Bart asked.

He likely meant, *How many people will be shooting at us?* Jason thought.

"Entirely possible. Remember that Grainne is a frontier society. There are dangerous animals on the planet, so people go armed. Some hunt food. There aren't many cops, and all veterans keep their military weapons and can be called for duty for trouble, under District Council orders. Just assume anyone can be armed, and with better stuff than we have presently. Out in the Habitats, there is a certain black market element that can get violent."

"Sounds like my kind of system," Elke said.

"Why do you think I retired here?" Jason grinned. "It's not bad at all, and cheap. But you *are* held accountable for your actions. So don't fuck up."

"Is it necessary that we hijack a live broadcast?" Bal asked. "Can we not just schedule a press release?"

"Not here, sir," Aramis said. "It won't work."

They all looked at him.

"Look, I did some journalism in school, and we studied press releases. If we do that, the word goes out to expect the release. Then the initial release goes out. Then the video of the conference.

So then the UN clamps down on broadcasts. Their ships simply won't transmit the news. This has to go out so fast they can't shut all the sources down, and it's still a crapshoot. If they get word through some smaller system, it'll still be a 'rumor' they can squash, and we're stuck here, unable to go home. The broadcast, not private trans or wire, remember, has to hit several systems at once so it can't be denied easily, which means they'll be busy doing damage control, have badly conflicting admissions and denials, and then figure it's easier to burn some BuState asshole than deny it."

"So we must take over a broadcast in progress?" Bal asked.

"I concur," Alex said with a nod and a nervous glance at the hatch. "Multiple light-speed delays means multiple copies against multiple denials. We prove you're alive and *then* you can start doing press releases for various nations."

"Another reason for live," Jason said, "is that studios, even foreign owned, really don't like to interrupt broadcasts. They view local ratings rather highly, and regard and assume censorship is the responsibility of the receiving station. For example, two of the nations on Mtali don't allow any nudity to be shown. Certain political issues are sensitive on Earth. The anti-Monarchist groups are not allowed to be seen on government stations in Caledonia. The attitude here is very much, 'That's your problem, not ours.' Even if our opponents get into the station, it'll take a court order, that they will never get, to shut down a broadcast. If they physically interrupt it, they'll face a suit for damages."

"Sue-happy bunch, aren't you?" Alex asked.

"Yes, we are, and it works to our advantage at this time," Jason grinned back. "Worst case, they interrupt, but Bal can remain resident here and they can't touch him."

"Why not do that?" Elke asked, "And then go about publicity?"

"They'll claim he's a double or impostor. Hard to disprove and they have official color to their claims," Shaman said. "Yes, our best bet is not the easiest, but it is the messiest and most public."

"Not to mention that we'd have to explain ourselves then. So let us do this," Alex said.

"It will take another ten days," Jason said.

"Why so?" Alex asked. "Ship departures?"

"No broadcasts like that from the station. Technical and astro only. They have some local entertainment but it's all wired or local transmission. You want a proper broadcast, we have to get boots on the ground on Grainne."

Elke sighed. "What's involved in that?"

"You're going to love this," Jason chuckled.

"Yes?" Aramis prompted him, first to do so after a long pause.

"We buy tickets and land. All there is to it."

"That's *it*?" Alex asked. "You said it wasn't complicated, but . . ."

"Yup. I'll get a private assay on the remaining bullion, convert, get the cash, minus the five percent fee we're looking at for out-system transfers, we buy tickets and board, no questions asked. After that we have to schedule our approach and hit a station. Getting down is easy, and sooner is better, in case they do come looking for us," he added.

"So the solution to this element does not involve explosive or shooting?" Elke asked.

"Correct."

"How . . . interesting," she said.

"If we need to, I can get some company funds from the local office," Alex said. "It means coming out, but they should cover for us now."

"They may not," Jason said. "I would assume that every company commo is being scanned. Besides, I can use my assets here." He could also check in with his family, hopefully before anyone gave them bad news. On the other hand, after the news might be better, so they realistically seemed shocked. Dammit, he didn't want to bring them into this. They deserved better, and he'd have to make amends.

"What if they do shut things down?" Bart asked.

"Simple," Elke said. "I blow up as much stuff as possible, you shoot everything full of holes, and we get outside in time for a competing station to cover the story." She grinned brightly. Bart chuckled.

Jason cringed and said, "If we have to. But I cannot stress enough that we minimize damage. Really."

"Besides," Bal said, "it will work much better with dignity. These things are important in the political scene."

"All we can do is all we can do," Alex concluded with a serious expression.

A series of bumps, shoves, and clanking noises interrupted the conversation. Two crew, Gina and one of the cargo crew—Nicolo

maybe?—came through and undogged safeties before opening the
hatch. There was a whoosh of equalizing pressure and a slight
but steady flow of air into the ship.

The redhead faced them and said, "The Captain's compliments
and will you please, and I quote, 'get the fuck off my ship now,
or else,' unquote." She was smiling a nervous smile. She made an
open gesture with her arm.

"We're moving," Alex agreed.

Micro-G maneuvers took them through, with Jason first, Bart
helping Aramis second, Bal with Shaman, and Alex and Elke bringing up the rear. They were into the station proper in moments,
and it was like any other station: a long corridor of docking ports
with islands of benches. The deck was polished space rock, and the
walls, because they weren't bulkheads, were cut and semifinished,
evidence of the hollowed-out planetoid that was Station Ceileidh.
Another difference was that the ship itself was inside a long dock
carved into the planetoid instead of outside a constructed station,
and the cargo was being handled somewhat differently . . . and
that was no longer their problem.

Everyone except Jason and Aramis concealed their weapons.
Jason tucked his in his belt, which was a little unusual but there
were enough other people wearing pistols it wasn't obvious, and
Aramis's carbine was too large to hide, so he slung it muzzle
"down" and presented himself as what he was: a security guard.
In five minutes they were through several passages of maze as
rotational gravity increased, and stopped in front of a hotel. The
classic Hyatt logo was carved into the passageway rock.

With a sign to wait, Jason slipped to the desk, made their transac-
tions, and returned. With another sign, the team split into elements
and took three different routes into the hotel. When Alex and Elke
knocked on the door, he opened it and ushered them in.

"Why a Hyatt?" Alex asked. "Worth the money?"

"Yes," Jason said. He gestured toward the beds and couches
everyone else was sprawled across. The curvature of the floor
could just be seen at this level. The G was about forty percent,
enough for comfort without wasting kinetic energy.

"Several reasons," he continued as they joined the mass flop.
The tension was bleeding out in a hurry. Weeks' worth of stress
relieved, for the moment. "First, a suite is more cost-effective and
safer than multiple rooms. Second, classier joints are less likely to

call Station Safety. They like to maintain the illusion of decency. Third, lower-class places are often flophouses. I haven't been through here in a while, only came through a few times briefly, and don't have time to determine which ones are safe, which ones are filthy, and which ones are loaded with smugglers."

"I thought everything was legal here. Why smugglers?" Elke asked.

"Since everything is legal here, the deals are negotiated before the stuff is smuggled elsewhere. Between Outsystem thugs, homeless sex workers, smugglers, cashiered ship crew, and dishonest profiteers, I don't recommend anywhere without a brand name and ISO certs. Both."

"Both?" Alex asked.

"Anyone can hang up a sign claiming ISO certs . . . for a while," he observed.

"True. What a fascinating system you've picked to live in."

"Hey, this is the system's main port. All ports are alike. The scum of the waste spaces."

"True enough. What's next?"

"Order us some decent food for delivery. I recommend Eight Lucky Chinese, Tapatios, Ati's Grill, or one of the Earth chains." He headed for the door. "And don't let anyone in, would be my recommendation."

"I'd figured that part out," Alex said with a disgusted look.

Many ships came through Grainne's Jump Point One. It matched Jump Point Six in Sol space, and thus brought not only Earth traffic, but traffic from anywhere in that direction, including a number of systems with only one Point connected directly to Sol.

Not many ships departed Salin for Sol. Fewer still continued on to Grainne. Of those few, only one had blown through the gate with "system failures." Even though it had continued to have problems in Iota Persei space, it was certainly noticeable. Since it had been flagged for examination anyway, it was a beacon to Weilhung. He knew that they knew he was onto them. It was a matter of time.

While the Colonial government didn't monitor activities or do much tracing, it was certainly possible to contract others to do so. He could even, had he chosen to, have hired bounty hunters to take them down. The threefold problem with that was he'd first have to warn them of the quality of their prey, which would raise the price and the necessary quality of who he hired, that he had no control over potential leaks at that end, which could scrub things, and that he'd be yielding a mission to a contractor. That issue was what had started all this—contractors taking military missions. He didn't dare go there and keep his career intact.

Besides, there was a point to be made.

There was no reason not to hire investigators to surveil the RC people, though. That was easy enough. Whether it was done with cameras or naked eye hires wasn't relevant. Nor was it cheap, but Weilhung had the assets of a government behind him. His opponents were down to carry-on bags and some cash, though he did not rule out them acquiring more assets. They'd been very resourceful so far.

They were on Station Ceileidh. If they were still there in a few hours, he'd have them. If not, the chase would resume. That would almost certainly be on the surface of Grainne, because he couldn't imagine they'd try to hop another ship anywhere. That avenue was closed off with AF ships waiting beyond each of Grainne's Jump Points.

One problem was that the press still invoked their "rights." No one dared breathe a word of why this ship was of interest because that would make things worse. Asking them to clear everything through an additional filter—because BuCommerce couldn't be brought in on this; too many people knew already. The rogue contractors would have to be physically stopped at whichever outlet they went to for publicity. He figured to plan for all the big ones and have personnel in position.

As annoying and aggravating as this had all been so far, the one bonus to it all was that when Major Weilhung, UN Forces, U.S. Army Recon Force got into the game, he'd get that much more credit for bringing them down.

It didn't take Vaughn long, and Bart was impressed. Vaughn came back within the hour holding a briefcase full of credit chits and coins.

"Spot price minus five percent. They even covered the assay fee. The stuff also isn't likely to leave the system soon enough to matter."

"And they didn't think it was stolen?" Shaman asked.

"No, I suggested to them it was for a covert military mission. The variety of stuff I had made that a good bet. The watches and jewelry went to a local jeweler, and I offered him ten percent to hold them for three weeks. We might even get them back."

"You still use coins here," Anderson noted, turning one over in his hand. "I'm amazed."

"They're struck with a gauss field so they have an encoded signature. Every cash counter can check them. So it's not worth forging them. Once asteroid mining took off, Earth should have gone back to real metal coins, not plastic."

"Instead we have rechargeable cards. Lighter weight."

"Yeah, but no character." Vaughn flipped a Cr5 coin through the air to land on the table with a ring. There was silver in there. That was classy, Bart agreed.

"I checked insystem flights," Marlow said. "We can be on one tonight at nine divs, or tomorrow at three. Once I get used to your screwy clock."

"What, ten divs of one hundred segs? Easier than Salin's sixty-four minutes and twenty hours and god knows what months. I needed about a week to get used to it."

"Just so everyone knows," Marlow said, "I have to relay the bad news, too."

"Go ahead," Bart said.

"We are all missing and presumed dead."

Into the silence that followed, Anderson said softly, "Does that mean they intend to make us dead?"

After a moment, Vaughn said, "Likely not. That's why they've left options open. They can't jail us if we're dead, and don't want to admit the gaffe. This means they can smear us with more dirt if they do find us."

"They'll claim we faked our own deaths, probably," Marlow said. "Right."

Bal said, "I am so sorry. This just seems to get worse, doesn't it?"

Shrugging, Bart looked at him and said, "I expected as much. It is harder on you and Jason, having families." He looked around.

The expression on Jason's face suggested that there would be vengeance.

Horace shook his head all the way down. Cash on the counter, seven tickets, board the craft with weapons in carry-on luggage and pistols worn. All they'd been asked for was to clear the chambers and holster or case them. There'd been little surprise.

He shared a cabin with Bart and said, "I can't help but wonder about that. It almost seems like an invitation to have ships pirated."

"I wondered about that, too," Bart replied. He was stretched out on a large bunk with his hands behind his head and legs sprawled. He looked very happy to have so much room. "I suppose there aren't many places one can take such a craft, unless you have your own maintenance, support, and fuel facility. And if so, why steal one?"

"All colonies overreact against the controls of Earth," Horace said. "If they were like the rural parts of Africa, they'd have far stricter controls. Of course," he shrugged, "it hasn't helped much to stop civil wars."

"Pfah. You don't fight effective wars with rifles and pistols," Bart said. "Not without support weapons, artillery, and some recon and power in the sky."

It was a good start to an intellectual conversation, which lasted most of the ten days in. They took turns guarding Bal, though it was obvious no one recognized him nor cared, and there weren't any other passengers who were a believable threat. Some were families, some business types constantly sending messages, and there were a couple of college kids coming back from Novaja Rossia. The two of them hit it off and spent most of the time in a cabin together, after swapping space to be alone in that cabin.

I could use a woman, Horace thought with wry amusement tinged with bitter frustration. When this assignment is over, hopefully in a few days, I intend to be far less spiritual, and far more carnal.

The only real excitement was in the transfer from the system craft to the landing shuttle. The orbital station was not much to speak of: very sterile, small, and mechanical, being designed for a safe transfer between craft, as a support point for those craft and not much else. However, their intent to go through together came to a halt when they realized the lock was only big enough for three to five with luggage. Bal got cut out of the group and directed into the lock with no one else from the team.

After a hesitation, some looks, a quick shuffle, Aramis took his place and went ahead. That made it obvious to everyone that they were up to something. Horace kept a studied neutral expression and pretended not to be aware of the stares. He kept expecting customs agents or cops, even though neither existed here. There were safety officers who were akin to cops, but not on hand, nor would they show up unless called. Apparently, their little dance had not been enough to merit it.

Once locked aboard, one here, one there, it was a matter of taking seats and the typical cramped, annoying, mildly nerve-making descent through atmosphere, gravity returning, going away, sharp pressure on speed-killing turns and lifts halfway around the planet, before a long, screaming approach to Jefferson Starport. That was the best choice to find a studio making broadcasts for export, and was the only choice of a landing for today. Westport was the other starport, and it only handled traffic every two to three days, as the western edge of the Serpent continent was colonized.

Taxi and hotel. Elke had no real time to see much of Jefferson or Grainne, other than to note the stiff gravity, bright Iolight, and mostly modern architecture with some old Colonial blocks being replaced as fast as possible. It was cool, this being autumn, and the local flora were a riot of blues and yellows mixed with the greens and reds of Earth transplants. This was definitely a multibillion dollar economy, not the waste they'd just left. Bal looked very sober, and never took his eyes off the scenery. The city was small but modern, with large greenways between it and the port, most of it agricultural.

This time, they went to a cheaper location, but it was easy to tell from the outside it was of decent quality, and the cabbie recommended it. They cycled in in three groups and got organized. Elke stretched as she sat, and then started unsnapping her boots to change socks. Her boots were very well broken in and comfortable by now. They were also very sweaty and stale. The climate system had sensors for contaminants and the fan speed increased with only the barest hint of breeze. The smell evaporated in seconds. This wasn't a pricey place, but it was very roomy. That was an advantage of being out here.

Jason came in last. "Okay, I've got my phone back in service, and I called a friend. We're borrowing a car. At some point, he'll need the car back or the money."

"How upset will he be if it's money?" Elke asked.

"Not very," Jason said. "I warned him it was business, without saying what."

"Good. How are we doing on cash?" Alex asked.

"Down to about two thousand credits," Jason said. "Just enough for some ammo, food, and a few bribes. We've got to make this work. However, I also have hyperweb access and my friend is bringing a spare computer. I can acquire more money tomorrow."

"So we can find a schedule at one of the larger studios," Aramis said.

"Yes."

"I'll do that, if you like. UN station preferred? Just so it's harder to deny?"

"Why would that be harder to deny?" Bart asked.

"It's a perception," Aramis said. "If it's on a Grainne station, it means it's faked. On a UN station it's credible."

"Even though a UN station will have better security than a local one," Jason said. "And of course, by 'better' I mean 'worse but more of it.'"

"I was wondering if you'd got into my medications," Shaman said. "'Better' indeed."

"What is our approach to be?" Bart asked. He was finishing up a sandwich he'd snagged at the spaceport. Both he and Aramis had started packing away calories once insystem.

Elke said, "I would see first if we can just walk in. That would be easiest."

"I doubt it," Jason said. "They tend to have guards against fringe groups making statements on camera. Quite a few are willing to bust in and pay the court costs for minor trespass in order to disrupt the propag— I mean news. Of course, that means they don't panic and cut power at the first sign of intruders."

"I would assume they run a strict schedule, and vet everything as they do insystem. In Sol System, I mean," Aramis said. "Bal is not going to be allowed on camera unidentified, and there's no fake ID we can use that will be of interest. His real identity will be a problem." Bal looked up at the mention, but offered nothing. He'd been going through stages of depression and elation. Seeing the money in the economy around him had depressed him again.

"So we'll have to bust in loudly and with lots of distraction," Jason said. "Afraid so."

Elke grinned brightly from the room's computer terminal.

"Luckily, I just found a store that sells explosive listed on the hyperweb. It's within walking distance." She might have to move here and look for work.

"Explosive," Alex said. He didn't sound ready for this.

"Just enough for distractions," she said. "And intimidation, of course. Meridian and Thirty-Eighth Streets. Alcohol, Tobacco, and Firearms, Inc."

"Earthies keep going there thinking it's an official office," Jason commented. "But their prices are decent."

"Make up a list," Alex said. "We've got a budget."

"And we need a plan," Shaman said. "One with supplemental plans so we don't have to resort to wholesale violence."

"Yes, and I cannot stress that enough," Jason said. "I'll order more food. I promise it will be cheap, but it won't be ship food or military rats."

"I will appreciate that," Bal said. He mostly stayed out of the debate. He was along for the ride at this point.

Elke knew her part of the plan. She'd have enough explosive to destroy everything they didn't need. Beyond that was up to Alex.

Jason's friend showed up discreetly with the car, handed over keys, and left after a warm hug. No chatter, no name given. The man had to be a professional himself. He also left a case of beer. Alex doled out two bulbs each and took inventory in the lot behind the hotel.

"That's a little more than a 'car,' " he said.

"It's technically not a truck," Jason replied.

"Technically, it's balls," Aramis said, grinning. "I don't recognize it, but I like it. Oh, yes, yes I do."

"If I didn't know better, I would say that bumper was designed for ramming," Bart put in, resting his foot on it and shoving to test the resistance.

"Then you don't know better," Jason grinned.

Elke read the logo and name plate on the glacis, because it was certainly more than a hood. "Is this 'Goliaphant' a dangerous animal?" The logo glinted in the bright Iolight. She was cold, despite that. Jason had been honest about the UV, gravity, and thin air, but it was invigorating. Even in the city it had a freshness not found on Earth.

"Can't you tell?"

"I am glad we are in an urban area," she grinned.

The Goliaphant was angular but blocky and an AM General product. It had the distinctive look of a rally vehicle, and was beefy enough to be a light military vehicle. She'd been worried about using a civilian vehicle, but this would do nicely.

"Will we need to crash through a gate?" Bart asked.

"We might," Jason admitted. "And this will do it. Our biggest problem will be that, while weapons are legal to carry, what we'll have will definitely be attention-getting. And when they try to stop us, we're going to be blatantly obvious."

Alex asked, "What is our legal position with UN personnel, vis-à-vis armed force and the law?"

"There is a cutout there," Jason admitted. "Unless they are paid residents, they have no standing to appear in court. The station and the broadcaster both count as Corporate Persons and could bring charges for damages, but that's a harder case to prove. They'll want to be paid for damaged equipment. If we don't actually kill anyone, we're not too bad off. But a lot of their help are locals under contract with standing to sue."

"Elke, dial the blasts down."

"I will," she said. "But I want my protest officially filed with Corporate." She'd comply, but so far she'd been able to use an amazing amount of stuff that went bang. She wanted to finish the race that way.

"I'm serious," Alex said. "And you watch it, too, Aramis."

"Yeah, I'm allergic to being indentured. Can I stun someone heavily?"

"Good idea at this point," Alex nodded. "Nonlethal force preferred, try to limit armed force to attention getting and cheap accessories—couches, walls, not cameras or stages."

Jason said, "Okay, we have a good vehicle, we have three general targets. Our time frame is limited by our funds. I'd say we have a week at most to make things march."

"So let's go back inside and work things out," Alex said.

"Okay," Aramis said from one computer, which was netted to Jason's, hardwired for security, cable snaking between the desks. "We have a choice of ABCNN, NBCBS or AIMSN. AIMSN has a reputation of being antigovernment."

"Sure, about five percent of the time," Jason said. "They're pretty much indistinguishable from this end."

"Right, but I'd say we hit one of the progovernment stations so it'll have more impact," Alex suggested. He was surprised at how much information his people had on this subject.

"I concur," Jason said. "Who's the most suckup?"

"NBCBS. Who are, coincidentally, also the biggest fuckups on accuracy and have been hacked several times." There was no love lost between Alex and them, it seemed.

"Hmm . . . perhaps ABCNN then. Didn't they have that story about—"

"Yes," Aramis cut in. "Complete inside info and they paid cash for it. Of course, they're also the most antimilitary. So fucking them would give me a warm fuzzy feeling."

"Would you like some lube?" Shaman chuckled.

"No, I want it to hurt." Aramis sounded vicious. He must have been caught in one of their stories.

"When is a good time?"

"I dunno," Jason said. "I don't watch much video, and a lot of it's cryptic. You pick out a title."

As the production schedule scrolled past, Elke said, "That one." A few moments later, Aramis said, "That one." Shaman spotted two.

"All four are talk shows where losers are exploited for humiliation factor," Alex observed. "What a comment on our species."

"On *your* culture," Jason said. "I'm not American anymore, and they're producing those strictly for the Earth market. They won't get much slice here."

"Nor am I part of it," Elke added.

"It is popular in Germany, but I am not fond of such," Bart said.

"And Africa is full of enough real tragedy," Shaman said.

"Likewise," Bal finished. "I believe it's for you." He indicated Aramis and Alex with a grin.

"Do we want busy time of day, or late night?" Aramis asked. "Slow traffic, or lots of concealment?"

"I'd say late night," Jason replied. "Less fight, less bystanders, people slower generally. Get in fast and do it."

"And we need to make sure they've started and are live," Alex said. "I also need an ephemeris or whatever it's called on ship departures so we know we're getting some transfer."

They settled on the popular Lewis Spaniel show, out on tour. Spaniel had stopped on Grainne for a session entitled, "I Moved Here for the Drugs and Hookers and Now I Need Help."

"I'd think that was obvious," Elke snickered. "And here's yesterday's title. 'Teenagers Who Declared Themselves Adults to Become More Attractive to Older Men.'"

"Are you sure we can't shoot him, the guests, and the audience?" Shaman asked, stepping back slightly as if distancing himself from a toxin. "This is rather foul."

"Tempting, but no." Alex looked bothered by the titles. "He gets lower every time I'm forced to endure him."

"But he has high ratings, likes doing live gigs for the 'rawness,' and there are five major ships in the pipe as he's on. They get the live feed, they record until they jump, and then dump it, and it's rebroadcast."

"How many immediate viewers?" Bart asked. "Won't it be held for the slot and caught before then?"

"In Sol space, definitely," Jason agreed. "But other colonies will have it on contract or syndication, and will find that one segment interesting. The point is to make enough noise to governments. The public viewers won't care, unless they see shooting on camera."

"You keep encouraging me with talk like that," Aramis said. "I know, I know. Minimize collateral damage."

"We need the vehicle," Alex said. "Cash. Body armor. Explosive. More ammo. Field medical kit needs updated. I want maps inside and out of the entire area, and maps for nearby buildings. Double-check on the ship departures and show schedule."

"We should be fast, and pick a large audience," Bal said. "Popular shows, no matter how sordid, will give the visibility we need."

"I still say we should wait," Shaman suggested.

Alex shook his head. "No. Schlenker wants her money, her crew are going to drink and talk. She can't get back into UN space until we clear this up. Our departure has to have been noted. Another two days, tops, is all we have, and I don't think it's going to get any better. That show shoots in two days and we're on it. Jason, can your friend roll us and do it quietly?"

"He can. I can access some funds too. I drew a new card at the bank."

"Alex, that card is bound to be tagged," Elke said.

"That card is tagged," he agreed. "Which is why I had my wife authorize a new one in the name of my backup ID, which I picked up at the Citizens' Building. I drew from her account, and I drew cash so as not to register any businesses they may catch."

"Backup ID?" Aramis asked.

"None of your business, kid," Jason grinned.

"You didn't call your family, did you?" Aramis asked.

That was a sore point, but a legitimate question.

"As far as anyone knows, no," he replied. "We have signals set up for just such an emergency. Specifically, my first transaction was in an exact amount that tells her I'm alive and being discreet. So my family knows, but no overt contact was made." That was likely a good thing, as painful as it was. He was sure she'd be as ready to kill as he was, and that would have to wait.

CHAPTER THIRTY

The plan, as always, started out well enough.

"Two blocks, everyone stand ready," Alex said from the passenger seat. He felt really odd about doing a combat escort mission through the streets of a modern, prosperous city with no visible threats. Nevertheless, they had no idea what they were facing, and needed to be ready. Alex assumed all their preparation was overkill, and a few pointed pistols would acquire what they needed, or at least earn enough curiosity to get some support.

He was also ready to use as much nonlethal force as necessary. If really necessary, they had two carbines, and Elke had a new shotgun and some explosives. She'd been joyous at finding the same model available, promised favors she couldn't be serious about to purchase it, and had taken it to bed with her to cuddle all night like a teddy bear. She might really need some therapy when this was over.

Traffic was smooth. The streets were broad and well laid out in this city that had been designed from day one to be a national capital. That was advantageous. Alex reflected that if every city was like this, his business would be much easier. Of course, it would also be less profitable. Not that it was profitable at present, but he still had hopes.

"We're blocked," Bart said. Alex looked to their left for the upcoming turn.

"Shit."

The ABCNN gate was closed, locked, and had guards posted.

Behind them, the building stood as a long rectangular prism fitted against a large, low dome that held the studios and gear.

"Someone knows we're coming," Jason said.

"How?" Aramis shouted.

"What do we do?" Bart asked.

"We should abort and escape," Bishwanath said. "I am not worth this."

"Shut up, Bal. Shut up, Aramis. We need a solution fast." Alex burst into sweat, pulse hammering.

"What do I do?" Bart asked again. "I have seconds only."

"Ram it," Elke said.

"Concur," Jason agreed.

"No time to reschedule. Blow the gate," Alex said, stomach churning. They were all going to die. "Aramis, you'll take the vehicle for your position."

"Got it."

"Yes, sir," Bart said.

Bart drove almost past the gate before he suddenly swung across traffic and nailed the throttle. The Goliaphant used two very small turbines that, with lots of tweaks, spooled up quickly. He used one hand to lock the waste gate manually then powered in the start fluid in a steady flow. The vehicle was traveling close to a hundred kilometers per hour when it hit the gate.

The bars burst, followed by the car's tires as the antientry spikes in the road deployed. Both guards dove aside but turned stunners on the vehicle as it passed. Most of the effect was grounded by the Goliaphant's cage, but Alex felt a tingle at least.

"Straight for the door!" he shouted.

"*Ja,*" Bart replied. They bounced jarringly over a curb, threw dirt out of a flower bed, smacked a glancing blow off a tree, and bumped back down onto paved surface, shedding bits of tire and throwing sparks from the scandium alloy rims.

Bart drove right through the entrance, window plastic shattering and flying in a cloud.

"An antique drive-in theater!" Aramis shouted.

"*Move!*" Alex shouted and kicked the door.

Six people in suits jumped out feet first and advanced as a block. Aramis, still partially disabled, stayed back with the vehicle. His job was to be a distraction.

Alex led the rest. They needed to get further inside fast. They wore typical Earth-style suits. They carried large bags. No one watching by camera or from a security box should trigger on any of it. Once inside, they were just suits in a studio, the ultimate in camouflage.

"Spread out slightly," Alex muttered, glancing toward Jason and grinning, as if holding a normal conversation. It wouldn't do to look like a pack of goons. He pushed open the door to the main office hallway, which was directly in line with the actual studios at the rear. Those were the doors ahead, at the far end. It was working!

"So, there we were, and I had to wonder what the heck he was talking about, I mean . . ." the meaningless fake conversation was easy. Just pick some event and start jabbering. Thirty meters to the door. Keep walking. So far, so good. Once through that door, they would use persuasion or guns to make people listen to Bal on camera, with ships recording it at light-speed before they jumped system and spread the word.

Jason's reply to his conversation, however, threw a wrench in the works.

"That can't be . . ."

Alex looked toward the door casually and let his gaze linger. *Oh, shit.* "It is."

One of the rent-a-cops at the door was familiar. He was a Recon sergeant from Celadon.

And the supervisor behind him was another one.

"Aw, shit," Jason muttered.

"Cover Bal, Bart, go," Alex said.

The man didn't have to be told twice. He and Shaman were both off at a sprint, literal cannon fodder to attempt to ground any stun charges thrown Bal's way.

"We'll abort if we have to. Going through hard," Alex decided aloud. "Elke, would you be a dear?"

Her only reply was to flick her hands forward, which was followed by cracks and poppling sounds behind the two running mercs that escalated with each move until serious bangs were shaking the air and side doors.

And Bart pulled out a carbine.

"Goddamit, no!" Alex said, as Shaman followed Bart's lead.

The two Recon troops were reaching for their own weapons, but jerked when hit, their armor going hard. Then they started moving again, stiffly, as it started to relax.

And the two contractors shot again and again as the others ran up behind in a hurry.

"Gun," Bart demanded, holding out a hand. Elke shifted just enough, the cacophony of explosions slackening as she drew her pistol and flipped it over. Jason pulled his out and tossed it to Shaman.

Balls out, Alex decided, sighing but also relieved. Shooting he understood. He put a burst toward the nearest local guard, who was rapidly moving and would certainly be calling for backup. The burst was toward, not at. He couldn't kill the man. Legality aside, the guy had been decent.

Then they were through, as Bart and Shaman kept the two soldiers pinned in place, able to make only slow, jerky movements as their knee-to-neck armor seized up with every impact. Of course, the practical limit on that was ammo. While they were partially immobilized, Elke and Jason were able to get close enough to stun them with batons, and then Shaman whipped out an injector. In the moment before he passed by, Alex could see a very disgusted look frozen on one soldier's face.

Smooth. Very smooth. Nothing could go this smooth without a serious problem just waiting to crash down on them. Just how big a force was inside? Would it be wise to abort? But it was obvious their cover was blown . . . how thoroughly?

No, if this message were to work, it was now or not at all.

The Recon squad, assuming it was one squad, was twelve. Two were down. Likely, each entrance would have a couple inside behind the locals, so they would either be arriving in pairs or waiting to attack en masse. The longer it took for a response, the bigger and more effective that response would be. Nor was there any way to intercept it. This had to go fast. The main doors had to be guarded, so going through them would create a brief disturbance ended by stunners, on a show famous for such events. They'd put the team down and fix it in the mix.

"Jason, keep me warned on threats. Escalate if you have to, but we're still trying to pull this off. Bal, down this hall."

Elke and Bart came past at a sprint. Elke had doffed her jacket and looked very female in a suit shirt, even with body armor underneath. Her bag was empty on the floor and she carried her shotgun slung right, demo bag left. Bart had ditched his and the tie, and he was wearing his bag on his back now. That made sense.

With cover blown, there was less reason not to look military. Behind them were more explosions, seconds apart, designed to slow any pursuit; professionals would quickly deduce they weren't a serious threat. And the prohibition against bullets, Alex remembered, was one way. They were the armed intruders.

Gas started billowing. It was normal tear gas with a smoke screen, not a nasty incapacitance agent. Still, they'd expected a few civilian guards with minimal gear, not a couple of squads of professionals. Everyone was on to them.

Elke turned to the left and blew a locked door open with a shotgun blast straight through the bolt. Bart and Shaman took up position as Jason and Alex urged Bal through with Alex leading. He went cross-eyed looking for threats, but this was a detour and thus should be less well defended. Of course, they had to get back en route . . .

Bart kicked in another door which revealed an office of some sort. Two occupants, male and female. He stunned them both and then swung around to use a wrecking bar from his bag to shatter the polymer panel that was the opposite wall so he could kick through it. It splintered and left jagged edges to be avoided.

Luckily, no one had been in the hallway behind it.

"Up the stairs," Bart said and led the way up and to the right.

"Dammit, no, we need to stay . . ." Too late. The only thing worse than going the wrong way would be to split up, so Alex followed. This was not getting any easier. They were truly fucked. Oh, well, at least if they pushed for trial here, they could serve out sentences doing labor on a frontier world instead of in a UN jail in France.

There were definite sounds of pursuit behind them now. Though the level of shouting seemed to indicate local hires, not military professionals. Jason seemed to have been correct. No respectable Grainnean veteran took a security job that didn't allow him to be armed. The response was slow and not very coordinated, so far. That would change with Weilhung's unit in the mix.

Bal was just about being carried. While not in bad shape for his age, he was worn a bit ragged from the ordeal of the last few weeks, and not nearly in the shape of the younger troops. His feet banged over steps, but he never quite tripped. Bart and Elke lugged him, with Jason switching off as they were needed for specialty tasks.

Then they were up, with people pouring out of executive offices to see what the disturbance was. It was getting crowded, even though anyone with any brains should be running away.

There was some hesitation about the armed intruders, but locals were used to armed guards in suits and weren't instinctively flinching. The Earthies were following that cultural lead. If the locals weren't scared, there wasn't a problem, was there?

The sounds of pursuit increased, and there was a tinge of tear gas to the air, drifting up. The good news was that that reaction served to create more panic behind. But this crowd was parting out of courtesy, not from fear.

Jason shouted, "Folks, this is a fire drill. Please vacate the building. This is a fire drill."

One intern type in a suit with his hair cut in a skunk mohawk and his forehead tattooed in knotwork gave a typical sarcastic, you-want-me-to-do-what? look.

"Fire drill? Right," he said.

Elke tossed something at his feet that whoofed into a ball of burning liquid and spread into a half-meter circle on the carpet, almost engulfing his feet.

"Fire drill," she repeated, with a quirky smile and raised eyebrow.

Then the crowd ran.

"You!" Jason shouted, grabbing one of the people fleeing past him. "Grab a fire extinguisher and deal with it!"

The team kept moving down the hall into some kind of storage area. Bart dodged to one side and grabbed a power cord attached to a portable wall-sized monitor. Following his lead, Shaman found a cargo strap looped around a pallet of office supplies and cut the latch loose with his knife.

"Right!" Jason shouted and pointed.

Somewhere along the line, Bart had found a printed directory. He held it in one hand and his reader in the other and split his attention three ways. He obviously didn't see the stunner-armed guard ahead who was sizing up the group and deciding what action to take.

Alex zapped him and he stumbled, but tried to recover. He zapped again and put the man down. Bart jumped far too lightly for a man of his size over the still form, as if he'd known all along that someone would take care of the problem for him . . . and maybe he had. They'd been through so much shit that they were almost gestaltic.

Then a burst of real small-arms fire caused everyone to duck and dive.

That would be the rest of the squad, Alex thought. What now? They were split between both sides of the hallway with no hard cover, though side rooms would make excellent concealment for a few seconds . . .

"This way," he said, grabbed a gibbering Bal and reached for a door handle. Shaman was still with them, and Jason. So they had the native guide. That left the firepower under Elke, and . . .

Another burst came far too close.

. . . and Bart had a map and seemed to know what he was looking for.

"Go, Elke. We'll catch up shortly."

"Roger," she agreed. The two of them faded back through a door on their side.

Alex, Jason, Bal, and Shaman went through the door, which led into some sort of utility room. Jason grabbed a large spike and a hammer off a bench, jammed the spike into the door at an angle, setting it with one tap and then beating it twice.

"Ceiling," he suggested, vaulting onto the bench and helping Bal up. He punched out two panels and slid them aside carefully.

"Concrete ceiling," he added. This must still be the front side of the building, not the main working area. "Shit. Hold on . . ." He scanned around, grabbed a torch, and shone it in circles, then said, "Hatch, over that way. Bal, give me your hand."

Alex helped Bal ascend into the twilight of the utility space, then began easing himself up on his hands. Not too soon, either. There was beating at the door. In a moment, that turned to hinges being shot off and a wall being gutted. Shaman barely made it, grunting with the effort as Alex heaved him up.

But he was up, and slid the panels back carefully, trying not to disturb too much dust. He was already sticky with insulation and dirt clinging to the sweat coating him.

Below Jason heard, "Concrete ceiling, it's safe to shoot."

"Soon as I figure out where."

So there were at least two troops down there, and now was a good time for an incapacitance grenade. He backed carefully along a steel girder while drawing one from his ruck. Right side pocket, and only one more after this.

A bullet wanged off the girder a meter ahead of him. He

didn't hear the rest of the burst, but did see the holes. Now was the time. He popped the pin, counted, "One," punched his hand through a soft tile and counted, "Two," and let it go.

Then he shimmied back as fast as he could, not worried about damaging wires or cables or if anyone saw him.

The *pop!* of the grenade was followed by loud cursing and scrabbling noises. Apparently their opponents had not expected them to use gas in the studio and had neglected to bring the appropriate gear. So it was likely that two more were out of commission, bringing the effectives down to no more than eight.

Assuming it was only one squad, and not counting any local security who would reinforce them.

Elke's voice came over his headset. "We're going to meet at Location Three in five minutes."

He tried to remember Location Three. That was the control room above the studio catwalks. From there, it was straight down into the main studio, Number Two . . . which was the one they needed.

Aramis skittered feet first over the seat and into the front of the vehicle. The engine was still running, and he slammed the transmission into reverse while nailing the throttle. First, he wanted outside where he had room to maneuver, and public visibility so he couldn't be convicted for anything he didn't do. Although, what he was going to do was plenty.

Dammit, he should be in on this, not sitting it out. The damage to his side was healing and every body was needed for this. He tried to pretend that looking over his shoulder to back didn't send stabbing pains up his side and around almost to his left nipple, back to the kidney, and up his neck.

The shredded, ruined wheels slammed against the curb of the decorative flower island out front but didn't immediately scale it. They did jolt him into further spasms of pain, but he rode through it, ignoring his pounding pulse and the sweats that came with it. The smell of damaged plastic grew stronger, along with assorted metallic scents and fuel.

He saw the two guards from the gate running up fast, batons out and shouting into radio collars. *Time to dismount.*

The nearest one fired, but Aramis was on his knees in the dirt, behind the open driver's door, and the heavy plastic didn't conduct the beam. He reached underneath, aimed by feel, and shot and missed, but the guy dodged aside and rolled for cover. The other was trying to flank him. Aramis shot at him, and that one dodged the beam, too, diving into the back of the flowers a few meters away.

Perfect.

He dropped the baton, reached back to the box between the seats, and grabbed a stun grenade. His left side hurt just from pulling the key, dammit, but once done, a careful right-handed lob sent it over the mound. As he used his left hand for suppressing fire, the baton zapping every half second or so. It was a good throw, even accounting for the higher gravity. As the grenade arced down he ducked his head and drew his arms in.

He was safe from the direct blast. His toes tingled a little, but it was manageable.

The stunner blast that smacked the closed rear door next to him was a little less so.

He yelped, fired blindly, rolled while his ribs stabbed, and shot again with better accuracy. The half-stunned survivor went down twitching and Aramis stunned him again. Meanwhile, he heard sirens howling as civil backup arrived. That would be City Safety Patrol, almost all of whom were ex-military, according to Jason.

Glancing around the trees, landscaping, and truck to be sure he was safe, he grabbed a couple more grenades, rose, and headed for the building at a limp, bent over his side. Looked at from this position, the front was a mess, doors and frames shattered, windows fragmented and even some rock damage, not to mention scrapes on the walkway from the now totally ruined truck.

He almost tripped on the curbs, stumbled inside, and slammed against the welcome desk, now empty, just in time to hear real rifle rounds slap into the brick façade a few meters away. Not good.

Building security to his left shouted and came after him as a few remaining gawkers squawked and ran. He counted three threats. There was only one thing to do: run. After tossing a stun grenade, of course.

Three rounds came close as he crossed the threat zone of the atrium again, past the desk, and toward a dead end. He zigzagged to get the solid cover of the greeting center between him and the impending blast. Then he heard shouts as the incoming fire met the pursuing security. Then he heard the grenade bang. He grinned.

One wounded Aramis had mission killed five local security and tied up the cops for a few seconds. If he could now get a good position, here, against a table with a stone statue atop it, he could possibly take more out.

It was a moral victory. A guard jumped over the railing above and landed bare centimeters away. He and the guard stunned each other simultaneously, batons in contact for maximum effect. He passed out with a rictus of pain and triumph on his face.

Elke and Bart dodged the opposite way from Bal's group, which was toward the rear of the building and away from the studio or the control room above it. For now, she and Bart had to make as much of a distraction as possible without killing anyone or destroying anything.

That latter had already gone to hell, Elke decided, as her pounding heart kept time with her pounding feet. Fabric fluttered across her arms, and she realized her shirt was open to her belt. She'd popped all the buttons doing something. Her body armor was clearly visible.

Bart fired behind her with his pistol. Good. Just because they couldn't use nonlethal force didn't mean the enemy needed to know that. Though rules or no rules, if one of those Recon *mamrds* shot at her, she was going to kill him.

They seemed to like locked doors around here. Luckily, her breacher loads could shatter locks and the mechanisms attached. Just as they hit the door at the end of this corridor, literally, Bart crashing atop her and knocking her breath out, she jammed the shotgun muzzle against the lock and shot. The noise was hellacious from conduction, even with her earbuds in, but the door blew open.

It was dark as she erupted through left, Bart going right, ready to shoot anything with either the riot gun or the baton she held underneath. Her eyes adjusted in a moment, and the space wasn't actually dark, just lit by dim directional lights with dark walls. Seeing no immediate threats, she shouted, "Clear!" as Bart did also. She then took two seconds to attach her baton to the standard clip on the shotgun.

They were in an open area under a roof, a loading and work area behind the soundproofed and sealed studios. They were between outside cargo doors, and no threat was imminent. She dialed her gun, turned, and shot recon over the studios twice in different trajectories. One round smacked through something overhead, the other was unknown. Images flashed on her glasses, and she sorted them. Daylight, delete. Black, delete. Crowd near the front, good, that was away from them.

"*What the fuck is going on back heurff!*" someone shouted as Bart stunned him. Elke's charge was a moment behind. At five meters, he'd be down for minutes. There was another corridor and it was closer to where they wanted, but they needed to be sure. This was turning into an athletic event.

"This way!" she shouted, heading back to the right, past Bart. She scrolled the last two images . . . inconclusive, but this way was not filled with hostiles yet. What they needed was a massive distraction back here to draw attention away from Bal, while she and Bart tried to regroup. That distraction couldn't be a fire, damage to the building power or antennae.

An idea occurred to her and she loped toward the wall.

When it came down to it, the power, a camera, and an antenna were the minimum mission requirements. Beyond that, they needed more notice, and she had a reputation to uphold. Besides, distractions were best loud.

In ten seconds she had three breaching charges in five-meter increments slapped against the extruded wall with glue. That glue was also tacking up on her fingers and shotgun, but it could be peeled or dissolved later. Right now, it was time Recon thought Bishwanath had his own army.

"Fire in the hole," she whispered to Bart while grinning. He took off at a sprint with her on his heels. She grabbed four more small charges, called up a code on her programmer, and stuck each detonator in in turn. Those charges she just dropped on the ground.

Jason kicked a hole in the ceiling below and dropped, pointing and shooting at the two figures below. They turned out to be employees on their way out the door, but he hadn't had time for that distinction.

"Hallway!" he shouted and yanked the door, as Alex went through with Shaman and he brought Bal last. Elke and Bart were shouting on their mics, so they were still working.

Elke said, "Be advised large team out front and allied force in the rea—" as a bang and rumble shook the building.

"Holy shit." The original plan, he recalled, had involved as little damage as possible. Someone was going to pay hugely for this.

Ah, well. That did mean a better chance of notice . . . assuming they got through. But what the hell had Elke meant by "allied force"? Was that just a distraction? It had to be.

"Ladder," Alex pointed. "Goes up to the maintenance mezzanine."

"Perfect!" Jason tried not to shout. "Bal first, go!" It was a ladder with a web of safety rails around it, and a hatch only three meters up.

Bal looked dazed but did as he was told, clambering up as fast as he could. Jason went second. He held the hatch and stood ready to close it.

"Someone coming," Shaman hissed. "We'll meet you there. Go," he said, as he handed up the coil of cable, then slid down the ladder, turning to appear as if he hadn't used it yet.

Then the shooting and shouting started underneath. Jason closed the hatch with a curse and a flip of his stomach.

Below, he heard the zapping bang of a stun grenade, but whose?

No time. He needed to get Bal two hundred meters across that way. There was a catwalk near the arching roof but no handy way to get there. Or, there were the climate control ducts hanging on heavy straps. Those straps were not rated for a man's weight, certainly not for two, but he'd done it once or twice during maintenance, and this was an emergency.

Which of course meant it would fail. He was sure of it. Nevertheless, he urged Bal to shimmy up atop a decent-sized duct leading from an air handler, and followed.

"Watch yourself," he said with a wince as he ripped his palm on a loose edge. Even plastic could be sharp, and this stuff didn't get beat around enough to dull it down. There'd be jagged edges at every seam.

Elke was truly insane, Bart decided, head ringing from the triple blast. He also intended to shoot anyone who tried to get her therapy. Her lunacy had kept them alive many times now. When all you had was explosive, everything looked like a bank vault, it seemed. He wondered how much she had left.

"Catwalk," she said. "You cover down here and stop anyone. I'll cover the top." She unslung her shotgun, the strap tangling for a moment on the remains of her shirt.

"*Ja,*" he agreed. That was likely best. Staggered defense for a few more seconds could let them finish this. He handed over his ersatz rappelling rope, which she dropped over her shoulder as she swung onto the ladder and started climbing. She ignored the power lift. It would make noise and be otherwise detectable, but she had a stiff climb without it, in higher than normal gravity. Bart crouched and ran to a pile of crates he could use for cover.

Clattering booted feet sounded from two directions, and it sounded like a lot of them. From his "rear" came a series of small explosions and shouts. Someone had found Elke's mines and was delayed. He squatted behind a stack of slatted plastic pallets that were great concealment but lousy cover, as absolutely anything could shoot right through them. Of course, he thought, as he laid out pistol, shotgun, and baton, that made them a great rest, because absolutely anything could shoot right through them.

Elke had stun rounds in this cassette, but he wasn't sure how many, nor could he easily read the indicators. On the other hand a shotgun was loud. Bart let the first man, almost certainly local security, get into clear view, then deliberately shot just behind him. He shrieked, stumbled, and dove for cover against the wall of the end studio. Bart recalled the map for a moment. No, that was not the studio in question, and holes wouldn't matter.

Someone else was close behind and shot back, then tossed a stun grenade that landed short. He felt the tingle through the gaps in his position, but it wasn't disabling yet. Bart had nowhere to retreat, however.

It took two seconds to empty the remaining rounds in the shotgun, snapping the trigger and letting the cassette spin sequentially until empty. Ambient light grew brighter as he shot, as several rounds tore holes in the studio wall across from his position. Shouts and curses indicated he'd had good effect. No one wanted to face that kind of artillery, even in full armor, and non-Recon people in suits were likely not wearing more than torso armor to start with.

He wasn't sure at first why he was cringing, until his brain caught up with his reflexes and realized several weapons were being emptied at him not far ahead. Another grenade banged and zapped, and his left fingers went half numb. Something clublike slammed into his leg, and he knew he'd been shot.

That was enough. He shouted, "*I surrender!*" loudly and raised the shotgun butt first. He raised it off to one side, in case they decided to shoot.

"Drop the weapon and come out!" came the reply.

"I am wounded," he said. *Ja*, his leg was hit, muscle torn red and blood pouring out. He hoped they had a medic. Oh, *scheisse*, it hurt. He felt nauseous under the sweats and needed to lie down.

"Nice try. You better hope you can walk out, or we'll use shitgas."

That would certainly slow things down while they masked, but Bart had a better plan on removing combat effectives. His leg jolted with pain anyway, so he shuffled forward on his knees, leaving both firearms and using the baton as a short walking stick. Even that was excruciating, but he had to hold out a few moments more.

As soon as he peeked around he saw weapons. There were six here, plus the one he'd scared who'd been stunned by the incoming fire. Enemy fratricide was so useful when you were outnumbered. He just hoped he could arrange more.

"Put the baton down *now!*" someone shouted, recognizing it as a probable weapon.

So Bart jerked and fell forward, extending his arm and the baton in it. That aimed the baton directly at his foes, and made him the smallest target possible in the open. The floor was dusty but also cool, which felt good. He was near to throwing up from the pain.

As the first of them approached, he flicked the button for the light and started pressing the trigger.

Two men recoiled from the actinic flash, one stumbled from the charge, and a second one dodged aside. He could see four more weapons pointed at him, and more than one of them fired their own charges.

At least his leg stopped screaming at him as he blacked out.

"This is it," Alex said to Shaman, amazed at how calm he sounded. Whoever had discovered them was twitching on the ground ten meters away at a blast from Shaman. No one had seen Jason and Bal that he knew of, so it was time to create distractions and vacate this area.

He fired a shot into the wall behind, paused a second for a response, then fired five more times in a vertical line to break a hole. He crashed through, leaving skin. His face, arms, and chest stung and burned and he was bleeding in ten places at once, but

Shaman could tape him up afterward. Right now, he needed an outside wall of some kind, or a stairway. This was a vacant office with a desk and computer but nothing to indicate human occupation. It was just one box of many. He pulled the door on the far wall and Shaman led the way through in guard position into another hallway of this rat maze. No civilians, no threats. Behind them, however, was a large amount of noise as security people arrived. He yanked the initiator on an incapacitance grenade and tossed it in as he closed the door. That was area denial at least. Three meters to the right, Shaman opened another door, fired a preemptive stun at something and waved. Behind him he heard the beautiful sound of someone violently heaving their guts and banging on the door in panic.

In two more twisted passages they reached an outside wall with a rolling overhead loading door. Somewhere was a ladder or elevator, but it wasn't here. He heard definite sounds of troops in both directions. This area was hotter with fumes and a hint of fresh outside air.

Gulping, he hit the lift button, grabbed hold of a ridge on the door and jammed his boot toes into another. If he could ride this up, there might be something to hang onto.

From outside he heard, "Shit, there's one!" and someone fired at Shaman with a real weapon. Shaman ducked, rolled, zapped in that general direction, and ran. Three people pursued him, local security in plain coveralls. Three more bashed through a wall and caught sight of the fracas and followed. Now they were chasing him, and none of them noticed Alex rising up with the door.

The full height was ten meters. Alex reached six in a panic, looking across both levels of offices, until he saw enough bracing and scaffolding to take his weight at least, a couple of meters higher. He wouldn't fall unless shot, and he could snipe at the minimum. Not that many meters away, he could see Jason and Bal creeping along ductwork.

Then three blasts almost blew him off the door. A cloud of dust billowed to his right and a gaping hole opened in the wall. He cringed and clutched, eyes closed against the dust until he remembered he was on a *rising door* and had to find a handhold at once. He took a glance through slit eyes, saw a girder, and snatched at it. He kicked off, wrapped his legs around and started shimmying backward. Below he saw the concrete floor, a cruel bitch he didn't want to get intimate with. He didn't loosen his cramped hands until he felt a vertical truss that let him stagger carefully upright. From there, he had to step gingerly along the five-centimeter-wide joist using wires and angled braces for balance. He took a much needed break to calm down. Sweat was pouring into his wounds and the combination gravity and atmosphere getting to him.

He almost fell when he heard more shooting and explosions. But those were a good thing, because it meant this wasn't over. That was also a bad thing, as it meant this wasn't over. Any time now, sensor gear would be brought in and start showing vital signs, including his. They were on minus minutes and counting.

He cautiously eased forward. Ahead was the overhead of the offices, and beyond that the soundproofed double walls of the studios. At this point, his greatest fear was that someone, probably on the other side, would take out the power or antenna and leave them with no message to send. He had to hope their plan was to be as discreet as he'd hoped to be, and be struggling with the reality for a few more minutes.

Someone was busy, Jason thought. A triple blast indicated Elke, he hoped, and not some other agency. He heard general shooting now, coming from all directions. The six of them had managed to tie most of the security up, but there was bound to be some at the studio entrances, still. Elke was right. They needed to be overhead fast, and rappel down. They only had to get Bal in, and not get dead in the process. That would do the trick. At least he hoped it would. This was the final drive and they had no Plan B now. Not even Elke had that much explosive.

"Come on, Bal," he urged. He'd taken the lead because Bal was having serious trouble with the heights and swaying supports. Well, so was Jason, but this was the only feasible way.

"Coming," Bal agreed, and kept moving. It was taking ongoing support to keep him going, though. The man was near mental exhaustion and looked ready to give up. He was lagging from a combination of the environment, the duration, and the stress. However, now was not the time, dammit. Harsh measures were called for.

"Bal, if you fuck this up at this point in the game, I will kick your ass, and then I will shoot you myself. You are part of this team and you are not fucking it over because you've had a bad day."

A look of pure rage crossed Bal's face, then slipped back underneath as he nodded. Jason could see his jaw grinding as he walked, though. He'd hit close with that one. Good. He'd do it again if he had to.

A strap popped and the ducting creaked as it repositioned. Jason held out a hand and clutched at Bal's, then pulled him forward. Another snapped and he had to skitter back himself, spreading their mass out over as great an area as possible.

"Hand and knees," he said.

A bullet whanged by, the weapon's report echoing in the large dome. "Over here!" someone shouted.

There was more fire from another direction, then two groups were shooting at each other. Just ahead was the thick mesh of a catwalk with railings. That was safer for walking, if more predictable.

"Hurry, Bal," he urged again. "We're there."

Alex had almost reached a work platform welded against another upright when the weapons fire started. Far across the dome was a man with a carbine in a good shooting position, aimed in the direction of Bal and Jason. He had to do something about that, but the only weapon he had at this point was a pistol. A shot at that range was almost ludicrous, but he only needed to be close. Better, still, that he did not hit. He leaned across the small floor and took careful aim, then fired.

In moments, he was taking fire in return. They couldn't see him, but could deduce it soon enough.

A crashing blow on his shoulder told him "soon enough" was now. Spots flashed in front of his eyes as he passed out from the pain.

Horace had no idea what to do other than seek people out and put them down. At this point, they wanted to not draw attention to Bal by crowding him. Jason should be enough, and with Alex up above, or more, he could work best down here.

The question was, how many of them had his picture, had memorized it, and would recognize him now? If he could get close . . .

"Help, security, I see a man!" he shouted in his best American accent. Most of the execs in this field were American, after all. His suit was dirty but that was not unexpected.

Damn, they were good, he thought with disgust. Two Recon troops just appeared, one through a wall leaving a hole, and one dropping down off nearby scaffolding. They pointed weapons at him.

"Where?" one asked.

"Right there," Horace said, pointing with his empty right hand up into the framework above. When they followed his finger, he swung his baton out with his left hand, flashed the light and zapped at the same time, just as they swung at him.

He did get both of them. They got him. The irony of the combat doctor getting shot center of mass was not lost on him. He felt a sledgehammer blow to the chest and went down.

Elke reached the top and hopped lightly over the secured gate onto the catwalk. The coiled cable and her bag tangled somewhat, but they were annoying rather than a real hindrance. She confirmed there were six walks radiating from the center, and that Bal and Jason were on another one heading to the cross-route that would put them above the studio. The plan had been to meet at the supplemental control room off to her left from here, but they saw each other and headed straight for the access at the center of the studio. Power was still up and the broadcast was still going on. Aramis had been right. Interfering with a broadcast was the one thing the government did not want to do, and they weren't going to discuss it with local hires around. Add in the debate between bureaus as to who controlled what, and it was still an exploitable situation. She moved as fast as she could while keeping silent, senses alert for threats. Not that she could do much with just a couple of small charges; all her weapons were behind her, and she hoped Bart would take care of her shotgun.

That was the moment she heard him burn off the cassette down below. So he was still in the fight. Her rear was secure.

Panting, heaving for breath, she fell against Jason for a comradely hug that was hands on forearms, then pulled the cable over her head.

"Lose weight before going down," she said. She ripped the fastener on her torso armor as she did. "These cables will be good once at most. I hope."

Jason was glad to see Elke. He was more glad to see a second cable in case they needed it, and someone to escort Bal down. As the lightest, Elke was the right choice for that, and he'd keep control up here. She'd figured that out and was already doffing gear.

"Bal, come here," Jason gestured. He started tying a bowline on a bight, to make an ersatz seat. It failed on the first attempt until he reversed the loop, then it worked but used up most of the cargo strap. He wished Bart was here. Bart had been wet navy and had practice tying a lot more knots a lot more times. Swearing, he yanked it open and tied a single bowline. "We'll have to get you down quickly."

"How strong is that power cord?" Bal asked, looking worried on top of all the other emotions cascading over him, as Jason dropped the loop over his shoulders.

Jason started coiling the cord in, trying to get a good, loose pile to feed from. He was going to have to lower Bal manually.

Someone saw them and shouted, "Over there, above Studio Two."

"I'm going to lower you faster than it can stretch and break," he said. "But slow enough you are not hurt."

Elke swore, stepping into an improvised abseil in the other cord, shoulder, crotch, thigh, and back up. In her hurry, she'd done that before tying the far end to a brace. Now she was fumbling to do that.

"I trust you," Bal said.

"Which is why you're sweating," Jason grinned. "Hang off the edge and let go when I tell you." Bal did do as he was told, age apparent as he bent awkwardly over the railing and hung by hands and feet, right above the access hatch. Jason measured out cord. He had plenty, and might need some for himself shortly. He took a moment to tie a loop around the railing with the other end. He tugged at the railing because it seemed very flimsy, but it held against his weight.

Stun charges started cracking nearby. None had the range so far, and no one was using lethal force yet.

BangCrack.

That was a bullet, he thought. Now they were shooting. Twenty meters away, trying to shoot through the web of structural walls, hangers, trusses, cable runs, and pipes was a Recon assault team looking very odd in tactical harnesses over suits and shirts. That didn't make them less deadly, and he didn't think they'd stop for cameras. Jason and Elke dropped directly onto the roof of the studio, hoping the blown polymer would take the mass. Bal had flattened out on the catwalk, and Jason helped him wiggle through and down. Then Jason had to reach up, untie the cable, and reposition it so it didn't bind through the railings.

Seconds, we have seconds, he said to himself. *Do it!*

"Elke, we need a distraction as soon as you get down there. Something Spaniel will pay attention to long enough for Bal to say hi, and not think it's an attack."

"Oh, distraction?" she asked. "Like what?"

"Make Aramis proud."

She stretched in her harness, rolled her eyes, sighed and said, "I suppose for the Cause I can go with maximum mayhem, screaming, girly crying, and bare tits if need be. But I *better* see a bonus."

"Consider the audience," he said.

"Consider me on the hyperweb," she replied, looking disgusted as she stared at him. "I'll do it. On three." She snatched a light-stick from a thigh pocket, cracked it, stuck the end in her mouth, and ripped it with her teeth. She let it hang there oozing bright blue goo as she raised the hatch. Light and sound and positive airflow spilled up from the sealed facility, illuminating her. She was wrapped in cable over pants and bra, sheened with sweat, disheveled, and bruised.

Another bullet cracked past and Jason shouted, "That's three, go!" and grabbed the hatch, as she growled and jumped.

Bishwanath gulped as Elke dropped down the hole, and again as he was chivvied off the roof, down and through. He dropped, panic making him shake, until he felt the cord behind his shoulders yank and stretch. Somehow, he could feel it stretching faster than Jason's jerky lowering, and panicked again. Below, Elke spun and the floor below her twisted dizzyingly, and people were looking up. They started cheering, pointing, shouting. Obviously, they thought it was part of the show. There were three bizarrely dressed individuals on a couch near center stage, and two others off to the side on chairs. It looked like an orgy of body paint had been in progress.

"Get the camera on that!" the director hissed and pointed up at them.

Well, he was on camera. Though this was not how it was supposed to be. He gulped as he fell, because he was sure the cord was parting. Elke touched down with athletic grace and threw the cable off herself with a dramatic wave. Her bra came with it leaving her in suit pants and boots.

"There's been a terrible accident!" she shouted, arms wide as she tossed her head. She'd spilled the lightstick down her chin and her breasts were glowing a bright Cerenkov blue over pink nipples and tanned skin, rivulets running down into her pants.

"Get the camera on *those!*" the director shouted, looking simultaneously shocked, confused, and thrilled.

The cable did part just before he landed, and Bishwanath banged one knee as the point of his chin struck the other. He felt blood on his lip and stood, slightly groggy.

Spaniel was halfway toward them, flanked by his shaven-headed, mean-looking goons who actually wore black shirts that proclaimed, "Goon." Into his microphone, he said, "First we have an explosion behind the studio, now we have some unusual guests. This is certainly one of the more interesting systems on our space tour."

Get up, get up! Bishwanath urged himself, forcing all his remaining strength. *Just five seconds.*

He rose and held out his hand. "Good afternoon, Mister Spaniel," he said, grinning a friendly grin at the camera to his right. "I'm President Bishwanath of Celadon. I hope you will pardon the unorthodox methods of my bodyguard, but the situation itself has been most peculiar."

His grin turned an amazing combination of triumphant and vicious. That look was what would be remembered for decades, not the angry shouts and screams that followed a few seconds later. "The rumors of my demise have been greatly exaggerated," he quoted. There were close to a thousand eyewitnesses here in this studio to attest to his presence. LeMieure was going to wet his pants.

"Mister President, this is certainly most interesting," Spaniel said taking his hand in recognition while staring at Elke, hands on her hips, who looked challengingly at him as she heaved for breath, chest rising prominently, scarred with welts from the cord. He might run a show that resembled a zoo full of howler monkeys, but he was neither stupid nor slow to exploit an opportunity.

"Won't you please take a seat."

One of the cameras exploded as three men came through the roof in a shower of polymer. People screamed and an NCO shouted, "*Stop*, it's over, dammit!"

President Bishwanath grinned again.

CHAPTER THIRTY-ONE

Weilhung was dictating his daily reports, a process that took two hours that wasn't scheduled, in a day too short, when a message blinked in. He finished speaking the paragraph, glanced at the header, and saw it was from recently promoted Sergeant White. He wondered what she was calling about. They'd been in touch, and she'd had useful info for the palace evacuation after action review, very helpful in removing him from the incident with Bishwanath. She'd been cool about that, apparently helping because he'd asked. Fair enough. The politics of it all sucked, and she'd really been out on a limb he didn't care for. Maybe she had details on the newly arriving President Rajani?

Still. "Hello, this is Major Weilhung."

"Major, you're just in time," she said as she came on-screen. She was in micro G, her hair floating loosely. "I'm aboard *Strident*, and this is a conference with Mister deWitt, Colonel Weygandt, and Mister leMieure." Their faces flipped on-screen as she said, "I thought you'd all like to see the following."

The image flipped to an interview before anyone else could offer a greeting. One of the two was some annoying talk host. The other was . . .

"Holy shit."

He couldn't believe it, but part of him was thrilled. The man was alive! Damn, those Ripple Creek fuckers were good. Weygandt didn't seem to agree. He was cursing heatedly. DeWitt was chuckling. LeMieure sounded incoherently apoplectic.

It ran for about ten seconds, as Bishwanath talked about being told he was dead. Six groggy, wounded, and beat-to-hell contractors sprawled across the studio, some of them leaking blood, while a second feed showed a car blown to hell, massive holes in the building, and some of his Recon guys stunned or trussed. The conscious ones, he was relieved to see, said not-a-damned-thing. Sykora was next to Bishwanath with a mismatched jacket over a bare chest covered with blue lightstick goop. What the hell was that about? Marlow bled from a shoulder wound, Mbuto's armor oozed reinforcing fluid, while someone checked him over for further wounds. Anderson was already bandaged and Weil was shaking himself awake from a heavy stun, with one pants leg dark from congealing blood.

White came back on full screen, the other minimized faces all showing some sign of shock. "Would you care to comment, Mister deWitt?" she asked.

DeWitt's face was stunned and amused, even half asleep. His bedroom showed behind him. "Yeah, I'll comment," he offered. "I guess Weilhung's already covered because he was not directly in the area, was cut out by the contractors and had orders that didn't involve taking action. Colonel Weygandt opposed the idea, mostly because he didn't want to get burned, but we pay off on results, not intentions. I expect he has all the documentation he needs. I didn't actually give any orders and officially opposed everything I could. Sergeant White documented that for me, and helped with the extraction. I guess that just leaves Mister leMieure. I suppose he's fucked."

"DeWitt, I'll have you gone over this!" the fat man screamed.

"Sure, from jail. So, how's that going to work for you?" deWitt cackled with glee.

Weilhung was still shocked himself, but when the toad looked at him and said, "Weilhung, if you'd—" he trod on it.

"Fuck you, you gutless worm. I'm not sure who in the chain went along with that idea, but it made me want to puke, and I'll be glad to see them gone. I've got my differences with the colonel, but he stayed out of it and I'm not going to try to make him a scapegoat. Sounds like I'm covered. I can't be nailed for not assassinating someone, and BuState smuggled my people insystem. Everyone seems to be less visible or approachable than you. You were told the press would be as happy to take you down as to glorify you. Guess that's coming."

"Thank you, Major," Weygandt said. He did still look as if a car was bearing down on him. "I also have my differences, but I don't see that this is a military matter at our level. We were reassigned by someone at Cabinet or New York level. If I were involved, there's specific legal advice I'd offer. But of course, I'm not." His grin looked relieved.

LeMieure was panting, crying, about to go into hysterics. *What a piece of shit*, Weilhung thought.

"If I go, I'll see to it that reports are made! You will all fucking pay. You were all told what . . ."

"Oh, good to have that on file, *sir*," White said cheerfully after a light-speed delay. "I'll copy everyone on this as soon as I stamp it against edits. My commander is also with me as a witness, by the way."

"I have not been charged or read any rights!" leMieure practically screamed.

"Of course not, *sir*," Weygandt put in, copying White's formal but derogatory tone. "So you have the right of free speech. You may wish to exercise it with discretion."

It took leMieure four swipes to kill the connection, while he clutched at his throat with the other hand. His eyes looked as if they'd pop from his head.

"Colonel," Weilhung said to break the stretching silence, "what do you think of the idea of contacting Ripple Creek and offering supporting documentation. I just happen to have a couple that might help?"

"Negative, Major," Weygandt replied with a shake. "I'd suggest holding on to that. After Mister deWitt contacts their attorneys in confidentiality, and they contact us, so we are only on record as responding to inquiries, then send them your files."

"Excellent, sir," he agreed. Whew. He hadn't done anything wrong, but it wouldn't have taken much of a misstep to land him in jail, too. An adrenaline ripple that felt like a combat reaction jolted through to his fingertips and up his neck. "Then I should get back to work."

"By all means."

"Good-bye, Major," deWitt said.

Weilhung said, "And Sergeant White, thank you. Thank you a lot. Can you get me contact information for Mister Marlow?"

"I can," she said. "I don't have it at present, but I'm sure I can find it shortly."

"Thank you."

EPILOGUE

Alex took several deep breaths as he entered the office. He knew exactly what this would be about.

It wasn't actually necessary to stand at attention, especially with a healing shoulder. Ripple Creek was a civilian enterprise, but Alex recalled a previous major screwup where he'd had to stand before a superior and take it. So he faced Don Meyer, Ripple Creek CEO, who was a fine operator, the man who contracted all this work, and a pocket billionaire.

The office wasn't a place to make him comfortable. There was nothing wrong with it, except that it was suit central, not military at all in layout, though it felt that way, and this was his general, if one thought of it as a chain of command. Adding to the discomfort was Massa's broad form sitting in a chair to one side.

"You wanted to see me, sir?" Alex said. He'd tried to think of something better, but that was neutral enough and acknowledged the meeting. After that, he'd play it by ear. He wasn't too worried yet. No charges had been filed, there was a certain amount of visibility, and Bishwanath had promised to pull any strings and help cover costs. But Bishwanath wasn't exactly the SecGen or a federated nation president.

Meyer sat back in his chair, looked up from the screen set into his desk and said, "AIC Marlow, it sounds like you had one hell of a deployment."

"Yes, sir. That would be a good way to put it." He'd brought everyone home. That had to count. Most of them were still recovering from wounds and damage, but they were alive and mostly intact.

"Everyone came back alive, and the principal survived some major political backstabbing. That's the good news to start with," Meyer said, and rubbed at his eyes.

"I imagine the bad news is that certain elements are highly pissed at me."

"Several," Massa nodded from the side. "Assemblypersons, senators, heads of major corporations . . ." His expression was part grimace, part grin.

What was that implication? But RC wasn't a major corporation technically. Although . . .

Meyer spoke again. "We also have a huge amount of publicity, although Sykora vehemently refused the nude modeling contract that came in."

No one laughed. Even if she wasn't here, Elke commanded a certain level of respect and fear.

"How's the other publicity coming across, sir?" Alex asked. That could make or ruin them all.

"Very well, truth be told," Meyer nodded, failing to hide a grin. "Contract inquiries by the hundreds by paranoid execs and a few heads of state, as well as several highly placed appointees with cash to burn. Cash they probably shouldn't have," he snickered. "But BuState is officially unhappy with us and has sent us a letter to that effect. They are going to 'review our status and contracts.'"

"Ah, shit, I'm sorry, sir."

"No, you're not." Massa locked eyes with him. "You're not stupid, and you knew exactly what you were doing. Your contract was cancelled, and you carried on anyway, with another unofficial contract with the same principal, knowing that the connection between you and Ripple Creek was tangible. You had to know our primary contractee would be annoyed at you circumventing their operation." He stopped and let the silence hang. Alex needed a moment to decipher the corpspeak.

Alex picked it up. "You're right, sir. But I didn't feel like walking out on Bishwanath, or anyone, and leaving them to die, and I didn't think that being quite that mercenary would inspire confidence in anyone other than a government contract, and likely not many of them."

Meyer nodded. "You're correct. We didn't enter their plans

at all, and if they were willing to sacrifice Bishwanath, I'm sure they were willing to then dump the blame on us. The initial reports already showed that, and I've since seen documents we acquired," he didn't say "stole," "that indicate they were ready to start inquiries about you and your team. Had you contacted us, that's exactly the information I would have given you."

"Sorry, sir. I was afraid of getting an answer I wouldn't like."

Meyer's voice was firm. "That's the part we have a problem with, Agent."

"Yes, sir." Was that "Agent" for "Agent in Charge" or a demotion to "Agent"? If so, that wasn't too bad. Yet.

"Within any reasonable means, you *will* keep this office informed of your actions and intents, so we can direct it from here. Had you inquired about that order, I would have given you some appropriately worded hints about what to do with your free time. I don't like being bent over the desk by bureaucrats, and I am not getting fucked for their entertainment." Meyer jabbed his finger against the desk for emphasis, making knocking noises from the impact.

"I can understand that, sir."

"Which is why I'm very glad to have AICs with the foresight and courage to tackle a situation like that. You put your ass on the line several different ways for your principal, and that's coming out in industry publications, even if not in the mainstream."

"That's good to know, sir." A positive spin. Hopefully, this wouldn't mean another "resignation."

Meyer said, "I'm sure you'll like this part," and Alex let out his breath in relief. Sarcasm wasn't Meyer's way. So the good news was?

"I've had inquiries about your availability, and heard hints. I'm bumping you a slot. I'll likely still use you as an AIC for special contracts, but you're officially a District Agent."

Well. It was never bad to be told your monthly contract rate was equivalent to a skilled craftsman's or middle exec's *annual* salary.

"Thank you, sir. I'm very glad it worked out for the best."

Meyer nodded. "I did interview your team and principal and noted that you considered the repercussions on the company. You juggled ethics with cold professionalism, and then got the job done without any support we could be blamed for. I was able to sit here shrugging my shoulders, grinning like an idiot and denying any involvement. The illegally done surveillance—which we are filing charges on—showed *nothing* to stain us. We followed the letter of the contract, you followed the spirit, and between them, we look like executive protection *gods*." He grinned as he said it.

"But the nail chewing I was doing when I thought you'd skipped out entirely and were going to wreck all of that was a nightmare. I was running on drugs for a week."

Alex was relieved. He'd figured it wouldn't be all bad, but this was a break after entire weeks of shit. "Got it, sir. I'll try to have better commo before disaster hits."

"That's what I want to hear. Did Bishwanath mention a bonus to you?"

"No, sir. He mentioned he'd cover us if we got him out and he was able to acquire assets."

"Well, he is President now, and he wants you six back until things steady down. He prefers the distance professionals give him over any local groups, including his own. He's forced BuState to contract it, and his government is tossing in a twenty-five percent kicker, plus a hundred K for each of you for the mission. Oh, and a medal from his new government."

"Damn, sir. I'd thought it was going to be a balls-up." Holy crap. He'd known Bishwanath was a man of his word. He wouldn't have even attempted this otherwise. Still, it had never been about the money and he hadn't thought of it in those terms.

"Not quite. Will you take the contract?"

"Oh, hell yes, sir. I'll ask the rest, but I think we'll do it."

"You do realize the nation's in the midst of a civil war and experiencing large amounts of chaos? If you thought it was screwed up before, you won't like it now."

Alex grinned and said, "We'll manage. As long as it's not boring."